The Gatekeeper

First Published in Great Britain in 2019 by
Schnauzer and Schnauzer

ISBN: 978-1-9160572-0-3 (Paperback)
ISBN: 978-1-9160572-1-0 (ebook)

Text design by Ellipsis, Glasgow
Printed and bound in Great Britain by Clays Ltd, Bungay, Suffolk

To my late Mum and Pop. Reunited in
celestial Sheekeys. You made me what I am today – neurotic.
In my heart always.

The GATEKEEPER

Russ Kane

SCHNAUZER&SCHNAUZER

PROLOGUE

"Dream or nightmare, we have to live our experience as it is, and we have to live it awake."

– Lawrence M. Krauss, A Universe from Nothing: Why There Is Something Rather than Nothing

The Chevy had just had enough. Maybe it was the fact that it hadn't been serviced in five years, maybe it was that Doug had inherited it from his Dad when he went off to college, a long time ago. Or perhaps it was that 1975 Chevrolet Caprice four-door sedans weren't meant to be still working in the 21st century. Whatever the cause, it was deader than Kevin Spacey's career.

"Where the hell are we, Doug?" Loretta had awoken from a delightful dream that featured warm sand, the ocean lapping around her ankles and Elvis, her recently departed and much-missed dog, whose entertaining excitement at the first sight of waves was a balm to her soul.

Doug consulted the satnav, not a standard feature back in 1975 as they hadn't invented geography back then.

"Well, we appear to be in Hellam Township."

"Where the fuck is that?"

Loretta may have had the innocence and enthusiasm of a child, but she had the potty mouth of a stevedore, not that most people knew what a stevedore was these days.

"We still in Pennsylvania for fuck's sake?"

Doug squinted at the satnav as if the oracle would speak to him.

"Yup. Sure are. York County to be precise. We just passed Franklin so we're on the right road."

"In a piece of crap that has broken down. Again. Like that's a goddam surprise. Why the fuck you insist on keeping this piece of trash is beyond me. It's just plain dumb. We coulda got one of them Japanese type cars. They never break down. Lynn's got one, says it fucking fabulous."

"Well, good for Lynn. It'll be the distributor. It don't like the rain. I'll lift the hood and fix it. We'll be fine Loretta."

Doug reached under the dashboard and popped the hood. He opened the car door and, grimacing against the rain that fell heavily, walked to the front of the Chevy, lifting a hood you could land a Chinook helicopter on.

He stared intently, shining the flashlight over the 350 Turbo Jet V8 hulk of an engine. Yes, there it was, a distributor lead had come adrift. He'd just re-attach . . .

"Looks like you need a bit of help there, mister."

The voice had come out of nowhere. Doug jumped, hitting his head on the hood as he did so. He may have even cut it on the hood release catch, he thought.

Doug straightened himself up and turned towards whoever was kindly offering assistance. He swung the flashlight towards where he could see the outline of a face in the heavy rain. The l.e.d. beam cut through the gloom and illuminated the face of the good Samaritan.

Between the sound of the rain bouncing off the Chevy's roof and Neil Young's *Keep On Rocking In The Free World* playing on the AM radio, Lynn didn't hear Doug's scream.

Neil was going for it.

There's a lot of people sayin'
We'd be better off dead
Don't feel like Satan,
But I am to them

Loretta joined in the chorus. She was back in High School when Neil Young wasn't Neil Old.

Her reverie was interrupted by a loud tapping on the window. The kind of tapping sound metal makes on glass.

"For fuck's sake you moron! Jeeze Doug. You fucking scared the crap outta me. What? You fixed the goddam car yet?"

A face appeared close to the passenger window. So close its breath steamed up the exterior of the glass in small, round halos.

Loretta stared. She wanted to speak but no words came out of her mouth.

"Hello Loretta honey. Aintcha gonna say hi to your Daddy?"

Loretta started to mumble. "But . . . but you're . . . you're . . ."

"Dead. Yeah. I know. And now it's time we had what you might call a little family reunion."

ONE

"This horror will grow mild, this darkness light."
– John Milton, Paradise Lost

"And . . . action!"

"This is Borley Rectory, a Victorian mansion in the pretty village of Borley in Essex. The rectory was destroyed by fire in 1939, but gained a reputation for being haunted after a series of locals reported some unexplained paranormal goings-on. In fact, the hauntings caught the nation's attention when the story of Borley was covered in the *Daily Mirror* by noted paranormal investigator Harry Price . . ."

"And cut!"

"What now? For God's sake, what's the problem?"

Nick Gold was not in a good mood. It was late, it was cold and the new director that Good Foot Productions had lumbered him with was driving him round the bend. Gold and Adam Farthing, the aforementioned director, had differing views on how the programme should be made. Adam considered it a piece of art that should merit a BAFTA and help him up the greasy media ladder towards his goal of directing a gritty drama set in the north of England where everything was . . . gritty. Nick Gold saw it as fifty-three minutes (plus ad breaks) of populist pap on a satellite channel nestling between 'Ancient Aliens' and 'UFO Files Uncovered'.

'Nick Gold – Paranormal Detective' had been running for over four years on TV, gaining a small but loyal audience. The public, it seemed, could never satisfy their desire to be frightened

– in this case mostly by shaky camerawork, night-vision lenses that turned the screen green and close-ups of Nick urging in a throaty whisper "What was that? Did you hear it . . . ?"

Friends called him the 'Hoarse Whisperer'.

Over four series of thirteen shows each, Nick had travelled the length and breadth of the United Kingdom in search of 'mysteries', 'spooky sightings', 'the unexplained', in fact any old crap that kept him and the production team busy and gainfully employed.

It had started, as most things in life tend to, as the result of a simple mix up. Nick, then in his late-twenties and with a BA in Philosophy and Theology from Oxford University under his belt, had written what is generously described as 'social observation pieces' for various magazines – articles of mere puffery proclaiming the great importance of this bar, that restaurant, this art installation, that tailor, this designer, and so it went. A friend had seen a casting call for a new DIY/Interior Decorating TV series catchily entitled 'Paint It, Patch It, Flog It' – catering for the thousands of people who saw 'doing-up' property as their way out of penury.

Nick's knowledge of DIY and interior design was limited to knowing the location of his nearest branch of IKEA and thus avoiding it like the plague. That, of course, didn't stop him from arriving one spring morning at the casting session in the rehearsal room located at the bottom of London's North End Road. As usual it was full of hopefuls sitting around in leotards waiting to fulfil their dream, or that of their mothers, of being in the chorus of a new West End musical, joining a dance troupe on the floating council flats that now passed as cruise ships or being the 'next big thing on TV'.

Nick smiled at one or two of the young female dancers, most of whom looked like a loud sneeze would snap them in half. The rehearsal centre was a warren of wooden-floored corridors, large mirrored rooms, small rooms with just enough space for an upright piano, and a café where a large mural by a convicted celebrity paedophile was yet to be overpainted.

A note written with a Sharpie and pinned to the entry hall notice-board proclaimed, 'TV Presenters Audition Room 7'.

With all the assurance that being in one's early twenties and a large Jack Daniels for breakfast brings, Gold swaggered into the room. Three producers from Good Foot Productions sat at a trestle table.

As he crossed the uneven floor, one of them said without looking up, "And why do you think you will bring our little show to life? What will you be bringing to the party?"

Without missing a beat, Gold replied, "A bottle of red, a bottle of white and some happy pills."

The man in the middle of the trio looked up and smiled, displaying a set of perfectly white, even teeth. Clearly his mouth was no stranger to London's Harley Street. He exuded that easy air of 'Success'. The signs were there if you knew what to look for: the quality cotton shirt that, despite the weather, seemed uncreased; the under-stated, but very expensive classic wristwatch; and a haircut shaped by a barber that clearly knew his trade.

"What . . . no guacamole?"

Nick smiled at the man's sharpness.

"I'm Larry . . . I'm the, what's the word . . . guv'nor . . . of this jolly team. Tell me [looking at his notes] Nick, is it, in three words, why we should hire you?"

Despite the hour – for Nick Gold this was too early in the day to be under scrutiny – the three years he'd spent doing as little as possible at a small college at Oxford University had not blunted the quickness of his mind when he was in the mood to utilise it.

Gold mirrored the easy smile of the 'guv'nor'.

"One – I'm here. Two – I look great on camera. Three – you need a safe pair of hands that will carry the series, never drop the ball and deliver every single time."

Larry nodded slowly.

"That was more than three words."

Gold looked straight at him. "Precisely. I'll add value and all for the same price."

Larry turned to his fellow panellists and spoke in a low, inaudible tone. His body language was impossible to interpret. The discussion was over quickly.

"Welcome aboard, Mr Gold."

He had got the gig.

It was only when the contract arrived a week later that Gold saw the show had nothing to do with house décor and the floppy shirt cuffs of Lawrence Llewellyn-Bowen. Unless it was that LLB had died and Nick was to attempt to contact him in the great wallpaper shop in the sky.

And so was launched 'Nick Gold – Paranormal Detective'. It was work. It paid the rent on Nick's modest (a much less pejorative word than cramped) flat in Balham, South London. It kept him in booze, beer and, occasionally, as he referred to them, 'broads'. Perhaps he'd read one too many Raymond Chandler novels as an adolescent. Odd that Chandler was only associated with California and Hollywood, yet had been educated at Dulwich College just three and a half miles from Gold's flat. A coincidence not lost on Gold.

Adam Farthing approached Gold with what he thought was a friendly, concerned, caring smile, which Gold trusted as much as a rabid pitbull wagging its tail.

"Nick . . . Nick . . . Nick . . . may I have a word?"

Gold gave the director a return smile with all the warmth of Anna Wintour.

"Nick . . . how can I put this . . . I want to *smell* the fear."

"You want to what?"

"I need to feel the terror. I want my audience . . ."

"Excuse me?"

"*Our* audience to be scared. To feel that at any second the true dark horror of Borley Rectory will be revealed."

"Adam – the true horror of Borley bloody Rectory *has* been revealed. It's in the middle of freaking nowhere, it's sodding freezing and I've already missed the Crystal Palace game on TV tonight."

Adam drew back. He blew out his cheeks and let out a long theatrical sigh.

"Well . . . I see . . . one of us is not taking this seriously."

In hindsight, that probably wasn't the wisest thing to say to a hungry, cold, football-deprived Nick Gold.

"Not taking this . . . what?!! You listen to me you twat! I've been presenting this programme for years . . . there is no fear . . . there is no horror . . . you know why . . . because there is nothing out there. Nothing. Zero. Zilch. The square root of fuck all. There is nothing that goes bang in the night, no ghoulies, no ghosties, no arse-clenching apparitions . . . it's all an industry built on bullshit. And the audience love it. So we give it to them. That, my friend, is how it works. Give the punters what they want. They want fear, we give them fear. They want creepy corridors, we give them more corridors than 'The Shining'. So please don't tell me how to do my job. OK?"

Adam Farthing stared at the ranting Gold, making a mental note not to send him a Christmas card or to invite him to any future screenings. Arrogant little shit.

"Fine, Nick. It's my job as director to get the best performance out of my cast and ensure the public have a first-rate viewing experience. But if you wish to take that barrow-boy attitude then so be it. I can see that this is a fruitless conversation."

Farthing turned away and in a loud voice called to the crew. "OK everybody . . . let's take fifteen for a coffee and a comfort break. Back on set in fifteen please."

With that he walked away.

From the parapet of Borley Rectory, a nun looked down on the proceedings. It was the most excitement she'd had since she was walled-up alive in the Benedictine Monastery in 1362 for her affair with a monk. He hadn't been let off so lightly and had been executed.

Still, the time was approaching when they would be avenged.

They would all be avenged.

TWO

'Brown Sugar . . .'

1971 KARAKUM DESERT – TURKMENISTAN DESERT

Mick, Keef and the boys were on top form with their latest track which was blaring out from the cassette player in the digger.

Anatoly sang along. He had no idea what a houseboy was but he sang about it anyway. Not that he spoke any English, but like many Russians, he made a brave stab at copying the words on the radio that he managed to hear, which is why he sang in an accent that, like Mick, ranged from Dartford to New Orleans, in no particular order.

He liked The Rolling Stones, although, as his father had pointed out on many occasions, they were the very embodiment of the disgusting decadence of the corrupt West, which was, of course, why Anatoly liked them so much. Anatoly was a realist. He knew that The Rolling Stones would only last another year or two, so he might as well enjoy their music while they were still around. He smiled to himself. Jagger was getting on at twenty-eight; imagine anyone going to see them when he was in his forties.

The group – in fact Western music in general – had provided a lifeline of escape from the grey boredom of growing up in Omsk where his father was a local party official. The premier, Alexei Kosygin, was a decent enough man and his father was fiercely loyal to him and the Party. In America, Richard Nixon had swept to power in 1969 and now was stronger than ever after two years in office. Anatoly's father, to his surprise, liked Nixon, describing him one evening over dinner as 'a man you could trust who acted in the best interests of his country, even if that country was our enemy'. Maybe he was right. Anatoly couldn't care less. He just wanted to get the hell out of Omsk.

One day, Afanasy Kozlov, his best friend since they had attended the 58th School in Omsk City, showed him an article in the *Siberian Times*. While they drank a particularly unpleasant cup of chicory-flavoured coffee and ate bland cheese sandwiches, he read aloud that geologists were drilling for oil in the desert of Turkmenistan. In Karakum their optimism had been rewarded and an enormous deposit of oil, rivalling those located in Iran, had been discovered.

"The desert, Anatoly! Think of it. Sunshine. Money. And we get the hell out of here. It will be an adventure!" extolled Afanasy as he drank the last dregs of his ersatz coffee.

Anatoly thought about the prospect of leaving; yes, it would be a change. They might well need able-bodied men out there in, where was it, Karakum…it certainly sounded exotic. Most of all it was a long way away from Omsk, which had to be good. He would discuss it with his father who, he believed, would see it as an act of great patriotism – not that working in the local bakery was not patriotic. The People needed bread as much as they needed the teachings of Lenin.

To Anatoly's delight, his father, at first sceptical, saw the benefit of his son applying to join the team in the desert. He didn't mention that he planned to rent out his son's bedroom on the quiet to supplement his meagre income from the Ministry. The rental would be deemed far too entrepreneurial by his superiors. The face of unacceptable capitalism.

Letters of application were written, interviews attended, intensive background checks made not just of Anatoly but his parents, grandparents, his former teachers and of course his circle of friends. The Soviet Union was nothing if not thorough. He passed scrutiny. Unfortunately, Afanasy was not so lucky. It appeared that his aunt had attended a secret meeting in 1969 that had resulted in several arrests and one permanent disappearance. No, Afanasy Kozlov would not be representing Soviet oil exploration interests in the desert.

With a firm handshake from his father, who was already calculating the rental income resulting from his son's departure, and an emotional hug from his mother, who urged him to 'take care' and 'not to forget to write', Anatoly found himself bound for Derweze, Turkmenistan in the heart of the Karakum Desert with the grand official title of Trainee Mechanic.

It was hot. After the frigidity of Omsk, quite ludicrously hot. Anatoly was stunned by the brightness, almost blinded by the light. The team had been issued with darkened goggles which were proving invaluable. He'd seen blue skies of course, but never a hue of such extraordinary intensity, almost, he thought, a new shade of blue. However it was the sun that was so difficult to comprehend. The sun shone in Omsk as it did, he assumed, across all of the Soviet Union. Never had he seen a sun so fierce, so dazzling, so unremittingly aggressively extraordinary. Anatoly felt that he'd landed on another planet. Was this what those American spacemen – he'd forgotten their names – experienced when they had landed on the Moon two years ago? If they actually had landed of course. Popular rumour had it that the Soviets had landed there first but the cosmonauts had soon perished, so the event was hushed up.

The plan set out by the geologists leading the exploratory group was straightforward. Even Anatoly understood it, and he had hated geography at high school. He assumed that as the words sounded similar, geology and geography were probably the same thing. Maybe you used different maps, or hammers or something.

The site had been chosen as the experts believed that it held vast deposits of oil, enough oil in fact, to tip the balance of fossil fuel power in the Soviet's favour. The Kremlin were firm believers that the more self-sufficient the country could be, the stronger it would become. So they were happy to bankroll this geological exploratory mission.

The days in the desert rolled by, boiling hot days and freezing cold nights. The stars put on a dazzling display every evening, shining with a clarity and in such profusion that Anatoly had never experienced at home.

After weeks of maintaining the equipment (a skill Anatoly had learned at his high school and at compulsory engineering classes), plus making endless mugs of coffee and tea for the crew, a skill he excelled at thanks to his mother, he noted a palpable excitement throughout the camp. Local dignitaries had arrived from the capital of the area, travelling 150 miles across the inhospitable terrain to witness the event.

They were going to drill deep. It was time to bring home the mother lode to Mother Russia.

The equipment had been in place for several days now, waiting for the chief geologist to confirm the precise place where the drill head should be located. Anatoly had sensed the heightened tension in the camp and watched the arrival of a helicopter cadre of military advisors, who presumably advised with the help of the Kalashnikov automatic rifles that were much in evidence.

The Avtomat Kalashnikova sent a very clear message to the geologists and the crew: you might be in the middle of nowhere, but you're a bullet away from Moscow.

Anatoly's job today was to stand close to the drilling site and be 'on hand'. The crew had grown to like this young man with his can-do attitude and ready smile.

At 11am precisely, the command was given for the drilling to commence. The silence of the Karakum Desert was shattered by the loud mechanical sounds from the drill's motors and the drill bit biting into the rough desert surface.

The chief geologist announced with barely disguised pride the phrase he'd been rehearsing in his tent for the past two days. "This is truly a great day for the Soviet Union. A day in which we will tap into a power that we can only dream of."

In hindsight, they were words that would turn out to be remarkably prophetic.

Everything was looking good. The drill was burrowing inexorably into the earth, and soon the promised fields of as yet untapped oil would be reached; the expedition marked as a success; and attendant promotion for the chief geologists. Maybe a bigger apartment might be on the cards. Perhaps even the use of a government villa by the Black Sea in the summer.

Which was pretty much the last thoughts that he or anyone else had.

There was indeed oil down there. But sadly, what the collective geological brains had failed to spot was the one tiny flaw in an otherwise immaculate plan. They were drilling over a vast cavern of natural gas. A cavern so huge that if punctured it would threaten a vast area including the local villages and small towns.

But, as it turned out, that was the least of their problems.

Over the coming days, the Soviet press agencies, led by the Telegraph Agency of the Soviet Union, known universally as TASS, ran the story. The story had been written in the Department of Information and News, located in a heavily guarded section of the Kremlin by a team hurriedly summoned in the middle of the night by their superior. Even for a team used to working any hour of the day or night, it was unusual to have four armed guards outside the department's double wooden doors. The three armed guards inside their office was a first, even for men and women used to the unusual communication habits of the world's second largest superpower.

From the expressions on the faces of the heads of department, there was a very serious problem that needed 'editing'. "Remember, you are not re-writing history, merely helping the People find it more palatable" was a phrase often heard.

*

Some of the older members of the team, writers taken from all walks of life including journalism as well as the arts, were already on board in the late 1950s when their last major 'palatability exercise' had them working twenty-two-hour days.

It was known, strictly internally of course, as the Mayak Disaster. Externally, it was not known as anything at all for another two decades.

As part of the Soviet Union's atomic bomb programme, the Mayak plant was built between 1945 and 1948. It was constructed in a great hurry and, naturally, in total secrecy. Five nuclear reactors were built to make, refine and machine plutonium for weapons. Later the plant began to specialise in reprocessing spent nuclear fuel from nuclear reactors and plutonium from decommissioned weapons.

In the early years of its existence, the Mayak plant released quantities of radioactively contaminated water into several nearby small lakes and into the Techa river. That was seen as acceptable. After all, the rivers didn't run all the way to Moscow.

The workers at Mayak were under tremendous pressure as the nuclear arms race between the Soviets and the USA was at fever pitch. Severe health hazards were the norm and accidents were commonplace, news of which never reached the outside world.

On 29th September 1957, the unthinkable finally happened.

The cooling system for a tank storing tens of thousands of tons of dissolved nuclear waste failed, resulting in a chemical, but mercifully non-nuclear, explosion, with an energy estimated at about 75 tons.

This released vast amounts of deadly fission products that casually drifted off the site, creating a contaminated region of 20,000 square kilometres. Fifty-five people died of radiation-induced cancer; sixty-six were diagnosed with chronic radiation syndrome. Ten thousand people were evacuated from their homes, and nearly half a million people were exposed to radiation.

The Head of the Information and News Department summed it up succinctly as "In the history of fucking messes, this is the fucking worst".

The Soviet Union did not release news of the accident and flatly denied it had happened for the next thirty years. However, you don't dump fission material into the atmosphere without consequences. Residents of Chelyabinsk district in the Southern Urals reported observing polar-lights in the sky near the plant, and American aerial spy photos had documented the destruction of the disaster site by 1960. The Mayak nuclear accident was categorized as a Level Six Serious Accident. The International Nuclear Events Scale only goes up to seven.

The older writers had been virtually chained to their desks ensuring that the scale of the accident was never known to the outside world. It was the worst nuclear accident in the USSR's history. That was until 26th April 1986, when the radioactive shit truly hit the fan at a place that became synonymous worldwide with death – Chernobyl.

This time, there was no hiding it. The instructions that the writing team, or News Analysts as they were officially referred to, were straightforward as the Head of Department, a grizzled pro, addressed them. Better to have information delivered verbally – no paper trail.

"Sorry to drag you from your beds but that's life. Right, there's been an almighty fuck up in the desert. Never heard of the place but now it'll be news. Fucking great explosion. Geological team wiped out. A few survivors. And they're talking total bollocks and are fuck-all-use to man or beast. Your job – sort it. I want copy on my desk before dawn. Background material will be handed out. When you've read it, shred it. That's it, now get going."

Within two hours, the official line from Moscow had been written, sent up the chain of command, amended, approved and sent out first via TASS then the other media channels. It read as follows:

*

'A team of Soviet geologists working in the Ahal Province of Turkmenistan have discovered a vast supply of oil deposits using our most advanced detection and technological drilling techniques. The oil supplies that will be released because of our scientific endeavours will make the Soviet Union completely independent for its consumption of natural resources for the next one hundred years. The Premier of the Soviet Union, Alexei Kosygin, has sent his personal congratulations to the geological team who are to be honoured upon their return.

The petrochemical scientists have earned additional praise from the Kremlin for their swift and decisive action at the drilling site. It was discovered that to reach the vast oil deposit, the drilling process had to pass through a deposit of natural gas. To facilitate the process, the gas, comprising mostly of methane, was set alight and will burn-off within 48-hours. This process, known as flaring was developed by our geological engineers.'

It was widely agreed in the department in Moscow that this was an excellent, well-crafted succinct press release.

It was unfortunate that not a word of it was true.

The truth would probably never be known. It certainly would never be understood. However, the facts, as far as anyone attached to the project could say, were not in doubt. One minute the drilling had begun. The next, all but one of the team were dead. The survivor, a young man called Anatoly, had been helicoptered out of the desert in poor condition. The medical team quickly assessed that he was not just in deep shock, but that the trauma had made him temporarily insane.

No one at that time in 1971 could have predicted that the gas fire, which was due to burn out within 48-hours, would be burning brighter, hotter, and more fiercely nearly half a century later.

Nor could anyone have foreseen that where the oil drill had bit into the desert surface, a crater measuring 230-feet across and

65-feet deep now stood. A fiery pit that burned so brightly it could be seen for miles.

No member of that 1971 expedition would have appreciated that all wildlife within a five-mile radius would, quite literally, drop dead within 24 hours.

What might have been handy would have been if any of the team knew the meaning of Derweze, the location where they were drilling.

Derweze means gate.

And some gates are best left shut.

THREE

"Solitude sometimes is best society."
– John Milton, Paradise Lost

Present day in Balham, South London and the sun was not shining. The area, once the butt of a famous sketch by the comedian Peter Sellers in 1958 when the UK was still in black and white, hunkered down under a typical London overcast sky. It wasn't raining. It wasn't cold. It was just grey. A shift on the colour-palette scale from black and white.

Nick Gold had settled himself down into the café close to his flat located off the High Street.

There was, in Nick Gold's lexicon of life, only one way to start the day. Coffee. Espresso. Usually a double espresso.

If he had to describe Hell, apart from being forced to watch any television programme which contained the name Simon Cowell in the credits, it would involve having to commute. It was immaterial whether it would be by car, bus or underground train, the nub of the problem was that it would mean he would be unable to start his day in a café having a morning coffee. Not just any café. In this regard, Gold was more particular than the worst wine snob in The Hamptons.

Gold avoided the coffee shop chains, unless there was simply no alternative, in much the same way he avoided crying babies on long-distance flights or young children whose concept of in-flight entertainment was to kick the back of his seat from Heathrow to JFK.

Coffee shop chains, in his opinion, were staffed by people who, when it came down to it, knew as much about making great coffee as Jeffrey Dahmer knew about haute cuisine. They attempted to make the experience 'personal' which only exacerbated the soulless, corporate nature of just being there. Their latest attempt at 'personalising the customer interface experience' was to ask you your name which they would then write, with varying degrees of accuracy, on the side of your cup, so that the barista, which normally meant a very sweet, smiling girl from Eastern Europe with a degree in physics, would call out the customer's name. Gold usually gave his name as Spartacus. And sometimes other customers would get the gag and join in.

No, the coffee shop could not form part of a chain, it had to be run by the proprietors who actually gave a shit, it had to be small, cosy, yet not claustrophobic. It had to feel authentic. Gold wanted to experience the patina of years of serving good coffee the moment he walked in.

No one said Nick Gold didn't have his obsessions.

Over the years, Gold had made a shortlist of where he was happy to have his early morning coffee and on this occasion he had chosen a small, higgledy-piggledy establishment called, rather mysteriously, Romeo Jones, which was tucked away just off Balham Street. The proprietor, Patrick, ran it with an effortless charm and greeted not only each customer by name, but knew their order before they'd uttered a word. The small wooden chairs creaked, the little round wooden tables wobbled, the wooden floor was not entirely even and the loo was outside and reached by walking through the very narrow kitchen. It was absolutely perfect.

"Ah, good morning Nick. All good I hope?" beamed Patrick as Nick walked in. "The usual?"

"Great . . . and I'm going to go wild today, Patrick, and have your scrambled eggs on sourdough toast. I'm feeling reckless."

Patrick smiled, and bustled off to the kitchen, smoothing his blue and white striped apron as he did so.

*

Gold settled into his favourite chair at his favourite table, the one right by the counter that held the most delicious selection of cakes, pastries, scones and every other delicacy designed to pile on the weight. He took out his mobile phone and began looking at emails, Twitter, Facebook and texts. Just like everyone else on the planet.

In fact, Gold's choice of cafés in the area had been reduced by his promise to a particularly attractive waitress that, as he was on TV, he could expedite her brother's proposed visit to the United Kingdom. It had resulted in a few amorous evenings, but no brotherly appearance. Hence, he was not currently top of the popularity charts.

The contretemps with that total idiot Adam Farthing had not endeared him to Good Foot Productions either. The little snot had dumped him right in it, claiming he was 'difficult to work with, unprofessional, not focused and jolly rude'. There were apparently rumours that Gold had been 'drinking to excess' during production. Bloody little git . . . probably a vegan from the look of him. Not that being a vegan was wrong, of course. Except if it applied to Adam Farthing.

A rather tense meeting at the offices of Good Foot Productions tucked away on the third floor of an anonymous building in Dean Street, Soho, had not improved the situation. Was he still happy? Were there any problems at home he'd like to share? How much on average was he drinking on a daily basis? Was there a clash of personalities with Adam Farthing?

Spare me from this touchy-feely garbage thought Gold as he smiled politely and did his utmost to seem civil, professional and interested.

As he sipped on his espresso that Patrick the Proprietor had brought to his table, Gold started to read through his emails. Naturally he had his personal account and, being a scintilla in the public eye, had his professional, public email address. Not that he bothered to reply to most of the messages. That, most certainly, was not in his contract. Besides once he'd deleted the 'I think you're hot, I live in Devon, do you fancy a special cream tea, just the two of us' . . . 'I hate you and vomit whenever I see your stupid face on my TV screen you Commie prick' . . . 'Can you help me find my cat?' sort of messages, only a few remained. No, he didn't want an all-you-can-eat Indian buffet via Groupon nor did he require a penis enlarger or to meet Russian girls who just wanted to be friends. However, one message caught his eye.

Dear Mr. Gould. [Oh FFS! Really?]

I am in desperate need of your help. Something happened to my husband Terry and myself while we were on holiday in Turkey. You may have read about it. They say it was a bomb, but I know it wasn't. Terry was killed, but not by a bomb. No one will believe me. They think I'm suffering from grief and talking nonsense, but I'm not. I'm an experienced NHS nurse and I know the truth. I need your help to prove what happened. Please contact me ASAP. I know you must get hundreds of letters and messages, but please, I am begging you to please contact me. I don't know who else to turn to.

Yours sincerely
Joanne Walsh

There was an address in Leeds, a phone number and an email address. Mrs Walsh was evidently leaving nothing to chance. Gold mulled over the possibilities as his breakfast arrived, the scrambled eggs looked perfect on the sourdough toast. Should he have added bacon as a side order?

What might have happened in Turkey? Several scenarios ran through Gold's mind. It was a bomb and she can't deal with it. Truth, as he knew all too well, was often unpalatable. There was a fight as a result of too much booze and the hot sun, it got out of hand, she's covering up. Mr Walsh ran off with the woman who ran the local taverna and faked his death. Perhaps nothing so romantic: maybe he couldn't face another winter in Leeds and had chosen to stay in Turkey.

These scrambled eggs really were blinding.

With nothing in particular to do that morning, Gold reached down into his leather messenger bag and took out his MacBook Pro – the *de rigueur* laptop for any young media hack ever contemplating applying to join Soho House, The Hospital Club or The Groucho Club.

Gold wasn't a member of any of them.

He hit the power button and was soon Googling, 'Turkey – Bomb Blast'.

Instantly, a number of entries appeared on his screen. He scanned the headlines.

'Islamic State Blamed for Tourist Bomb Atrocity.'

'Turkey Being Pulled Into Middle East Conflict' ('no shit, Sherlock', thought Gold).

'English Tourist Killed at Holiday Resort' (hmm . . . that must be Terry Walsh, Gold assumed. So there was some truth to the email. Well, that made a change).

Nick clicked on the entry and began to speed-read.

'Terry Walsh . . . on holiday . . . leaves wife Joanne . . . Nurse very shocked (No, really, you think, her husband was just blown up in front of her, that'll put a dent in your holiday plans).

He read on.

Gold sipped on his espresso which he realised to his intense irritation was now cold. Catching Patrick's eye, he made a gesture to indicate another was needed in a hurry.

So, what did this all add up to? A couple from the north of England go to Turkey to take in the thermal springs, the husband gets blown up by a terrorist's bomb, the wife, a nurse, won't accept it.

Shit happens.

So what was he supposed to do about it? Ignoring it was probably the safest option. Don't get involved. It really wasn't any of his business.

Patrick placed the hot espresso down on the table. The aroma lifted Gold's spirits and the first sip gave him a pleasant caffeine rush. Now he was off those delightful recreational substances that had, for years, formed the foundation of his social hours, coffee was right up there with 'the good stuff'.

He glanced at the counter and a lemon drizzle cake seemed to speak to him. Within moments it was sitting on a plate from Patrick's eclectic collection of crockery where nothing matched – all part of the Romeo Jones café's charm.

But, on the other hand, this woman, Joanne Walsh, was a bona fide NHS nurse. She knew how many bedpans made five. But even nurses are liable to go into severe shock if their husbands are blown up right next to them. While on holiday. Christ, losing his suitcase once on a flight to Malaga was bad enough and took him two days to get over.

What to do?

The lemon drizzle cake really was very moist with a nice tart, sharp feel . . . maybe another slice would . . . fuck it, he'd write back. Why not? What's the worst that could happen?

Nick Gold could not have the slightest clue what the worst was going to be.

FOUR

"Awake, arise or be for ever fall'n."
– John Milton, Paradise Lost

Gold's one-bedroom flat in Balham was what estate agents describe as 'beautifully presented . . . bright . . . a-must-see . . . a-rare-opportunity-to-buy . . . charming . . . close-to-local-amenities'. He had often wondered how the people who write this misleading crap didn't win the Booker Prize every year. It was small and bright because he kept the lights on twenty-four hours a day, the local amenity was the Day of the Raj curry emporium which, handily, was directly below – although not particularly handy for Gold's waistline. As for 'charming', that was a matter of some debate.

His kitchenette served as his office, the small table piled high with books, paperwork, ignored unopened brown envelopes from HMRC (what was the point in opening them, they were highly unlikely to be the bearer of great news) and newspapers, marked in blue Sharpie at pieces that had caught his attention.

Opening the laptop, Gold began to write an email to Joanne Walsh.

Dear Joanne

No.

Keep it formal. Don't open the door to familiarity.

Dear Mrs Walsh

Good start.

Dear Mrs Walsh,

Thank you for contacting me. I was sorry to learn of your husband's death . . .

No. Not death. Too in your face.

I was sorry to learn of your husband's passing in Turkey. Would you furnish me with some more facts regarding why you do not believe it was a bomb that caused the fatality?

Kind regards

No no no.

Yours sincerely,

Nick Gold.

He clicked on send and the message left Balham and travelled up towards the north of England in a millisecond.

He was standing up, pouring a cup of coffee from the Huehuetenango beans that he'd bought during his last trip to Soho at the Algerian Coffee Stores on the corner of Old Compton Street ('established 1887' as the small red pack of fresh beans proudly proclaimed) when he heard the familiar chirp announcing a new email had arrived.

As addicted to his laptop as everyone else on the planet, Gold strode across the kitchen, a move accomplished in under two strides.

It was from the not so merry widow.

Dear Mr Gold

I can't tell you how much receiving your email has meant to me.

Oh crap.

It is too complicated to write down exactly why I am so convinced that what happened to my Terry was not as a result of a bomb, despite what the papers say. Could we meet?

Bollocks. Here we go.

I appreciate that you are a busy man, so I would travel to London. Also, I fully understand that you would have every right to think I might be a stalker or just plain mad . . .

You ain't freaking kidding.

. . . so, I would propose that we meet in a place that makes us both feel comfortable, such as a coffee shop at a station.

Hang on. This sounds horribly reasonable. Bugger.

Please let me know when you might be free and I will work around your schedule.

Thank you in anticipation,

Joanne Walsh.

Gold sipped from the slightly-chipped coffee mug, the one that he had left after *she* had left, and contemplated his response. He was between series of 'Nick Gold – Paranormal Detective' so he had some time on his hands. Good Foot Productions were not amongst his closest chums, but they were prudent enough not to throw out the irritating baby with the ratings water. He could easily spare an hour or so to meet Nurse Walsh, listen to her probably bonkers tale of woe and maybe use some of the story in the next series. Actually, come to think of it, that was a brilliant idea – goodbye freezing cold, draughty English ruins. Hello sun-soaked Turkish health spas, sorry, very scary ghost-infested haunts. He made a mental note to pitch the idea of expanding the show to overseas locations after he'd met with Nurse Wretched.

Gold replied to Joanne Walsh, gift-wrapping his brief response with how he was touched by her plight . . . how he supported the NHS and its marvellous nurses . . . that he happened to be free in two days' time (although in reality he was almost snow-blinded when looking at his diary) and they could meet at Café Rouge upstairs at Victoria Station and would 1pm be convenient . . . looking forward to meeting her blah blah blah.

Unsurprisingly the response was rapid and in the affirmative.

Nick looked at the chipped coffee cup. It wasn't much to show for two years. Two long, short, wonderful, awful, gut-wrenching, heart-breaking, life-affirming, angry, tender years. Life eh? Bollocks to it all.

Two days later, Nick Gold arrived at Victoria Station via the Tube (as London's Underground system was universally known), and navigated his way through the seemingly endless throng of travellers. This was, after all, London's second busiest station and had been a hit with the public since it opened in 1860, so expecting it to be quiet, even at lunchtime, was unrealistic. But then, he was a paranormal detective, so realism usually took a back seat.

He walked up the stairs to where Café Rouge was located, in a dark corner of the large terminus. This was a popular chain of ersatz French restaurants which reflected a Parisienne atmosphere as much as putting a beret and a string of onions on a statue of the Queen might achieve. Still, they gave it a go.

It didn't take long for him to locate the object of his trek. Joanne Walsh was seated at a table in the darkest corner of an already dark restaurant. She had that aura of someone anxiously awaiting the arrival of another party. This would vary, generally speaking, from low-level pleasure at the imminent arrival of a mate to have a laugh with to the Defcon Four Code Red All Systems on Standby Mode of a person waiting for a blind date.

Gold had been on three blind dates in his life; before he never needed to again.

As he crossed the restaurant, Joanne Walsh stood up, almost knocking over a wooden chair in her haste to greet her would-be saviour. Clearly, she recognized him from TV and his social media profile so it wasn't a deduction worthy of an astonished entry by the ever faithful Dr Watson.

Nick did his best to set his face into a smile. "You must be Joanne?" he said, trying to keep his tone both approachable but formal.

"Yes. Yes, I am." The Yorkshire tone was unmistakable. Gold couldn't help himself. He was a Londoner. It meant that as soon as he heard the broad vowels, he half-expected this perfectly nice woman to bring out a couple of ferrets, a racing pigeon and don a flat cap. It was an utterly ridiculous cliché of course. Well, the ferret part.

"You found it all right, then?" he added, immediately regretting uttering such a trite comment. Duh! Obviously she found it, you're sitting opposite her, you twat.

"Would you like a tea or coffee perhaps?" Was she going to ask for a pint of Monksman Slaughter or Frothingham Best Ale?

"Yes, thank you, a cup of tea would be lovely. I ate on the train down. Made myself a quiche and a small Greek salad."

Nick smiled inwardly at his ridiculous fantasies about anyone north of Watford.

The waitress took their order and smiled delightfully. Did she recognize him? Did his black leather jacket give him a dangerous edge? You idiot . . . tip . . . she wants a tip, you dumb-arse.

Joanne was twisting the gold wedding band on her finger in an unconscious nervous fashion. Round and round it went. Twisting endlessly. Gold was drawn to it.

"Thank you so much for seeing me. I really appreciate it. I didn't think you'd reply. I mean you must be so busy and everything." The words came out in a rush. A release of pent-up nervous energy.

"That's OK. I had a bit of spare time," added Gold with unnecessary cruelty.

Joanne Walsh looked down at her hands.

"So, Joanne, how do you think I can help you?"

Slowly, her head began to shake from side to side in an almost imperceptible motion, as if saying no. Gold waited patiently. Mercifully, the pot of tea and Gold's double expresso arrived from Miss Smiley and the spell seemed to be broken.

"Would you like a piece of cake?" enquired the TV personality. This was England after all. Nothing existed, no problem too difficult, no crisis too deadly, that couldn't be solved by tea and cake.

"No thanks, Mr Gold. I'm OK. Gotta watch my figure these days."

Don't go there. Do not fall into the trap. "Fine. So, how can I help?"

Joanne Walsh took in a deep breath as if preparing to perform a high dive in the Olympics.

"First of all, I want you to know that I'm not mad."

Good start.

Gold smiled benignly at her opening gambit. It had been his experience during the thirty-two years that he'd been on Planet Earth that anyone incorporating the sentence "I'm not mad, you know" was, generally speaking, East Ham, one stop short of Barking.

It was the same when people uttered that worn-out phrase 'Contract? You can trust me, you know. I'm very trustworthy.' Not only was that tautology but it was an immediate signal to phone a lawyer. A good one. Preferably a Rottweiler.

"I'm sure you're not, Mrs Walsh. No one has said you are."

"Oh no. They have. My sister-in-law wants to have me committed. She's a right cow. We've never really got on. She's after Terry's money, not that there is any. I mean, we both worked and so there were two incomes coming in so to speak but if you knew what they paid us nurses you'd laugh. I blame the government, not just this one but all of them. You see they think we won't go on strike but . . ."

Gold closed his eyes. "Mrs Walsh! Please . . . can you tell me why you needed to see me. I hate to rush you but I have to edit a new show," he lied.

Joanne straightened herself up as she was snapped out of her rant.

"Sorry. Of course. Sorry. I'm an NHS nurse, Mr Gold. I've worked at Leeds General Infirmary for the past eleven . . . no . . . twelve years. I've seen it all."

Gold silently hoped that he was not about to be regaled with gory tales from A&E. He had a low threshold for blood-related matters. And with good reason.

"Yes. Seen it all over the years," she continued. "You name it and I've seen it."

"I'm sure you have, Mrs Walsh," replied Gold attempting to move the story on. "So, if I may jump ahead, what you're saying is that you are, as it were, a fully trained professional not prone to flights of fancy."

Joanne Walsh stared at him as if he'd just spoken in Mandarin.

"Er, what I'm saying is that I know what I saw. That's because I saw it."

Gold smiled encouragingly. "Yes, I think I'm ahead of you here. So, mindful of the time and your tea getting cold –"

"Bollocks to the tea."

Gold's jaw dropped a fraction. What on earth prompted that outburst? The words had been spat out with force. Joanne Walsh took a deep breath once again to steady herself.

"Sorry . . . sorry . . . it's just that . . . that . . . no one will believe me. They think I'm going mad. But I'm not. I'm really not."

There was something in the sincerity with which the nurse spoke, the conviction in her tone that made Gold think either she was absolutely as mad as a box of frogs, or, tantalisingly, she was telling the truth.

"Go on Mrs Walsh. Just go ahead and tell me what happened, what you saw."

Joanne blew out her cheeks and exhaled slowly, steadying herself once again.

"Me and Terry were on holiday as you know. We'd been out to lunch and –"

"I'm sorry to ask you this, and please don't take offence, but had you both been drinking?"

Mrs Walsh shot Gold a look that was both furious and hurt at the same time.

"What are you saying. That we were pissed? That I was drunk and didn't know what I was doing? Is that it?!"

The nurse started to push the chair back as if about to get up from the table. Gold put what he hoped would be a reassuring hand on the sleeve of her jacket.

"Not at all, Joanne." (If ever there was a time to build bridges it was now, he thought). "But you've got to understand, I am contacted by hundreds of people and most of them are, well, you know, nuts. But I want to hear your story. Really. I do. Please sit down. Talk to me."

Joanne Walsh looked at him, seemed to consider his words, and slowly sank down into her hard-wooden chair.

"Fine. We'd been out to lunch –" She paused, but this time Gold was as silent as the grave.

"It was a beautiful sunny day, clear blue skies, couldn't be nicer. We'd been chatting about re-decorating our front room at home, I'd see some wallpaper in John Lewis that I'd liked, when we saw him. Right there. As clear as I'm seeing you. We both saw him. Me and Terry."

"You saw who exactly, Mrs Walsh?" asked Gold quietly.

"My brother. Peter. Standing right there by the side of the road. He was smiling. Smiling with that crooked funny look he always had."

"And you didn't know he was in Turkey? So that was a big surprise I'm guessing?"

Joanne looked at Gold in pity and confusion.

"Yes, Mr Gold, it really was a big surprise . . . since he is dead."

Later, Gold would recognise that this was the moment when his life changed forever. Hindsight is a brilliant thing.

"Mrs Walsh, I'm really sorry, I don't think I'm following you here. Who was dead?"

The nurse leant forward so that she could whisper the words, as if somehow saying them at any greater volume would be an unpardonable sin.

"Peter. My brother. He's dead. He died a few years back in a car crash. His van was totalled on the A65."

Gold was having great difficulty grasping what the woman opposite him at the Café Rouge in Victoria station was saying.

"Can I see if I'm following you? You saw your brother in

Turkey, but he had died a few years ago. But you saw him?"

Joanne Walsh began to nod her head. "Yes. Terry and I saw him. As large as life. He even spoke to us."

"He spoke to you? What did he say?"

The nurse gave out a short mirthless laugh.

"That I was looking well. That Terry had lost weight. And that he was hungry."

Gold raised his hand and summoned the waitress. "Bring me a Jack Daniels. Straight up. One cube of ice. Thanks."

He didn't offer anything to Joanne Walsh.

"What happened then, Mrs Walsh . . . after this chat?"

Joanne looked down at the bare wooden table.

"Mrs Walsh? What happened then?"

She spoke very slowly and quietly.

"He ripped out my husband's throat."

The JD arrived. Gold picked up the glass, which infuriatingly had three cubes of ice in it, and swallowed. His throat burned as the liquid went down.

"Er . . . did he use a knife of some sort?"

Again, another pause.

"No Mr Gold. Peter used his teeth. Like an animal. They were pointed, like . . . like a shark's that you see on those nature shows on TV. Horrible pointed teeth. And he used them to rip out my Terry's throat. Right next to me."

The bourbon had hit Gold's stomach.

"And what did you do then?"

"I screamed. Well, I tried to scream and I started to run . . . run as fast as I could. I remember one of my flip-flops that I'd bought in Tesco fell off."

"And then?"

The nurse bit her lip. "Then there was an almighty flash. And a huge bang. Dust was everywhere. I couldn't see properly."

Gold drained the glass to the last drop.

"That was the bomb, then?"

She shook her head. "There was no bomb. The flash came from the temple. From right near where we'd seen my brother Peter. It was all the same thing."

Gold sat back in his chair. What in the name of The Twilight Zone was this? A nurse and her husband see her dead brother in broad daylight on holiday and the dead brother then turns all Dracula and rips out hubby's throat with his pointy shark teeth? Bullshit. This was nuts.

"You don't believe me, do you Mr Gold? You think I'm a head-case. I can see it from your face. But I know what I saw. Peter was there."

Gold considered his reply carefully. "Mrs Walsh, what you're telling me is, frankly, well, incredible. I don't know how to reply to you."

Brilliant. Well done. Quite the orator.

"Could it be possible . . . and hear me out . . . that your brother wasn't killed in the car accident? That he was still alive and wanted to, I don't know, disappear?"

Joanne Walsh shook her head. "No Mr Gold. Not possible. I had to identify Peter's body in the morgue. He was very, very dead. I'm a nurse. I know a dead person when I see one. Especially with a bloody great chunk missing from their skull where the rear-view mirror of the van went through it."

"OK . . . OK . . . so, what would you like me to do?"

Mrs Walsh sat up again and looked directly into Gold's face. Actually, it was rather disconcerting.

"I want you to investigate it. I want you to dig into it. I want you to go to Turkey and –"

Gold held up his hand as if directing traffic.

"Whoa . . . whoa . . . hold on. Go to Turkey? How would that happen exactly? Who will be funding that?"

Gold stopped just short of adding, "What's in this for me?"

"I have savings. You're welcome to them," answered Joanne Walsh without any trace of anger.

"No Mrs Walsh. I'm sorry. I can't take your savings. I just can't."

Where the hell did that come from? Are you mad? Grab the cash and dash. Take the mon and run. Take the loot and scoot.

There was something about this woman from Leeds that Gold, to his own utter amazement, found somehow believable. Her story was, of course, bonkers. However, she seemed, he had to admit, perfectly sane. Here in this café in a London mainline station her crazy tale of dead brothers becoming husband-eating zombies seemed ridiculous, but the teller of the tale far from it.

"I'll tell you what I'll do Mrs. Walsh. Leave this with me. I'll look into it. If I find out anything, I promise I'll let you know. If I need some funds, I'll call you first. I'm sorry to be blunt, but it's not that I don't believe that you believe what you saw was real, but undertaking an investigation like this takes time and money. A lot of it. I mean, this isn't like finding a missing dog."

Joanne Walsh's face relaxed a little and the muscles in her cheeks stopped twitching as they had been for most of the conversation.

"So you believe me, then?"

The million-dollar question.

Gold did his best to re-arrange his face into his most reassuring look. "Mrs Walsh, you seem like an eminently sensible person. You're a nurse. Clearly something awful, truly awful, happened during your holiday in Turkey. I'll see what I can do."

That was pretty good. Shoulda been a politician. Talk loads, say nothing.

Gold stood up, indicating beyond any doubt that the meeting was concluded. Mrs Walsh followed suit and extended her arm for a handshake.

"Thank you. Thank you so much Nick. May I call you Nick? It means so much to me. I already feel a lot better. Well, as I'm in

London, I thought I'd fit in a spot of shopping. You know, might as well."

Oh god, the merry widow.

"Yes, I'm meeting my niece. We thought we'd make a day of it. She's obviously very upset, what with losing her Dad and all in the car crash. Oh, there she is . . . just by the stairs. Well, I look forward to hearing from you."

With that Joanne Walsh, NHS Nurse, stood up and left Nick Gold alone with his bemused thoughts.

FIVE

"The mind is its own place, and in itself can make a heaven of hell, a hell of heaven."
– John Milton, Paradise Lost

Nick Gold walked up the road from his flat and caught the Northern line from Balham Station direct to Leicester Square. From there he could walk to the production offices of Good Foot in Dean Street. He might even treat himself to a steaming bowl of miso soup and some udon noodles at his favourite Japanese restaurant on the corner of Lisle Street. He liked it there; you weren't allowed to tip the staff.

Walking along a crowded pavement, standing on a train platform, sitting in a bar, anywhere really, he often felt he saw a fleeting glimpse of her. The lingering smell of her distinctive perfume in a shop, a half-seen reflection in a store window, a passenger disembarking from a train, all these would make Gold's heart skip a beat in shock, with a pathetic expectation that the past could be undone, that all could be as it once was. L.P. Hartley had written, *'The past is a foreign country: they do things differently there'* and Gold was painfully aware that therein lay a profound unmitigable truth.

It hadn't been his fault. That's what he'd told himself, time and again, until it became a litany.

No, it had not been his fault. It was hers. It was hers, all hers.

Gold's eyes began to mist. Irritated, he brushed away a tear.

She'd been twenty-five when he'd first met her. One of those totally random encounters. He was in a local coffee shop when he turned around and bumped straight into her, knocking the coffee she had in her hand all over the floor. He apologised profusely, offered to replace the coffee as it was all his fault, took a closer look at her, offered to pay her dry cleaning if the coffee had stained her clothes, gave her what he hoped was his best smile and suggested they had their coffee together at a table.

She tantalisingly hesitated and then acquiesced.

That was how it all started.

Gold had, in subsequent years, often ruminated on this chance encounter. It was, like most things in his life, a mixture of audacity, accident and alcohol. Not necessarily in that specific order.

As he glanced around at the other customers, some ready for the gym, experience had taught Gold that only two things in life never lied: very small children and Lycra. They were both equally unforgiving.

He had drifted in his thoughts. Thinking about her was very painful. It hurt. She was beautiful. Not in a conventional manner, but in a way that he knew he'd never get tired of. Her features taken individually were nothing exceptional, but put together, the effect was devastating.

Short dark hair in a sort of bob, he supposed it was called. Sparkling green eyes . . . yes, green . . . what was that all about? Then there was her smile. It was like Las Vegas. Luminescent. Her name was Suzie ('with a zed'), she was a graphic designer and worked from home for a boutique digital advertising agency in Hoxton.

She agreed to meet him for dinner later that week. Dinner ran into breakfast and that, as they say, was that.

Gold was in love. Suzie was deliciously captivating, infuriating, had an appalling temper, was passionate, exciting; in a nutshell, he was hooked. No one he'd ever met before or since looked so good in jeans, t-shirt, boots and a leather biker's jacket.

Despite his offers, Suzie refused to move in with him. She was fiercely independent. So, the two spent roughly an equal amount of time in each other's flats. Gold wasn't a fan of this arrangement but it was her way or the highway. Frankly, the highway held much less appeal.

Then it started. The mood swings. Gold never knew which Suzie he was going to meet: the adorable, sassy, sexy woman he loved or the maudlin, angry, irascible, vitriolic woman that, if he was totally honest, scared him a little. When in this state, she was so utterly unpredictable. So explosive. So mercurial.

These 'episodes', as Suzie referred to them, lasted varying lengths of time, a few days to, at their worst, two weeks. Then, like the sun breaking through after a storm, they were gone. Vanished without trace. Burnt away like morning mist.

Of course, the make-up sex was phenomenal.

Gold suggested that Suzie sought professional help, the reaction to which saw Gold with a swollen lip and black eye.

Where had it all gone wrong from being so right? At first, it was almost amusing: the flare-ups, the stupid, pointless rows and afterwards, making-up. It was a process that bonded them closer than ever. Tighter than Gold had ever felt with another human being, or, now he thought, would ever feel again. A depressing thought that had not helped his drinking pattern in the ensuing years.

Little by little, life with Suzie stopped being fun. The madness began to creep into every crevice, every single pore of Gold's existence. He called it 'madness' as that was the only word that seemed to embrace the depth of Suzie's behaviour. Besides, he had studied theology at Oxford, not medicine. What did he know? They would be sitting watching TV together. (Suzie liked American crime dramas such as NCIS, CSI, Criminal Minds) and Gold would catch her, without any provocation, glaring at him with a look bordering on sheer hatred in her eyes. It was unnerving. He would ask what was the matter and receive the inevitable monosyllabic response of "nothing".

Then there was the jealousy. A waitress would smile at him, a friend in the street would come up and say hi, a pal would phone for a chat, anything could be the lighted match to the petrol can of the emotional storm that would follow. Not immediately. The rage, pure unadulterated rage, would follow hours, even days, later. It was groundless, but Gold could see that to Suzie it was very real. Then the rage turned physical, inwardly and outwardly. Suzie would have large black circles under her eyes and look as if she'd aged ten or fifteen years overnight. Her face became hawkish, sharp, hostile. Outwardly, it manifested itself in ways that never failed to shock Nick. From nowhere, Suzie would launch a series of punches and slaps as she screamed obscenities at him. Gold tried his best not to engage by retaliating, trying not to fight back, but to mollify and calm her instead. However, the human spirit is never that strong. It would get physical. Never in a good way. The nadir of Suzie's behaviour was one night, following a casual conversation about family, she turned from the sink where she was washing up and squirted cleaning bleach into Gold's eyes, causing him to stagger to A&E where he proclaimed it was the result of a silly household mishap to the enquiries of the suspicious nursing staff.

Despite all this, he loved her. She completed him, filled the void in his soul and when she chose, looked so steaming hot that they would often leave social events early to race back to either of their apartments.

However, the illness deepened. It was clear to Gold that Suzie was staring into the bottomless abyss of clinical depression. Or so he thought. In fact, what she was staring into was infinitely worse. But hindsight is a curse.

After much persuasion and argument, Suzie agreed to visit her doctor, who in turn suggested she see a therapist. Gold would accompany her to each appointment, as though his presence might assuage the mounting crisis. Had he known, he would have saved his time. And himself. For a while, the therapy sessions seemed to help, but after a few weeks the rage returned, now worse than ever.

They were queuing to see a film at the local cinema when it started to rain. Suzie turned to Gold as if it were his fault, as if somehow he had control over the weather, and began to berate him hysterically. People in the queue turned around. She railed upon them "What the fuck are you motherfuckers looking at? Well? Fuck you. Fuck you all."

Gold tried to calm her and then move her from the queue, but it was too late. Suzie had gone into meltdown. It was almost as though she had no self-control, as though someone else was in charge of her, flipping her moods at their whim. Gold put it down to her medication.

But then the moods would go, like a sudden downpour that is replaced by blue skies and sunshine. Voila, there she was again. His Suzie. Beautiful. All-encompassing. Dazzling. Addictive.

Gold cursed under his breath for having allowed these thoughts to invade his mind. This wasn't the time or the place. But then, it never was. He took a few deep breaths to clear away the fragmented images. He needed to focus, to be in the here and now. To be what the outside world perceived as Nick Gold. To wear that thin carapace that just about protected him. The process worked. Within a few more footsteps, Gold was back and ready to board the train . . . in every sense.

The London tube system dates back to 1863 and was the world's first underground railway. The Metropolitan Railway, opened between Paddington and Farringdon, served just six stations. Shame it hasn't really improved thought Gold, as he found himself wedged between a woman eating a quarter pounder (with vomit topping apparently if the smell was anything to go by) and a suited businessman, the last of a dying breed, trying to read his broadsheet newspaper. Why in the name of Rupert Murdoch would anyone with an IQ that hit double figures bring a broadsheet newspaper onto the tube? Twat.

Gold exited Leicester Square Station, managed to circumnavigate the tourists who wandered aimlessly around the entrance, dodged up Lisle Street, cut through Chinatown to Shaftesbury Avenue, walked past several theatres and crossed into Dean Street and the offices of Good Foot Productions.

Like most of the buildings of what was left in London's once notorious, yet intoxicatingly exciting, Soho, the wooden stairs up to the offices of Good Foot Productions were uneven and hadn't seen a lick of paint since Jeffrey Bernard roamed the streets. Soho, like much of the most interesting parts of London, had caught the virulent infection of gentrification. Fascinating buildings were ripped down only to be replaced by bland, anonymous structures inhabited by investors who never bothered to live in them. The effect was to destroy local shops and make the area as dull and lifeless as a fast food burger.

Speaking of dull and lifeless, Gold was not looking forward to seeing Adam Farthing, his new director, again. The break from filming the TV series had been a blessing in disguise and Gold had enjoyed not having to endure Farthing's politically correct diktats.

As Gold entered the production offices, he was greeted by Mitzi the receptionist, who either had no mirrors at home, dressed in the dark or was wearing her outfit as a bet.

"Nick," she called out in her sing-song voice in which the end of every sentence sounded like a question. "Great to see you? How've you been? You here to see Adam? You're looking well? New jacket?"

Gold smiled. "Hi Mitzi. Thanks. Fine . . . yes . . . thanks . . . no."

Mitzi's expression clouded over as she tried to follow. A First in English Literature from Warwick University was no guarantee that one 'got' irony. It did, however, get her a job in 'meeja'.

"Coffee machine still not working?" he enquired.

Mitzi shook her head. "Yes, it's been fixed."

Gold wondered if it was Warwick UK or Warwick Alaska she'd attended.

An inner door off the reception area opened and out came Adam Farthing.

"Adam . . . good to see you, mate," said Gold with all the enthusiasm he could muster, which wasn't much. But he thought he'd at least make an effort.

"Hi Nick," replied Adam, flatly.

Nick was taken aback. Where was the over-cheery greeting? Where was the full-of-confidence strut? Adam Farthing seemed to have aged, and not in a good way. The shoulders seemed a little stooped, the eyes were slightly dimmed and he seemed to walk with some hesitancy. Was he ill? Worse, had he been fired? Gold was torn between pity and elation at the thought.

"Nick, do you think we could go out of the office to have a chat? Somewhere a bit more private?"

The little shit. He was going to fire him! Fuck that.

"Er, sure Adam. If you'd prefer." Ill or not, Gold had decided that he would end the encounter by punching the pretentious little twat in the face.

The two men left the office and walked through the busy street to the next road, Frith Street, home to Ronnie Scott's Jazz Club, a dozen or so restaurants covering every cuisine, and the best coffee in London at the legendary Bar Italia. There was even a swing song composed in its honour, sung by jazz sax player Ray Gelato and The Giants.

Back in 1949 when Lou and his wife Caterina opened the coffee bar, little could they have known that over half a century later it would be an institution. They would, however, certainly still recognise the place: the same Gaggia coffee machine, the red and white Formica fittings, probably some of the same customers, back then young guns, now old men, but still not men to be messed with. *Capiche?*

"There's a table at the back, let's sit there, Nick, if that's OK?"

Weird. Since when did Adam Farthing give a flying toss what was, or wasn't, all right with him? Actually, it wasn't where Nick liked to sit. He preferred the narrow counter that ran the length of the small café, perched on a red stool, watching the large TV that only ever showed Italian programmes, and, of course, Italian football. Rocky Marciano dominated the back wall in a large black and white photo. Adam ordered two coffees (anything else would be sacrilegious) and carried them to the small table at the back.

Nick adopted a deliberately casual manner but was feeling anything other than relaxed. The Paranormal Detective series might be crap, but the money was very useful. Now it was going to be taken away from him. He'd gone too far, over-stepped a line in the sand, pushed his luck too far . . .

"Nick, I know that you and I haven't always seen eye-to-eye."

Ya think?

Gold pulled an expression that was coolly non-committal. He'd keep his powder dry until the end.

Adam went on. "But, well, I've always thought of you as more than just a colleague . . . more . . . like a friend, really."

Where in the name of God was this going? Was he building up to fire him or ask him out on a date? Gold was now feeling a little lost.

Gold smiled. Not too much, just in case he had to launch into the 'I like you too Adam, but just not in that way' speech.

"We've known each other for a while now, Nick and, despite everything, I've come to like you, and more than that, to trust you."

No you bloody don't. You can't stand the sight of me, mused Gold.

"So if I told you something . . . something . . . special . . . I know it wouldn't go any further. Right?"

Here we go. No surprise really that they were one block away from Old Compton Street, Soho's exuberantly gay epicentre.

Gold had to break the tension which was becoming unbearable.

"Sure, Adam. It'll stay within these four walls. OK?"

Adam Farthing's shoulders visibly relaxed under his Jack Wolfskin jacket as though a weight had been lifted off them.

And then something happened that shocked Gold. Something totally unexpected.

Adam Farthing began to cry.

He slumped forwards and buried his head in his hands while his upper body started to shake. A man at a nearby table eyed this most unlikely of couples with a look that combined compassion with mild humour.

It was Soho. It happened.

Gold was stumped. What should he do next? Put a comforting hand on Adam's shoulder? Would that be totally misinterpreted? Was firing him proving too difficult? Crying? Who the hell cried in Bar Italia? Apart from grown men when Juventus, Inter Milan or Roma lost, obviously.

After what seemed like an eternity, a word that Nick Gold would become all too familiar with in the coming weeks, Adam Farthing looked up, dabbing his eyes with the back of his hand.

"Sorry . . . stupid of me . . . sorry."

Nick put on his most compassionate look. "Don't sweat it. No problem. Were the coffees that expensive?"

It was a sad little joke but the best he could come up with at such short notice.

Adam attempted a smile but failed miserably.

The silence was unbearable. Not quite as unbearable as Adam's egregious sniffing.

"Adam, why don't you just get it out? Just say whatever it is you have to say, eh?"

Adam took in a deep breath. Gold braced himself inwardly for the multitude of politically correct phrases that meant 'piss off, you're fired'. But what he heard was far more disturbing.

"OK. Here it is. You remember the piece we shot at Borley Rectory?"

"Yeah. Sure."

"Well, after we wrapped, you left for London and I went to a pub nearby with the crew and then realised I'd left my sodding phone at the location. I remembered calling a friend between takes, then you and I . . . well we had words . . . and I was so angry I forgot to pick it up from where I'd left it. Yeah, should've put it in my pocket but . . . look it happened. It just did. I'd left it with my e-cigarette kit."

E-cigarettes. Of course. Naturally.

"All the guys were leaving to get back to London so I drove back, alone, to the rectory to get it."

Gold was utterly bemused. Where the hell was this going? Was he crying because he'd lost his phone? *Jeez, get a life, mate.*

But Adam had stopped. He seemed lost in thought. Then, as abruptly as he'd stopped, he began again.

"Nick, I'm trusting you with what I'm about to say. I don't know who else to tell."

What? Had he done the deed with the continuity girl? Had he been drinking and driving after the pub and hit someone?

"I drove back to Borley Rectory. It was very late, but I had to find my phone and then I was going to drive home. I parked up and walked to where we'd been filming."

He stopped again.

Christ, this was like drawing out teeth.

"And what? You found your phone in your pocket?"

Adam's face had become a grey mask. The colour had drained from it. His eyes seemed to be focusing somewhere else.

"No Nick. I saw my grandfather."

Nick had no idea what to say.

"You saw your grandfather? At Borley Rectory?"

"Yes. I saw him as clearly as I'm seeing you."

"Well, that was a coincidence, Adam. Does he live nearby?"

Adam Farthing closed his eyes and squeezed out the next sentence as if it took every ounce of his strength.

"He's dead. He died five years ago. My grandfather is dead."

Nick stared at his producer. What the hell was he talking about?

Gold ran his fingers through his hair, took a deep breath, and spoke.

"Adam, let me see if I'm getting this. You saw your dead grandfather?"

Adam shook his head. "No Nick. Not just that. I spoke with him."

Oh, this was seriously messed up.

"OK . . . you'd been to the pub, you'd had a few drinks, you were tired, you were stressed about the phone . . . is that it?"

Adam gave a cheerless laugh.

"I drank Diet Coke. I never drink and drive. It's my rule. I was stone cold sober."

Gold was totally at sea.

"Adam . . . are you fucking with me?"

"Am I what? What? I knew it . . . I was a moron for thinking that I could confide in you."

The director began to get up from the table. Nick put out a restraining hand.

"Sit down, man. Come on . . . sit down, Adam. I'm listening. Talk to me. Take me through it. What happened?"

Adam Farthing seemed to age even further, as if the very retelling of the story was sapping the life force from his body.

"I got out of the car and started to walk to where I knew, or thought I knew, where I'd left my phone and ciggy kit. It was pitch black but I had the halogen torch I always keep in the car so I could see where I was walking. There it was. My phone. And the rest of my stuff. As I picked it up, I heard a voice say, 'You silly bugger. You'd forget your head if it wasn't screwed on.'

"I bloody well leapt out of my skin. I thought it must be one of the crew. You know, some of them went straight back to Town after we finished, didn't come to the pub. I presumed it was one of them. But then he came into the light from my torch. He spoke. 'Been doing all right for yourself, eh Addie.'

"I saw his face. It was my grandfather. Standing right there. Right bloody there. In front of me. He used to call me Addie when I was little."

Gold took a sip of his coffee. It was stone cold. He hardly noticed. His mind was racing.

Adam Farthing, a man with eff-all imagination. Mister On-Trend. A man who ran his life via his smart phone. This irritating man was somehow, infuriatingly, believable. Either that or he was having the worst meltdown Gold had ever seen, a meltdown that would require months in the Priory to fix.

"What happened next?"

Adam bit his lip. He answered very slowly.

"He tried to kill me."

Gold jerked forward in his chair. "He did what?"

"He picked up a stone and threw it at my head. It missed and hit my shoulder. I still have the bruise. Then . . . then he smiled at me."

Gold waved a hand, indicating that Adam should continue.

"I'll never forget that smile. It was the teeth. Horrible, repulsive teeth. Sharp. Pointed. Not . . . not human. The light from my torch seemed to pick them out in the darkness. And I ran . . . Nick I ran to my car. I ran as fast as I could. I could hear him coming after me, calling 'Addie wait . . . wait. Addie.' My hands were shaking so badly I thought I wouldn't be able to start the engine. But I did. I drove away like a maniac and in the rear-view mirror, I could see him. He was laughing. Laughing and pointing at me."

And then Adam Farthing, television director, Nick Gold's nemesis, broke down again and sobbed.

SIX

"Did I request thee, Maker, from my clay
To mould me man? Did I solicit thee
From darkness to promote me?"
– John Milton, Paradise Lost

After another coffee at Bar Italia, Nick had finally managed to calm Adam Farthing down enough so that he could be sent on his way back to the offices of Good Foot Productions. Nick used every trick he could muster – Adam was probably very tired, he'd been working too hard, the stress of producing such great television would affect even Martin Scorsese. No, of course he wouldn't tell anyone, no he didn't think he was going mad, yes it was strictly between them and, of course, he'd be absolutely delighted to work with him again on the next series and they were undoubtedly friends, not just colleagues.

Showbiz, dontcha just love it?

Christ! Gold settled the bill, he felt it was the least he could do under the circumstances, and decided that something a little stronger than coffee was required. It wasn't every day that someone you didn't like had a total meltdown in front of you.

Leaving the café with the obligatory 'Ciao' to the staff, Gold walked up Frith Street to Dean Street where The French House beckoned.

It was time to think and drink. The two activities were indelibly connected.

The Grade II-listed French House was a Soho legend. Charles

de Gaulle used the pub as a workplace during the Second World War, Dylan Thomas and Francis Bacon both drank there. Beer is only served in halves. Don't ever bother asking for a pint.

Gold liked its no-nonsense rules: no music, no gaming machines, no television and no mobile phones. London's finest conversationalists would gather here. But Gold was in no mood to talk. If he faced up to the truth, he was feeling very unsettled. He walked into the small, crowded bar and ordered a double Jack Daniels, straight-up.

The barman, a grizzled veteran of more Soho history than most, gave him a look that said another tough day, another drink.

Gold sipped at his drink in the small space he'd found to stand in the crowded bar. Everyone in The French House expected to be jostled, sometimes by a celebrity, sometimes by a normal person.

In life, thought Gold, there is weird, very weird and the downright pass me a double Bourbon. Was this some ridiculous yet very elaborate prank? It wouldn't be beyond the grounds of possibility. After all, Gold himself had seen far worse television submissions arrive across the desks at Good Foot Productions, his favourite being 'Stuck On You' where couples who have been through bitter, acrimonious divorces are super-glued together for a week.

First, considered Gold, as he ordered another double shot, there was Joanne Walsh and her insane story. An NHS nurse, who ought to be entirely sensible and pragmatic, although how anyone can work so hard for so little money would counter that assumption, goes to Turkey on holiday and just happens to bump into her dead brother. As you do. Now Adam Farthing, a man with all the imagination of a coffee table, gets attacked by his grandfather who also happens to be dead.

So, what to think? What in the name of Hammer Films was going on?

Gold took a deep swallow of his Jack Daniels and, by a miracle caught the eye of the Mr Happy-Go-Lucky behind the bar and ordered another double, straight-up.

First, was this a massive, well-constructed wind-up? That seemed impossible. Unless Adam Farthing had sneaked off to the Lee Strasberg Film & Theatre Institute in New York to take a crash-course in being the new Al Pacino, there was no way he could act so convincingly. Fake crying is really hard to do. Way harder than faking orgasms.

Gold focused his thoughts once more. No point in ruminating whether any of his exes had faked it. No. Impossible. He'd know.

Then there was the nurse. There was no connection between her and Adam. They'd never met. They didn't know each other.

So, in conclusion, there were only two possible explanations – the arrival of which required a packet of salted peanuts, which Gold ordered and began to eat. Part of his five-a-day.

Conclusion one: this was a brilliantly conceived, high-production prank. There were hidden cameras capturing all of the conversations, the meetings, the facial reactions. Genius. Had early Saturday night ITV written all over it.

Or.

Something very, very, off the Richter Scale of Weirdness was going on. Something so peculiar that it broke every known rule of life . . . and death.

There was only one thing to do – order another double bourbon and, just to ring the changes, some pork scratchings. A snack so revolting in concept that only the British could have invented it.

Gold left The French House and the fresh air of Soho, if that wasn't an oxymoron, hit him rather hard. Several double Jack Daniels will do that, even to a TV presenter. His mind felt fuzzy as he tried to process the day's bizarre events. It didn't matter how many times he ran the various scenarios over in his mind, the stories were just impossible to comprehend. Dead people, outside of a Stephen King novel, don't reappear to have a casual chat with their relatives. Then there was the killing thing. Just how pissed off were these relatives if they wanted to kill close members of their own family? It wasn't like the still living family members were all lawyers or estate agents. That would be justifiable homicide. No, these Walking Dead had rocked up, one in the UK, one in Turkey, one in broad daylight, one at night, and tried to kill members of their family. Not just kill, bite.

And then there were the teeth. Gold knew he didn't floss every single day, life was too short, but how bad would your dental hygiene need to be before you sprouted pointed fangs, as witnessed by the nurse and the director?

The questions ran around Gold's mind like an earworm tune.

The walk to Leicester Square tube station, only a short distance even in Gold's condition, did little to clear his mind. On the plus side, he hadn't been fired; on the minus side, he truly did not have a clue what the hell was going on.

Funny how certain words can haunt you.

The tube carriage was full. London was a 24 hour-a-day city. No longer tied to any pretence of Sabbatarianism, London never stopped. Of course, the tube trains did and if you didn't drive, there were the delights of the Night Bus – a thrill-a-minute voyage into the unknown.

Gold looked around at his fellow passengers. Was his late grandmother about to reveal herself from behind a copy of the *Daily Mail* and plunge her sharpened NHS dentures into his neck? Yeah . . . right.

Opposite him sat (yes Gold had managed to find an empty seat, a result so outstanding that he briefly contemplated tweeting about it) a couple of tourists scrutinising a London Underground map. It was a masterpiece of design, the brainchild of Underground electrical draughtsman Harry Beck, who produced the simple design in 1933. Beck based his design on the circuit diagrams he drew for his day job. Of course, the innovative map was rejected by the then publicity department as being far too radical. Naturally.

The tube map . . . why was it suddenly the focus of his attention? How odd. Something about it. Then the moment was gone and Gold was contemplating several matters of great importance: what to have for supper, what was in the tourists' massive rucksacks outside of a family SUV and why wasn't there air-conditioning on the London Underground? Multi-tasking, he liked to call it.

Getting out at Balham Station, Gold crossed the road and walked across the carpark towards the entrance of a large branch of Sainsbury's supermarket. It had been a helluva day.

But it wasn't over yet.

Not by a long way.

Close to the sliding entrance doors sat a dishevelled homeless man. He was maybe forty-five, maybe thirty-five, hard to tell under the grime and care-filled lines on his face. He looked, even to Gold's tired, bourboned-eyes, a wreck. Unshaven, a filthy woollen hat perched precariously on his head, some sort of very dirty blanket wrapped around his body, fingerless gloves on his hands. By his side sat a dog. A mongrel the size of a Labrador.

Gold glanced at the sad scene. The streets of London, like every major city, were home to thousands of the dispossessed; people who had somehow fallen through the cracks, through the supposed safety net of the State and had ended up in a perilous, appalling place.

The man looked up.

"It's you."

Gold paused. "Sorry?"

The man's expression seemed to change. It was tiny, almost imperceptible, but it was there – somehow at variance with his appearance.

He spoke again, his voice clear and classless. "It's you, you know."

Gold thought it best to humour the man. He smiled while thinking, there but for the grace . . . He reached into his trouser pockets to find some change. He could afford this small gesture. After all, he hadn't been fired today.

"I don't need your money. We've come to tell you that it is you."

Gold had had enough. "Mate, take the money. Get something to eat or a hot drink. Go on. Take it."

"We don't need your money."

Gold froze. He had heard an innocuous phrase, delivered in a polite, non-threatening, reasonably-voiced manner. Nothing exceptional.

Except it was the dog who had spoken.

Gold couldn't move. Around him shoppers were entering and exiting the supermarket. Babies in buggies cried or slept. Cars patrolled the car park looking in vain for a parking place. It was a normal everyday suburban scene. Christ! Just how drunk was he? Three doubles – no big deal.

Gold tried to speak but nothing came out. He stood rooted to the spot and stared at the homeless man and his dog.

A woman walked past, patted the dog on its head and dropped some coins into the plastic food container the homeless man had at his feet.

Still nothing.

Gold shook his head in an effort to clear it. Sod this, he'd ease up on the alcohol for a day or two. He gently placed two pound coins into the plastic box and backed slowly away. The man just smiled up at him. The dog licked its balls.

Gold entered the supermarket and headed straight for the wine section. On balance, this wasn't the day to quit drinking. Was he having a breakdown? Around him shoppers were doing what shoppers do – shop, wandering up and down aisles filling their trolleys or baskets, arguing with their kids, standing in everyone's way checking their phones. It was all perfectly normal. Sainsbury's was simply a large supermarket, not the Seventh Circle of Hell. Except in the run-up to Christmas.

As Gold walked down the Crisps & Snacks aisle to rendezvous with a large pack of Doritos, he let out an exclamation that made the pensioner near him turn and stare.

"You total moron. Idiot! Of course. The guy outside could do a bit of ventriloquism. What the hell was I thinking?"

The elderly lady stared at him.

"Er . . . sorry . . . it's nothing . . . I thought a dog had just spoken to me. You know . . . outside. A dog . . . crazy huh?" he offered the woman by way of explanation.

The old lady continued to stare at him, then as she turned muttered, "Fucking crack head."

They don't mess around in Balham.

Gold was suddenly flooded with relief. Yes, of course. It was so blindingly obvious. What was wrong with him? Nothing that a good night's sleep wouldn't put right. What an idiot. Talking dog! Not even the desperate TV companies would bother to make a show about that now, not since Mr Ed, the talking horse, back in the late fifties.

With his essential provisions loaded into a five pence plastic bag, Gold left the supermarket with a sense of trepidation as he looked for the homeless man. He was gone. Him and Lassie the Wonder Dog.

Good.

He started to walk towards his flat.

Gold smiled ruefully to himself. Life had re-balanced. He was OK. Stupid panic over. Yeah, a talking dog. Obviously, that's going to happen . . . outside Sainsbury's . . . in Balham.

Maybe he'd taken the money from his plastic box and gone to get a hot drink. Maybe the dog needed a walk. Or an elocution lesson. Who knew? Who cared?

Walking up Balham High Street the lights from the restaurants, bars and shops put Gold in a good mood. Soon he'd be home in his one-bedroom mansion flat, the wine would be open, the TV on and God would be back in his heaven.

Approaching the entrance to the mansion block, Gold's slightly jaunty pace began to slow.

No . . . it couldn't be. This wasn't possible.

Sitting on the first step that led to the double entrance doors of Gold's mansion block was the homeless man.

And his dog.

Gold stopped dead on the street. The plastic carrier bag suddenly felt like it contained lead weights. His heart pounded and his mouth went dry.

Slowly, one rather faltering step after another, Gold approached the man.

Somehow Gold found his voice.

"Mate, I gave you some change. What do you want? Why are you here?"

The homeless man stood up.

He was, to Gold's surprise, taller than he had appeared at first glance. More muscular. His posture belied his circumstances – it was straight and purposeful.

None of this made Gold feel any easier.

Then he spoke. The voice had changed. No longer the slightly tremulous weak voice of the vagrant outside the supermarket. It was soft yet commanding. It seemed to fill Gold's ears and enter directly into his brain as if he was wearing an expensive set of noise-cancelling headphones.

"I told you . . . it's you."

"Yeah . . . I heard you the first time, mate. I know it's me. Now I don't want to be rude, but why are you following me?"

The moment he'd spoken, Gold knew that was a ridiculous sentence. This man hadn't followed him. He was already here when Gold returned.

Him and the dog.

"Following you? Because you're . . . an important man. We need you."

What the hell was this? Some new form of headhunting from another TV production company? A joke? A nut job?

"I'm not important. Just because you may have seen me on TV doesn't make me important."

There was a silence. Somehow the homeless man seemed to prevent Gold from moving by his mere presence. There was no direct threat, but Gold felt a distinct low-level, sub-textual unease.

"Who's we?"

Silence.

"You said 'we need you'."

Damn. I've engaged him in conversation. Idiot. Sod this.

Gold began to walk towards the double front doors of the street entrance to the flats.

"It's you."

Right. Enough was enough.

"Mate, do me a big favour . . . piss off. Hang around here and there'll be trouble."

Instantly, the ears of the dog pricked up and from its throat came a low, rumbling growl. A growl far outweighing the not inconsiderable size of the dog. Gold was instantly reminded of any of the big cat shows he'd watched as a kid presented by David Attenborough. It was feral. If a canine can be feral. Well, whatever it was, it was fucking frightening.

Gold stood still. Half wanting to run as fast as he could into the flats, half remembering that a dog can sense fear and so standing stock still was apparently the safest option.

The homeless man stood silently, motionless. His eyes seemed to bore into Gold's skull.

Laser eyes.

Oh good, why not wind yourself up a bit more. Laser eyes. Jesus!

The homeless man's eyes seemed to Gold like nothing he had ever seen. He recalled from his university studies that in the bible

Matthew said, 'The eye is the lamp of the body. If your eyes are healthy, your whole body will be full of light. But if your eyes are unhealthy, your whole body will be full of darkness. If then the light within you is darkness, how great is that darkness!'

Yet this was no darkness. Neither was it a light that Gold had ever experienced before. It was as though Gold could see *through* the eyes of the man, and what he saw dazzled him. Stars shone, galaxies swirled, nebulae floated, planets rotated while their suns orbited them. The universe presented itself.

Finally, the man spoke.

"Gold's chemical symbol is Au. Its atomic number is seventy-nine. You are thirty-two. In some ways, Mr Gold, it is like you – when pure, it is bright, yet it is also dense, soft, malleable."

What the hell?

"Gold is a transitional metal. You, Mr Gold, are also transitioning. It is one of the least reactive chemical elements – you have so far failed to react to what has been placed before you. Do you know how gold was formed?"

Nick Gold stood in his own street, outside his own flat, and felt as if he was alone on Mars. All he could do was shake his head, very slightly. The homeless man grunted.

"Hmm. I thought not. Gold is produced by nucleosynthesis during supernovas. Big stellar explosions. Are you with me?"

Gold stammered. "What . . . er . . . no . . . no I'm not with you. I don't under –"

The lecture continued without further pause.

"It means that it was formed from the collapse of certain classes of stars. It was there at the very beginning of everything, Mr Gold. The very start. It was present in the dust from which the Solar System formed. Think of that."

Gold had now given up any rational thought processes. This was, as they say, seriously fucked up.

"Do you know why gold is located underground. Deep underground?"

A slight shake of the head.

"Because the earth was molten when it was formed. Do you see? Molten. That's why gold sank towards the planetary core. And that wasn't the only thing that sank deep, deep down, Mr Gold. No . . . it wasn't."

Somehow, God knows how, Nick Gold began to emerge from his state of paralysis. This was bullshit.

"Look, Professor Brian Cox, I don't actually give a flying toss about how gold was made or where it is. I don't care. You understand? What I do care about is going home and getting the fuck away from you. It's late, I'm tired, I've had a very trying day and, to be blunt, I really don't need this shit."

The dog once again emitted a deep, rumbling growl.

"And you can tell Krypto the Wonder Dog to shut it as well."

The homeless man's face was expressionless. Not the slightest sign of anger, disappointment, irritation. It was a blank mask.

"We value gold because of its easy handling, its rarity, and resistance to corrosion. It is precious."

"Are you deaf? I don't give a shit! I don't care about gold! Let me pass! Now!"

Something of a flicker of a smile crossed the homeless man's face.

"I'm not talking about gold, the element . . . I'm talking about you, Nick Gold."

Gold was stunned.

"What? You're what?"

"You, Nicholas Gold. You are precious. You are resistant. You are rare. That's why it is you."

Nick Gold, thirty-two, television presenter, media-savvy Londoner, weighed over in his head what he had just heard.

"I wonder," he said slowly, "if you would do me a favour? Go fuck yourself."

With that Gold strode straight on, brushing the homeless man aside, ignoring the growling hound, put his key in the lock, which he'd had in his hand ready to stick it in the eye socket of the stranger had things gone all Pete Tong, and ran up the three flights of stairs to his flat.

SEVEN

"O sun, to tell thee how I hate thy beams
That bring to my remembrance from what state
I fell, how glorious once above thy sphere."
– John Milton, Paradise Lost

Gold dropped the plastic shopping bag the instant he closed his front door and let out a long exhalation. That was weird. No, weird didn't cover it. It was . . . freaky. What was he, twelve? Freaky? Unnerving, Unsettling. Disturbing. Why not just come out and say it? Scary.

Yes, there you go . . . scary. OK . . . there . . . said it . . . scared. How did this lunatic know his name? Why had he picked on him? And why, come to think of it, had Sainsbury's put up the price of their wine?

Speaking of which, Gold picked out the bottle of Rioja that he'd bought, found the corkscrew that was buried deep in a kitchen drawer, realised it was a metal screw cap, cursed, unscrewed the top and poured himself a large one.

The red wine seemed to have the desired effect as its warmth flowed down his throat and into his stomach. Yes, he was feeling much better. Thank you, Spain, for your finest export. Perhaps he should feel even better by partaking in Columbia's finest export, stashed in a drawer? No. He needed to focus and was feeling paranoid enough as it was.

Gold opened the bag of Doritos, poured another large glass of

Rioja (the first one seemed to have magically vanished) and sat at his small kitchen table.

He began to scribble notes trying to marshal his thoughts:

1. NHS nurse sees her dead brother who tries to kill her. Bomb explosion? Shark teeth? Turkey. Drunk?
2. Adam Farthing sees his dead grandfather. Tries to kill him. Teeth? Nervous breakdown? Guilt?
3. Random homeless man knows my name. WTF? Dog!!
4. Buy more washing-up liquid.

Gold's thought-processes were often like a firework display. But, in truth, he had noticed that his Fairy Liquid Power Plus was on the low side.

He put down the pen and took another gulp of red wine, once again feeling the warm glow the Rioja brought.

Was there a link? Was there something that would make these seemingly random events make any sense?

Several handfuls of Doritos later, Gold opened his laptop and, forgoing the dubious and hugely time-consuming pleasures, of Facebook and Twitter, went straight to Google. This evening just wasn't the right time to look at photos of strangers' kids, dogs or how much they apparently hated the American President and TV Talent Shows in equal measure.

His fingers hesitated over the keys. What to enter? Fangs? Teeth? Ghosts? Bullshit?

Sod it! He was feeling utterly uninspired. The canvas was too broad. There was no convenient category to start researching. The search engine of choice was highly unlikely to have a section labelled 'Dead Relatives Who Come Back to Life to Scare the Crap Out of You'.

Wiping his Dorito-covered fingers on a kitchen towel (which his posh cousin Ceril insisted on calling a 'napkin' since 'serviette' showed a lack of breeding, apparently), Gold thought that the equivalent of digital doodling might bring inspiration. At the very least, it would stop him sitting around like an idiot twiddling his thumbs or, Heaven forbid, thinking about the creepy homeless man . . . and his talking dog.

So, without much enthusiasm, Gold headed for the Reddit website on his laptop. It was the Reddit sub-division called 'Not The Onion' that Gold derived most pleasure from. Bizarre stories, all apparently true, garnered from around the world.

Sure enough, a cornucopia of the weird and the wonderful appeared on his screen. Frankly he was spoiled for choice. Digital doodling at its finest. *Boy Arrested and Charged For Throwing Paper Plane In Class*; *Bristol Police Taser Their Own Race Relations Manager By Mistake*; *Woman Is One Hundred Percent Allergic To Her Husband*; *Research Shows Cyclists Pollute London More Than Cars.*

All true. All totally bonkers. Three-dimensional examples of just how crazy the world had become, especially, thought Gold, in the past five to ten years. It seemed so much more straightforward when he was twenty-two . . . or maybe even thirty.

He clicked on the articles taken from media reports across the globe. They defied belief but were backed up by appropriate court papers or official statements from police forces or newspapers. The fact that they were true just made them all the more extraordinary.

Then Gold's eye caught another headline and weblink.

Woman Arrested For Husband's Murder. Claims Her Dead Father Killed Him.

What? Seriously?

With a knot forming in his stomach, Gold clicked on the accompanying link and began to read.

York County Times

Loretta Johnstone, 35, has been arrested and charged with the murder of her husband Doug, 38. The couple were driving through Pennsylvania and had reached Hellam Township when their vehicle broke down. It was while Mr Johnstone was attempting to repair the car that he was viciously attacked by his wife, sustaining horrific injuries to his neck that almost caused decapitation. In her defence, Mrs Johnstone has repeatedly told police that her late father, Walter Trout, appeared, attacked her husband and then spoke to her before also attacking her. The police have put the crime down to a domestic dispute that got out of hand, but the defendant has refused to move on her story, which she claims is true. Police doctors are baffled by the serrated teeth-like marks on the victim's neck and face but are convinced that Mrs Johnstone's story is just that – a story.

The trial is set for six weeks' time.

Gold sat rigid at his kitchen table.

You have got to be fucking kidding me.

No way. No. Nonsense. First, it was America and this is the country where every weirdo has been abducted by a UFO, seen Elvis or carries enough firepower to start WWIII. Secondly, it was just the sort of cock and bull story that a deranged wife would invent to cover up the brutal murder of her husband. That or 'The Devil Made Me Do It' your Honour.

It was crap. Obviously.

Gold sat back in his kitchen chair.

When the great consulting detective Sherlock Holmes was faced with an especially vexing conundrum, he would sit and contemplate while smoking his trusty briar pipe – calling the most perplexing of these cases 'a three-pipe problem'.

Gold had a similar methodology. A three-glass problem. With extra handfuls of Doritos. Not as snappy or alliterative as 'a three-pipe problem' but equally as effective.

A dead relative kills someone. Jagged teeth marks. Defendant adamant in her story.

Bookmarking the link, Gold decided to consider things a little further.

Although the musical 'Avenue Q' insisted in a big number that 'The Internet is For Porn' (not entirely untrue), Gold was an adept hand at using it for genuine research for his television work, adding to the scripts, digging up more facts to flesh out his pieces to camera, making each episode feel a little more based on fact rather than fiction.

Where to start?

The first stop was to see if the case had attracted any more attention other than a small paragraph in the 'Not The Onion' section of Reddit.

Google soon came up with a few reports on the incident, most of which reiterated the same 'facts' while varying in tone and degrees of sensationalism.

The *Bradford Era* more or less repeated what Gold had read on Reddit, with the addition of a few facts to fill out the copy: where they were driving to; where they had been living; an interview with a neighbour who described them as 'nice ordinary folks who kept themselves to themselves'.

Why did every everyone describe their neighbours in this manner? Had the Hellfire Club, the Nazi Party, Genghis Khan or Jack the Ripper lived next door, the description would have been the same. "I used to see Mr Hitler occasionally putting out his recycling bin on a Tuesday, but other than that –"

The *National Enquirer*, however, didn't hold back. *Demon Driver Devours Dad* (apparently the Johnstones had a son, Scott, who was staying with the wife's sister). The article, if such a term can be bestowed upon anything in the *National Enquirer*, went on in gruesome detail to list the injuries sustained by Mr Johnstone and those inflicted upon his hapless wife, now languishing in a county jail awaiting trial on a charge of Murder in the First Degree. 'Ragged strips of flesh . . . jagged teeth marks like those from a shark . . . blood splattered car . . . parts of the husband found all over the road . . . Kim and Kanye said to be shocked . . . *et cetera, et cetera*.'

There it was again: 'jagged teeth'. Either this was a tremendously unlikely orthodontal coincidence, or there was a link. A weird, 'Twilight Zone meets Dean Koontz let's all change our underwear' link to be sure. But what else could it be? Did all these people not just have bad teeth, but teeth that would look pretty good on a Great White swimming off the Great Barrier Reef?

Gold was on a roll. Which reminded him that Rioja and Doritos do not a supper make. He headed for the fridge (no time to cook) and pulled out some cheese, butter and Branston Pickle. Within sixty seconds, a veritable feast of a crusty roll, cheddar cheese and a generous dollop of pickle was on a plate. Gold munched as he hunched.

What else? What else might provide a link between Mrs Walsh, Adam Farthing and the psycho in Pennsylvania?

The three had never met. Had the square root of sod all in common. Their paths had never crossed. So what was it? Gold chomped on the cheese roll, so lost in thought that he really didn't taste it.

Nothing. Shit. Nothing was coming. An NHS nurse. A TV producer. An American housewife.

Then, like a tiny light at the end of a tunnel, an idea began to form. A light that grew like an approaching express train.

It wasn't *who*, it was *where*.

Of course there was no point in looking for a link between these people. There wasn't one. Despite the locations of these attacks, incidents – Gold didn't know how to refer to them – being spread across the world, maybe, just maybe *where* they had taken place was of some significance.

Gold took another swig of the wine, failing to note the aromatic botanic flavours with a nose of raspberries, but noting it was making him slightly pissed.

Where did these occurrences take place? Grabbing his spiral-bound notepad he began to search the web and make notes.

Mrs Joanna Walsh had seen her husband killed by her dead brother in the ancient city of Hierapolis, near modern-day Pamukkale in Turkey.

Adam Farthing had been attacked by his dead grandfather at Borley Rectory in Essex.

Finally, Loretta Johnstone had killed, or not killed, or whatever, her husband via her dead father, or not, in Hallam, York County in Pennsylvania.

So, Turkey, the UK, the US of A.

Great.

Nothing sprang to mind. Gold massaged his temples as the wine, and the thinking, combined to start off a headache of epic proportions.

And not just anywhere in the UK but Essex. The one county that was guaranteed to start more jokes than any other. Essex man. Essex girls. Hardly the stuff of legend.

Was it the Olympics? No, to Gold's certain recollection, the Olympics had never been held in Essex.

Was it perhaps lay lines? Which in itself prompted Gold to make a very juvenile joke in his head about Essex lay lines. No, absolutely not.

Maybe his search should be more specific.

This was starting to remind Gold of his theology studies at Oxford when he'd pore over books into the small hours as he cross-referenced Jospehus, biblical quotes and scholarly texts.

Maybe it was the Rioja that was making Gold wander aimlessly down memory lane, or perhaps the bizarre double encounter with the homeless man, but wander he did, in an uncharacteristically mellow mood. Time, and recollections, can play tricks with the mind, but Gold was firmly convinced he could recall sitting in his highchair, playing with a red toy racing car that had an engine that lit-up when the wheels were turned, when he became aware something was very wrong. It wasn't the words that were being exchanged, it was the body language of the people exchanging them – a babysitter and a woman in a blue uniform. It was the way that the babysitter collapsed, gasping sobs punctuating the ensuing silence, that had stayed with Gold.

In later years, Gold would come to understand that this was the moment the police had come to his home to report that his parents had been killed in a car accident on the North Circular Road near North Finchley. As he grew older, he had investigated every aspect of the accident but to no avail. Its cause remained a mystery. The weather was fine, the roads dry, it was still light, but somehow Debbie and Andrew Gold's Rover 200 had careered off the three-lane road, overturned and hit a tree at high speed.

The Coroner's report that Gold had read a hundred times at least concluded that the couple had died instantly from the impact. No other vehicles were involved. Eye witnesses claimed it seemed the vehicle deliberately left the road and aimed straight for the tree. Gold knew that simply could not be true. What sense did it make? His parents had only popped out for a coffee and to do some food shopping. The sheer randomness of life. Except it wasn't.

Life from that moment took a very different turn. Much like the Rover.

Gold's parents had no siblings, so he was sent to a second cousin of his mother's. His memories of those years always seemed to be in black and white, never in colour. Lloyd and Hazel Carson were a deeply religious couple, steeped in the ways of the Bible. Their hearts were in the right place, that is beneath their rib cages, but they were firm believers that 'a child should be seen and not heard'. There were no hugs and kisses. There were no Mr Men goodnight stories. Just readings from the Bible. Tactile was not a concept that they embraced. The couple had no other children, so could lavish all their religious fervour upon young Nick throughout his childhood. They meant well, were never cruel, never hit him and ensured that he was always fed well and clothed modestly. As parents, the best description would be remote. Not as in a TV remote, because, naturally, Mr and Mrs Carson refused to have one in their home. For them BBC Radio 4 was sufficiently racy, and that was only for the *Six O'Clock News*.

The couple belonged to the Church of Christ, whose website proclaims, 'The Church of Christ is God's sole representative on the earth today'. For Mr and Mrs Carson, there was no doubt whatsoever that this was an absolute truth. To them, all other denominations were either heretic or demonic, with all their members on a one-way ride to Hell. In their eyes, they were the Way, the Truth and the Life and they were not a denomination because they *were* the church.

Young Nicholas Gold soaked all this up. His young very agile brain like a sponge. It was all he had ever known. All he had ever been taught. Childhood passed in the blink of an eye and the teenage Nicky Gold, as he liked to think of himself back then, was deeply religious. He had embraced it. While his school friends went through the daily horrors of adolescence, Nicky had religion as his best friend. He even attended, of his own volition, the Church of Christ. It provided for him and quenched the thirst *to belong*. Here, as a bright young member of the community, he 'belonged'. The Church loved him and he bathed in their intellectualised affection. In its own remote, non-tactile way, he felt it loved him. And to be loved is the greatest desire of mankind.

Hazel and Lloyd Carson had little need to encourage their adopted son to study for his exams. With four A* grades in his A level exams, university beckoned. The three of them sat down together over tea and ham sandwiches to complete the scholarship paperwork that Nicky proudly posted off to Oxford.

To celebrate his successful application and admission to study Theology and Philosophy at St Hugh's College, Oxford, Mr Carson poured three glasses of sherry. Mrs Carson later described herself as feeling 'tipsy'.

Back then, eighteen-year-old Nicky Gold was certain of his vocation to become a priest. To make a difference. To serve God and the community. It would fulfil him.

But the road to Heaven is paved with good intentions.

Free of his adopted parents, Oxford University turned Gold's life from black and white to glorious technicolour. It was as though his senses had suddenly exploded into life. There were girls, many girls, there were endless parties, there was far more to drink than sherry, far more to smoke than cigarettes and certainly far more to put up one's nose than decongestant.

This was life! This was what feeling alive really meant! It was fantastic!

And best of all, he still had his faith.

Until Suzie. Until then.

Gold shook his head to clear away the memories and the Rioja. Coffee was required, was made, was consumed and he returned to his work renewed. Where was he?

So, start at the beginning. Mrs Joanne Walsh. On holiday in, where was it, somewhere unpronounceable in Turkey – Pammukale.

Gold typed in the name of the resort. Oh crap. Endless entries from holiday companies with photos of perfect smiling families having a great time by the pool, buffet, taverna . . . no cliché left unturned. Now he'd be inundated with pop-up adverts for flights, car hire, hotels and diarrhoea medicine for eternity.

He dug a little deeper. 'Pammukale + Hierapolis'.

Oh hello.

> *'Pamukkale is a town in Western Turkey known for the mineral-rich thermal waters flowing down white travertine terraces on a nearby hillside. It neighbours close-by Hierapolis, an ancient Roman spa city, which was founded about 190BC. Ruins there include a well-preserved theatre and a necropolis and sarcophagi that stretch for two kilometres.'*

*

Gold sat back. What in the name of Vincent Price was a necropolis and the other thing? He knew Metropolis, but that was a large motorbike showroom in Vauxhall, South-East London. The only well-preserved theatre he could think of was the Hackney Empire.

This wasn't helping.

But this was.

'Hierapolis means "ancient city" and was believed to have been founded by the god Apollo.'

Then, quite suddenly, at the click of his mouse, there it was.

Gates of Hell found at Hierapolis.

'The mythical "Gates of Hell" have been discovered in the ancient Phrygian city of Hierapolis, now Pamukkale in South-Western Turkey. It is said to closely match historical descriptions of what was known as Ploutonion in Greek and Plutonium in Latin.

'In its heyday, a small temple with traditional Greco-Roman pillars was said to have stood next to a wall with steps leading down to a cave doorway filled with foul and noxious gases.'

Mate, try the Northern Line at rush hour.

'Describing the site, the Greek geographer Strabo said, "This space is full of vapour so misty and dense that one can scarcely see the ground. Any animal that passes inside meets instant death. I threw in sparrows and they immediately breathed their last and fell."

Bit harsh.

'Now a team led by Italian archaeologist Francesco D'Andria, Professor of classic archaeology at the University of Salento, has discovered what they believe to be the ruins of the site. Announcing the discovery at a

conference on Italian Archaeology in Istanbul, Professor D'Andria said he and his team had managed to pinpoint the location by reconstructing the route of the thermal spring.'

And then the really good bit.

'Archaeologists now believe that a large statue found at the Phrygian city, previously believed to depict Apollo, is actually Hades, Greek god of the underworld.'

Oh yeah . . . now we're cooking with gas.

'Among the ruins the archaeologists found a cave with Ionic semi-columns on which were inscriptions and dedications to the gods of the underworld, Pluto and Kore. Professor D'Andria told Discovery News: "We could see the cave's lethal properties during the excavation. Several birds died as they tried to get close to the warm opening, instantly killed by the carbon dioxide fumes."

Professor D'Andria has conducted extensive archaeological research at Hierapolis and two years ago he claimed to have discovered there the tomb of Saint Philip, one of the 12 apostles of Jesus Christ.

In conclusion, is this actually the Gate of Hell? Archaeologists say the temple doorway belching noxious gas matches ancient accounts of 'portal to the underworld'.

Archaeologists announced the otherworldly significance of this holy spot. The same gases that heat the famous hot springs of Pamukkale originate from a cave beneath the Ploutonion, and because the vapours are toxic, the people of Hierapolis believed that they had been sent from Pluto himself and the site was treated as a ritual entrance to the underworld. Pilgrims would travel from all over the classical world to make sacrifices to Pluto; animals led into the cave would drop dead from the toxic fumes, while acolytes of Pluto would prove their devotion to the god by entering the cave and emerging alive (perhaps thanks to their knowledge of pockets of breathable air within the cave).'

Gold sat back once more. 'The Gate of Hell'. You're kidding, right?

He stood up, walked over to the kitchen counter, and poured a very large glass of Rioja into his glass. Damn, why hadn't he bought a few bottles? This really wasn't the best time to have given up smoking, either. His empty fingers began to tap out a rhythm on the table surface that Buddy Rich or Ginger Baker would have been pleased with. Well, maybe not Ginger Baker.

Sitting down once more at his laptop, Gold began to Google more about this so-called Gate of Hell. In his mind, this was as likely as the Loch Ness Monster, a fabulous marketing ploy to entice visitors to Scotland. The chances of seeing the mythical beast were about as high as seeing a Scottish Square Sausage march down Sauchiehall Street in Glasgow singing 'I Will Walk 500 Miles'.

As he researched and made copious notes, the cross-referencing only bolstered the notion that back in Greek-Roman times, this place, this Hierapolis, now a popular tourist resort, was considered to be the gate to Hell.

Clearly, they'd never been to Croydon during rush hour in the rain.

Gold had several problems on his hands as he tried to process things. First, despite his years of strict religious upbringing and emerging from Oxford with a solid degree, he had long stopped believing in Heaven and Hell. Suzie had seen to that. Although he was not ready to jump into bed with Richard Dawkins, he felt there was a strong case to be made that, when looked at in the cold light of day, religion was merely an extension of the superstitions created by Man when he was ignorant, afraid of everything and understood next to nothing about the world. For Gold, science was the way forward. Science explained everything in a rational, mature, intelligent manner. Secondly, there was his cynicism that had grown in recent years. It was a tourist trap, surely? No more than a brilliant notion to bring in the punters, like his adoptive parents. Well done to the celestial tourist board. In fact, the God that so many worshipped, reminded him of Hazel and Lloyd Carson: distant, cold, unaffectionate and demanding. It was all about Him. Thirdly, it was the 21st Century. The Roman and Greek gods were back there with Spartacus, Ben Hur and Russell Crowe. It was all swords and sandals. As charming as the myths were, they had no more truth to them than Harry Potter.

And yet.

And yet . . .

All these years later, Gold could still recall the Oxford University prospectus for the degree course he had been yearning to take. Reading it as he sat with Mr and Mrs Carson had excited him beyond his expectations.

The study of Philosophy develops analytical rigour and the ability to criticise and reason logically. It allows you to apply these skills to including the existence and nature of God and the relevance of religion to human life.

The study of Theology provides an understanding of the intellectual underpinning of religious traditions, and of the social and cultural contexts for religious belief and practice.

He had excelled in both disciplines. As his personal tutor, Professor Mark Whittaker, had wryly observed "Mr Gold, if only you would commit fully, you would be a quite brilliant scholar instead of being merely very good. But I suspect you will always be seduced by the easy, glittering path."

Indeed. He had been.

And now he presented pap TV to the gullible masses. He snorted in derision at how his life had turned out. The haunts of Soho were a long, long way from the priesthood. As John Lennon said, 'Life is what happens while you're busy making other plans'.

This *really* was a crap time to have given up smoking. The finger drum solo continued. Another slug of Rioja.

Gold rubbed his chin and felt the roughness of its stubble on his hands.

What if . . . . what if there was another reference? What if geography really was the key?

Hurriedly, he scrolled back through his browser history. Yes, there it was on the Reddit 'Not The Onion' site. The insane story of the woman who murdered her husband yet claimed it was perpetrated by her dead father. As you do.

Gold ran through the article again. It still sounded off-the-scale mad. But at the back of his mind, a thought was forming.

Here it was. Hellam, York County, Pennsylvania.

Let's take a look, thought Gold.

"No fucking way!"

But there it was.

*A local legend claims that in the woods off Trout Run Road in Hellam Township, Pennsylvania, sits one of the Gates of Hell. According to popular fiction, the gates appear near the site of a tragic asylum fire, and if you step through all seven gates, you land straight in Hell. There's only one gate, a rather ordinary-looking thing a local doctor installed to keep people off his property. (*Weird US *explains that the gate is supposed to be invisible during the day.) That hasn't kept curious trespassers from sneaking onto the property, however, in search of a direct route to Hell.*

Gold sat and stared at the text. It was preposterous. Of course it was. So why was his stomach clenched like a fist and why, as he suddenly realised, was he breathing fast in jagged little breaths? OK. This is seriously freaking me out now, thought Gold. Yet he was, despite his protestations to the contrary, a journalist. That meant it was hardwired into his DNA that he had to dig a little deeper.

Had he bothered to read the research notes for the location of his last TV show and not just turned up half cut on Tramadol and Jack Daniels, Gold might have been better prepared for what he was about to read.

Borley Rectory was a Victorian mansion that gained fame as 'the most haunted house in England' after being described as such by author Harry Price. Built in 1862 to house the rector of the parish of Borley and his family, it was badly damaged by fire in 1939 and demolished in 1944.

The large Gothic-style rectory in the village of Borley has been alleged to be haunted ever since it was built. These reports multiplied suddenly in 1929, after the Daily Mirror published an account of a visit by paranormal researcher Harry Price, who wrote two books supporting claims of paranormal activity. Although a place of religious connotation, villagers in the surrounding area believed that the rectory, and the ground it was built upon, was cursed as it was believed that it provided direct access as a gateway to Hell.

"Fuck me!"

Gold suddenly felt more in need of a cigarette than at any time in his life. Was there a pack still somewhere in the flat? Bugger, he'd thrown out the last pack weeks ago. OK . . . OK . . . calm down.

Gold felt anything but calm. His brow was perspiring, the tension in his stomach had not abated and his ragged breathing was, if anything, even more pronounced. He dug into the research notes folder and found a sheet of typed A4.

Ghosts at Borley Rectory

There is no shortage of ghostly experiences. One of the earliest and perhaps most famous sightings was that of a nun, which may seem strange given that there used to be a monastery on the site. According to local folklore, a nun from a nearby nunnery fell in love with a monk from the monastery, and the pair attempted to elope together. They were found and sentenced to death. The monk was reported to have been sent to the gallows in the monastery whilst the nun was sealed into the walls of the nunnery alive.

All reports stretching over 100 years seem to cement its place as one of the most haunted houses in Britain, and maybe even the world. Could the extraordinary events that are on record as occurring be due to the location of the Rectory over what was believed to be The Gate to Hell?

*

Gold sat in his kitchen and slowly looked around him. It was still perfectly normal. It was what you would expect to find in the flat of a man in his early thirties. There was the kettle, the toaster, the large pot of Marmite and next to it the jar of peanut butter. There was a loaf of white sliced bread. There was the DAB radio. Nothing was out of place. In the sink were the dirty dishes of the past few days. There on the side was the nearly-empty bottle of washing up liquid.

Gold felt he needed to perform a mental check list of normality. He needed his equilibrium restored. But the old panic was beginning to creep back. He recognised the signs – the sweats, the rapid breathing. He stood up and went to the bathroom. After a few moments he found his Propranolol. Popping one in his mouth, he walked back to the kitchen and swallowed it with a large gulp of wine. Soon the beta-blocker would have its calming effect and allow him to think clearly. The panic attack would subside. Propranolol and Rioja – an always winning combo. Should be available on the NHS, thought Gold.

Reaching across the kitchen table, he hit speed dial and waited until a weary sounding, or was it wary, voice answered.

"Adam, did I wake you?"

The voice at the other end mustered a response.

"Huh?"

Gold pressed on. He felt inspired.

"Adam, it's me."

"Who's that?"

Oh great. Why couldn't people instantly recognise who was calling by the simple salutation 'It's me'? At least Gold hadn't launched into a conversation without any nominative reference.

"Adam, it's Nick," and for safe measure added, "Gold."

There was a pause that was so pregnant it could have re-populated Milton Keynes.

"Hello Nick," Adam replied without enthusiasm.

Gold was beginning to get a trifle irritated. This wasn't how he'd imagined the conversation going.

"Adam, listen, I've been thinking about our chat today and –"

However, the Adam Farthing on the phone right now was a very different person to the sobbing wreck he'd been in Bar Italia.

Not letting Gold continue, he cut right across him.

"Oh that. Forget it. It was nothing."

"What do you mean 'it was nothing'? You were in pieces. You were crying. That wasn't nothing . . . that was . . . er . . . something!"

Gold, always the wordsmith.

"As I said Nick, forget it. I think I had a touch of food poisoning. Made me feel a bit off."

"Oh really. Is that so? Interesting. The reason I was calling you was that I've been thinking about what you told me and, after some research, I think I can help."

That should do it.

Pause.

"Nick," Adam's voice had a slightly harder edge to it now. "As I just said, forget the whole thing. It was a mistake. I'll see you soon."

"Just hang on a moment, Adam . . . you haven't heard what I've got to say!"

But Adam Farthing, young media Turk, was not for turning.

"Sorry Nick. It's late. I'm tired. You sound pissed. Bye."

But Adam was no match for Nick Gold. You don't survive in the media without either having lunch, or being lunch.

"Don't you fucking 'bye' me! You were a mess this afternoon, crying like a Kardashian who'd just chipped a nail. You saw your grandfather. Newsflash – he's dead! He tried to kill you – call that nothing? A dead guy tries to kill you, nothing?"

Adam hadn't stopped fighting yet.

"As I just explained, I wasn't well . . . .and if you bloody dare ever, and I mean *ever*, repeat any of what I may or may not have said this afternoon, I will not only sue you for slander, I will make sure that you never work for Good Foot Productions again. Get it?!"

Gold decided there was only one way forward. He'd tried the nice approach. Although he believed firmly in the maxim 'Don't wrestle in the mud with a pig. You both get dirty and the pig likes it.' It was time to cut to the chase.

"Listen-up, numbnuts, this is how it's going to go. You are going to listen to me and then you and I, together, are going to make sure that I get the advance to research my next series. You can direct it, I don't give a shit. But this could be the biggest break of my career, and when I say *my* career, I mean *our* career if you play it smart. But if you stand in my way on this, if I think, for one tiny second, that you've fucked me over, that you've whispered in the wrong ears about me, then let me explain very clearly what will happen. I will take Larry out for lunch. He will drink more Barolo and Amarone than they stock in Tesco. I'll then take him to a club where we'll hoover up about a year's export of Columbia's finest . . . and I will, in glorious Ultra 4KHD, tell him every last tiny detail of your breakdown . . . how you fell apart . . . how you cried . . . how you are no longer a safe pair of hands. Do *you* get it?"

The other end of the phone fell silent. Gold could just about hear Adam Farthing's laboured breathing. That's the great thing about gambling, knowing when to show your hand or keep the cards close to your chest. And Gold was a gambler. It was in his blood.

After what seemed an age, Adam spoke.

"You utter, utter little shit."

Praise indeed.

Gold considered very quickly how to proceed. He'd kicked the crap out of Farthing. Now time for a 'there-there' and a sweetie.

"Adam, listen. You're a decent guy. I believe that what happened to you was real. You didn't imagine it. It scared the hell out of you. Look, it would scare the hell out of anyone. But here's the thing, since we met – and thank you for coming to me and trusting me – I've been busier than a one-armed paperhanger with an itch doing research. You will faint when I tell you what I've found out. This is award-winning stuff, Adam. This is you and me getting a BAFTA, or a National Television Award . . . Graham Norton, Ant and Dec, champagne, increased profile, increased salary."

Gold was good. There wasn't a button he wasn't pressing.

Another long pause. Gold could almost hear the cogs turning in Farthing's head. That's the essence of any negotiation, the one thing no one can resist: 'what's in it for me'?

They don't call it 'me'-dia for nothing.

"I'm listening," replied Adam Farthing.

Of course he was.

As Kenny Rogers sang, 'You gotta know when to hold 'em, know when to fold 'em.'

EIGHT

"Our state cannot be severed, we are one,
One flesh; to lose thee were to lose myself."
– John Milton, Paradise Lost

That evening, Gold was to spend two hours on the phone with Adam Farthing, but not before he'd emailed a Non-Disclosure Agreement across for his erstwhile director to print, sign, scan and return.

Show business. Five percent show, ninety-five percent business.

Nick walked Adam through his research: how he'd linked seemingly disparate events around the world together. How, in a totally insane way, it made some sort of sense.

Adam was many things, but he wasn't stupid. As Gold's story unfolded, he was already blocking out scenes in his head, working out locations, considering if it should be a one-off special or a six-part series. He didn't like Gold, in fact part of him loathed him, but showbiz wasn't about friends, it was about the right connections. Nick Gold was, potentially, his way up the greasy pole. Job done.

They agreed to meet the next day in town, eschewing Bar Italia for a small Japanese restaurant on the corner of Lisle Street. At a corner table they drank miso soup, ate assorted sushi and sashimi, and finished with Chicken Katsu Don washed down with warm Saki.

It was Soho, it's enshrined in the by-laws that alcohol will always be consumed at a meal.

As they ate, Gold explained in further detail what his initial online research had uncovered. There were two ways to consider it.

First, that it was in the realms of the conspiracy theorists – people who saw a conspiracy in everything, the Kennedy assassination, UFOs, Area 51, the Bilderberg Group, 9/11, the Aurora super-secret aircraft project, recycling wheelie bins. You name it, there was a YouTube channel or a website about it with thousands of often deluded but passionate followers.

Secondly, that Nick Gold, TV's Paranormal Detective, had inadvertently stumbled across something weird, wonderful and utterly terrifying. For real.

Of course, there was a third way to look at it all.

That it was a load of absolute crap, with no basis in reality, but would, nonetheless make a great TV series. The public would lap it up. Why not? They loved 'Ancient Aliens' (no proof whatsoever) 'Jesse Ventura's Conspiracy Theory' (even less proof), 'NASA's Unexplained Files' (pure conjecture). The list went on and on; enough, in fact, to fill hours of the output of dozens of TV channels, night after night.

Underneath it all, Gold and Farthing both wanted a piece of that pie.

What it required was 'fleshing out', putting 'some meat on the bones' and any other saying that meant, in a word, investigation.

Of course investigations cost money. One golden rule about TV production was never invest your own money; always use someone else's. True, it meant that Gold and Farthing would receive a smaller percentage of the ultimate deal, but it made their roles risk-free. You know, just in case.

As the second bottle of warm Saki and the freshly prepared food started to work its magic, it seemed the best way forward was to pitch the idea to their boss, get a budget for a recce, and see what it turned up.

It sounded simple and straightforward enough, but it involved the handing over of money. In that regard, Soho was no different from the Square Mile; persuasion was essential and a solid argument was a necessity.

Bullshit talks, money walks.

It meant considering the best way to pitch the idea to the CEO of the production company. He would have to like the idea and then believe that it could be sold, successfully, as a package to a terrestrial or satellite broadcaster. This alone was a risky business. The BBC had a delightful habit of replying, "Our production team is working on a very similar idea, but thank you for your submission".

Funny how often that happened. Maybe they were psychic?

So, should it be a written proposal or a verbal presentation? Formal or over lunch?

They opted for a combination of both. A verbal presentation with reasonably detailed documentation and a rough outline budget. It wasn't that Gold had changed his opinion of Adam Farthing but at this point in their endeavour he could prove useful. For reasons beyond Gold's comprehension, Larry seemed to have faith in Farthing's ability and saw him as a 'rising star'. The bottom line was that Adam Farthing wasn't considered a 'loose cannon' in the same category as Nick Gold. So, logic dictated, that if Gold had Farthing sat in at this stage, Good Foot Productions might take the concept more seriously and that meant the initial funding should be easier to obtain.

It was TV. In the end, it always came down to money. The bottom line was the bottom line. Profits meant happy days; losses meant P45s all round. If you wanted 'art', then go to a gallery.

Within a week, the document had been written. One page of A4 in Arial 12 point. No TV proposal could ever be longer than one page; apparently, any reader would instantly fall into a coma if it strayed onto a second page. To back up the outline was a neatly bound document of some ten pages, covering background, geography and a last page summary of the financial and budgetary requirements. Always put the budget on the last page: hook 'em; reel 'em in; get 'em excited first.

Gold made an appointment to see Larry, selling the meeting as 'an idea so big it's beyond huge'.

On the appointed day, Gold and Adam Farthing met up for a pre-meeting coffee, worked out a rough plan of attack, and headed to the office.

The pitch went surprisingly well. Gold did most of the talking, injecting the razzmatazz and excitement he knew would interest Larry. Adam Farthing added the required media buzz words to make it sound . . . media-ish.

After twenty-five minutes of hard sell, Gold concluded with the mandatory, "It's not just great, it's fantastic. It's got winner written all over it. Whaddya think, Larry?"

Silence.

Larry drummed his manicured fingers on the sides of his leather chair while scrutinising the back page of the document. Just the back page.

Finally, Larry spoke. "So, let me get this straight. You think there's a connection between totally random events across the world. You think that there may be some truth in the bullshit defence this American woman is spouting in . . . where was it . . . Pennsylvania?

Adam looked anxious. "Er yes, that's right. Pennsylvania."

"And, just so I've got it, the dead are wandering around killing people?"

Adam jumped in. "That's the point! Yes!"

A gentle tapping of perfectly manicured nails on the mahogany desk. "OK. You want me to fund an investigation into these . . . what's the right term . . . events, things, deaths?"

Gold simply nodded.

Larry Shaitan burst into laughter.

Which probably wasn't a good sign.

"Guys," said Larry after he'd composed himself, "I don't know what you've been smoking or shoving up your nose, but this is the biggest load of garbage I've read in months . . . and trust me, I'm snowed under with submissions from people who have got to be certifiable."

Adam looked aghast. Shit! He'd thrown in his lot with that idiot Nick Gold, let him persuade him, no . . . blackmail him, into joining him in this hair-brained idea, and now his credibility would be down the toilet. Fuck!

Larry continued, removing his designer glasses as he spoke. "It's ridiculous. More than that, it's insane. Beautifully insane."

Adam had made up his mind. Sod this, time to jump ship.

"Well, I must say that when Nick came to me with his idea, I was very sceptical as you can imagine. It is ridiculous really but we thought, well Nick thought, it was worth taking up thirty minutes of your time and I wanted to, er, help him because as you know I'm a team player."

Gold shot him a glance. If looks could kill, then Adam would be in a body bag.

The little shit.

Larry smiled. "You're right Adam. It is ridiculous. It's crazy. And that's why Nick gets the big bucks. It's fucking brilliant!"

Adam Farthing looked as if he'd been hit round the face with half a side of frozen salmon.

Larry stood up, walked across the room and man-hugged Nick."Come here you. You fucking crazy genius. I love this guy!"

Nick simply smiled.

Another man-hug. Shaking hands didn't really cut it in Soho.

Adam sat in his chair unable to move. Actually, unable to think for a moment.

"Nicky, Nicky, Nicky . . . you're a pain in the arse, but you're *our* pain in the arse. What goes on in that mind of yours, huh? How do you come up with this shit? It's batshit crazy. Hell, ghosts, death, teeth, gates, spooks . . . it's got the sodding lot! Our demographic won't just like this, they'll fucking *love* it! This could be our break into terrestrial if we play it right. Discovery Channel will take it, History Channel, well it's right up their street, but I think maybe ITV2 or Channel 4. You clever bastard, Mr Gold."

Adam Farthing sat silently in his chair. If only he knew, the way Nick Gold knew, when to hold 'em and when to fold 'em. But he was no gambler. What he was right now was sick to his stomach. Had he maintained his silence for just thirty seconds, he'd be currently sitting at the table with the grown-ups, instead of at the children's table.

Larry went on, a broad beaming smile filling his tanned and remarkably line-free face. "I think this calls for a light lunch gentlemen. I'm sure the Ivy will squeeze us in."

There was a horrible silence.

Then Nick spoke. "That would be great. Adam, you were saying how much you like their Wye Valley asparagus with soft poached egg and black truffle mimosa only the other day."

TV Media Rule No I. Keep your friends close and your enemies even closer.

Anyway, Gold could afford to be magnanimous in victory – he wasn't paying for lunch.

NINE

"Long is the way and hard, that out of Hell leads up to light."
– John Milton, Paradise Lost

The 'light lunch' merged into an early supper then a drinking session at the Groucho that saw Larry, Nick and Adam stumble onto the pavement outside 45 Dean Street at around 11:15pm that night. None of them would remember much of the Amarone-induced nonsense that was spoken, but if the humongous hangovers the next day were anything to go by, all three had to assume it had been a pretty good night.

They had even extravagantly donated to the homeless man outside the club, and patted his dog.

With the budget approved for the exploratory investigation, Gold called Joanne Walsh with the news.

"Mrs Walsh, it's Nick Gold, Paranormal Detective, you came to see me about –"

"Mr Gold, I know who you are. I assumed you weren't interested anymore."

Well, it had been a while.

Gold was at his most oleaginous. He wanted this one on his hook.

"Oh my goodness no, Mrs Walsh . . . or may I call you Joanne? I've been discussing your case in great depth. In fact, what I was calling about was that I am going to Hierapolis to have a look around and see what I can dig up – sorry, probably not the best phrase to use – but yes, I'm going to investigate for you. Sorry I didn't get back earlier, but I'm sure you appreciate that these things take time."

It turned out that NHS nurse Walsh did indeed understand the time needed, was delighted that Nick Gold was 'taking her case' (as if he was out of a Conan Doyle novel), wished him the very best of luck and would look forward to hearing from him in due course.

A few days later Nick Gold was at London Stansted Airport, which overseas travellers assume is in the heart of London and not, as it happens, located at Stansted Mountfitchet in the local government district of Uttlesford in Essex, a good thirty miles north-east of Central London.

It was a two-part journey to his destination. The Pegasus Airlines Boeing 737-800 first flew to Sabiha Gokcen International and then, after a reasonably short wait, he was onwards from Istanbul to Denizli, landing at Cardak Airport.

After a short, yet exciting Turkish taxi drive later, Gold checked into the exotically named White Heaven Hotel. For a man investigating Hell, the private joke was not lost on him.

There were the usual amenities, an outdoor pool, a sun terrace and a garden described as 'peaceful'. In keeping with ancient Roman/Greek tradition, free Wi-Fi was accessible throughout the premises.

None of which was of any interest to Gold. What was of interest was that the Pamukkale Travertines and Pamukkale Lake were just eight hundred yards from the hotel.

It was what Nick called his 'Gold'-en Rule' that if information was to be acquired, the best info hub was a bar. This solved two issues simultaneously – first, he could get a drink and secondly, he could ask questions and, hopefully, get answers.

Pamukkale, meaning 'cotton castle' in Turkish, seemed to Gold to be a *non-sequitur* if ever he heard one. Anyway, he was here, in Denizli Province in south-western Turkey.

Hot springs and travertines, terraces of carbonate minerals left by the flowing water and dead people in desperate need of orthodontic work were apparently all about to rock up.

People have bathed in its pools for thousands of years. As recently as the mid-twentieth century, hotels were built over the ruins of Hierapolis. When the area was declared a World Heritage Site, the hotels were demolished and the road removed and replaced with artificial pools. Now you can't even wear shoes in the water as it would mess up the deposits.

Gold headed to the hotel bar, ordered a local Efres Pilsen, and asked the barman if he knew of any especially good guides, not the hokey tourist guides, but someone who properly knew his onions or, in this instance, his kofta.

Oddly enough, the barman's uncle was, as it so happened, the best guide in all of Pamukkale. Fancy that. In fact, if Gold wanted to get the most out of his visit to the site of Hierapolis, then Uncle Mehmet was the best choice he could possibly make and would he like him to call him and would he like another drink?

Having arranged for Uncle Mehmet to meet him at the hotel at 10 o'clock the next day (no need to go crazy and get up early), Gold felt suddenly tired, grabbed a snack in the bar and went off to his room where he watched Turkish television. Turned out that Turkish TV was pretty much like British TV – but without Clare Balding appearing in every programme.

After a rather pleasant breakfast by the pool, he went to wait for Uncle Mehmet by the hotel entrance.

The weather was warm, not too hot, the sky dotted with a few light clouds and a light breeze added to the overall effect of 'I'm not in England'.

He didn't have long to wait. Whatever Gold was expecting, Uncle Mehmet was the exact opposite. Yes, there was the manly greying full moustache, but the fifty-five-year old's hair was immaculately and stylishly cut, the Ralph Lauren Polo shirt appeared genuine, the Timberland deck shoes looked new and the chinos were ironed to within an inch of their life. He was a dude.

"Ah, Mister Mister Gold, I am Mehmet, yes? It is a pleasure to meet someone as famous as you. My nephew was very impressed."

Gold was taken aback.

"I'm really not famous. Really."

Mehmet smiled, showing a set of suspiciously perfect, too white teeth.

"Mister Mister Gold, we may be close to a very ancient site, but we have here what we call the Internet. Yes. 'Paranormal Detective'. I had to ask my wife what that was. Would you like to see a photo of her?"

Gold had about as much interest in seeing his guide's wife as catching leprosy, but he smiled encouragingly. No point in getting off to a bad start.

Mehmet took out his mobile phone, pressed a few keys and with a flourish showed the screen to his client.

"Bloody hell!" exclaimed Gold before he could stop himself. This guy was a player. Mrs Mehmet looked all of twenty-three, and was so smouldering in the photo it was a wonder the phone's screen didn't melt.

"She beautiful, yes?"

Gold nodded in the affirmative.

"I lucky man. Now Mister Mister Gold, shall we be on our way?"

All thoughts of Hierapolis had momentarily slipped from Gold's mind as he considered a tour of Mrs Mehmet.

"You want to see Hierapolis, yes? We go. Good."

As he had picked the hotel primarily for its location, it was only a short journey on foot until the two men arrived. Annoyingly, it was Gold who felt slightly out of breath while his twenty-year older guide showed absolutely no signs of exertion.

In fact, he hadn't stopped talking during the journey, pausing only to light up several Samsun cigarettes with a classic Dunhill lighter.

Dude indeed.

Listening to the monologue, Gold had learned about his guide's family history, how he met his wife, how his children from his first marriage got on with her, why Nana Mouskouri didn't really need to wear glasses and how the Turkish tourist industry had been hit by the rise of 'those crazy Isis bastards'.

"Mister Gold, there she is . . . Hierapolis. Beautiful, yes?"

Indeed, she was.

"Mister Gold . . . Hierapolis means 'sacred city'. It was believed by the ancients to have been founded by the god Apollo. It was famed for its sacred hot springs, whose vapours were associated with Pluto, god of the underworld. Are you familiar with Hades, Mister Gold?"

"You mean Hell?"

Mehmet shook his head. "No, no, Hades was the god of the underworld. He gave his name to it. A common mistake. It was Hades that abducted Persephone who was the daughter of Zeus and Demeter. Her mother was furious".

Gold smiles. "Yeah, well I guess she'd be pretty pissed off."

Mehmet ignored the response. "Yes. Indeed. She made the crops wither and the earth barren. Zeus intervened and tried to bring Persephone back to the world of the living."

"Uh-huh. And how did that work out?" Gold thought he knew the answer.

"Not too well, Mister Gold. Persephone ate the seeds of a pomegranate that Hades had given to her, binding her to him for one third of the year."

"And they tell you fruit is good for us."

Unabashed, Memhet continued. "It was decided that Persephone would spend four months in the underworld and eight months on earth with her mother."

"Hmm . . . those custody battles can be a real bitch."

"But interestingly, to answer your earlier question, Persephone became Queen of the Underworld."

"So she and Hades cut a deal? Makes sense. Actually Mehmet, I was just messing with you. Apologies. I knew the story. It came up during my university days."

Gold flashed his guide a broad smile which, to his relief, was returned.

Mehmet returned to the job in hand.

"These days Hierapolis is a World Heritage Site . . . is very popular tourist destination, yes?"

Gold nodded.

He'd been here five minutes already and hadn't seen one zombie.

"We will see many interesting classical ruins but, if you so wish, also the thermal Sacred Pool in which you can swim. There is a wonderful view of the spectacular white terraces of Pamukkale, and, as a souvenir perhaps, a visit to the most excellent museum. I know the lady who looks after it. I arrange a very good discount."

Gold smiled encouragingly.

"What takes your fancy?"

"Mehmet, what I want to see is the cave. I really want to look around the place where the fumes, you know, the ancient gases, came from. That, my friend, takes my fancy."

Mehmet nodded. "Of course, but first we look around, yes."

The tour started in earnest.

"Hierapolis is mentioned only once in the Bible in a letter from St Paul. Also, ancient tradition associates Hierapolis with the biblical figure Philip. Not your Prince Philip."

Mehmet chuckled at his own joke.

"It could be Philip the Apostle, one of the original twelve disciples, who is said to have been martyred by upside-down crucifixion or by being hung upside down by his ankles from a tree. Or Philip could be Philip the Evangelist, a later disciple who had four virgin-prophetess daughters. Early traditions say this Philip was buried in Hierapolis along with his virgin daughters, but confusingly they call him 'Philip the Apostle'."

"Yes. I know. From early on he came to be confused with Philip the Apostle. Basically, it stemmed from him being an esteemed member of the apostolic company. So he may have been described as an apostle in the wider sense of that word, you know, beyond just the original twelve Apostles. Probably doesn't help that he's first mentioned in the Acts of the Apostles as one of 'the seven' who were chosen to attend to affairs of the church in Jerusalem."

Mehmet looked at his client as if he'd just pulled a rabbit out of a hat.

"Theology student. You get to remember stuff like that."

"And now Mister Gold –"

"Please Mehmet, call me Nick."

"OK, now Mister Neek, some history, yes? Hierapolis may have been actually established close to the 4th century BC by the Seleucid kings. The name of the city may derive from Hiera, the wife of the son of Hercules and grandson of Zeus, the mythical founder of Pergamum. Or it may have been called the 'sacred city' because of the temples located at the site."

"Er, yeah, about those temples –"

Mehmet was in his stride and not easily put on pause.

"The hot springs here at Hierapolis were believed to have healing properties, and people came to the city to bathe in the rich mineral waters to cure themselves. Hierapolis was dedicated to Apollo, who was said to have founded the city. The Temple of Apollo that survives today dates from the 3rd century AD."

As much as he tried to stop himself, the moment Gold heard 'Apollo', he was picturing the venue in Hammersmith, southwest London and remembering the AC/DC concert he'd seen there recently.

"Mister Mister Neek, also worshipped at Hierapolis was Pluto, god of the underworld."

Jesus . . . finally!

Gold smiled encouragingly. "Ah yes, Pluto. I'm all ears."

Mehmet looked puzzled.

"I'm listening . . . to you . . . about Pluto."

Crazy English. "This was probably because of the hot gases released by the earth. The chief religious festival of ancient Hierapolis was the Letoia, in honour of the goddess Leto. The goddess was honoured with orgiastic rites."

"Anyway, this place was finally abandoned in 1334 after an earthquake. Excavations began to uncover Hierapolis in the 19th century."

"Great . . . thanks . . . er, the Pluto part . . . when can we –"

"I see you are a man of great hurry, Mister Neek. You young men, always in a rush. That's what my beautiful wife tells me."

Nick had a sneaking suspicion that the pulchritudinous Mrs Mehmet might be an authority on this subject.

"So, Mister Neek, when we were walking here, we saw gleaming white travertine terraces of Pamukkale, yes, right next to the ruins of Hierapolis. You know how this happen? Let me tell you. The effect is magnificent, yes. It is created when water from the hot springs loses carbon dioxide as it flows down the slopes, leaving deposits of limestone."

Either Mehmet was a genius or he could regurgitate *Encyclopaedia Britannia* by rote.

"The layers of white calcium carbonate, built up in steps on the plateau, gave the site the name Pamukkale or, as we say, 'cotton castle'."

"Unfortunately, we are no longer allowed to walk on the terraces. Too bad, no?"

"Yeah . . . tragedy," replied Gold, suddenly craving one of his guide's strong Turkish brand of cigarettes.

"I tell you, a good place to start our tour is the small but very, very excellent Pamukkale Museum. Coins, jewellery, sarcophagi –"

"Mehmet, I really don't want to see the museum right now. Maybe later, OK? Can we press on to the ruins themselves? You know, like I mentioned earlier?"

Mehmet looked crestfallen for an instant. There went his commission.

"Of course, Mister Mister Neek. Whatever you say." The teeth flashed their iridescent smile and the two men walked on.

From out of absolutely nowhere, Gold had an irresistible urge to look over his shoulder. He had no particular reason to do so, simply an odd feeling that he was being followed. As he turned, he thought he caught a glimpse of someone . . . someone he knew . . . but that would be completely impossible. It must be the weather. He turned around as Mehmet continued.

"Most of what you can see here is from the Roman period, as the original city was destroyed by earthquakes in 17 AD and 60 AD. The site is surrounded by Byzantine walls, outside of which is an extensive necropolis. The nearest complex from us here includes the Sacred Pool, a colonnaded street, and a basilica church. The Sacred Pool is warmed by hot springs and littered with underwater fragments of ancient marble columns. Behind the Sacred Pool is the nymphaeum, a monumental fountain that distributed water to the city.

"Next to the nymphaeum is the Temple of Apollo, the patron god and divine founder of the city and finally, Mister Neek, south of the temple, is the Plutonium, a sacred cave believed to be an entrance to the underworld, the domain of the Roman god Pluto or as the Greeks called it, Hades."

Yes! Finally! About effing time, thought Gold. It wasn't that he was a philistine or anything, but one lot of ruins looked much like any other. What was there to see? Bits of stone, some rocks . . . big deal. With the insane amount of building work in London, Gold was tired of seeing rubble.

Sensing that he had really captured his client's attention, Mehmet ratcheted it up a gear.

"Ah yes. The famous cave. It is, as you say, a mystery worthy of Shirley Holmes."

"Sherlock. Sherlock Holmes."

"Is what I said. The cave emitted poisonous vapours in ancient times, and still does! For this reason, the entrance is sealed off. The priests of Cybele could enter the sacred chamber safely, but animals who did so, died.

"But look, the theatre of Hierapolis is well-preserved, especially the stage buildings. The theatre could hold twenty thousand spectators and had reserved seating for distinguished guests in the front row."

"If you come to London, I must show you the O2 Arena. Same deal."

But there was no stopping Mehmet.

"To the north of the main ruins and along the modern road is the north necropolis, the largest graveyard in Anatolia . . . more than twelve hundred tombs."

Gold held up a hand. "Mehmet, you are one heck of a guide. This is great. No, really, it's great. But what I need . . . what I really want, is to get close to is this plutonium thing . . . this cave. That's what I need. That's kinda why I'm here."

The guide paused, stroked his full moustache and in a subconscious movement, ran his fingers through his hair.

"Mister Neek, what you ask . . . is not possible. The cave is closed to the public. Too dangerous. The gas. The fumes. No. Closed long time now. Many years. We can look from a distance but no closer. We go to Museum. I tell you, the gifts there are the best in all Turkey."

"Mehmet, I have no desire whatsoever to go to the museum, the gift shop, the café . . . I don't care. Not to be rude, but it's not why I'm here. I need to see the cave close up."

Mehmet smiled indulgently.

"Ah, perhaps we come back at midnight, when here is closed and we break in, yes?"

Yes, indeed! Brilliant plan!

"Can we do that, Mehmet? I'd make it very worth your while."

Mehmet laughed out loud. "Mister Nick. You English. You

watch too many of those bad films. You know . . . the ones where you are scared. My wife she loves them. The more she screams, the more she loves the film. And those books, too. You know, what's his name . . . Stephen . . . Stephen –"

"King?" interjected Gold.

"Yes, that's the man. It is always dark, midnight, alone. Crazy! That's for books Mister Neek, this is Turkey . . . this is real life. Is not film. Come, let's get a coffee or a drink in the museum. After that, we go look at cave as near as we can."

Bollocks. This wasn't going well. Not at all. But on the plus side he wasn't in Balham, he didn't have to face rush hour on the Northern Line, the sky was blue (mostly) and come think of it, a Turkish coffee sounded like a good idea.

"OK, Mehmet. Let's grab a coffee."

They walked into the cool of the museum. Maybe a ten-minute break wasn't such a terrible idea. When you're used to the constant grey of London, somehow the blue sky and sunshine was both invigorating and tiring simultaneously.

Gold spoke. "What can I get you, Mehmet? Coffee? Drink? Snack?"

"Snack? What is 'snack'? No, just Turkish coffee, medium, please. And some water. Thank you, Mister Neek, so very much. Most kind."

Nick queued up with the other tourists and finally could ask the young man behind the counter for two Turkish coffees, one medium, one sweet, and two bottles of water. Oh, and a couple of those baklava too.

The coffees were made, and with a laden tray, Gold started to walk back to the table where Mehmet was seated.

He never made it.

TEN

Which way I fly is hell; myself am hell;
And in the lowest deep a lower deep,
Still threat'ning to devour me, opens wide,
To which the hell I suffer seems a heaven."
– John Milton, Paradise Lost

Mehmet was startled by the sudden loud noise in the otherwise quiet café. It was the unmistakable sound of glass, crockery and cutlery crashing to the floor. In Britain, it was universally followed by a loud cheer. No one knew why, but that's the British for you. In Turkey, however, it was greeted by polite stunned silence.

Mehmet looked to see the cause of the commotion and was very surprised to see it was his client, Nick Gold.

But that wasn't what surprised him the most.

It was the expression on Mister Neek's face. All the colour had drained away so it resembled a dead-white death mask. But it was the look on it that literally sent a shiver down the elegant back of Mehmet the Guide. Nick Gold looked terrified. His eyes were wide open, his mouth half-open as if he wanted to scream but no sound was coming out. Beads of sweat were running down his forehead but he didn't seem able to brush them away. He stood as rigid as the statues on display around the museum.

It was as if he'd seen a ghost.

Mehmet finally found the presence of mind to stand up and walk briskly across to where Gold was rooted to the spot.

"Mister Neek, are you OK?"

There was no response.

Gently, Mehmet put a hand on Nick's shoulder and very slightly shook him.

The customers in the café were all staring at this odd scene. Slowly, a murmur of voices grew as they began to comment to each other at what was unfolding in front of them.

"Mister Neek . . . sir . . . are you ill? Can I get you some water?"

The water that Nick had purchased was lying on the floor amidst the shards of glass and pieces of crockery.

"Come . . . come and sit down. I'll fetch you something to drink straight away."

Gently, for his client was clearly either very ill or in deep shock, Mehmet led his client back to their table. Gold walked as though he was in a trance. With each faltering step, it seemed he might collapse onto the floor.

The guide settled him in a chair, rushed across to the counter ignoring the queue and took a bottle of Ceysu Mineral Water, explaining to the staff that it was an emergency. They, in turn, were all too aware of the need for urgency. The last thing they needed was a medical event in their café.

Mehmet poured the water into a glass and handed it to Gold saying, as one would to a child, "There you go, drink that. That's it, drink it . . . slowly now."

Nick Gold held the glass like an automaton. His eyes were focused far, far away. Wherever he was, it wasn't in the museum café in Hierapolis.

With the glass emptied. Mehmet filled it again with the mineral water. Maybe his client was dehydrated?

Gold drank the second glass, this time more like an adult, and gradually the colour began to return to his face. His eyes started to refocus and with a large intake of breath, he suddenly spoke.

"Fuck me!"

Mehmet breathed a sigh of relief. His client evidently wasn't going to die in front of him. Hopefully.

"Are you feeling better, Mister Neek? You gave us all quite a fright. Should I call for an ambulance?"

This last question was spoken partly out of genuine concern and partly as he did not want the responsibility for having a dead body on his hands. Not on his watch.

Gold smiled. An odd, bizarre little smile.

"Ambulance? No, I don't need an ambulance thank you, Mehmet. Not an ambulance."

Mehmet was far from satisfied at his client's behaviour.

After an uneasy silence while his client seemed to slowly compose himself, Mehmet ventured another question.

"Would you like to continue our tour of Hierapolis, Mister Neek? There is still much to see."

Again, that odd little half smile.

"No, thank you. Actually, I've seen quite enough for one day."

"Are you sure?"

"Mehmet . . . I've seen what I came for. Now, I'd like to go back to my hotel, have a very large drink and a lie down. Not necessarily in that order. Haven't made up my mind."

Mehmet was in two minds. Half of him was dismayed that he was unable to show his client all the wonders of this magnificent ancient city of Hierapolis so near to his home town of Pamukkale, but the other less emotional half was in no small way relieved. Mister Neek was a perfectly nice young client, but Mehmet did not want the responsibility of nurse-maiding him should, most unfortunately, he become ill again, or even worse, die. The paperwork alone would be a monumental pain in his Turkish '*popo*'.

"Of course. Whatever you so wish. Why not finish your water and then we will get you back safely to your hotel?"

Gold smiled. This time, in a way that didn't make the experienced guide with the beautiful young wife feel exceptionally uneasy.

The journey back was mercifully uneventful except that the English client kept looking around him, as if searching for someone or something. Was it a particular ruin that had caught his fancy? A specific statue? By the end of it, Mehmet was, in a way, partly glad to be saying goodbye to this client who was clearly unwell.

Well, he felt that was perhaps the most polite connotation he could ascribe to it.

At the White Heaven Hotel, they paused outside.

"Mister Neek, if there is anything more I can do for you, then please do not for a moment hesitate to call me. You have my card now. I am here for you day and night. I hope that you feel, er, better soon, yes?"

Gold shook the proffered hand from this most charming Turk.

"Mehmet, thank you. Thank you for everything. Sorry . . . sorry if I went a bit weird back at there at the museum. It must have been something I ate . . . or the heat . . . you know. Thanks again."

With that, Gold turned and with a sudden turn of speed, entered the hotel, headed straight for the terrace and ordered a double Jack Daniels, no ice, straight up.

He downed it in one.

Immediately, he ordered another and after that, another.

It was only after his third double JD that he began to feel the slightest sense of relaxation, that his neck muscles began to ease from the steel that they'd become.

The view from the terrace overlooked the 'peaceful' gardens as they had been described, but Gold didn't really see them. He might as well have been sitting at Wandsworth Roundabout in a traffic jam.

He exhaled slowly, called the waiter over and asked if he could bring some nuts or crisps. Anything. He was far too wired to eat properly. Over his fourth double bourbon, Gold's mind strayed back to two years ago. Back to her. The One That Got Away. Back to Suzie.

It was during a particularly bad 'episode' that it happened. Suzie was being impossible and frankly Gold was relieved to be getting out of London for a few days.

He was away on location in Scotland filming an episode of 'Paranormal Detective.' The shoot had gone well and the cast and crew thought it would be a rather good idea to have a party that night before they returned home the next morning.

Gold was in an ebullient mood. King of the Hill. The Man. The wine was flowing, various substances generously distributed, and everyone was in a what might be termed politely 'party mood'.

The party continued upstairs in his hotel room. This was a smaller, more intimate party, just Gold and Jenny, the continuity girl.

The next morning, Gold caught a plane down to London while the rest of the crew either drove or caught the train. That, presumed the Paranormal Detective, was that.

It wasn't.

Not by a long way.

Jenny the Continuity Girl wanted precisely that – for the relationship to have continuity. She had Gold's number from the printed call sheet that all the crew were given, and soon began calling him, much to Gold's dismay, initial astonishment and increased irritation.

What the hell was she on? It was location sex. That was it. It was like conference sex but without having to endure arse-achingly dull presentations about projected sales figures and the team-building exercises.

Along with the phone calls were the texts, ranging from the sexy, the romantic, the how-dare-you-treat-me-like-shit, to the venting of serious anger at the apparent rejection.

Gold tried to be polite and placate her, but Jenny was not for turning. Eventually, after a particularly long barrage of abusive texts one day, Gold lost it and simply replied "Fuck off and leave me alone".

And they said romance was dead.

Fuck off she did. No more calls, no more texts. Result.

A week or so after he returned from Scotland, Gold was having lunch with Suzie in Balham. She was still in a very bad place. Not Balham, mentally.

She toyed with the salad, pushing it around her plate. The conversation was stilted, filled with awkward pauses and seemingly endless silences. Gold tried every conversational gambit that he could muster, but this episode was way too deep. Suzie looked rough, bags and dark circles under her eyes, her normally immaculate bob a greasy bedhead mess; she also couldn't afford to lose the weight she evidently had. Her insecurities seemed to have grown and had her gripped in their thrall. In fits and starts of sentences, the clues were there: she didn't feel she was attractive anymore, she felt that her talent was a thin façade, a pathetic sham, that one day she would be found out. Why couldn't she have children and if she did would she be deserving of their love? Wouldn't they deserve someone better than her? What was she actually achieving in her life, not materially, but as a person, as a human being? What was the point of it all?

As he looked at her across the rough wooden table, his heart went out to her. He wanted his Suzie back. His Suzie? She was never his, just on loan, he was beginning to suspect. But, despite it all, she was The One.

Why? That's the thing about love, you can never define why. It just is.

Still, if Nick Gold was concerned that the lunch was full of conversational gaps, he needn't have worried. It was about to get considerably livelier.

Gold's first indication that his luncheon was going to get far, far worse, was when he heard a waitress say in a loud voice

"Madam . . . excuse me . . . madam!" This was followed by a female voice replying, "Get the fuck out of my way."

And there she was. Standing at the table. Jenny. This was a most unwelcome continuity.

"Aren't you going to introduce me?" she said in a loud vodka-flavoured voice.

Gold and Suzie looked up at her.

"No? Oh well, let me make the introductions. I'm Jenny. I'm the one Nick was fucking in Scotland. What's the matter Mr Paranormal Detective, didn't your super-senses pre-warn you?"

Nick spoke: "You're drunk. Go away."

Jenny barked an unpleasant laugh.

"No, I don't think so. After you fucked me all night, I thought it might just be polite to return my calls. But not you. Not the great Nick Gold. Fuck 'em and chuck 'em, eh? Well, not me. Not this time."

Suzie was staring at the ranting woman. The entire restaurant was staring in rapt attention. This was cabaret of the finest quality.

"Nick, who the hell's this bitch?" demanded Suzie.

Oh, that's gonna help.

"This is a crew member from our last shoot and –"

"I have a fucking name, you prick! My name's Jenny. I am a highly-qualified continuity person. And I don't like being treated like a piece of crap. Anyway, who the hell are you?"

Suzie smiled a rather sick grin. "I'm Nick's girlfriend. So, Miss Highly Qualified Cunt-inuity Woman, I strongly suggest you get the fuck out of here or so help me, I'm going to stick this fork right into your fucking eye socket!"

Jenny looked as if she'd just been punched. This wasn't how she had planned it. This wasn't what was meant to happen. She was meant to be the one in charge.

Suzie stood up. At 5 foot 9 inches, she was taller than Jenny. It was the look in her eyes that was more disturbing. They were dead.

Suzie spoke in a very low, calm voice, which made it even worse. "If you are still standing there in five seconds' time, I swear you will be leaving here in a body bag. Do you understand me, you dozy twat?"

Jenny started to say something but Suzie had started to count.

"One –"

She had picked up the fork from the table.

"Two –"

She gripped it as if it were a dagger.

"Three –"

The fork started to rise.

Jenny's vodka-induced bravado instantly disappeared. This had gone disastrously wrong. She was in serious danger of getting hurt, or worse.

As a last resort, Jenny spat out: "You're welcome to him. He's crap in bed anyway." With that, she turned swiftly away and marched out of the restaurant.

The hubbub of conversation rose in the restaurant. The water-cooler moment in offices throughout the area would be full of this within thirty minutes.

Gold sat, not knowing what to say or do. Finally he spoke. "Suzie, I –"

That was as far as he got.

Suzie simply said, "Goodbye Nick," stood up and left.

Gold sat quietly at the table. Was he really crap in bed?

For two days, Gold tried to contact Suzie but without any joy. No answer on the phone, she wasn't at the ad agency and no answer at her flat in Battersea.

On the third day, there was a ring on the intercom on his flat. "Mr Gold? This is Inspector Viner of the Met Police. Can you let me in please?"

The police. What the hell did they want?

Inspector Viner was accompanied by PC Francine Warner. Both were in uniform.

After the usual introductions, the Inspector spoke. "I understand, sir, that you know a Suzanne Fuller?"

It took a moment for Gold to realise he meant Suzie.

He nodded.

"I regret to inform you, Mr Gold, that she was found by the railway track yesterday. It appears that Miss Fuller threw herself in front of the express train that passes along that line. I'm sorry for your loss. We've notified her parents in Esher, but she left a note that was addressed to you. We traced you from the contacts on her mobile phone."

Gold couldn't speak. Suzie. Dead. Under a train. Horrific images flashed across his mind as the engine smashed into her slender body.

After a time, Gold asked. "The note. May I see it?"

WPC Fran Warner handed him a photocopy of the original.

Gold read it and his entire body turned to lead.

'Nick. I always felt worthless. That somehow I'd failed. But with you I thought I had a chance. You of all people seemed to understand me. You put up with my stupid episodes. That woman at the restaurant made me realise I meant nothing, not even to you. That's what hurts the most. That it was all a lie, just like the rest of my life. I've come to a decision, Nick. I've been thinking about it for a long time now. I'm going to the place where I really want to be. It's a better place than this. It's different in so many ways. I'm going to join my true love. The one who really does understand me.

I've been fooling myself. Well, as The Who sang, I won't get fooled again.

Bye Nick. Take care. I never said it, but I did love you.

Gold started to sob. He answered the police questions and they left.

He cried for days. Drank and smoked himself into virtual

oblivion. A sense of loss mixed with deep self-loathing. Two years on and inside he felt no different.

He still missed her. He felt incomplete. There was still the emptiness inside him that only she had been able to fill.

Which was why he was so shocked to see her smiling at him through the windows of the museum café today at the runs of Hierapolis.

ELEVEN

"Better to reign in Hell, than to serve in Heaven."
– John Milton, Paradise Lost

Gold finished his drink. It had become dark and he wanted his bed. He wanted to draw a line under today as it was all too much to try and process. Leaving the veranda, he went upstairs to his bedroom.

He switched on the TV and watched an episode of NCIS in Turkish. Lying on the bed, despite the four double bourbons, he had trouble sleeping. He was too exhausted. Of course, it wasn't Suzie, I mean, that would be impossible. She was dead. Very, very dead. As dead as getting hit by an express train can make a person. You couldn't get much deader.

And yet.

It was her. Her smile. The hair. The piercing green eyes. The familiar black leather biker jacket she'd bought from Zara in Westfield Shopping Centre when they had gone there to catch a film and grab some supper one Saturday.

This was insane.

He went back to the TV. Gibbs was shouting orders to Duckie and Very Special Agent DiNozzo . . . in Turkish. He got the gist of it.

There was a gentle knock at his bedroom door. What? Who the hell was there?

Slowly, with the onset of a mother of a headache coming on, he walked across the room and opened the door.

Christ!

Framed in the doorway was a very beautiful stranger. A stranger, yet one he had been admiring earlier that day. It was the stunning young wife of Mehmet the charming guide.

What was she doing here? At his hotel? At his bedroom door?

Gold recognised her straight away. The long dark hair, the full mouth, the enticing cat-like eyes.

"May I come in Mr Gold? I hope I'm not disturbing you? It's a little late," she said. Her voice was soft, husky and, quite frankly, beguiling.

Gold was too stunned to say anything except a rather ungallant, "Sure."

"I'm Zehra," she said as if that covered all explanations. "You were with my husband today. He was your guide."

"Er . . . yes. Um . . . that's right. Mehmet. Very nice guy."

How very British.

"Yes, Mr Gold. My husband is as you say, 'a very nice man'."

Well, this was awkward.

If Gold had thought this was already the weirdest, most fucked-up day in recent memory, then clearly he was mistaken in that assumption.

"Zehra . . . is that the right way to say it . . . er, don't think me rude, but what exactly are you doing here? Is Mehmet OK?"

She smiled. "Yes, Mr Gold. Mehmet is well. But it is *you* that is my concern."

Gold frowned. "Really? Me? Why are you concerned about me?"

Zehra sat down on the edge of the bed.

"Because I understand that you were ill today, at Hierapolis, in the café. Mehmet told me. So, I thought I would come here and see if you were feeling better . . . and if there was anything I could . . . do?"

Gold was seriously regretting the intake of bourbon. It was clouding what was left of his judgement.

What was this woman doing here? Surely Mehmet would have come over to check up on him, not sent his wife, but she was seriously hot. Bloody bourbon!

"I'm feeling a lot better thank you. And, er, please thank your husband for his very kind concern. That's . . . er . . . very kind of you . . . both."

Was it suddenly hot in the room?

"So, Mr Gold, you saw my husband. He is most charming . . . yes?"

"Yes. Yes, indeed. A . . . er . . . very charming man. And very good looking. A good-looking man."

Zehra gave a half smile and sighed. Gold had watched porn that didn't have the effect her sigh had just had on him.

"Yes, he is a good-looking man Mr Gold . . . for his age. May I call you Nick?"

The bourbon was making Gold's head feel as if Gene Krupa was playing a drum solo inside his skull.

"Well, Zehra, thank you so much for coming round to check up on me. As you can see, I'm fine, so please tell Mehmet . . . your husband . . . that I'm fine and I'll probably call him tomorrow."

Zehra slowly stood up. How could anyone just standing up from a bed make it look so damn sexy? She walked slowly towards Gold.

"Tell me, Nick, how did you feel when you saw my picture on my husband's phone? Hmm? Did you like it?"

Gold laughed. "Sure. Of course I did. What's not to like?"

She walked a step further. "And how did it make you feel, Nick? Hmm. What did you think of me? You liked what you saw, yes?"

Gold just nodded.

"And do I disappoint?"

Gold managed to shake his head.

"So what are you going to do about it, Nick? I'm here. You're here. You've had a bad day. Perhaps your day could . . . improve?"

Before Gold could even respond she closed the distance between them and he felt her soft, full mouth on his.

This was one helluva day.

Nick liked Mehmet. But God, this woman was sex on a stick. It was so wrong but hey, he hadn't invited her to his hotel. He didn't even know her. And her tapered fingers were effortlessly undoing the belt on his jeans, unzipping the fly and pulling down his Calvin Kleins.

"Why don't you lay down on the bed Nick? We'll both be so much more comfortable, yes?"

Gold didn't need asking twice. He reached to undo her dress but playfully she moved his hands away.

"Uh-uh. Not yet. First I need to . . . how you say . . . take care of *you*. To help you forget your horrible, horrible day. I think I know just the way to take your mind off things."

As she said this, she slowly licked her lips.

Oh, she was good all right. This was, morally wrong or not, going to be memorable.

Gold lay down on the bed as Zehra pulled his jeans and boxers even lower. Then, with tantalising slowness, she began to kiss him as she headed south. First his lips, then his neck, his shoulder, his chest, his stomach until she began to lick around her point of destination.

Oh, she was *really* good.

Gold, ever the narcissist, thought that maybe he could watch the hot action on the flat screen TV that was mounted on the bedroom wall. Not that it was being broadcast to a stunned Turkish nation, but that the reflection of the fabulous woman pleasuring him on the blackened screen would make this even more erotic.

Zehra took him in her mouth. Gold glanced at the blank black screen and stared.

And stared again.

In the reflection, Zehra's long, lustrous hair was now in a short bob. Her Turkish curves had narrowed to a slimmer frame.

He let out a grunt of pain as he felt something sharp on his hardness.

He looked down at the woman licking him. She smiled back at him. The perfect triangular pointed teeth, like white daggers, reflected in the bedside light. "Hi baby. Miss me?"

Suzie!

"What the fuck!" yelled Gold. "You're dead. Train. Dead."

Eloquence had gone out the window along with normality.

Gold leapt up, moving quicker than he ever had in his entire life. Adrenalin will do that to a person about to have their penis bitten off by their dead wife.

Suzie stayed on the bed, arching her back like a cat about to pounce.

"Oh poor little Nicky. So confused, huh baby? Dead. Alive. What's the difference?"

Gold stared at her. "What's the difference? What the hell do you mean? It's very fucking different."

Gold was yelling as shock ran through his nervous system.

Suzie smiled enigmatically as she started to stand up from the bed. "Of course. Silly me. To you it's all black and white isn't it, hun? You're alive or you're dead. So simple. But it's not. Don't you get that yet? It's not simple at all. I mean . . . look at me. Do I look dead?"

Gold was edging away. His legs felt as if they had turned to lead and he was struggling to breathe. "I, er, I dunno."

"Well, let's think for a moment, shall we? Thirty seconds ago you were ready to fuck me. Feeling a little limp now, are we, baby?"

Christ, dead or alive, Suzie could be such a total bitch.

"That wasn't you. That was . . ."

"Yeah. Couldn't resist. My bad. You're so utterly predictable, Nicky. Your face when Mehmet showed you his hot wife on his phone. Bloody classic!"

"You saw that? You were there?"

Suzie stood up and flexed her shoulders as if limbering up.

"We see every fucking thing, Nick. Haven't you worked that out yet either? I told you in my note, but you were too obtuse to understand. I kept trying to tell you for the two years we were together, but you never got it."

Gold felt the room starting to spin slightly. "Got what? What didn't I get?"

Suzie moved silently, gracefully, a few inches closer. Somehow she seemed taller than her five feet nine inches.

"He wanted me."

Without warning her right arm lashed at astonishing speed. Gold, on pure instinct, managed to avoid the blow.

"Wanted you? Who wanted you? Your boss at the design company?"

Suzie laughed. A loud, rasping laugh. It sent a shiver of absolute fear through Gold's body.

"You are so fucking pedestrian. So horribly ordinary. So devoutly middle class. No, Nicholas, not my boss . . . I said 'He' wanted me. My Lord. My true love."

"Who . . . God? You've got religion?"

Suzie screamed. It made Gold wince. The sound penetrated his head so that he physically felt his brain vibrate.

"Noooooooo! Not your God. The true Lord. The only Lord. The Ruler of Mankind. Lucifer!"

Gold couldn't move. Couldn't speak. He was so utterly and desperately lost.

"Night after night he would come into my dreams. Showing me another life. A better life. A life that someone like you could never understand. You thought I was having a breakdown. 'Poor old Suzie' you all thought. You utter fucktard. You didn't have a clue what I was going through. For two years he pursued me, haunted me, seducing me with images that were so . . . so . . . magnificent. How could this shit that you call 'life' compare to that majesty? Don't you see how trivial you became. Poor Nick with his sad little problems. Mummy and Daddy all gone. Oh boo fucking hoo. I was being shown an existence beyond your wildest imagination. Of power so intoxicating, of possibilities beyond anything anyone has ever even written of."

Finally, somehow, Gold managed to speak.

"And this . . . this person, you chose to join him?"

Suzie spat out a laugh. "Person? Christ, you have no idea what you're up against. Not a clue what you've got yourself into, have you? I came here to warn you . . . to tell you . . . leave it the fuck alone. Leave it! Walk away!"

"Who the hell are you? What are you? You're not Suzie. Not the Suzie I knew."

"You wouldn't even begin to understand who I am. Yes, I was Suzie. Now, I am Persephone. Satan's consort. What girl could turn that down?"

"Any fucking girl on the planet, except you, you raving lunatic!"

Gold tried to run to the bedroom door but in an instant Suzie was across the bed and trying to claw at his face. In an instinctive movement of self preservation, Gold swung himself to one side to try to evade the shark-like teeth that were about to strike, and his hand grabbed the glass bottle of mineral water on the bedside table. In an arc he brought it down as hard as he could on Suzie's head. The glass shattering on her skull.

Suzie groaned. Her head now had a large jagged gash, but no blood.

"Wanna play rough, big boy? We got plenty of time, baby."

With a snarl, she launched herself at him again, baring her razor teeth, her hands like talons.

Acting on pure adrenalin, Gold snatched the bed sheet off the bed and managed to throw part of it over her head. He moved to his right, picked up the upholstered wooden chair that formed part of the bedroom, and in the instant that Suzie was caught in the sheet, smashed it down where he assumed her head would be. Again and again. He lost track of how many times he used the chair as a club. He kept hitting the shape until his arms gave way.

The movement under the sheet stopped. Gold stood there and, from sheer exhaustion, dropped the chair to the floor.

The bed remained motionless. Gold tried to gulp in some air. His lungs and throat felt on fire. He was soaked in sweat.

Gingerly, with his heart beating so loudly he could hear nothing else, he picked up a corner of the sheet and slowly drew it back.

Whatever he was expecting to find, it wasn't this.

Nothing.

The bed was quite empty.

TWELVE

"Of neither sea, nor shore, nor air, nor fire,
But all these in their pregnant causes mixed."
– John Milton, Paradise Lost

Gold was adrift on an ocean, clinging to a small piece of wooden decking that somehow he had managed to salvage. The ocean was mercifully calm and the gentle undulations of the waves were soothing and relaxing. Soon his entire body was in tune with the rhythm of the sea. If he died out here, alone, that would be just fine, he was at peace. Here on the endless ocean, under a cloudless sky, that would be like coming home to an endless beautiful rest.

The ocean began to change its pattern. Swirls of colour mixed in with the azure blue. Was it the reflection of the sky or perhaps shoals of fish as they swam beneath him in the fathomless depths?

The texture of the sea started to alter. It felt surprisingly dry, somehow almost bristly.

It had turned from liquid into a solid state. It *was* solid.

Painstakingly slowly, Gold raised his head a fraction of an inch as his fingers dug into the surface of whatever was keeping him afloat. Gradually, as his vision returned and his surroundings came into focus, the sea became a carpet.

After what seemed an age, Gold's brain managed to process that he was lying face-down on the bedroom floor in his Turkish hotel. How he got there, he had no recollection.

Then, like a tsunami, the memory rolled over him in a rush that physically took his breath away.

The guide's young wife had come to his room. Yet it wasn't her. It was Suzie. But Suzie was dead. Been dead two years. She had tried to kill him. In this room. Teeth. Razor-sharp, pointed shark-like teeth. Then he remembered precisely just where she was when he saw her unmasked. The thought made him shudder and bile rose in his throat.

It was too much to comprehend. All Gold could manage was a long, drawn out groan.

For a while he considered spending the rest of his life right here, lying on the carpet, never opening the door to his room again. He'd be safe.

It wasn't really an option.

Mustering all his determination, which at the moment was at zero, Gold slowly hauled himself up off the floor and managed to sit on the edge of the bed. After a while, the bedroom came back into focus.

What in the name of God had happened? Had he been drugged? Was he, like maybe Adam Farthing, having some form of mental breakdown? It can't have been a nightmare, the broken chair and smashed mineral water bottle that lay in pieces attested to its reality.

And yet . . . and yet . . . it couldn't possibly be real.

As he sat rubbing his head, and checking that his penis was indeed still attached to the rest of his body, a quotation crept into his mind: *'Life and death are one thread, the same line viewed from different sides.'*

So, where was he?

Think . . . think . . .

Joanne Walsh gets attacked by her dead brother, a woman in Pennsylvania gets attacked by her dead father, Adam Farthing nearly dies at the hands, or teeth to be precise, of his dead grand-father and now Gold's very dead, ex-girlfriend Suzie rocks up in his hotel bedroom and tries to kill him at worst, or bite off his manhood at the very least.

He gave an involuntary shudder. "Fuck me, those teeth."

It was all the more disturbing to Gold as it brought back memories of just how great sex had been with Suzie. Now, he wasn't sure if he'd ever be able to enjoy fellatio again, certainly not without a taser or baseball bat close to hand.

Thoughts ran around his head like a firework display, each one demanding attention, but gone in an instant.

There was no connection between any of these incidents. He'd never been to Pennsylvania. Frankly it was about as high on his wish list as spending the day on a trading estate in Slough.

It was a fact that the human condition only allows a person to process so much information at any one time.

Back when he was at university, Gold had read Alvin Toffler's book, *Future Shock*. Toffler theorized that the human brain has finite limits on how much information it can absorb and process. Exceed that limit and the brain becomes overloaded, thinking and reasoning become dulled, decision-making flawed and, in some cases, impossible.

Even worse, he suggested, information overload will eventually lead to widespread physical and mental disturbances. He called this phenomenon 'Future Shock Syndrome'.

Gold was dwelling on this. Future Shock? I've had a fucking great, massive, mahoosive shock, he mused.

Fact: people don't come back from the dead. Even Justin Timberlake had trouble making a comeback.

But.

Why would three people with virtually no, or very little, contact share the same experience?

When you eliminate the impossible, whatever remains, however improbable, must be the truth.

Somehow, in some weird, messed-up, insane way, the dead were returning. And not in a good way.

He had to get back to the Temple of Apollo in the ruins of Hierapolis. For that, he wouldn't need a guide. He knew how to get there. Besides which, Gold felt that he couldn't look Mehmet in the face any more after the 'visit' of his wife to his bedroom last night. OK, it wasn't actually her . . . or he *presumed* it wasn't her . . . unless she was a magician good enough to headline in Las Vegas.

It was early morning. Gold passed on the buffet breakfast. Eating wasn't a priority today, finding answers was. Somehow nearly having his penis bitten off by the undead had curbed his appetite.

Maybe he could patent it as a diet.

After the journey to the site of the ruins, Gold headed straight to the area of the temple, surrounded by the gleaming white stunning travertine terraces. There was no way he was going to go back to the café. Not after what he had seen through its windows the previous day. Not after he'd seen *her*.

As it was early, the usual throng of tourists had not yet risen from their beds or, unlike Gold, were munching their way through a breakfast at least three times the amount they would normally eat at home.

Under Roman rule, the city had flourished. There were temples, a theatre and people flocked to bathe in the hot springs which were believed to have healing properties.

The doomed Mr and Mrs Walsh had travelled to Pamukkale for its well-known hot springs. It was still a thriving enterprise, centuries on.

The remains of a pool and the steps placed above the cave which match the descriptions of the site in ancient sources were still visible.

Gold knew he couldn't enter the cave where the gate of hell was depicted in legend; he was anxious for answers but not suicidal. Fact or fiction, one thing was for sure, any animal going too near dropped dead from the poisonous gases.

He walked as close as he could get to the site of the Temple of Apollo – the Plutonium. It was a crumbling ruin. A double door underneath a large stone lintel. A set of five, broken stone steps led up to the entrance.

Gold stood looking at the bricks, the stone, the earth in the early morning sunshine. His mind raced. What was he expecting to see? The Devil himself, accompanied by a strong aftershave waft of sulphur? Suzie rising from the ground like a Christopher Lee Hammer Horror film?

No. There was nothing to indicate that this was the epicentre of all things diabolical. It was a ruin with little tufts of rough grass and a few weeds dotted about in the dry ground that surrounded it.

Gold sat down on a nearby piece of ground that wasn't hallowed, sacred or particularly remarkable. The stones had been laid out so that tired, hot and bothered tourists could simply sit and take a rest.

He stared at the site before him, taking in every crevice, every piece of stone, every last detail.

"So, beginning to believe are we?"

Gold jumped at the intrusion into his reverie.

Automatically, without looking at the speaker, he responded, "What?"

South London for pardon.

"I said, you're finally beginning to believe, are you Nick?"

What the hell?

Gold spun around. When he had sat down, he had been quite alone. No one was even approaching this area of the ancient site. How had this guy sneaked up so quietly without him even noticing? Out of nowhere, an old schoolboy joke about Hush Puppies flitted across his mind. Extraordinary what the human brain does when trying to process the unfathomable.

Gold's mouth opened. But no words came out. Just an exhalation of air. The thumping in his chest as his heart went into hyper-overdrive was physically painful. Finally, after what seemed an eon, words came out.

"You have fucking got to be fucking joking. What the actual fuck?"

South London for I am incredulous at what I am currently observing.

Gold somehow managed to regain a modicum of composure.

"No dog this time? Or has he got his own TV talk show now?"

The homeless man smiled.

"No. But you know how complicated it is travelling with animals. All the inoculations and stuff."

Gold was in too deep a state of shock to stand up. His legs felt as if the bones had been removed and all that was left was unsupported flesh.

"Really. Gosh. Well, that must have been a real headache for you. Where did you put him – in the Kennels for the Fucking You're Weirding Me Out?"

Again, the response was an enigmatic smile.

"OK. Enough of this shit, my friend. Who are you?"

"I am precisely that."

"Sorry Yoda? What?"

"I am your friend."

If Gold had had a packet of Marlborough Lights on him, he would have put two in his mouth and lit them simultaneously.

"My friend? Is that right? Well, call me crazy but I don't recall receiving a Christmas card from you or a cheery text on my birthday. Hang on, yes, it's coming back to me now . . . we met on the 12th of Never back in the month of It-Never-Happened. Who the fuck are you?"

"Barachiel."

Gold frowned.

"What? Come again? Like the former President of the USA?"

The homeless man smiled gently, as a father would to a young child.

"No, Nick. That was Barack. A good friend of mine incidentally. My name is Barachiel, but you can call me Barry."

"And you can call me KissMyArse. Barry? Barry? What kind of bullshit name is that?"

The homeless man's face clouded.

"It's my name, Nick. Please don't wear it out."

Gold ran his fingers through his dark hair and across the stubble on his chin.

"Look . . . Barry . . . on a scale of one to ten, I am losing this at number five trillion. You freak me out outside Sainsbury's back home, you turn up outside my flat . . . and now . . . now . . . you appear like some dumb-arse magic trick in Turkey? You got a thing about me or what?"

"Nick, do you know what my name means?"

Gold snorted a derisory laugh.

"No . . . Barry . . . I don't. Why don't you enlighten me?"

Barachiel the homeless man smiled.

"What's with the smiling, you freak?"

"I smile Nick, because that is precisely why I am here. To enlighten you. And to inform you of your duties and responsibilities."

Finally, Gold managed to get to his feet.

"Oh really? That so? Well Barack O'Nutcase, let me stop you right there. Let me tell you what my responsibilities are. One, to make TV shows about spooky shit that doesn't really exist. Two, to research yet more bullshit so that I get another long-running series commissioned. Three, to avoid nutbags who decide in their delusional minds that they need to stalk me. How does that sound. Pretty close?"

The homeless man stood up. Gold was surprised at how tall he appeared. And for a homeless guy, he was in remarkably good physical shape. Muscular. Purposeful. Strong.

How old was this guy? It was as though his face waxed and waned between elderly and youthful and with no Beverly Hills plastic surgeon in sight.

And what was it with his voice? It fluctuated from the

anonymous accent of any of the eight thousand homeless men living on London's streets to one of gravitas, a mixture of James Earl-Jones and Morgan Freeman.

"I see," he replied thoughtfully. "And tell me Nick, where does Suzie fit into these *responsibilities* of yours?

Gold stood stock still.

"How the hell . . . what do you know . . . who the fuck *are* you?." The words tumbled out.

Again, the infuriating enigmatic smile.

"I think I've covered that point, Nick. My name is Barachiel. What do I know? Well, right now my friend, a lot more than you. How was it last night with Suzie?"

Gold stared at the homeless man who somehow didn't look so homeless. The long-sleeved Ralph Lauren shirt tucked neatly into a dark pair of trousers, well-polished Church brogues, was that a Rolex Daytona on his wrist?

Then there was the hair. Outside Sainsbury's, it had seemed matted, the dreadlocks grimy from the detritus of living on the street. Now it appeared to be in great condition. Gold knew that a change of scenery could work wonders but not on this scale. It was as if Barachiel . . . Barry . . . was physically morphing in front of his eyes, even as they spoke.

"How was it? You're asking me that? Well, let's think about it shall we? A woman you've never met comes into your hotel room, proceeds to give you a blow job and in the middle of it changes into your dead girlfriend who then attempts to bite off your cock with teeth she's presumably borrowed from a great white shark . . . on balance, after careful consideration, I would say, from memory, I've had better evenings. That's how it was . . . *Barry*!"

To Gold's intense annoyance, Barry broke into loud laughter. Tears began to roll down his cheeks, which now, oddly, had a chiselled, male-model appearance.

"Yeah . . . yeah . . . the dead can really mess you up my friend."

Gold considered what he had just heard.

"The dead? You know she's dead? Suzie, I mean."

Barry nodded. "Oh, she's dead all right. In a manner of speaking."

"In a what? Listen Actimel –"

"Barachiel."

"Whatever. You're either dead or you're not. It's like being pregnant. You either are, or you aren't. So, don't give me this voodoo mumbo-jumbo bullshit 'in a manner of speaking' crap."

Barry sat down once more, leaving Gold standing facing him and looking far from happy.

"Last night Nick, was Suzie in your room or were you dreaming?"

Gold snapped back. "I wasn't bloody dreaming! She was there! Right in front of me. As real as you are."

Barry gave a very small smile and glanced at his white-gold watch, which gleamed in the brightness of the Turkish sunshine.

"Well Nick, if you weren't dreaming, and she was in your room, as real as I am, and you assure me categorically that she's dead, then . . . what was she?"

Nick frowned. This was getting weird, which considering the past few hours, was saying something.

"I'm not following."

Barry replied. "It's quite simple. Was she dead in your room or was she alive?"

Nick was having trouble answering. Of course she was dead. Had been for two years. As he had reminded himself for every one of the one million, fifty-one thousand and two-hundred minutes since he had found out.

"Suzie is dead . . . but last night . . . last night . . . " his voice faltered. Gold couldn't find the words.

Barachiel did.

"Last night, Nick Gold, she was both dead *and* alive."

THIRTEEN

"Never can true reconcilement grow where wounds of deadly hate have pierced so deep."

– John Milton, Paradise Lost

Gold felt dizzy. The ruins were starting to revolve around him. His focus felt fuzzy. The day felt suddenly very warm. Sweat started to form on his forehead and to run down the back of his neck. This was all too freaking insane.

Barry put out a steadying hand and Gold, like a child, allowed himself to be assisted as he sat down.

"Drink this." Barry produced a bottle of very cold mineral water. Gold hadn't noticed him carrying it before, but gratefully took it and drank. It was the best, most refreshing water Gold had ever tasted.

Allowing a few moments for Nick to regain his composure, Barachiel spoke in a calm, even tone, as a lecturer would to an intelligent third-year student. Subconsciously, it resonated with Gold.

"Are you familiar with the concept of Soul Sleep?"

Nick shrugged. "I think I saw them play once at Ronnie Scott's. The drummer was particularly good."

Barachiel's tone changed. Harder, less warm. "Not everything in life is a joke, Nick, as you will soon discover. What you are embarking upon is no cosmic comedy. Snappy one liners will not help you. Not this time."

Gold looked at this stranger with a mixture of insolence, anger and, oddly, respect.

"Have you heard the term before?"

Gold nodded. "We touched on it briefly when I was at university. It's the belief that the souls of those who die will 'rest' in an inert state until Christ's future return."

Barachiel nodded his approval. "Very good, Mr Gold. Soul Sleep is also called Christian Mortalism or psychopannychism. The idea has been held by a variety of religious groups throughout history. It is not a new concept. Far from it."

He continued.

"Until the final resurrection though there is a temporary heaven – Paradise, and a temporary hell – Hades. At the resurrection, this body is 'awakened' and transformed into the everlasting body a person will possess for eternity, whether in Heaven or Hell. But suppose, Mr Gold, that someone, someone with unlimited power, had found a way to awake those in Soul Sleep . . . to bring them back, so to speak. To bring them into a state that made them appear to all intents and purposes 'alive' . . . but of course, as you would understand it, they're not. You see my point?"

"Not exactly."

"I suspect that your studies also touched on as you say, Persephone?"

Gold was being reminded very clearly why, during his three years at Oxford, he had often bitterly regretted opting to study theology.

"Yeah. Sure. Randy old Hades gets the raging hots for this chick Persephone, so he abducts her and takes her down to Hell. She gets seriously moody and refuses to eat anything at all. Her mother goes nuts looking for her for a whole year and finally tracks her down. They're about to blow that particular popstand when Hades urges Persephone to appease her terrible hunger by eating a single pomegranate seed. Big surprise – it was a trick. No shit. Duh! Anyone who tastes the food of Hades must remain in the Underworld. So she has to agree to a sort of divorce settlement/time-share deal and spend some of the year with her Mum and the rest with Hugh Hefner down in Hell. That's about it.

Barachiel stared at Nick Gold, the expression on his face flitting from appalled astonishment to amazement.

"You have a sense of the contemporary dramatic, Mr Gold. Do you see why I raise the subject of Persephone?"

"No idea. Maybe you felt the conversation was flagging?"

"Again, enough of the jokes, Mr Gold. Freud will have a field day with you one day. As he so rightly says, the superego allows the ego to generate humour. A benevolent superego allows a light and comforting type of humour, while a harsh superego creates a biting and sarcastic type of humour, just like yours. I introduced the subject because I wanted you to appreciate that Persephone was not the last beautiful woman to catch the eye, so to speak, of the Lord of the Underworld. Across the centuries there have been many. Including one close to you. One you know well."

Gold stared at him. "You mean Suzie?"

"You studied the ancient texts, Mr Gold. You comprehend what I am saying to you, do you not?"

"So she was telling the truth. Holy shit!" muttered Gold.

"Well, unholy shit would be more apropos."

Barachiel sensed he was losing his audience and changed tack.

"Look at that flower over there."

Barachiel indicated a lone red rose that protruded defiantly from the stony ground.

"What do you see?"

Gold looked at the petals a few feet away from where they both now sat.

"A red flower. Do I win a prize?" He said weakly.

"Indeed," replied the homeless man. "You see a red flower. A rose, in fact. A dog, however, can't distinguish green, yellow or red objects based on their colour. A snake, my friend, sees in infrared, using thousands of microscopic sensors, at least ten times more sensitive than the best artificial infrared sensors humans have ever built."

"Sorry to interrupt you, David Attenborough, but is there a point to this?"

Barry brushed an invisible speck of dust from his shirt cuff.

"The point, Nick, is this: what does that red flower actually look like?"

Gold shrugged.

"Who is right, Nick, you, who sees a red flower, the dog, who sees it in black and white, or the snake, who sees it glowing in infrared?"

"I give up. Who is right? Enlighten me, Bazza."

Again, there was that annoying fleeting smile.

"I intend to. The answer is, Nick, that they are all correct. How we see that flower is precisely how it is. It is both red, black and white and glows in the infrared wavelength of light. Thus it is with Suzie. She is both dead and alive. To us, she is dead. She died in front of that train. She is buried. She is mourned. But where she is . . . well, she is not dead."

Gold drank at the bottle of mineral water until every last drop of its sweet-tasting content had been drained.

"Thus? *Thus?* Who on earth says thus? OK, Barry-Boy, I'll take the bait. Happy? Where is she? Where exactly is my two-year dead girlfriend? Bournemouth?"

"No, Nick. She is in Hell."

Gold stood up and stared at the homeless man.

"Go fuck yourself, you jerk-off freak."

Turning, Gold began to walk away.

He had reached twenty yards from where they had been seated when Barachiel fell into step walking beside him, without making a sound on the stony ground.

"Your reaction is understandable, Nick. It's a lot to take in. Think about it, just for a moment. Suzie tried to kill you. Joanne Walsh's brother tried to kill her close to where we are now, Lynn is accused of killing her husband Doug in Pennsylvania . . . and then there's your friend Adam Farthing. He saw what he saw. They all did. They all saw the red flower."

"He's not my friend." Gold had stopped walking. "That little shit Farthing. He's a colleague. He's not my friend."

Barry produced another bottle of mineral water. Gold hadn't seen him carrying the first bottle let alone this second. He took it, unscrewed the top, and drank deeply.

At least Gold had the good grace to say thank you, which was followed by a long exhalation.

After a while, and his composure restored to some degree, Gold turned to the homeless man.

"What do you want from me, Barry or whatever name you're calling yourself?"

Barachiel nodded, as if the question made perfect sense.

"We need you, Nick Gold. When I first spoke to you outside the supermarket in London, I tried to tell you that."

Gold shook his head.

"Here we go! More crap. Can't you just give me a straight-answer to a simple question? How hard can that be? You've followed me from London to Turkey, you've been busting my balls now for God knows how long, at least give me a clue what this insanity is all about? What do you want from *me*?"

"Well Mr Gold, in a nutshell, we want you to save the human race."

Somewhere nearby, a Caspian Snowcock began to chirp. There was a gentle sound of the breeze as it blew across Hierapolis. In the distance, a Dutch tourist was on her mobile phone to her daughter in the Erasmus University of Rotterdam telling her not to forget to send her grandmother a birthday card. Otherwise, the air felt so quiet it was as though it was holding its breath.

Finally, the silence was broken.

"So, just that? Save the human race. Good, because for a moment there, I thought it might be something, you know, big like getting you a ticket to the Brit Awards or tickets for the Harry Potter play. Sure. No problem. I don't unfortunately have my diary on me at the moment, but I could probably fit this saving humanity thing in, say, next Tuesday. I can give you a morning or afternoon slot. Does that suit?"

Gold turned away and started to walk, this time with purpose. As he strode across the pale white stony ground, he called out to Barachiel behind him.

"You had me going there, Baz-Boy. But I can now say with one hundred percent confidence that you are, what I believe our American chums call, a total whack job. Get some fucking help my friend. And leave me alone! You get it?"

On this verbal flourish, Gold spun around to make sure the stranger understood the message.

The ruins of Hierapolis were completely deserted. Of Barachiel, the homeless man, there was no sign. The path where, just a moment ago he had been walking behind Nick, was completely empty.

FOURTEEN

"He who receives Light from above, from the Fountain of Light, No other doctrine needs, though granted true;"
– John Milton, Paradise Regained

Later that afternoon, Gold was on a flight back to London. It had been, he mused, an interesting trip. Aside from homicidal dead girlfriends, transforming nympho Turkish delights, and a homeless guy from Sainsbury's in Balham appearing out of nowhere, it had been fairly uneventful.

Much of this was, however, to have a major impact on Gold's life. He would change from shopping at Sainsbury's to Waitrose henceforth.

The trick now was to convince Good Foot Productions the recce had been an outstanding success, represented excellent value-for-money, and would form a solid base from which to launch the new series that would be warmly embraced by the show's target demographic audience and therefore attract the level of sponsorship any independent television production company would need to fund the project.

The usual media bullshit that Gold spoke so fluently.

As soon as he reached his flat, Gold began to compose a detailed email to Larry Shaitan in which he set out his thoughts in an ordered, succinct manner. His Oxford degree hadn't been a complete waste of time.

As he was sitting at his laptop, Gold, like most of the population, checked his Facebook page and Twitter account.

Facebook was, as ever, full of 'fishing expeditions' as he termed them, most of which were a variation on 'Feeling down' to which some poor sap would take the bait and enquire 'You OK, hun?' or the infuriating 'Am off to a very important meeting – can't say more' to which Gold always shouted at the laptop screen, "Well, don't sodding tell us in the first place".

Amidst the humour, pathos, ego-massaging and adverts from Californian start-ups, something caught his eye.

It was a friend request.

From someone calling themselves 'Barry Sainsbury'.

Really?

Gold clicked to see if the profile would add some flesh to the bone. It didn't. Not even a photo or a single mutual friend.

Twitter, the digital equivalent of Dodge City, proved equally as barren in the 'Barry Sainsbury' department, although there was someone of that name who, as of very recently, had started 'following' him. He, however, appeared to have no followers of his own.

What had Barry called himself? Ah yes, 'Barachiel'.

Barachiel.

At first, he assumed it was some sort of South London hip name, but in the recesses of his mind, it felt oddly familiar, like a half-remembered song. It took a few clicks of the mouse for it to come flooding back. There it was.

> *'Barachiel is an Archangel known as the angel of blessings and is also the chief of all of the guardian angels. Barachiel means 'God's blessings'.*
>
> *In art, Barachiel is usually depicted scattering rose petals that represent God's blessings showering down on people, or holding a red rose (to his chest).*

"Oh, holy crap. You have got to be shitting me," said Gold aloud. He began to read in earnest. The names, the ideas, quotes all coming back into focus. Material that he had studied and debated for three years, especially with Professor Mark Whittaker, with whom he had formed an intellectual bond at Oxford.

"The problem, Mr Gold, is that you refuse to allow the idea that any of this might actually be true to enter into your discourse. Your cynicism, your intellectual rigidity, your seeming inability, in fact I'd go as far as to say your inherent anger, prevents you from opening your mind simply to the possibility to look at this in a more, shall we say, charitably positive manner."

Gold refreshed his memory

'The third Book of Enoch, an ancient Jewish text, describes Archangel Barachiel as one of the angels who serve as great and honoured angelic princes in Heaven. The text mentions that Barachiel leads 496,000 other angels who work with him. Barachiel is part of the seraphim rank of angels who guard God's throne, as well as the leader of all the guardian angels who work with humans during their earthly lifetimes.'

"No sodding way," murmured Gold. "Half a million people working for him? That homeless guy outside the supermarket with the talking dog? Now he employs more people than the National Health Service."

'Since rose petals symbolize God's blessings, Barachiel will sometimes use rose petals to signal his presence in your life, say believers.'

The red flower – it was a rose, growing alone in the stony ground of the Turkish ruins, remembered Gold.

'Barachiel came to be associated with rose petals because of his depiction in the ancient Jewish texts, the Sibylline Oracles: "He holds blossoming rose branches, a token of God's blessing."

'Roses, which contain the highest level of energy vibrations of any flower, serve as symbols of God's love in all of the world's major religions.'

*

Yes. Of course they did. Just four miles from Gold's flat in Balham stood Dulwich Village, an oasis of contemplative study and Volvos. As well as Dulwich College, an extraordinary Venetian-styled school founded in 1619, there was the Dulwich Picture Gallery, the country's first purpose-built art gallery that had opened in 1817. Gold had spent many a rainy English afternoon there staying dry and studying the collected works of art on display. Now it came back to him. Roses. Featured in so many of the religious paintings. Roses. He should have remembered earlier.

Gold stood up, walked the few paces to where the Jack Daniels was standing near the sink, and poured himself half a tumbler. His head was beginning to ache and the unpleasant knot was back in his stomach. Angels, Archangels, stuff he hadn't thought about in years. These days he put it right up there with Father Christmas, the tooth fairy and an honest politician.

And why him? What on earth had made him the apparent centre of attention (a position that Gold often revelled in) of all these utterly bizarre events in London and Turkey? There's odd, there's weird and then there's hit-your-head-against-a-wall, it's less painful and too out-there to comprehend. Gold felt that trying to get his head around this was like trying to teach a cat mechanical engineering.

Dr Jack started to work its warm way through his body after the first not inconsiderable gulp.

Gold continued to read and as he did so, it started to feel familiar, like finding a favourite t-shirt that you thought you'd lost. The knowledge acquired during his early upbringing and through his formal education had never truly gone away; he'd merely chosen to bury it after they'd buried Suzie.

'There are seven angels or Archangels as related to the seven days of the week: Michael (Sunday), Gabriel (Monday), Raphael (Tuesday),

Uriel (Wednesday), Selaphiel (Thursday), Raguel or Jegudiel (Friday), and Barachiel (Saturday).'

OK. So, the dude was a weekend Angel. Party-on, Barry!

'An angel is a pure spirit created by God. The Old Testament theology included the belief in angels: the name applied to certain spiritual beings or intelligences of heavenly residence, employed by God as the ministers of His will. The English word "angel" comes from the Greek angelos, which means "messenger".'

And I thought it was DHL. Gold sipped some more Bourbon. Greek. Another subject he hadn't thought about in years.

'In the Old Testament, with two exceptions, the Hebrew word for "angel" is malak, also meaning "messenger".'

Indeed it is. Another sip. A pause. A re-fill. More sipping. Religious research was thirsty work.

'In the Book of Revelation the elders of the seven churches of Asia were called angels (Revelation1:20).'

Ah, of course. The *Book of Revelation*. The Stephen King of the *Bible*. Gold scanned page after page on his laptop screen. And there it was.

'Archangel Barachiel is the angel of God's blessings. While asking God to bless all our good efforts, let us also appeal to Archangel Barachiel for help. However, we must accept the Lord's blessing not only for prosperity but also for our cross, the sorrows without which there is no salvation. And may Archangel Barachiel give us strength to carry our blessed crosses.'

*

Well, that sucked. Crosses? No salvation? A real bundle of laughs. Gold reflected, his thoughts partly aided and abetted by another glass of Lynchburg's finest export, that there were two ways of considering this. The first was that he, Nicholas Oliver Gold, out of the 7,484,325,476 inhabitants of Planet Earth, had been specifically singled out by the Archangel Barachiel for reasons yet to be specified, or that, second, it was all a complete load of bullshit and he should take a couple of Nurofen and go to bed.

He voted for option two.

Over the next few days, Gold kept a wary eye out for the homeless man, but the most dramatic occurrence was a shouting match between two women vying for the same parking space outside the Franco Manca Pizza Restaurant on Balham High Street. Life seemed to have settled down so that at least Gold didn't feel his brain was about to explode with yet another revelation. Bad choice of word, he mused.

Larry had read Gold's detailed email and summoned him, and Adam Farthing, into Dean Street for what he called a face-to-face to grease the collaborative process. They used to be called meetings.

Mitzi indicated that Larry was on a conference call and Adam and Nick should wait to go in until he'd finished. Larry's voice could be heard in the reception area clearly as it rose in volume. The conversation, it would appear, was not going well.

"You listen to me, you fucking ingrate. This is what you wanted. This is what you craved. So I made it happen. You got what you wanted. And now you're on the phone whining to me that it's a tough role. No shit, genius. Of course it's tough. I'm not here to wipe your arse every time someone bitches about your Tweets. Sort it out. I fucking told you, be careful what you wish for. I warned you. Don't blame me if you didn't listen. That's on you. You understand me? Do you need me to come there and explain this face to face? Yeah . . . didn't think so. I gotta go. I'll check up on you tomorrow. I got stuff to do now. Yeah . . . yeah . . . no . . . *you* take care."

"I think he's finished. You can go in now," smiled Mitzi.

They entered. Larry rose from his desk and shook both men warmly by the hand.

"There's my boys. Nice tan, Nick. You trying to look like me these days, huh? Well, who could blame you?"

This time Adam Farthing kept his mouth mainly closed. He was many things, but stupid was not one of them. If his boss liked Gold's ideas, then by golly so did he. It would be rude not to.

The face-to-face went exceptionally well. Ideas were run up the flagpole and saluted, cross media solutions were maximised, cross-platformed ROIs were streamlined, distributed partnerships were envisioneered and, of course, web-enabled convergence was cultivated.

In other words, they'd market the fuck out of this TV series.

Much man-hugging took place that day in the offices of Good Foot Productions, a raucous lunch was had upstairs at The French House and Gold was once more the golden boy. Adam was content, for now, to bathe in the radiance of the Sun King.

As they all stood, unsteadily, outside Soho's venerable drinking hole, Larry put his hand on Gold's leather-clad shoulder and said, solemnly, "Our boots on the ground is the most value-added thing at our company. Do your best to monetize it. I've got my eye on you, Nick . . . never forget that."

Gold nodded sagely as if he understood one syllable of what had just been said.

For Gold, all that mattered was that his boss had increased his research budget and that meant only one thing.

America.

FIFTEEN

"Into this wild Abyss
The womb of Nature, and perhaps her grave."
– John Milton, Paradise Lost

A few days later, Gold found himself at London Heathrow Airport boarding an eight hour, twenty minute British Airways flight to Philadelphia International Airport. America seemed the next logical destination for the TV series recce. It gave the show an international feel, it meant that the vibrant US TV market could be tapped into and, best of all, the inhabitants of the market spoke a form of English.

The Good Foot production office had been surprisingly supportive and had clearly caught Gold's enthusiasm. Adam Farthing was so far up his arse that all that was now visible of him were his ankles. Naturally, their effusive enthusiasm didn't stretch to business class, just pleb class or as the folk at BA term it, World Traveller.

Gold travelled light. Just hand luggage on wheels that he'd bought in TK Maxx in Croydon. It avoided the Russian Roulette of the baggage carousel.

At Pennsylvania International, Gold hired a car, and while yearning for a Corvette Stingray or Ford Mustang, he settled instead for a two-door hatchback Chevrolet Spark which was about the size of a can of Diet Coke.

Living the dream.

With the satnav that the car hire company had thrown in, for an extra fee naturally, Gold calculated that it was 104 miles from the airport to Hallam Township, and set off along Interstate 76, then the I-176 and then smaller roads towards Hallam. He noted, with enormous delight, that in Lancaster County he passed a town called Intercourse. That alone was worth the trip.

With a watchful eye on the budget (Gold was no team player and GFP could well afford it, but sometimes when playing the long game it was best to conform) he had pre-booked a room in the Comfort Inn which seemed the most reasonably-priced hotel in the vicinity.

Once settled, Gold began to consult his notes, while marvelling at the difference between a UK budget hotel, which has all the charm and amenities of Colditz, and its American equivalent, which was spacious, comfortable and offered everything the weary traveller could require.

His plan was straightforward. Meet with the police officer who had conducted the investigation into the murder of Doug Johnstone at the alleged hands of his wife, Loretta and then gain access to the prisoner to try to get her side of the story. To the best of his knowledge, Loretta Johnstone was still maintaining her innocence, insisting her father had perpetrated the crime. Unsurprisingly, the police and the District Attorney were not buying into her 'my father came back from the dead' line of defence.

After a good night's sleep thanks to the Melatonin 10mg tablet that Gold popped before watching endless infomercials on the large TV in his room, most of which promised to give him a body like a Greek god, he grabbed a small American breakfast, which meant enough food for a family of four. Full to bursting, he drove to Hallam Police Headquarters.

Having watched the movies *Deliverance* and *My Cousin Vinny* one too many times, Gold was wary of rural US police departments. GFP had been in touch from London so Gold's arrival was not going to be unannounced.

The police HQ was a modern two-storey building finished in a light-coloured stone which reminded Gold of the city of Bath. This being America, he could park the tiny Chevrolet almost outside. Just like London . . . said no one ever.

Soon he was sitting in the office of Chief of Police Ken Anderson, a man of not insubstantial build, with a matinee idol sweep of grey hair and matching walrus moustache.

One thing that any Brit travelling to the USA always finds unnerving is the sheer amount of fire power on display. It was a long way from the London bobby on the beat, armed only with a notebook and pencil.

The Chief's office was no exception. On the wall was a rack of assault rifles and on a side cabinet Gold noticed a neat pile of boxed ammo.

"So, Mr Gold, you've travelled all the way from London England to speak to me. I'm mighty flattered but I think you're on a wild goose chase son, if you ask me."

Every American, it seemed, assumed the full name of the United Kingdom's capital city was London England.

Gold decided to be as charming as possible. The jetlag wasn't helping him in that endeavour. Neither were the breakfast pancakes that seemed to be stuck to his ribs and had turned to cement.

"Well sir, yes I have. We're really impressed back home by the way you seem to have this all wrapped up so quickly."

Chief Anderson's moustache moved a centimetre as he allowed himself a smile of satisfaction.

"And as you can imagine, the viewers of our . . . *my* . . . TV show will find the whole thing fascinating. I mean, Mrs Johnstone is still saying she's innocent, right? And that her father, her *dead* father, killed her husband?"

Chief Anderson moved forward in his chair.

"Yup. That's right, son."

Son FFS!

Gold kept smiling.

"Darndest thing I ever heard. I mean, we told her, come clean, plead guilty and the court'll go a tad easier on you. But hell no, she flat out refused. Kept saying her Daddy had appeared and killed her husband. Biggest load of bullcrap I ever heard."

Gold smiled encouragingly, nodding as if in agreement.

"Well, it's certainly very peculiar."

"*Peculiar*? Son, when I see some dumb-ass with his jeans hung so low I can see his damn ass-crack and he thinks it looks good, that, my friend, is *peculiar*. This is plain insane. I mean, does she think this is gonna work in court?"

Gold saw his chance and dived in.

"So, you think she's mentally ill? My viewers will find this case fascinating . . . and of course you'd feature very heavily. You know we have a great respect for law and order in the UK," Gold lied.

The grey moustache was gently stroked as the Chief pondered this.

"But, I thought your show was all about the, what do you call it, the unexplained? You gonna make us all look like idiots? Don't think we don't know what you TV folk do."

Bugger!

"No, not at all. We see this as taking the series onto a higher, more serious, more in-depth level. How the law and order is maintained here in America. In fact," (Gold was warming to his improvised theme), "how the paranormal is no longer an excuse for murder."

There were times when even Gold was astounded at what came out of his mouth.

Chief Anderson grunted.

"So, when are you fellas thinking of filming all this here hoo-har?"

Result. He was on the hook.

"Well sir," (no harm in sir adding into the equation) "when I get back to London . . . England . . . and tell the team how co-operative you've been, I estimate we'll be back in a few weeks. Certainly well in time to cover the trial. And speaking of which, when can I get to meet this, er, Loretta Johnstone?"

A cloud scudded across the Chief's weather-worn face.

"I mean, Chief Anderson, it would give the show such gravitas . . . er . . . such appeal and really highlight the difficulties that you and your team here in Hallam encounter when dealing with cases like this . . . cases that really seem to be open and shut. If I can meet Mrs Johnstone, then I could really tell the story much better . . . from *your* point of view."

More moustache stroking.

"That ain't in my hands, son. You'd best take it up with her defence attorney. See if they'll let you anywhere near the crazy bitch."

Gold was taken aback by the venom that the Chief added to his last sentence.

"You don't seem to like her, Chief."

Chief Ken Anderson sat back in his chair and gently rocked back and forth.

"Not like her? Let me tell you something son. I've been a law enforcement officer all my life. I've spent close to thirty years on this force. Worked my way up from rookie to chief. Did it the hard way. Paid my dues. But in all this time I have never, and I mean never, seen a body so goddamn mutilated. The officer who was first on the scene is still off sick. He was throwing up his guts for two days solid. The victim's face was practically eaten off. So no, you'd be right, I don't like her one little goddamned bit."

Bloody hell. "Right, well that sounds, er . . . horrific. Poor chap . . . er . . . guy," responded Gold, desperate to make the right impression.

There was a slightly uneasy silence as Chief Anderson continued to rock gently back and forth in his chair.

"So, Loretta's defence attorney, where might I be able to find him?"

"*Her*, son, it's a her. No one around these parts wanted to touch this case with a goddamn cattle prod. Ain't gonna be no career boost, that's for sure. But there's this gal, think she's from New York or someplace originally, that came along like the Seventh Cavalry over the hill. Personally I think she's as nuts as that crazy bitch we've got locked up."

The Chief reached for a notepad, wrote a few lines, tore off a slip of paper and handed the sheet to Gold.

"That's her, Ms Trobe, and where you'll find her. Good luck with that, son. Now, if you'll excuse me, I've got a meeting with some councillors . . . seems some moron's been spraying graffiti on one of their houses and they ain't so happy."

Gold left amidst much hand-shaking, effusive thanks and promises to stay in touch and keep him posted. The usual meeting extrication routine.

Outside in the Pennsylvanian fresh air, Gold consulted the piece of paper. The name and address meant, of course, nothing. Back in the hirecar, Gold put the address in the satnav and set off. He felt that by turning up at the defence attorney's office, rather than getting a straight no on the phone, was the best course of action, Gold drove for fifteen minutes to a part of town where he felt it was best to lock the car's doors.

The satnav's not unattractive female voice informed Gold that he had arrived at his destination.

Jesus.

Fancy it wasn't. It was run down and in desperate need of a coat, or indeed an entire wardrobe, of paint.

There was only one door beside which was a cheap-looking sign proclaiming Lesley-Ann Trobe – Attorney At Law.

This must be the place.

Gold tried the door. Unbelievably, it was unlocked. Either Ms Trobe didn't give a toss about security or the contents of her office were so shit no one would bother coming in to rob the place.

Dust seemed to fill the heavy air. Unlike the rest of America, there was no Arctic blast from an air conditioner the moment you walked in from the street.

"Can I help you? Are you Mr Gildea who left a message yesterday about a libel case?"

Gold craned his neck to see the person behind the voice. And there she was. Ms Lesley-Ann Trobe was a ten on the self-appointed Gold Standard scale of hotness. Early thirties, dark hair pulled back into a 'I'm working here' ponytail, large blue eyes highlighted by large black-framed glasses and a figure that was a mixture of living in the gym and eating cheesecake. Who knew how that worked?

"Hi. Ms Trobe? No, I'm not Mr Gildea. My name's Nick Gold, I'm from London . . . England. Chief Anderson gave me your details. I'd like to talk to you about the Loretta Johnstone case."

Off came the glasses. On came a very disarming smile.

"If you're from the *National Enquirer,* would you do me a huge personal favour and get the fuck out of my office."

Hmm. Quite the legal orator.

"Whoa, hang on a mo . . . I'm not from any publication like that. I'm from British television. We are fascinated, that is our viewers *will* be fascinated, with the case. I've flown here from England because I'm in the process of researching similar cases."

There was a pause. The gentle hum of a desktop printer filled the void.

Finally, she spoke. "Hang on a *what?*"

"Er, a mo . . . a moment."

Back went on the glasses. "I see. British vernacular. Do you have an appointment? Did you send me an email? Do I know anything about you? Was I expecting you?"

Great. This was going spectacularly well. Ms Trobe was a real ballbuster.

"Ms Trobe. What if I were to tell you that I have reason to believe that your client is telling the truth?"

Off came the glasses again and the defence attorney started to chew on one of the arms of the frame.

"What did you say your name was?"

Gold tried a smile. Please stop chewing on your glasses.

"Gold. Nick Gold. I'm from Good Foot Productions in London and I present a series of, may I say, very well-received TV shows called Nick Gold – Paranormal Detective."

Rather disturbingly, Lesley-Ann Trobe burst into a throaty laugh.

"Are you shitting me? Paranormal Detective? Seriously?"

This was not the time to lose one's temper. He needed her help to get to Loretta Johnstone. Another attempt at a charming smile.

"Yup. That's what it's called. Crazy, I know. It's a very successful show. Good ratings. But I've been travelling around the world," (yes, a slight exaggeration but he had to close the deal) "researching events . . . other cases . . . that sound very similar to this. That's why I'm here. And no, I don't have an appointment, no I didn't send you an email or call ahead. Until thirty minutes ago, I'd never heard of you, but, all that being said, here I am."

Back went the black-framed glasses into the mouth.

"You wanna coffee?"

Gold nodded. "That would be great."

"There's a diner across the street. Food's bad but the coffee's pretty good. You're buying, Mister Paranormal Detective."

In the diner, which had the catchy name of The Hallam Diner (clearly hours of creative thought lay behind that choice), Gold sat in a small booth covered in red vinyl opposite Lesley-Ann Trobe. Over the coffee, which lived up to its mediocre reputation, Gold decided to go for broke and tell the defence attorney all he knew – leaving out only the blow-job from hell in Turkey. Too much, too soon. If he could get the lawyer on his side, and gain access to the alleged killer, then he really would have one hell of a show.

As Gold spoke, he became conscious that his confessional

report might have the opposite effect on Ms Trobe – that she might see him as another raving lunatic. Accordingly he interspersed his narrative with a few well-timed, 'I couldn't believe it myself' . . . 'I thought Joanne Walsh must be crazy at first' . . . 'I was one hundred percent sceptical' and the home-run, 'As a seasoned professional television investigator, I have my reputation to uphold'.

The lawyer sat across in the booth listening intently, without saying a word. Not even a grunt or murmur. Tough crowd.

Finally, Gold finished on what he hoped was a neat finale, "And that's why I'm here sitting opposite you right now."

The lawyer motioned to the waitress to bring more coffee.

"Mr Gold . . . do you know why I took this case when every other lawyer in town refused to go near it?"

"Because you believe your client? Because you believe in justice? Because it touches on the very reason that you became a lawyer in the first place?" replied Gold.

That throaty laugh again.

"No, you arsehole. Money. I took it for the money. My client is batshit crazy. She's as guilty as Charles Manson. She nearly ripped off her husband's face in that car."

Gold felt utterly crestfallen.

"So, you're not going to help me Ms Trobe?"

The aforementioned lent forward and lowered her voice.

"Are you out of your fucking mind? Of *course* I'm going to help you! This is great publicity. Puts me on centre stage. It's like OJ's lawyers – that's how Mr Kardashian got his big break, and look how that worked out for the entire goddam family! If we play this right, this could be huge. Maybe even get me out of this one-horse town to LA or back to NYC."

Gold made a mental note never to believe the plot lines of any Hollywood legal movies again.

"So whatcha wanna do?"

Gold replied without hesitation. "I want to meet Loretta Johnstone. I want to hear direct from her what happened that night."

Lesley-Ann Trobe smiled. "Well, Mr Gold, what are we waiting for? Let's move your paranormal arse and make some phone calls."

SIXTEEN

"For so I created them free and free they must remain."
– John Milton, Paradise Lost

Back in the dusty law offices across the street (Gold mused on the last time he'd seen dust in an office – even in Soho it was a thing of the past, like video recorders, cassette tapes and moral compasses), Lesley-Ann started to make a series of phone calls, jabbing the buttons on her phone as if testing an avocado for ripeness. Gold sat across the desk from her trying not to look like a spare wheel while also trying not to indicate how attractive he found the thrusting attorney. He was, after all, in America, where he was just as likely to be sued for breathing as he was for sneezing inappropriately.

After thirty minutes of calls being made and returned, Lesley-Ann Trobe faced Gold with a look of triumph on her face.

"We're on. I've cleared it with all the right channels. You can meet Loretta Johnstone tomorrow at 11am."

Gold smiled back. "That's great news, what I was hoping was that –"

Trobe held up a hand as if directing traffic. Gold obediently did an emergency stop.

"Hold your horses there Pete Paranormal. Let me set out the ground rules, just so you know which way this is gonna go."

Gold's stomach knotted slightly. What was it with lawyers? They can be sex on a stick and still be abominable human beings.

The defence attorney continued. Clearly, she was used to being heard.

"First thing, this is *my* client. Not yours. Not the BBC's –"

"I don't work for the BBC –"

"Whatever. I don't give a shit, frankly. My client. My rules. Clear?

Gold nodded his assent.

"Whatever deal you make with your paranormal mumbo-jumbo Darth Vader Twilight Zone TV show, I want twenty-five percent. Put me down as a consultant, executive producer, catering crew . . . I don't care. Twenty-five percent. That's across the board globally, including the merchandising rights, any publishing deal and TV and movie rights. Shit, if they turn this into a Broadway musical, I still get twenty-five percent."

Gold went to open his mouth to respond.

"That's non-negotiable Mr Gold. Unless you want to negotiate up?"

Gold shook his head. This clearly was not Ms Trobe's first rodeo.

"Next – I am to be included in all communications, letters, emails, smoke signals, Morse code, I don't care. Everything. No exceptions. Finally, and let me be really clear on this point, if I find you've chiselled me out of one single dime on this, I will rip your lungs out. We got a deal?"

He smiled. "Lesley-Ann, I like your style. Straight to the point. No dancing around. You're my kind of . . . " (he just stopped himself in time) " . . . lawyer."

He held out his hand. "Deal."

The attorney stared at the outstretched hand as if it was a plate of fish that had gone well past its sell by date.

"Aww, how sweet. A gentleman's agreement. Is that how you do things in dear old little England?

"Well, Pepe Le Pewnormal, we aren't in England no more, we're in Pennsylvania, which is, last time I checked, part of the

US of A. We do things a mite different round here. I'll have contracts drawn up by 9am tomorrow morning. Sign them, we go see Miss Loretta at 11am. Don't sign them and it's *adios amigo* and happy trails."

Gold wondered if the original *Terminator* film was based on this woman.

"Sounds great to me, Lesley-Ann. You go ahead and sort all that out by 9am and we'll be on our way."

He withdrew his hand.

Time to go for broke.

"As you like to be direct with me, perhaps I can be likewise with you. I've just arrived in town and don't know a soul so I was wondering if you'd like to have –"

"Have dinner with you? No. Go to your hotel and fuck you as you're a poor boy all alone in the big bad city? No. I have plans."

But Gold was a South London boy. Screw this.

"Sorry, what I was *going* to ask was if you'd like to have someone in your firm recommend somewhere for me to eat tonight – I always find personal recommendations so much more reliable than tourist guides, don't you? You have my contact details. Pleasure meeting you. I'll be here tomorrow morning at nine sharp. Have the papers ready for me. Have a good evening, Miss Trobe."

With that, Gold stood up and walked out of the attorney's office.

You don't mess with blokes from Balham.

Of course, no fine dining recommendations were sent to Gold's mobile, so he found a restaurant close to the Comfort Inn and ate as only you can in America, demolishing portions that would satisfy the hunger of a small village in the UK.

After another night of watching infomercials – the steam cleaner really was a bargain – Gold managed to find room for an American breakfast, this time avoiding the heart attack-inducing pancakes.

Hoping to catch the somewhat feisty Lesley-Ann Trobe off-guard, Gold rolled up outside her offices at 8:50am. A full ten minutes before he was expected. To his irritation, he could see the attorney standing outside smoking a cigarette, while talking on her phone. It was a miracle she wasn't chewing gum as well.

Gold decided to be bold, bright and breezy, giving her a slightly exaggerated wave and what he hoped was a welcoming smile.

It wasn't returned.

Whatever Ms Trobe had up her arse, Gold was now past the point of even considering removing it.

Without a word, Ms Trobe threw the cigarette onto the ground and walked into her office, still talking. Gold didn't wait for an invitation and sat down in the chair by her desk. Eventually, the call ended.

"So, you made it."

Gold smiled back. "So it would appear Lesley-Ann. Got the papers for me to look at?"

There was no point in wasting words. As Michael Corleone said to his hot-headed brother, 'It's not personal Sonny, it's strictly business'.

The attorney opened her briefcase and handed Gold a sheaf of papers. Wordlessly, Gold speed-read the contract. It was couched in the usual undecipherable legal terminology of 'why use one word when twenty will do', full of wherefores and here unto aforementioneds.

Gold was bored after the first paragraph but acted as if he was mulling over every sentence. Frankly, had the contract insisted that Gold handed over his step-parents as collateral, he would have signed it anyway. He needed to get to meet Loretta Johnstone and this was the key to opening that door.

After a reasonable pause, to which he added the flourish of dramatically turning back a couple of pages as if re-examining a particular point, Gold grunted.

"Hmm. Yup. Seems OK."

Without wasting a moment, the attorney handed Gold a ball-point pen.

"Well, in that case put your John Hancock where it's indicated and we've got ourselves a deal."

After signing what seemed several dozen times, but was only in fact three, Gold handed the papers back.

"We're done. Shall we go or do we have time for a coffee?"

The attorney considered this for a moment. "This is America Mr Gold, there's always time for a coffee."

Coffee having been consumed in the diner opposite the law office, Lesley-Ann got into Gold's hired car and they set off. This course of action had been determined by a succinct phrase from the lawyer, 'You're driving'.

Mrs Loretta Johnstone, accused of Murder in the First Degree, was currently incarcerated in York County Prison. Gold had pre-set the satnav for 3400 Concord Rd York, PA 17402. Thank God he didn't have to use a map while driving.

Gold had looked up the prison the previous night and was delighted to observe that the prison's mission was to 'house in a safe and humane manner all adult offenders committed for offenses committed in York County, and to provide inmates with the opportunity to participate in programs that will successfully help them reintegrate into the community'.

Gold wondered if that extended to literally eating off the face of your husband? Of the capacity two thousand, five hundred and twenty-two inmates, Gold wondered if he was about to meet the most dangerously insane?

During a thirty-minute drive along Interstate 30, Gold observed the usual assortment of random businesses that were to be found in Anytown USA. They passed Dick's Sporting Goods Shop, Chili's Bar & Grill, David's Bridal Shop, the ubiquitous Staples and Ross Dress for Less until York County Prison hoved into view. It was a modern facility and, from the outside, looked like any nondescript corporate building. The inside, unsurprisingly, told a different story. Gates, guns, more gates, steel doors, security, more security and the all-pervasive atmosphere of a place that housed two and a half thousand people who didn't want to be there.

With formalities completed, including several security checks and body scans, Gold and Attorney Trobe were ushered into a bright bare room that contained a table fixed to the grey lino floor with four chairs arranged around it.

Gold's stomach was knotted. He had never been in a prison before and was finding it thoroughly unnerving. Nor had he been up close and personal with a killer. Well, alleged killer.

A door opened at the back of the room and, accompanied by two female guards who looked as if they could kill you with just a glance, the defendant, Mrs Loretta Johnstone, was brought in.

Gold was struck immediately by two thoughts. First, how the orange jump suit made her look like she was an assistant at a branch of a B&Q store and secondly, to his surprise, how, well, entirely ordinary she looked.

He had no idea what he was expecting – Myra Hindley, Rose West, Cruella DeVille – anything but this very unexceptional woman in her mid- to late-thirties. Her hair was pulled back and her face was make-up free.

As she sat down, Gold didn't wait. Lesley-Ann Trobe had brought him this far, now in his opinion, she could be jettisoned.

"Mrs Johnstone . . . may I call you Loretta . . . my name's Nick Gold, I'm from London . . . England . . . and I've come all the way here just to meet you. No other reason."

The attorney shot him a glance that would have stripped lead off a church roof, but he was off and running.

"Your story is extraordinary, Loretta. But what if I told you that I believed you? What if I said to you that I'm investigating similar cases to yours that have happened in Turkey, England, possibly Russia and here?"

The accused woman sat silently taking in Gold's words. He could almost hear the cogs in her brain slowly turning.

Finally, she spoke.

"Mr . . . Gold, was it? Mr Gold, I didn't kill my husband, Doug. I didn't. I swear it."

Gold nodded.

"What I'd like you to do for me, Loretta, is tell me exactly what happened that night. Every detail."

The attorney had had enough. "My client has told her story dozens of times, Mr Gold. I'm sure she doesn't feel like going through it all again."

Gold twisted in his chair to look at her. The mask of politeness was firmly back in its box. Instead, he became the media player that he really was, a man with the ability to sniff out a story like a veritable ant eater.

"Right now, the only thing that's between your client spending the rest of her life in jail, with no chance of parole, is me. I'm Loretta's best bet. Unlike you, Ms Trobe, and this may astonish you, I care about the truth. Unlike you, I've spoken at length with people who have told me the same story as your client. That's why I'm here. So, why don't we let Loretta decide if she can be bothered to tell me what happened or, like you, she's just too bored to bother?"

The attorney was seething. This was no dumb-ass Brit pushover. Clever act.

It was Loretta who broke the tension.

"Doug and me were on our way to spend time with friends of ours, Melvin and Sharman. We were driving in Doug's beat-up old Chevy. I hated that damn car. Told him a thousand times to trade it in for a Jap car. More reliable. But he loved that piece of junk. Anyway, we'd been driving for a coupla hours when the goddam car broke down, as per usual. Doug got out, opened the hood to take a look-see at what had gone wrong this time. It was late. It was dark. It was raining, I recall. So I stayed in the car. No point in us both getting soaked, right? I had the radio on . . . Neil Young I think it was . . .

when I hear Doug screaming. I don't mean hollering like he'd hit his head, I mean screaming. I'd never heard him do that before."

She paused as if remembering the last sound her husband made.

"Please go on, Loretta," said Gold softly.

"The screaming seemed to go on and on, like it would never end. Then it stopped. No noise. Just the radio. I saw a shape, like a shadow, coming around from the front of the car to my side. I thought it was Doug. He tapped on my window. Scared the living shit outta me. I yelled at Doug not to scare me like that. Then the light, I dunno, I think it was a flashlight, one of them fancy LED types you know, showed the face. I nearly died right there and then. It weren't Doug . . . it was my Daddy."

Loretta Johnstone sat still, suddenly looking considerably older than her thirty-seven years and more fragile.

Gold prompted her. "It was your father? That was the face that you saw? I mean, it was raining, it was dark, you could have been mistaken?"

The woman in the orange jump suit suddenly shouted, "I know what the fuck I saw! It was my Daddy, you understand me?"

Gold had inadvertently jolted back in his seat. The two female guards moved towards the prisoner.

But her anger was over as soon as it had begun.

Loretta was speaking very quietly now. "I know what I saw. I can't ever forget it."

"Tell me, Loretta," asked Gold, "what your father looked like."

She ran her fingers through her lank, greasy hair.

"It was him all right. But, somehow, he was . . . different. When he smiled at me . . . his teeth . . . I ain't never gonna forget those teeth. Like a shark. All pointy and sharp. Like that movie *Jaws*. Not . . . not human teeth. And there was flesh hanging from them . . . Doug's flesh."

Silence descended on the room like a shroud. Not a comfortable silence but the type it was hard to break.

Lesley-Ann broke it.

"Loretta, listen to me. We've talked about this a lot, right? It's not too late to change your plea. I'll try to work out a deal with the prosecution."

The attorney was all too aware that the death penalty had been re-introduced to the State of Pennsylvania in 1976. Since then, only three death row prisoners had suffered State sanctioned death by lethal injection, but this crime was so repugnant, there was a chance the prosecution might argue for the death penalty.

"I've gotta convince a jury that your father, who died five years ago in a work accident, came back from the dead and killed your husband. Loretta, your father is dead. He's gone. I know it's hard to accept, that you were close, but that's the fact – he's dead and dead people don't come back."

"Yes, they do."

Three words rang out in the interview room. The guards looked at each other. Was the Limey as crazy as the accused? The attorney spun around in her chair so fast it almost toppled over.

"What the hell did you just say?"

Gold cleared his throat. "I said the dead do come back. I know. I've seen them. They tried to kill me in Turkey. That's why I'm here. This woman is no more crazy than you or I. She saw her father that night."

The attorney could not contain her fury.

"You come here pretending to be a TV presenter and it turns out you're a crazy. What do you think you're doing? We're done here. Get the hell out!"

Gold wasn't moving.

"Listen to me very carefully, Lesley-Ann. I've interviewed several people, and they've all described the attacks in precisely the same way. The teeth are the link. Everyone saw the teeth, those shark-like teeth. So did I. Just like Loretta described. Believe me, I'm not a crazy. I didn't believe a word of it. I thought it was bullshit. But it isn't. The more I've investigated, the more the stories from around the world line up. They're too similar to just be cranks. No details of the teeth have ever appeared. How would total strangers, thousands of miles apart, know about them and all be able to describe them in exactly the same way?"

The attorney's shoulders seemed to slump.

"How did you escape, Loretta? Why aren't you dead along with your husband Doug?" asked Gold.

"I, er, turned the key in the ignition. I guess maybe Doug had fixed the engine or whatever. I hit the gas and I drove. I drove so fast. I was crying, I felt sick, there was blood all over the windshield . . . I put on the wipers but that just smeared the screen all over. I couldn't see. I needed to stop. That's where they found me, halfway off the road on the grass verge. I musta leant or collapsed against the windshield or hood. That's how I got all of Doug's blood on me.."

"And you've stated that your father spoke to you? Is that right?" asked Gold

"Yeah, he did. He said, 'Aintcha gonna say hi to your Daddy?' I tried to speak. I couldn't, I was terrified. I mumbled something about him being dead and he looked me in the eye and said '*Dead. Yeah. I know. Go figure. And now it's time we had what you might call a little family reunion.*'"

Loretta Johnstone started to shake. Then the tears came. They wouldn't stop.

SEVENTEEN

"What is dark within me, illumine."
– John Milton, Paradise Lost

They stayed with Loretta in the soulless room for another fifteen minutes, calming her down, muttering platitudes, saying that it was 'all going to be OK'. Mere words of course; the attorney didn't give it any credence. In her mind, this was a total loser of a case and her client would be found guilty. It was all about mitigation. At best she was mentally ill, at worst a cold-blooded psychopath. Now Lesley-Ann's main concern was how to extricate herself and her client from this mess while still smelling of roses. And the mouthy Brit wasn't helping.

They said their goodbyes and walked out of York County Prison. Gold thought that fresh air had never tasted so good.

"Well, I really must thank you, Nick."

Gold looked at her as they walked across the large car park to his rental.

"Really? How so?"

Trobe took out a cigarette and lit it. "For being so helpful in there. I mean, there I was thinking that my client would eventually listen to me and take a plea, but then you come along, clearly as fucking crazy as she is, with a story that's so . . . so . . . insane I'm beginning to wonder how you got through immigration at the airport. So, yeah . . . thanks."

Gold stopped walking.

"Listen to me Lesley-Ann, I'm not crazy. Your client's not

crazy. We are telling you the truth. Do you think my company would fund me to research this story if they thought I was a nutjob? No, they'd fire my arse. I know what I saw in Turkey. My clients, if you will, know what they saw. It's real. Yes, I know it sounds impossible, but it's real enough."

The attorney took a long drag on her menthol cigarette and blew out the smoke in a long weary-sounding sigh.

"You like giving it to me straight, so let me return the compliment. I don't give a shit if you believe me or not. It doesn't matter. Defend Loretta, don't defend her. I actually don't care. Why? Because it's not my problem. It's yours. What I *do* care about is understanding what is happening around the world. Why my dead girlfriend decided to pay me a visit in Turkey and then tried to kill me –"

"I don't blame her. I've known you for less than twenty-four hours, and *I* want to kill you."

Gold stared and then broke into helpless laughter. To his amazement, Lesley-Ann Trobe suddenly, quite without warning, laughed out loud too. The two of them stood in the brisk York County air, in the middle of the prison car park, laughing uncontrollably. It was like a pressure valve had suddenly been released. It was all too much to take in. Everything. So, in the face of the impossible-to-fathom, the only possible response is laughter.

The two walked to Gold's rental.

"You're serious, aren't you? I mean, you believe in this Twilight meets the Walking Dead crap, right?"

Gold nodded.

"You have to understand, Lesley-Ann, I'm a far bigger cynic than you will ever be. I'm on TV for God's sake! I rarely believe a word I say, but the viewers, well, they lap it up. They love it. They *want* to believe. They want spooks and ghouls and stuff that goes bump in the night. They want to believe in life-after-death, heaven and hell. Me? I think it's superstitious garbage that should have died out in the Middle Ages. Much of it was written for the

Greeks, cobbled together from loads of much older religions, and written by a guy named Saul who was known as Paul. Go figure. But I'm telling you, I know what I saw . . . and it scared the living crap out of me."

The attorney fastened her seat belt.

"Drive, Mr Paranoid Detective. I have an idea and on the way, I wanna hear blow by blow exactly what *did* happen to you out in Turkey."

"It's *Paranormal* Detective, by the way," replied Gold, while wishing she hadn't used the phrase, blow-by-blow. *That* bit he would be editing out of his monologue.

As they drove, Gold recounted everything. Meeting Joanne Walsh, Adam Farthing's encounter with his grandfather, more research that he'd undertaken and the entire episode in the ruins of Hierapolis. Of the hotel incident, there was no mention.

Lesley-Ann sat in silence, only once cracking open the passenger window so she could light up another menthol filter-tipped. The rental company would go ape shit but Gold thought he'd worry about that later. They probably sold Febreze in the States anyway.

Gold finished his edited highlights and waited for the attorney's reaction.

"Take a left at the next lights."

That was it.

"Er, so where are we going exactly?"

"There's a guy I know who's even crazier than you. You're gonna talk to him."

Right.

"So who is this crazy guy then?"

"Take the second right."

This was going well.

"He works for the local paper, *The York Dispatch*. You might wanna hear what he's gotta say."

Gold drove the little Chevy. He wasn't worried. After all, how much weirder could his life get?

The answer was, simply, off the scale weird . . . and then some. Luckily, he had no idea it was going to be the kind of weird that would keep you in the bathroom for days on end. With the door locked and a towel over your head.

"Pull over there," barked Ms Trobe. "We're here."

'Here' were the offices of *The York Dispatch*, started in 1876 and still going strong, both in print and online.

"I don't suppose you'd like to fill me in a little bit more on what we're doing? And more to the point, why?"

The attorney turned in the passenger seat.

"We're gonna see a guy I know. He's a crank. A crackpot but he's the best features writer I know. He's something of a legend around here. Worked at the paper since God was in short pants. He has a theory that will, let's just say, *appeal* to you. As for the why, that's easy. If I can gather enough evidence to bring in even a sliver of reasonable doubt in the minds of the jury, then I might have a snowball's chance in hell of getting out of this with my reputation in one piece. OK? Good. Let's go."

Gold wondered if she spoke to everybody like this, or was it just his lucky day?

They entered the newspaper offices and at last Gold felt on familiar territory. The buzz, the atmosphere, the computer screens, he was in his element.

They waited a few minutes until they were approached by a small man in his mid- to late-fifties with a matching grey goatee and moustache and a hairstyle presumably modelled on late period Albert Einstein.

"Hey, Counselor, I knew it was you. Could smell that mix of nicotine and perfume a mile off. You're looking good kid. This the guy you called me about yesterday?"

Gold shook the proffered hand.

"You must be that Brit TV guy, huh? I'm Arnie Woolfson. Good to meet y'all. LAT's already told me something about ya."

It took Gold a moment to realise that 'LAT' was Lesley-Ann Trobe.

"Come on through," invited the newspaper man. They followed him into a small office that looked like an explosion in a paper factory. Files, newspapers, magazines, photographs lay everywhere like leaves after a storm. There wasn't a square inch of visible furniture surface.

"Excuse the mess. I'm in the middle of an article. Research. You know how it is."

Gold wondered if Arnie Woolfson had heard of that new-fangled fad, the Internet? There had to be half a forest in here.

The three of them sat down, no easy task as every chair was covered in papers.

"So, Nick the Brit, you've got a theory, right? Stop me if I get this wrong. You think that the dead are coming back and killing people. That about it?"

There was frank, there was blunt, and then there was Arnie Woolfson, a veteran newspaper writer with a knack for cutting through the bullshit.

"I guess that's a reasonable summary Mr Woolfson. I assume that you share your friend here's opinion that I'm certifiable?"

Woolfson stroked his goatee and leant forward.

"No. I think you're right on the money."

The gentle hum of the air-conditioning system was all Gold could suddenly hear.

"I'm sorry, what did you just say?" Gold was sweating despite the room being a cool 65 degrees.

"I said I think you are correct. That's just what's happening."

It was LAT who broke the silence. "I told you you'd get on. Both as fucking crazy as each other. No offence, Arnie."

"No fucking offence taken, Lesley-Ann. How long you got, Nick?"

Nick's head was feeling a little woozy. This was becoming too surreal.

"I've . . . er . . . I've got plenty of time Mr Woolfson. Why?"

"Call me Arnie. Everyone does. Mr Woolfson was my father. Are you ready to have your mind blown, Nick?"

Gold now felt he was adrift in uncharted waters, once again clinging to a piece of wreckage like he had in the hotel bedroom in Turkey.

The attorney spoke. "Arnie has had a theory for a very long time. He'll tell anyone who'll listen, but we don't. You know why? Because it's as real as Hogwarts and all that magic crap. But then Mr Limey comes across the pond and, fuck me, you're as crazy as each other. So, what's a poor girl to do? Get the crazies together . . . and if it gets my client off the hook, then we got us a result!"

"Your altruism is commendable, Ms Trobe," replied Gold, keeping a poker face.

Gold had to begrudgingly admire the attorney's approach to life; the classic 'what's in it for me' *modus operandi*.

"Get a room you two," interrupted Arnie Woolfson. "OK, you wanna see what I got, fella, or what?"

Gold gave the newspaper man a broad beam indicating that, indeed, he did.

It was all the encouragement Arnie Woolfson required.

"You know why they haven't fired my ass round here?" Woolfson didn't wait for a reply. "I'll tell y'all. Because I'm the best features writer in this danged place, that's why. Yeah, I may be older than the rest of the kids who run around the place, and don't think I don't hear the little bastards calling me Gramps behind my back, but the editor and the owners know that I give the readers what they want. It's called journalism. It's called craft. And I care, Nick, I care about what I write. You getting me?"

Gold nodded.

Woolfson started to assemble papers and photos from around

his chaotic office and it reminded Gold of Sherlock Holmes's rooms at 221b Baker Street and the fury the great consulting detective would unleash upon his landlady, Mrs Hudson, if she had the temerity to disturb anything.

"OK, kid. Pay attention."

Gold let the kid slide.

"You know where we are?"

Gold frowned.

"Um...Hallam in Pennsylvania? Do I win a microwave oven?"

"Wise guy. Yeah, that's right, Hallam in York County, Pennsylvania. Know what it's famous for?"

"Ballbusting attorneys?" answered Gold.

"Smart ass! Come here."

Woolfson motioned Gold over to look at the array of papers and photos now spread on his desk. Attorney Trobe stayed where she was with a world-weary expression. She'd heard this a hundred times.

"Hallam . . . or as it was once called . . ."

"Hellam," said Nick instantly.

Woolfson smiled. "So, the kid's done his homework. Good. I like that."

Arnie continued, encouraged that he had a fellow-believer along for the ride. "The township was founded back in 1739, but maybe you know that? The tourist folk like to spout on about it being a pleasant little backwater in a corner of York, Pennsylvania, with its rich forestry, lakes, wildlife and waterfalls blah blah blah. But that ain't what this place is about. No siree."

Gold went for broke. "It's a Gate of Hell."

Arnie was stopped in his tracks. Slowly he removed his tortoise shell glasses and looked straight at Gold.

"You heard of the Gates of Hell? Well, I'll be goddamned."

Suddenly there it was. Said out loud. In an up-to-the-minute newspaper and online office in modern America.

The Gates of Hell.

Arnie Woolfson was on a roll. Finally, he had a captive audience of one.

"The Seven Gates of Hell feature is a popular piece of urban folklore. As you've boned-up about it, son, you'll know that there's a series of portals right here in Hellam Township, which open an entrance right down to the fiery pit of hell below. There's many different versions of the tale but Nick, only one is true."

Nick Gold's attention was one hundred percent.

"I have a theory, Arnie. But go on. I want to see if we're thinking on similar lines here."

Despite being three and a half thousand miles away, all this reminded Gold of being back in an Oxford tutorial with Professor Whittaker. The newspaperman and the Oxford don shared an enthusiasm for their subject which was contagious.

Woolfson continued. Lesley-Ann sat across from them, her face an inscrutable mask. Gold made a note never to play poker with her. "The gates belong to a former insane asylum on the outskirts of town. Right? They built it in a remote location so as to isolate people deemed insane from the rest of the world. Shame they didn't do that with Washington, huh?"

Woolfson chuckled at his own joke. The other two remained silent.

"Anyhow, one day in the 1800s, a fire broke out and, because they'd built it so remote out on Trout Run Road, firefighters couldn't reach the hospital in time to save it."

Gold jumped in. "Which is why many of the patients died in the flames, according to what I've read."

"Correct. Others escaped but were soon beaten to death. The townsfolk were none too happy about crazy folk running around free. You gotta remember this wasn't rehab. These weren't folks that were feeling a bit depressed or into coke or booze. These were bad, bad people, Nick. I mean real bad."

Nick spoke. "And these gates . . . my guess is that they exist. Do they?"

Woolfson nodded. "Damn straight they do. The guy who ran the joint was a real eccentric, a physician, rich as Croesus and an absolute saint by all accounts. You know the, 'Give me your tired, your poor, your huddled masses yearning to breathe free . . . ' sort. Way ahead of the times in treating nutjobs."

Twenty-first century sensibilities, even for an un-reconstructed man like Nick Gold, couldn't help but kick in. "Steady on Arnie, we call them psychiatrically-diagnosed or persons with mental health issues."

Arnie looked at Gold coldly. "Anyway, he lived on the property and built several gates along a path deep into the forest. Why d'ya think this place is called Hellam? It ain't called Sleepy Meadows my friend."

Gold was deep in thought.

Arnie went on, "Yeah, so the story is that some of these tormented, tortured souls were trapped inside the series of seven gates, which they haunt to this day."

Gold's skin was feeling suddenly very cold. The hairs on his arms were standing up.

"Oh, for fuck's sake!" Attorney Trobe weighed in.

Gold ignored the interjection.

"So, what's this thing about being only able to see some of the gates at night?"

Arnie Woolfson was delighted he seemed to have a real convert in the room.

"It's said that only the first gate is visible by daylight and this lies on private land just off the town's Trout Run Road. By night, other gates become visible in this quiet, wooded corner of the township. Passing through all seven will take the visitor straight to hell, and it's reported that nobody has yet passed five and returned to talk about the experience."

"And this doctor chap?"

"Chap? Well, the story tells of a doctor who simply showed up in the town one day. He had a whole bunch of new theories about treating *persons with mental health issues* and the money to set up his own asylum. He bought the land, on which he built a series of these darn peculiar gates leading deeper and deeper into the forest."

"Didn't Stephen Sondheim write a musical about that?" chipped in Trobe.

"That was *Into The Woods* you moron," replied the evidently irritated newspaperman.

"Take a look at these, Nick. They're photos from the archive. Taken around 1850 or so. I don't reckon you'd have seen them in your research. Took me years to track them down. Shows you the asylum and the staff. Oh yeah, it was real all right."

Gold moved closer and started to study the black and white photographs. He saw the building, an imposing stone manor house type affair, he saw the men and women posing stiffly for the camera in their medical uniforms.

"Oh yeah . . . this one's of the doctor who ran the place," added Woolfson.

Nick bent down to examine the face in the photo.

"No! No . . . that's . . . that's impossible!"

Lesley-Ann and Arnie Woolfson couldn't help but notice that the blood had drained from Gold's face which now matched the papers strewn around the office.

"Oh shit," the attorney muttered. "Oh shit."

EIGHTEEN

"From his lips
Not words alone pleased her."
– John Milton, Paradise Lost

Someone was calling his name from far away. "Nick . . . Nick . . ."

The voice was muffled, indistinct, almost as if it was underwater.

"Nick . . . can you hear me?"

There it was again. Calling to him. He thought it was familiar but he couldn't recall who it was. Maybe his birth mother? A friend?

"Nick . . . Nick . . . come on!"

Gold's eyelids fluttered open. He stared into the concerned face of Attorney Lesley-Ann Trobe.

"Ah Jesus . . . what's the matter with you? You OK?" she asked in the caring manner for which she was renowned.

Gold realised he was sitting in a chair, in the office of Arnie Woolfson at *The York Dispatch*.

"Yeah . . . sure . . . I'm fine thank you. Just a little tired, maybe," mumbled Gold.

"Those ten years at medical school weren't wasted on you. You back with us?"

Gold smiled weakly at attorney Trobe.

"Yes. Thanks. I'm fine. Must have been the heat . . . or the jetlag."

"Bullshit mister!" Arnie Woolfson interjected. "Don't bullshit a bullshitter, least ways not round here. You looked at a photograph and you turned white, fella. Whaddya see?"

"Oh, come on Arnie. Let's not make a drama out of this. The guy's big on drama."

Arnie wasn't budging. "Can it, sweetcheeks."

The age of egalitarianism hadn't quite reached this specific corner of the office. No wonder Woolson and Gold had hit it off, despite their age difference.

"He looked at a goddam photo, said it's impossible, looked as if he'd seen a ghost and practically keeled over. That, sweetheart, ain't nothing. That is *something*."

Gold had struggled to his feet but quickly sat down again, ignoring the papers piled on it.

Woolfson went outside to a nearby watercooler and brought back a plastic cup of cold water.

"Drink," was the only instruction from the grey-haired writer.

"OK, fella. Let's cut to the chase here, shall we? I wanna know what made you nearly freak out when you saw whatever it was in the photo. Spill the beans, son."

"It was nothing. Really. Forget it. Low blood pressure."

Woolfson exploded.

"You listen to me, you Brit shit. I've dedicated decades of my life to this project. I've been laughed at, mocked, ridiculed and still I didn't quit. You know why? Because it's real. And I shared it with you, a total stranger, because Lesley-Ann asked me to. So, don't you fucking disrespect me and treat me like a fucking moron or I'll throw your Limey ass out into the goddam street. You hear me!"

Gold did indeed hear him. The man was genuinely irate. It was now or never.

"OK Arnie . . . you're right. I apologise. I . . . I was a bit shocked."

Arnie blustered on. "Oh, really. I think your death-white face might have been a clue."

To his surprise, Lesley-Ann spoke up.

"Take it easy, Arnie. Give the guy a break."

Both men paused, slightly taken aback. Boy, was that out of character or what?

Gold took a deep breath. "I know the man in the photo. The man you say was the doctor who ran the asylum."

"You mean in your research, you've seen a photo of him before?" asked Woolfson.

Gold paused. "No. I've met him."

The room fell silent.

After what seemed an eon, attorney Trobe broke the stunned silence.

"What the fuck do you mean you've met him? That photo's from the 1800s."

"I know that," replied Gold. "I mean . . . there's no other way to say this . . . I've met him . . . several times."

Lesley-Ann looked at Woolfson with an expression that mixed incredulity with fear. Was the Brit TV guy actually mentally ill?

"OK son, where did you meet him?" asked Arnie.

"The first time was outside my local supermarket in South London where I live. The second time was in Hierapolis in Turkey."

"You mean you think you *saw* a guy who looks like the asylum doctor?" asked Trobe.

"No. I spoke with him. At length. Several times."

Woolfson cleared his throat. "And, er, this man, do you know his name?"

Gold paused. This wasn't going to sound either good or reasonable.

"Yes. I do. His name is Barachiel. He's one of the seven Archangels."

Trobe exploded. "That's it! I've had it with this voodoo George Romero horror movie shit. Fuck the pair of you. It's a real pity the asylum burned down because you both belong there. I'm outta here."

With that, Attorney Lesley-Ann Trobe stormed out of the office.

Her abrupt departure brought about an awkward silence. Gold felt stupid and Arnie Woolfson was in deep shock. Either this young Brit was delusional or he was the key to everything he'd been working on for decades. It was, at this point, pretty hard to call.

Arnie Woolfson sat quietly stroking his grey goatee. He was thinking very carefully.

"OK, Nick. I want you to tell me everything. Right from the start. In detail. Leave out nothing, I gotta hear it all. You understand me?"

Nick Gold nodded. As the two men sat in the newspaper office, Gold recounted the entire story. This time leaving out nothing, not even Mehmet the guide's wife transforming into his dead girlfriend Suzie. It wasn't just that Suzie, or Persephone, or whomever she now chose to call herself, had tried to kill him, it was that she had also tried to warn him. But warn him of what? What was he getting into? Going over-budget? Seemed a little over-the-top to get so excited about that. Gold looked at Woolfson for some interaction, for a clue, in fact for any damn thing, but he was as expressionless as the Sphinx. Another one not to play poker with.

"So, in a large nutshell, that's everything, Arnie. What do you make of it?"

Woolfson sat in total silence, having not interrupted even once until Gold had finished. Then he exhaled a long breath.

"Holy shit! All these years . . . all these years they've laughed at me. The crazy old guy . . . the nutjob with his Bogey Man obsession . . . I've heard it all. If I wasn't such a shithot writer, they'd have fired my ass years ago. I knew it. I always knew it. It's all true. It explains so much."

"Like what?" asked Gold.

"Jesus kid! Look around you? Remember the phrase the lunatics have taken over the asylum? Look no further than right here in the US of A. It doesn't strike you as odd . . . weird . . . what's happened over here? Nothing out of the ordinary . . . peculiar . . . springs to mind? Events that a few years ago wouldn't have got past a movie script committee are now for real? You think it's all a coincidence?"

Gold pondered. He avoided politics like he avoided beetroot.

"I thought, Arnie, that it was a democratic process and the people spoke."

Woolfson let out a mirthless laugh.

"Sure they voted. In their millions. Why . . . *why* do you think they voted the way they did?"

"Arnie, are you saying the White House is being run by . . . Hell?"

Woolfson shook his head.

"Don't be a dumb-ass Nick. Of course I'm not. He's so absurdly unqualified. Didn't even want the damn job. It all got out of control. It's these unseen powers that sweep these events along . . . that make the insanely impossible sane. It's cyclical. There's a pattern to it. Look around you Nick . . . fucking chaos everywhere. No one in control. Your country's just as bad. Politicians don't know what to do, how to control a restless population. The Middle East – a bunch of psychopaths running around cutting off people's heads, burning them alive, wanting to take the world back to the Middle Ages. You think this is all random?"

Gold paused. There was much to consider.

"Yeah . . . OK. There's a lot of trouble out there. But there's always been trouble."

Woolfson sighed. "Yeah, of course – but just think about it will ya? 1917 – World War One, Russian Revolution; 1937 – Hitler, Stalin, World War Two about to kick off; 1957 – the Cold War – all of us a button-push away from extinction; 1967 – the world nearly taken over by goddam Hippies, Jane Fonda shooting at our boys in Hanoi . . ."

Gold marvelled at how world events were always interpreted by the parties involved.

"What I'm saying is this, the chaos is unleashed every twenty years. Regular as damn clockwork."

Gold shook his head. "Arnie, it's *always* chaotic. Been like it forever. I don't buy it."

Arnie was on a roll now. He wasn't going to back off.

"Look Nick. You've got some . . . some . . . I dunno . . . sort of connection with all of this. This Barack character –"

"It's Barachiel. He's not a former President. He's an Archangel. There's a difference. Trust me on that."

"Whatever! This angel, he's chosen you. Fuck knows why. But hey, there you go. My wife chose me over thirty years ago, it's still a mystery but I'm sure glad she did. You are in some cockamamie way central, a key if you will, to all of this."

Gold burst out laughing. "Arnie, I'm a bloke who works on TV spouting bullshit to a gullible audience. I'm about as spiritual as a kick in the nuts. Maybe I was when I was younger, but not now. Trust me here, I'm not a key, I'm not the answer, I'm just doing a job. It's all got very weird, but I am not the solution. I am part of the problem."

Arnie Woolfson sat back in his chair and ran his fingers distractedly through his already unkempt hair.

"Lemme tell you what we're gonna do. Tonight, you and me are going out to Trout Run Road, to the old asylum. We're gonna see what happens."

Gold sat bolt upright. "Let me tell you, very clearly, that is *not* going to happen. Not in a million years my friend. Haven't you watched enough TV shows and films when some idiot is told 'meet me at the cemetery at midnight, and come alone'? Fuck that. I'm like 'no, meet me in the dairy aisle in Tesco at lunchtime on a Saturday'. Do I look that stupid?"

Woolfson looked disappointed. "So that's a no, huh kid?"

"We can go in broad daylight. And I don't mean dawn, or twilight, I mean full-on proper don't-scare-the-crap-out-of-me daytime. We can do that. But night time, forget it."

Arnie sat forward. "You got a deal. Pick me up here at ten-thirty tomorrow morning. We'll go and take a look-see. OK?"

Gold nodded. "Am I the only person in this town who can actually drive? I'm like Mr Uber since I've arrived. Fine. Sure. See you in the morning."

The two men shook hands and Gold left the offices of *The York Dispatch*. It was getting late, it had been one helluva day and Gold wanted nothing more than a cold beer or two, maybe a BLT or a burger and some sleep.

He stopped at a diner that looked promising and which should have had a young Sybil Shepherd working as the waitress to complete the cliché.

The food, of course, was ridiculously plentiful and good. Feeling much more content, Gold drove the little Chevy back to the Comfort Inn.

He had just settled into his room and switched on the TV to lull him to sleep when there was a knock on his bedroom door.

It couldn't be room service. There wasn't any.

"Yes. Can I help you?" he called through the door.

A familiar voice replied.

"Well, that depends if you open the damn door, numb nuts."

Gold was very surprised. There stood attorney-at-law Lesley-Ann Trobe.

"Did you forget your ballpoint pen or do you moonlight as a dry-cleaning service when you're not in court?"

LAT stood there.

"You gonna leave me standing here like a Clinton at a Republican convention or you gonna invite me in?"

Gold stood aside to admit her entrance. What the hell did the ballbuster want now?

She looked around. "Hmm. Like what you've done with the place. Am I disturbing you?"

Gold replied, "Do you mean was I going to sleep or is it that I find you as a person disturbing? Last time we met, today if memory serves, I apparently belonged in a lunatic asylum. Or did I misunderstand?"

LAT looked him. "Jeez, you Brits. So fucking sensitive. I lost my cool. Big deal. So what? You gonna bitch at me all night?"

"Actually, Lesley-Ann, the only thing I'd planned on doing 'all night' was sleeping. It's been a long day, I'm tired and I've got another big day tomorrow. So, without wishing to appear rude, why not tell me why you're here, then I can bid you a fond farewell."

"Are all you Brits gay?"

Gold stared at her. "Sorry?"

The attorney laughed. "Do the math. Why the fuck do you think I'm here in your hotel room? To discuss the American Electoral College Voting System?"

Gold was now totally lost.

"I'm sorry. It must be the jetlag but I'm a little confused. You've been busting my balls since we met. You clearly don't like me. You think I'm a raving lunatic. Frankly, I have no idea at all why you're here."

Lesley-Ann smiled. "Well, you know."

You have got to be kidding me! She's coming on to me, thought Gold.

"Are you trying to seduce me, Mrs Robinson?" was all he could think of saying.

The attorney shook her head as if dealing with an imbecile.

"You know what, fucking forget it. This was a massive mistake. I'm an idiot."

LAT turned and started to head for the door.

"Whoa . . . who's being sensitive now? Hold up a moment. You caught me off-guard. You're not an idiot . . . *I'm* the idiot for being slow. My fault. Sorry."

Gold had also picked up a Ph.D in bullshit at university along with his theology degree. It would be rude, indeed downright churlish, to refuse. After all, the UK and USA had a special relationship as they were always being told.

The attorney paused. Her back still towards Gold.

"So, you'd like me to stay?"

"Oh, definitely. Absolutely. Without a shadow of a doubt. One hundred percent."

"I'll take that as a yes then, said Lesley-Ann who turned around, walked swiftly over to a still inwardly-bemused Nick Gold, and gave him such a deep French kiss that he was genuinely concerned his tonsils were going to be sucked out of his throat.

American women. Go figure.

Suffice it to say that Ms Trobe seemed to be a ballbuster not just in the office. There was, however, one awkward moment when the attorney thought it would it would be appropriate to introduce oral sex into the proceedings. Gold immediately had an appalling flashback of Suzie aka Mrs Mehmet aka Persephone's razor-sharp teeth in Turkey and had to stop her, a move which brought about more accusations of all British men being impotent.

As they lay in the now dishevelled bed in the Comfort Inn, Gold just couldn't prevent himself from asking the lawyer the question uppermost on his mind.

"So, er, Lesley-Ann, what made you change your mind . . . about me?"

LAT turned onto her stomach and playfully pinched his nose.

"Oh, I haven't changed my mind about you at all. I still think you're either a deluded psycho or you're just off your meds. But I haven't had any action for a coupla weeks and I figured, what the hell?"

And once again they said romance was dead.

Gold knew that the French often referred to the sexual climax as *La Petite Mort* (the little death). Neuroscientists doing brain scans on women in the throes of orgasm found decreased blood flow to large portions of the brain. Thus, the little death. The decreased blood flow in the left lateral orbitofrontal cortex signified behavioural disinhibition during orgasm in women, and that deactivation of the temporal lobe is directly related to high sexual arousal.

All Gold knew was that his ego balloon had just been pricked big time. *La Petite Mort* was a bloody great *mort*.

"Well, thanks. I won't be expecting a card and flowers in the morning then, Lesley-Ann."

The attorney left the bed abruptly and stretched. She had, to Gold's relief, bedhead and the JBF look. Britain could be proud. US-Anglo relations were fully restored.

"You wanna grab something to eat . . . I mean *food*, Ron Jeremy. I'm starving. I always get hungry after sex."

"Good to know. Thanks for sharing," mumbled Gold.

"Jesus . . . are you sulking? Are you fifteen? Grow a pair. Get dressed. I know a place that stays open late and serves the best chilli dogs ever."

The mere thought of whatever new hell chilli dogs were, was enough to make Gold feel nauseous, but what's a boy to do? The lady wants chilli dogs.

"You drive."

"Now there's a surprise," replied Gold.

NINETEEN

"Farewell happy fields, Where joy forever dwells: Hail, horrors, hail."
– John Milton, Paradise Lost

To Gold's mild annoyance, the chilli dogs – hot dogs smothered in a volcano of chilli served on a roll the size and shape of a nuclear-powered submarine – were delicious. They ate the 'dogs' and drank German beer straight from the bottle. Gold had tried American beer. There were limits to even the most special of relationships.

"So, the plan for tomorrow. What time are we meeting Arnie?"

Gold paused mid-mouthful.

"We?"

"Fucking right, *we*. The way I figure it is this – either you two are idiots and the only thing you'll discover are your thumbs up your ass, or this will be the best show since *The Exorcist*. Don't look at me like that, I know it came out in 1974 but I like it. Get over it."

Gold chewed thoughtfully on the chilli which didn't seem to be getting any smaller on his plate. After the sex, he had only wanted to go to sleep, but now he was in an episode of *Man vs Food*.

"To be clear, are you there to cheer us on, laugh at us, or am I just irresistible and you can't bear to be apart from me? Ten-thirty at the newspaper office."

"Nick, we fucked. OK. That's it. It's what consenting adults do. It's not Bridget Jones. Right now, I'm deciding if I even like you, so don't be going on the web to find wedding planners here in town. Yeah? I'm gonna be there for several reasons. First, if you *do* find anything, then it may help my case with Loretta big time. Second, if you *don't*, then I'm gonna start looking for another defence strategy – insanity is looking good for me right now. Third, well, it might just turn out to be fun. And who doesn't like fun? Thanks for dinner, hun. That's my Uber outside. See ya tomorrow. Oh . . . and Nick . . . the earth moved . . . hate to think of my Brit Baby Boy sulking all night."

With that, and without a backward glance, Lesley-Ann strode off, climbed into a waiting Prius and was gone into the night.

"Yeah. No problem. Let me pay for a dinner I didn't want, why don't you?" said Gold to himself.

After a night in which the chilli made its presence known in various ways, Gold skipped breakfast and at ten-thirty sharp had parked the Chevy rental and was having a quick coffee with Arnie Woolfson in his office.

"You look tired, kid. Busy night?"

Gold felt himself blush. What, was he thirteen?

"Oh, no, not really. Probably just the excitement of it all."

Best to leave out the several hours of rather enthusiastic sex followed by the Mount Everest of chilli and Lake Michigan of beer.

Lesley-Ann strode into the office, looking, much to Gold's annoyance, perky and refreshed.

"Morning boys. All good? Say Nick, you look a little peaky. Someone you ate?"

Gold did his best to smile while Woolfson tried to read the subtext.

"Well, as we're now the Three Musketeers, let's vamoose and head on out to Trout Run Road," said the newspaperman.

"Don't tell me . . . I'm driving," said Gold, half to himself.

They piled into the little Chevy and set off out of town. Soon the urban environment became more rural. That was the beauty of America. Even in sprawling Los Angeles, you can drive out from the ludicrous excess of Rodeo Drive and be in the unspoiled canyons in under thirty minutes. Probably less.

After about half an hour drive along the two-lane blacktop, Arnie told Gold to slow down and began directing him, left here or right there, until they were deep in the forest. The light was having difficulty penetrating the thick foliage. To Nick, it looked just like the *Finding Myths & Monsters* TV series that the channel that aired his own show also screened. Surely Bigfoot would pop out from behind a tree and try to hitch a lift?

"OK . . . OK . . . take it easy. We're getting close. Pull over at the next cut-in in the road. We'll walk it from here."

"Really. Can't we just drive? You know, like normal people?" asked Gold.

"Not unless you want to rip the axles to pieces on this jalopy and take out the transmission. The road is shit from here. If you'd hired a goddam Jeep, we'd maybe have been alright."

"Well, if I knew I was going to go all Bear Grylls, I might have considered it."

"Who?" asked the attorney.

"Bear Grylls is . . . oh, forget it. OK. I'll pull in here."

He stopped the little car and the three of them got out.

"Is it far?" asked Gold.

"Do you ever stop fucking moaning? It is wherever it is. So stop your bitching and let's get a-cracker-lackin', mister," retorted the lawyer with her usual sensitivity.

They set off and, true to Woolfson's word, the road gave up and soon became a rutted track.

The trio walked for around twenty minutes, Gold cursing under his breath that he wasn't wearing his Timberland boots which were sat in his Balham flat.

"We're getting close," said Woolfson. "Nearly there."

"Thank fuck for that," muttered Gold under his breath.

"What are we supposed to be looking for?" asked the lawyer. "Gates, goblins, ghoulies?"

"What's the matter? Run out of Gs," retorted Gold.

"Play nice kids or daddy'll put your asses back in the car and no ice cream."

The track had completely given up even pretending to be a track. It was an almost invisible path, covered with leaves, plants and greenery, none of which Gold could name.

Then, quite without warning, there it was – a large iron ornate gate.

"Bloody hell!" called out Gold to no one in particular. "It's really here."

Arnie Woolfson spun round. "Of course it's here! Dy'a think I was making this shit up? It's the first gate."

They walked right up to it. It stood like the monolith in Kubrick's *2001*. No wall. No path. Just a large metal double gate maybe twenty feet high and ten feet across, standing alone in the middle of a Pennsylvanian forest.

"Do you think it keeps out the draught?" joked Gold weakly.

His humour was met with total silence.

"What now? Do we go on?" asked LAT

The newspaper man looked around. A light wind had picked up, causing the branches of the trees to start to move. The sky, which had started out quite bright, had darkened.

"Yeah, I guess so. Let's keep moving."

"The asylum. Is anything left of it, you know, after the fire?" enquired Gold as they pushed ahead.

"Nope. Just a few stones and stuff. Time, the weather, scavengers took care of what was left, and that was very little," replied Woolfson.

"And the gates, are they up ahead?

"Nick, I've no idea."

Gold stopped in his tracks. "Excuse me? What do you mean, you've no idea? Where are the other gates? The gates we talked about. The gates that lead to Hell?"

Woolfson suddenly looked tired and much older than he had in his office. "The thing is . . . the thing is . . . I've only ever found the one we just saw. I've never seen any of the other gates."

"But . . . but you said –"

"Yeah, kid. I know what I said. But I figured that you . . . you somehow would hold the key to finding them. That you stood the best chance."

Gold was livid. "So you've brought us out here on a wild goose chase? I'm a television personality . . . presenter . . . I'm not fucking Doris Stokes. I have no special powers. I'm not a character in a Marvel comic film. I'm from Balham. Trust me, Balham is not the centre of the spiritual world. Organic coffee and gluten-free bread maybe. I'm as much in the dark as you are . . . well, maybe not as much as she is."

"*She* has a name," piped up Lesley-Ann.

"OK. I fudged the truth a little to get you out here, Nick. But now we're here, how about we press on, huh?"

Gold let out a long sigh. "Sure. Fine. Why not? I'm in the middle of a forest, no idea where I'm going with a bullshit artist and a lawyer so what's not to like. Let's go."

Without looking back, Gold strode ahead. He was not a happy camper. He had never lost sight of the fact that this was, ultimately, a television recce, paid for by Larry at Good Foot Productions. He had to come back with great photos and information or the series would never be made, which was a career-threatening event to be avoided at all costs.

The path became more overgrown. The twigs and smaller branches were beginning to become a real pain in the arse as Gold pushed his way forward.

"Sod this for a game of tin soldiers," he muttered. "The only place I'm going to see more gates is in a garden centre in Croydon when I get –"

Ahead of him, in a clearing, was a gate. A very large gate.

"What the actual fuck –"

Gold walked towards it in disbelief. The clearing seemed to be an exact circle with the gate in the centre. Two things struck Nick Gold simultaneously. First, the gate, unlike the first one, was not rusted. It looked in surprisingly mint condition. Secondly, the clearing appeared to be on fire. No, not fire exactly but smoking slightly as if it had been on fire recently.

"Guys . . . guys! You won't believe it! I've found it! I've totally bloody found it!"

There was no answer.

"Arnie, Lesley-Ann . . . come on . . . follow my voice. It's here! I've found the gate!"

Nothing.

Not a sound.

Gold turned around. Surely his companions were only a few yards behind?

But they weren't. There was neither sight nor sound of them.

"Oh crap," thought Gold.

Suddenly, the gate started to open.

"Oh, you have got to be shitting me!"

There was no noise as the very large metal structure swung on its hinges. No *House On Haunted Hill* metallic creaking. Just total silence. It was as if the gate was made of air, weightless, silent.

Very slowly, Gold approached. He realised the John Bonham drum solo of his quickened heartbeat was back again. Dare he touch it?

Gold turned around again. "Trobe . . . Woolfson . . . where are you?"

"Mr Gold, I'm afraid your friends can't hear you anymore."

"Hell fire!" Gold was rigid with shock.

"Are you going to step through the threshold, and discover your destiny?"

TWENTY

"Our torments also may in length of time Become our Elements."
– John Milton, Paradise Lost

There are good days. There are bad days. And there are days that are so out there, you think someone has spiked your drink with LSD.

Gold's stomach was so tight he thought he was going to throw up. He tried to talk himself into being calm.

Come on . . . this is the 21st century . . . I'm in modern America . . . no, forget that last bit, that doesn't help. I'm a respected TV presenter . . . I know, there's no such thing . . . I'm with a lawyer and a newspaper man . . . but they've disappeared.

"Mr Gold, I'm waiting."

The voice had an edge to it, yet was inviting. Weird.

Gold dared to look. The large metallic gates now seemed to be illuminated, stark against the gloom of the forest. No, the gates themselves were giving off the light. It was growing in intensity, yet Gold could look straight at it, despite it being dazzling.

That wasn't normal.

There, bathed in the incandescent light of the gates, was a figure.

"You!" was all Gold could muster from his extensive vocabulary.

"Yes. Me." replied Barachiel.

"You!" repeated Gold.

"I think we've established that, Mr Gold. Would you care to follow me? Please?"

Even for someone who frequented the Groucho Club, this was very, very strange. Gold took a hesitant step forward.

"Whoa! Hold on a minute. Am I dead? Did I die in the freaking forest and no one told me? What's through these gates?"

Barachiel offered his trademark enigmatic smile. "You're not dead Mr Gold. And what is through these gates? You are."

"Christ! What is it with people like you? Riddles! Mystery! Can't you just give me a straight answer without going all Yoda on me? What's through the gates – Disneyland, a picnic area, a drive-through McDonalds? What!?"

Gold was trying to hold on to the last shreds of his sanity. Deep down, he longed to be back in Balham enjoying a coffee and a pulled-pork toasted sourdough sandwich at the Brickwood Café. In fact, he would rather be anywhere but here.

"Mr Gold. Please. Come with me."

Sod it. In for a penny.

Gold walked forward through the gates towards Barachiel, who this time had swapped the homeless man clothing for, of all things, a suit.

The human mind is an extraordinary thing. The typical brain is about two percent of a body's weight but uses twenty percent of its total energy and oxygen intake; it's seventy-three percent water, contains eighty-six billion brain cells, and each neuron connects with forty-thousand synapses; a piece of brain tissue the size of a grain of sand contains one hundred thousand neurons and one billion synapses all communicating with each other; and it generates about twelve to twenty-five watts of electricity, enough to power a low wattage LED light.

All of this, and yet Gold was thinking, *he's wearing a suit . . . in the forest.*

It was great to be at home back in his flat in London. Gold sat down heavily in his favourite battered leather chair (he'd salvaged it late one night from a skip in his street). It had the patina of wear, yet was ridiculously comfortable. By the side of the chair was his favourite bottle of single malt, Balvenie 12-Year Double-Wood. He reached out, poured a more than generous amount into the glass he'd appropriated from a local pub, the Bedford. He took a long delicious sip.

That was some weird-arse dream. Another sip of the single malt.

"I thought you'd be more relaxed in familiar surroundings, Mr Gold."

"Holy fuck!" yelled Gold, leaping to his feet. "No, no, no . . . wake up Nick . . . wake up –"

"You *are* awake, Mr Gold. Please sit down in your chair. Enjoy your drink."

Gold had never felt so disorientated in his entire life.

"As I said, I thought you would be more at home . . . *at home*, so to speak."

"Where am I?" asked Gold, panic just beginning to creep into his voice.

Barachiel smiled. "Where would you like to be, Nick? Let's just say that you're someplace where we can have a quiet conversation without being disturbed."

Gold realised he was gripping the arms of the chair so tightly he was leaving indentations on the cracked dark brown leather.

"Am I actually at home?"

"In a manner of speaking."

"Screw you. Am I actually in my flat at home?"

"No, that would be ridiculous."

It was Gold's turn to smile. "Yes. Ridiculous. Whereas finding you . . . in a suit . . . standing by a gate in the middle of a forest and then the next thing, I'm back in London, isn't?"

"I wanted you to be in familiar surroundings. To feel more relaxed. So, here we are."

"But this scotch . . . it tastes real. The chair feels real."

Barachiel made a small gesture with his hands. "What is real,

Nick? Remember the red rose I showed you in Turkey in the ruins? I tried to tell you then, but you weren't, shall we say, receptive."

"Tell you what, I'm going to drink the rest of this glass of not-so-real single malt, then I'm going to reach for the not-so-real-bottle and pour myself another."

Barachiel nodded. That would be fine.

After two very large glasses, the grip on the arms of his chair had lessened.

"You do this a lot, then?" asked a truculent Gold.

The Archangel thought. "No, not really. The last time was, let me see, when I gave the idea to Stanley Kubrick in 1968. You know, the end sequence of his film *2001*.

Gold was totally lost. The not-real single malt wasn't helping him focus. Especially on a very real empty stomach.

"Are you a little more relaxed now, Nick? Do you mind if I sit down?"

"Really? You have turned my brain into sushi. I'm in a forest and a second later I'm home . . . but you tell me I'm not home . . . and you ask me if I mind if you *sit down?* What I *mind*, Barry, is you totally messing with my life!"

Barachiel sat down.

"I owe you an explanation."

"No kidding? Who knew!"

"Nick, I want you to listen to me very carefully."

What was it about the Archangel's voice? It seemed to morph into dozens of different voices, yet sound like a cohesive whole, sometimes singular, sometimes like a chorus. And his face. It seemed to change. Black, white, brown . . . and yet it was, without doubt, unmistakably *his* face.

"Ah, my voice. Have you forgotten the description in *Revelation*: I heard a voice like many bodies of rushing water.

"Oh, great. You're reading my mind now?"

"Nick, thought, speech . . . they're the same."

Gold was regaining some of his composure. "Sorry, I may have taken theology at Oxford but I've still no idea what you mean. I must have missed that particular lecture."

Barachiel suddenly stood up.

"You have been chosen."

Gold sat motionless.

"What?"

Barachiel repeated "You have been chosen."

"Are you a bloody Scientologist?"

Barachiel raised an eyebrow. That was answer enough.

"Sorry, I'm a little freaked out here. When I say, a little, I mean completely. You know . . . totally."

"I understand. There is much you have to learn."

"You left out 'Young Skywalker'.

Gold's nerves were shredded and he was speaking without thinking.

"Nick, you have been chosen, and that is why I have been with you. I have been sent to help you with what you must do."

If Gold's heart could beat any faster, he wasn't aware of it.

"Er . . . hang on there . . . chosen . . . what I've got to do? I'm not liking this. I thought we went through this nonsense in Turkey. I wasn't buying it then and, newsflash, I'm not buying it now."

"Do you know what we just passed through?"

"Oh, you mean the big shiny metal thing that looked like a large gate. I'm going to stick my neck out here and answer . . . gate?"

Barachiel merely smiled. "Yes, that's right. It is indeed a gate. It is there for a purpose. Do you know what that purpose might be?

Gold was out of pithy epithets. He merely shook his head.

"The gate is there to keep you safe."

Gold looked up. "OK. You got me. Safe from what? Urban foxes? Republicans?"

"The dead."

The silence in the small flat in Balham was overwhelming.

"Look, Barachiel . . . Barry . . . the dead? Really? You still peddling that line? The dead didn't do such a bang-up job in my hotel room in Turkey I seem to recall. OK, there's something very, very, weird, going on, I'll give you that, but despite what you might think, I'm trying to hold on to being a rational guy. None of this is rational."

The silence grew almost oppressive.

"Nicholas Oliver Gold, you are The Gatekeeper."

"I'm the *what?*"

Was Barachiel growing? He seemed to be filling more of the room than he was a minute ago.

"You have been chosen to be The Gatekeeper."

Gold shook his head. "Oh, I'm sorry . . . did I miss that email? Perhaps it went straight to my spam filter. Chosen? Chosen by who? Lambeth Council, the CIA, MI5, Area 51? What the hell are you talking about?"

"You have been chosen."

Gold was getting irate, and increasingly nervous. "Yeah, thanks, I got that part. And what does this Gatekeeper of yours do? Pick up litter? Oil the gate with WD40 once a week?"

"No, Nick. I've already told you. The Gatekeeper saves the world."

Gold poured himself another very large, not-real single malt and downed it in one. His throat burned from the liquid.

"Save the world? That again? Spare me this nonsense for God's sake! Look at me! I mean, seriously, just bloody look at me? Do I even remotely look like someone who could possibly save the world? It would, I'll admit, look fantastic on my CV under previous experience or hobbies but otherwise sing another tune, my friend".

"I want you to listen. Don't speak until I have finished. Then you may speak."

There was something in Barachiel's tone that went straight into Nick Gold's brain. It said, very clearly, to be quiet. The or else was implicit.

"Everything you need, and will need to know, I shall now impart. In *Revelation* 12:7-12 it says 'And war broke out in heaven: Michael and his angels fought with the dragon; and the dragon and his angels fought, but they did not prevail, nor was a place found for them in heaven any longer'."

Gold held up a hand. "Barry . . . Baz-Boy (the bourbon was really taking effect now) let me stop you right there, old son. I read theology. In Oxford. Not off the back of a cereal packet. And this may surprise you but I got an upper Second. An upper Second. Yeah . . . at Oxford. I know this stuff. Right? I know it. So the great dragon was cast out, that serpent of old, called the Devil and Satan, who deceives the whole world; he was cast to the earth, and his angels were cast out with him."

Gold took another large mouthful of Bourbon.

"Ice? You got any ice?

Barachiel was staring at Nick with a gaze that Gold could not put into words. His gaze seemed to bore down to his very core.

"You understand, the Dragon . . . the Serpent . . . is Satan . . . or as we call him, Lucifer?"

Gold nodded. "Yes, of course I do. Lucifer. Great."

Barachiel continued. "Some believe God cast out his adversary Satan from heaven in 1914, the start of World War One. Not true. The devil clearly was removed from heaven many years prior to 1914."

"Tell that to the million who bought it during the Battle of the Somme," muttered Gold, darkly.

"In *Luke* 10:18, Jesus stated he personally witnessed this momentous event which occurred with all the quickness and power of lightning. He was literally ejected from God's throne."

"Barry . . . Barry, I'm going to be very, very honest with you here. I'm very freaked out by being here and I'm somewhat pissed. Frankly, it's not a great combination. Now, without in any way appearing rude, can you tell me something I don't know?"

Deep in his heart, Gold had a sinking feeling. This was not going to end well. At all.

Barachiel continued. "Satan's revolt took place when he was here on earth. In *Isaiah* 14, it says that he planned to go back to heaven where the throne resided. Once there, he would mount an all-out assault with his army of demonic followers to take control of God's throne by force so that he could rule everything. It's all spelt out in *Isaiah*. Tell me Nick, what do you think Lucifer was before he was literally thrown out of heaven?"

"Well Bazza, there's the thing. In *Ezekiel* 28:12-15, it describes Satan as an exceedingly beautiful angel, the highest of all angels, the anointed cherub, the most beautiful of all of God's creations. But that wasn't enough for him, as we both know. Me, because I studied theology, and you because . . . because, well God knows."

Barachiel gave a small smile. "Yes. You are of course quite right. That comes as no surprise to me. Now, while Lucifer was still on-side and obedient, God put him on the earth with certain responsibilities. But Lucifer had other ideas. Why did Satan fall from heaven, Nick?"

"Why? Why did he fall? I'll tell you why. Satan fell because of *pride*. He desired to *be* God, not to be a servant of God. He wanted, quite simply, to remove God from His throne and take over the rule of the Universe. But God wasn't having that, Barry, was He? Satan did not fall from heaven, Satan was *pushed!*"

Gold reached for the single malt. Religion was thirsty work.

Nick went on. It was all flooding back. "Then, with one third of all the angels that ever existed, Lucifer decided to rebel against God. The Lord tossed Satan from his heavenly abode when he and his angels arrived to attack it. How am I doing?"

Gold drummed his fingers on the glass he'd borrowed from the Bedford pub.

"Look Barachiel, I'm not saying that this isn't a great story . . . and you really tell it well . . . I mean, if I was casting for voice-overs right now, you'd be top of my list. But, I'm sorry what has any of this . . . fairy tale . . . have to do with me? I understand it, Barry. Really I do. But I don't believe in it any more. Not now. It's fascinating, but . . . but let's face it, it's not real, is it?"

It was as though the temperature in the room instantly dropped several degrees. Barachiel's eyes seemed to suddenly have a fire behind them.

"Fairy tale? You think this is a story . . . made up . . . to keep the people in submission? Don't you see, Nicholas Gold, that what I'm telling you is what happened, and more importantly, what *is* happening?"

Gold felt very uneasy now.

"Er . . . not really. What do you mean *is*?"

Barachiel seemed to calm slightly. "Do you think Lucifer has given up his ambition? That he's happy with the status quo? Every twenty years, the devil once again rises up from the earth to attack God's headquarters, only to get thrown down yet again. Read it Mr Gold – *Revelation* 12:7-9. 1914, 1934, 1954, and now."

"Now?"

Gold suddenly had a dreadful feeling where this was heading.

"Yes, Mr Gold, now. Lucifer will attempt, with his demons, to try to take control of the Universe."

"The entire Universe?" asked Gold

"Lucifer is not known for micro-management nor small-scale thinking. Yes. Every universe. All of them."

Gold sat up straight. "Hold on a minute. *All* the universes? There's only one."

Barachiel, quite unexpectedly, burst into laughter.

"Only one? There are an infinite number of universes, Nicholas. We live in a multiverse. You've heard of scientific theories like quantum mechanics and string theory . . . or Schrödinger's cat?"

Gold nodded. He thought maybe he'd seen a documentary on

it once on TV. Morgan Freeman or Kelsey Grammer probably did the narration to give the show gravitas.

He went to put the glass to his mouth but, to his surprise, it was a now a fine bone china mug containing the best black coffee he had ever tasted.

"I thought you'd had enough bourbon. So, tell me, what happened 13.8 billion years ago, Nick?"

"Um, Joan Collins' birthday? No, the Big Bang, right? The start of everything."

Barachiel smiled. "Correct. I have to say, it was one hell of a show."

Gold looked at the guest in his room. "Of course. You were there. Silly me. Naturally."

"Yes, we were there. Moving on. At that moment, in that impossibly small fraction of time, your Universe and an infinite collection of universes, came into existence."

"Barry, we covered this in my philosophy lectures. In summary Science 1, Religion Nil. Science goes through to the final."

Barachiel stood up and started to pace the room. Actually, not so much pace it, as fill it. Nick took a long drink of the coffee in an attempt to clear his head.

"Is that so? And where do you stand on the theory of multiple universes, then?"

"I'm pretty relaxed about it."

Barachiel gave Gold a hard stare that made him suddenly sit up straighter in his chair.

"Mr Gold, not everything in life can be dealt with, or deflected by, a casual remark. It may be a joke to you at the moment, but I assure you, very soon it will not be. So let me ask again, what do you know of the mulitiverse?"

Gold felt like a child being scolded by a teacher, but there was no mistaking Barachiel's firm manner.

"I know a bit."

Barachiel nodded.

"Well, Mr Gold, then you'll know that the two essential pieces of understanding to the multiverse are. . . ?"

Was he being tested here? As if the entire situation wasn't weird enough already, now he was subject to a verbal examination. What was next, a re-take of his driving test?

"Well Barry, if my memory serves me correctly, you need to understand cosmic inflation and quantum theory to have a snowball's chance in hell of getting your head round the idea of a multiverse. Right?"

"Interesting turn of phrase. Correct, Mr Gold. I see your time at university was not a complete waste."

Marvellous. An ironic Archangel. Not to mention judgemental, brooded Gold.

"Gee, thanks, Barry. How kind," retorted Gold. "Cosmic inflation is the idea that an infinitesimal fraction of a second after the Big Bang, the event where you and your boss had front row seats, space expanded at an exponential rate. It started everything astronomers can see today."

"Bravo, Mr Gold. But you forgot to add that in *your* region of space, inflation soon stopped but elsewhere it goes on indefinitely, creating an infinite cosmos. There are, therefore, an infinite number of universes."

Gold sipped from his coffee cup, which seemed to have refilled itself.

"Neat trick, Barry. What's next . . . the Sorting Hat?"

Barachiel allowed a corner of his mouth to move to either indicate a tiny smile, or his displeasure.

"You see, what *you* fail to add, Mr Angel, is that this is science. Not religion. Science! There's your lot with the getting the whole shebang built in seven days or there's science. I know who gets my vote."

Barachiel shook his head. "Ah Nick, you still don't see it, do you? What I am trying to get you to see is beyond this. There is religion and there is science but what lies within them both?"

Gold looked blank. "I don't honestly know. What?"

"Everything Mr Gold. Everything."

Gold sipped his coffee. It really was exceptionally good.

"I don't suppose you'd care to narrow that down a smidgen, Barry? You know, just for those of us who didn't see The Big Bang from the dress circle."

Did Barachiel just frown?

"What you do for a living, Mr Gold. Your television programmes. The supernatural."

"Are you a fan? Really, I'm flattered. They're nonsense, that is until I started investigating this . . . this feels real . . . insane . . . but real."

Finally, a tiny smile from Barachiel. "No, that's my point. They are *not* nonsense. Very far from it. That's the crucial point that I need you to understand, for your own good. The supernatural, as you quaintly call it, exists. It exists, Mr Gold, in the space of the multiverse. Humans see a tiny glimpse of it from time to time when the multiverses overlap, but I assure you, it is very real."

Nick Gold was silent. He slowly took another sip from his seemingly bottomless coffee cup and then he spoke.

"Are you telling me that the spooky stuff I put in my shows, that everything we read about that we think is fictional, imagined, legend, is actually real?"

"Yes."

"Fuck me!"

"Always the elegant wordsmith, Mr Gold. Consider this if you will. Where do you think you come from?"

"Balham?"

"I was thinking of mankind, the human race, rather than just you, Mr Gold. Where do you think the human race comes from? I'll tell you. Are you aware that nearly half of the atoms that make up your bodies may have formed beyond the Milky Way?"

"What?"

"Oh yes, Mr Gold. The atoms travelled to your tiny solar system on intergalactic winds driven by giant exploding stars."

"So, David Bowie was right? That we are Star Men?"

"I think your Joni Mitchell was even closer when she sang 'We are stardust'. The point is, Mr Gold, that your origins are much less local than you think. You came from the far reaches of your Universe. And some of you, came from the other, infinite number, of universes. In some sense, you are all extragalactic visitors, or immigrants in what you think of as your galaxy."

Gold let out a long breath and gently shook his head. "One minute, I'm in the woods and next I'm being told the origins of the human race. In my flat. Which isn't my flat. So tell me, while you're on a roll, where do you and God fit into all of this?"

Barachiel replied, speaking in a deliberate tone as what he had to impart, he knew, was vital for Nick Gold.

"Science is very useful for finding your place in your universe. However, only we can help you find your place not just in the multiverses, but in the spaces between. Whether you side with science or religion, Mr Gold, makes no difference. We exist. We have always existed. Before there was anything and after there is nothing."

"So, even if I accept everything you've just explained to me – and I'm not saying that I don't – *how* exactly do I fit into this?" asked Nick.

"You are The Gatekeeper. You will prevent Lucifer and his hordes from entering your world. You will keep the earth safe."

Gold sat there and did not say a word. After a few moments, he looked up.

"You are fucking with me, right?"

"No, Mr Gold. I am not. You have been chosen. That is all there is to it."

"Bollocks! Are you mad? Chosen? I still don't want to be chosen, thank you. Multiverses or not, I want to make my own little TV shows. I am not saving the world material. You've got the wrong guy. There's probably a Nick Gold who lives, I don't know, in Sydney or Seattle or Scotland who looks like Wolverine or Bruce Wayne or Dwayne Johnson. *That's* the guy you want. This is some terrible mix up."

Barachiel shook his head. "There is no mistake. *You* are The Gatekeeper."

Gold stood up and started to pace the living room of his small flat.

"Why me? Of all the people on the planet, why choose me?"

"That is not the question, Nicholas. The question is why *not* me? Do you think life, what *you* call life, is ordered, planned, ordained?"

Gold shrugged his shoulders.

"It isn't. When a child gets cancer, when a lorry's brakes fail and kills pedestrians, when a building collapses, when a tsunami strikes, when a bomb goes off in a train, when you win millions on the lottery – all of it is totally random. The reason you are The Gatekeeper is the same. Just because. It could have been anyone on the planet. But it's you. That's all. In life, Nicholas, there is no point in asking why me? It is, as the Americans say, a crap shoot."

Gold was still pacing.

"So, I have no special super powers, no magic ring, no special light-sabre . . . nothing? That's it?"

"That's it, Nick."

As the reality, if that was the correct term, of his situation began to sink in, Gold was, for the first time, genuinely frightened. Like so many people, the fear was expressed as anger.

"This is total bullshit. I . . . I . . . don't believe a word of this. Angels, Lucifer, gates . . . you know what, you're nuts. You've roofied my drink or something and none of this is real. Seriously, I have no idea who or what you are my friend, but I've had enough."

Barachiel stood very still, looking at Nick Gold who glared back at him.

"Then, Mr Gold, let me show you who I am."

There was a blinding flash and the room seemed to be filled with the dazzling brightness of a hundred suns. Gold was temporarily blinded. It was like the moment when a thermonuclear bomb is detonated; a flash of light so bright that looking directly at it is impossible. The room moved. The walls, the ceiling were gone. Gold was trying to squint to see what was happening. He could see only pure whiteness. Then he realised that it was Barachiel he was looking at – shining, glowing, pulsating with light. From either side of his body, vast feathered wings grew that seemed to stretch and to fill a space so unimaginably vast that Gold clutched onto the arms of the battered brown leather chair reeling with vertigo as if his life depended on it. The human brain has always encountered great difficulty in picturing huge distances. It can see the moon and understand it is quarter of a million miles from earth, or the sun, and understand that it is ninety-three million miles away. At a pinch, man can grasp the idea that the light from the sun, travelling at light speed obviously, takes around eight minutes to reach Earth. After that, the human brain struggles to comprehend the sheer scale of the universe.

As Gold sat in his small flat in a South London suburb during what had been seconds, minutes or hours (time was never, ever more relative than what he was experiencing just now), he was now witnessing the true majesty of the universe.

In its entirety.

It was no wonder that he was suddenly very close to mental collapse – the numbers involved were of an unimaginable magnitude.

From nowhere, Gold was reminded of the words of theoretical physicist and cosmologist Lawrence Krauss: 'Every atom in your body came from a star that exploded. And the atoms in your left hand probably came from a different star than your right hand. It really is the most poetic thing I know about physics: you are all stardust. Forget Jesus, the stars died so you could be born'. Barachiel was telling the truth.

Gold truly was stardust.

The thought left him almost as soon as it arrived.

But what was making Nick Gold's mind collapse was not the planets, stars, galaxies, black holes, cosmic webs or superclusters – it was that Barachiel filled all of it. Every last tiny particle of it. And by tiny it included the plasma droplets created by the Large Hardon Collider at CERN, more than one hundred thousand times smaller than a hydrogen atom.

The homeless man who had sat outside Sainsbury's in Balham now filled a space so vast it was beyond comprehension. Barachiel himself had grown until Gold felt not merely dwarfed by his presence, but rendered incapable of logical thought. The universe revealed in its full magnitude will do that to a person. The very air itself seemed to pulsate with energy. Finally, Gold found that words had formed in his mouth. Somehow, with great effort, he managed to speak.

"Holy shit . . . you're . . . you're an angel."

"Archangel," corrected Barachiel. "Welcome to my world."

TWENTY-ONE

"Of man's first disobedience, and the fruit
Of that forbidden tree, whose mortal taste
Brought death into the world, and all our woe,
With loss of Eden, till one greater Man
Restore us, and regain the blissful seat,
Sing heavenly muse."
– John Milton, Paradise Lost

Gold could not catch his breath. He was physically panting, trying to retain a scintilla of control of a situation that was beyond that which a human brain can process. He clutched the sides of the battered brown leather club chair as if he was on a roller-coaster. The effect of watching Barachiel transform into an Archangel was staggering. In a nanosecond, Gold had been shown the answer to Man's eternal question.

It was too much. Akin to teaching a dog algebra. Incomprehensible.

He was still trying to speak, but the words were caught in his throat.

"So . . . so . . . it's . . . all . . . all –"

"True?" interjected Barachiel. "Oh yes. All of it. The whole nine yards."

"So . . . so what happens to non-believers?"

"Oh, they're fucked. Big time."

Gold was losing any sense of reality now. The light was so dazzling. The wings were making the air rush past his face.

Barachiel broke into a loud laugh.

"I'm just messing with you. Believe, don't believe . . . it makes no difference."

Gold managed from somewhere deep in his consciousness to ask a half-way decent question.

"How can that be?"

"Some people think the earth is flat, that the sun orbits the planet, that humans are the only intelligent life form in the Universe and that Elvis is still alive. Their beliefs don't change the facts."

Gold wasn't sure he understood. But then he was finding it very hard to understand anything under the current circumstances. Answering his own name right now would prove difficult.

"So . . . where are we exactly . . . if you don't mind me asking?"

It probably didn't hurt to be polite to an Archangel.

"Are you sure you want the question answered?"

Oh crap. Here we go. Gold nodded.

"We are in a safe place . . . a viewing platform if you will. Think of where we are as one side of a vast aquarium. You're dry and safe, kept from deep-sea inhabitants and thousands of gallons of water by . . . what shall I say . . . a thick protective viewing window."

Gold seemed to recall the London Aquarium contained over two million litres of water. Great. Trivia. Never know when it'll come in handy.

"What are we, er, viewing?" There was a tremulous quality to Gold's voice.

"This!"

Barachiel made a movement with his arm. Gold looked and instantly vomited.

Blood. Gallons of it. Acres of it. Seas of it. Red, bubbling fresh blood. It rose and fell in waves. In the troughs stood, lay, crawled, putrefying what had once been people. Men, women, children

. . . children? Old, young, every colour, every ethnicity, were screaming. Their mouths open as they shrieked, howled, cursed and screamed at their fate. They were crawling over each other, their naked bodies covered in blood, filth and excrement. There were thousands upon thousands of them. Gold couldn't count them. It was a vast landscape of such unimaginable horror that even Hieronymus Bosch's fantastic imagery was insufficiently rapine, or gore-ridden, or a sufficiently festering realisation of what now confronted Gold.

He sat in his chair, frozen and aghast.

"I saw the opening maw of hell Herman Melville wrote, Mr Gold. And this is but a small fraction of it. Hell is huge: as vast and limitless as the Universe I've shown you."

Gold once again attempted to communicate.

"I . . . I don't understand. I don't know what to say."

"Well, of course not. Who would?"

"How long have these . . . these people been there?"

Barachiel spoke, but Gold was transfixed as a woman bit into the neck of an older woman and ripped her flesh off, then began chewing it, thrusting it into her mouth with a ravenous urgency, the blood covering the lower half of her face.

"That's one of the joys of Hell, Mr Gold. No European Court of Human Rights. No ambulance-chasing lawyers. Eternity means eternity. Do you have any idea how to begin to envisage eternity?"

Gold could only shake his head.

"A priest once explained it like this. Imagine a planet the size of Jupiter, made of solid steel. Every ten thousand years, a single dove is released and flies to that planet, its wings brushing gently against the solid steel surface once each flight. Eternity is when the planet has been finally eroded by the touch of the dove's wings and no longer exists."

"Fucking hell!"

"Crudely stated, but I concur with your sentiments, Mr Gold."

"And apart from bringing up everything I've ever eaten since I was a child, why are you showing me this?"

Barachiel made a movement and the vision began to disappear, but not before Gold saw a man pull the eyeballs from an old man and push them into his mouth like two dim-sum steamed buns.

"Because this is what Lucifer wants for the entire earth. This . . . and worse."

Gold reacted. "Worse? *Worse*!"

Barachiel smiled. "I thought it best to break you in gently. True Hell is not for the faint-hearted. This was, shall we say, an amuse bouche, a mere taster of the main course."

"Christ!"

"That, Mr Gold, is a whole different subject and one we might discuss another time. But not now. I wanted you to understand some of what you're facing and, shall we say, the scope of what awaits you. Do you know why the inhabitants of Hell behave like that?"

Gold merely shook his head. He was pretty much out of words.

"Well, let me ask you this, Mr Gold. Do you have a low threshold of boredom?"

Under the circumstances in which he found himself, bored was not a problem that Gold himself was experiencing.

"Er, well, you know, I like to keep myself pretty busy."

"So, Mr Gold, if for instance you found yourself on, let's say, a plane flying to Los Angeles from London, a flight time of eleven and a half hours, and there were no movies, no books, no magazines, no food – how would you feel?"

Gold pondered this for a moment. Or maybe he pondered on it for several hours, weeks or years; time meant nothing here.

"I'd complain to the airline . . . fine, OK . . . no jokes . . . I'd be bored out of my mind."

Barachiel nodded in assent. "Yes, you would. Now imagine that feeling for all eternity. Nothing. Just absolutely nothing. Just an eternity of ennui. With no chance of reprieve. That, Mr Gold, is the true hell of Hell. Boredom. The fiery pits, the torture, all created by men in the Middle Ages to scare, as you would say colloquially, the crap out of the human race. To keep them in check. To get them to toe the line, as it were. That's why the creatures that you just saw behave like that. It's better than nothing. It's something to do. And, of course, the boredom has driven them all quite, quite mad."

Gold dispensed with the stolen glass and drank straight from the bottle of single malt.

Finally, he had composed himself sufficiently to attempt to ask some vaguely coherent questions.

He was, literally, back in the room.

"This . . . this Gatekeeper of yours . . . he does what precisely? I mean by that, what the hell does he do to stop . . . to stop. . . ?"

Gold pointed to where Hell had been revealed.

Barachiel was returning to his human form. He was now dressed in a sports jacket, polo shirt and jeans. Even Archangels do smart-casual.

"Passing through The Gate can be seen as a process of enlightenment, if you will. Each Gatekeeper addresses their task in their own way. Sometimes they are less successful than others: 1939–1945 wasn't our finest moment and didn't go entirely to plan but we triumphed ultimately. Whereas this time, the stakes are very high. From Syracuse to Syria, it's been building and building. The signs were there for those who knew how to read them."

Gold was regaining a modicum of control, but he noticed that his hands were still shaking badly.

"Signs? Yeah? Well I know how to read Facebook, Twitter, WhatsApp and the instructions on my ready-meals. I don't do signs. What am I supposed to do . . . Tweet the Devil to death? I suspect that trolling him online isn't really going to stop him, but feel free to correct me."

Barachiel sat down. Was that a sigh he just made?

"Mr Gold, you have all the tools that you will need. You are The Gatekeeper. When the time comes, you will know what to do."

Nick Gold stood up. Half-infuriated, half-terrified, and wholly pissed-off. "Listen Barachiel, there has been some monumental celestial fuck-up here. A paperwork mix-up, I dunno. But trust me on this, you have one hundred percent got the wrong guy. It's a clerical error. It's –"

But Barachiel interjected.

"Let me assure you, there has been *no* error. You, and you alone, are The Gatekeeper. That is your destiny."

"Oh really? Is that a fact? Well, what happens if I refuse to be The Gatekeeper? What then?"

Barachiel's eyes darkened.

"Some have sought refuge in refusal. It does not end well for them."

"Oh yeah?"

Barachiel nodded. "You saw two of them just now."

Gold suddenly felt violently sick.

"Are you *blackmailing* me? You're kidding, right? An Archangel is no better than a mob guy?"

Barachiel smiled. "Mr Gold, I am not blackmailing or threatening you in any way. It is not we who transport the, shall we say, *refusniks*, to eternal damnation. It is Lucifer and his supporters who take a rather dim view of them. They make the travel arrangements."

Gold buried his head in his hands. After a few moments, he managed to look up.

"So, this is the Gate to Hell, right? And all I have to do is keep it shut, and my work is done. Is that it?"

Barachiel shook his head.

"No. That is most definitely *not* it. I will admit that here in the USA, we are living in, shall we say, interesting times. Even *we* were surprised by recent events. But the Gate to Hell is not here in Pennsylvania. In fact, there is not one gate, but many."

"Oh crap," exclaimed Gold.

"Mr Gold, do you honestly think that a realm as colossal as Hell has a single entrance? I just showed you a mere glimpse of the unfathomable size of the Universe. And of, course my young friend, that was just one of them. I thought that would be sufficient to grab your attention. We could, if you like, travel to the limitless parallel universes and have a look-see, but I suspect that would be *de trop, n'est ce pas?* Do you think that a demon as ambitious and driven as Lucifer would be satisfied with just the one gate? There are gates all over your world. You yourself know this. You have already been to two of them – in Turkey and in England."

Nick Gold groaned.

"Let me help you. The answer, Mr Gold, is Mr Beck."

The grass beneath Nick Gold felt damp. It was raining lightly and the drops fell on his face. He was dimly aware of voices in the distance.

"He's here! He's over here! I've got him!" It was a male voice that Gold didn't recognise. His vision felt blurred and his senses dulled. Then a face materialised. It was wearing a peaked cap with a badge. Gold could just about make out the words York County Police Department.

"It's OK, fella. Don't move. We've gotcha. Take it easy."

Then radio sets started chattering to each other, the staccato messages brief and to the point. In his confused state, Gold thought he heard fragments of 'White male, early thirties . . . confirmed he is alive . . . no sir, no injuries visible . . . yes, he's breathing unassisted . . . get the medics here ASAP'.

Gold's vision grew dim once more. He thought he felt pairs of hands moving him, lifting him onto a stretcher, but maybe that, too, was a dream. Then everything went very dark.

TWENTY-TWO

"So farewell hope, and with hope farewell fear, Farewell remorse: all good to me is lost; Evil, be thou my good."

– John Milton, Paradise Lost

"He's alive! He's alive!" A vaguely familiar voice was calling out with a note of incredulity mixed with elation. Gold thought he recognized the voice, but couldn't be certain.

"Nick . . . Nick . . . can you hear me?"

The voice needed a response.

Gold tried to answer, but all that came out of his mouth was a thin rasping sound. Slowly, he opened his eyes and blinked rapidly to regain his vision, which still seemed to be exceptionally blurred.

Bit by bit, like the way a photo used to download and slowly reveal itself in the early days of dial-up Internet, a face began to materialize. It was grizzled, and concerned.

Gold thought he knew the face's owner.

"Nick . . . it's me . . . Arnie . . . Arnie Woolfson."

Very slowly, Woolfson's face began to take shape.

"Yes . . . Nick . . . it's Arnie . . . you're OK now. You're safe."

The earth was moving. Bumping. Jolting.

It took a moment for Gold to realise he was in a vehicle. He was on his back. An ambulance he presumed. He could hear the sirens wailing through the roof of the vehicle.

"It's OK fella," continued Woolfson in a soothing voice.

The next voice wasn't quite so soothing.

"Where the fuck were you, numbnuts?"

Gold managed to turn his head slightly to see Lesley-Ann Trobe also sitting in the ambulance.

He tried to reply, but nothing came out. Just the rasping sound again.

Then a third voice spoke, a voice he didn't recognise.

"I'm just going to give you this, Mr Gold." There was a slight prick in his arm and Nick Gold fell into the arms of Morpheus.

Was it hours, minutes, millennia? Gold had no idea. There was a beeping sound and the hum of machinery. He was horizontal. In a bed? Yes, a bed.

The room began to come into focus. It was the smell that alerted Gold to his location. The unmistakable antiseptic smell of a hospital.

The beeping, Gold soon realised, was the monitor that he appeared to be wired-up to. He looked down and saw he was wearing a hospital-style light blue gown. His head ached.

"Welcome back, genius."

A female voice. The attorney.

Gold struggled to raise himself from the bed and, with an effort that surprised him, managed to lift himself a few inches off the mattress. Lesley-Ann was sitting on a chair in the corner of his hospital room.

"There he is. The man of the moment. Blue really suits you . . . brings out the jaundice in your eyes."

Gold attempted a response.

"Easy, tiger. Keep the monologues to a minimum. How ya feeling?"

"Where . . . am . . . I?"

"How original. You're in Paris. We've just had a fabulous dinner, took in a show and we're back in the hotel."

"Huh?"

"You're in a damn hospital, you moron. Where do you think you'd be? Palm Springs?"

Gold finally managed to speak. "How long have I –"

"Been worrying the shit out of us? Three days. To be precise, three days and three nights. Where the hell did you get to?"

Gold felt horribly confused.

"I . . . I don't understand."

"No shit. *You* don't understand? How dy'a think *we* all feel? One minute we're walking through the woods, the next minute you're gone, vanished . . . vamoosed."

"What do you mean? I don't follow you."

The attorney stood up and walked to Gold's bedside.

"Follow? Very droll. Like I said, Vasco da Gama, one second we're all following the trail in the forest, the next . . . you're gone."

"But you found me, right?"

"Duh! Yes. We did. After three days!"

Gold sat fully up in bed, wincing with the effort.

"Are you saying that I was gone for three days? Do you mean three hours?"

Lesley-Ann pulled a face. "What part of three days are you not following? Is it the numeral three or the noun days?"

"I don't get it. I was right there with you. Then I saw . . . oh crap!"

Gold stopped dead in his tracks. The attorney leaned forward.

"You saw the what? What did you see, Nick?"

Gold hesitated.

"I'm waiting, Mr Invisible Man."

"I saw The Gate."

There was a pause. Then Lesley-Ann spoke indignantly.

"Oh, for God's sake! We *all* saw the stupid gate! Piece of rusted out old shit. Big deal."

Gold frowned.

"Rusted? Old? What are you talking about? It shone. It was dazzling. It gave off the most incredible light."

The attorney's face hardened. "Oh great. You've got concussion. I'll get a doctor. I thought you'd got away with it too easy."

Gold reached out and grabbed the sleeve of her leather jacket.

"Wait, wait, wait! I'm fine. A bit muzzy but I'm fine. OK . . . a bit achy too but really, that's it. I'm not . . . er . . . delirious. I know what I saw. Bloody hell, what's everyone's obsession with Elvis today, Lesley-Ann? I wasn't on a UFO, I didn't see The Greys, I wasn't abducted. I didn't have alien probes up my arse. I *know* what I saw . . . and *who*."

Lesley-Ann removed Gold's hand from her sleeve.

"OK. It's the meds, exposure, you've been in the forest for three days, I get it. I do. Get some rest and I'll come back and see you when you're not babbling."

Gold, despite his condition, lost it.

"Don't you bloody well patronise me! I am *not* babbling. I've never felt saner. Get Arnie Woolfson in here. If you're too stupid to listen, maybe he will. Go on, piss off!"

The attorney gave Gold a look that would have cut through six inches of lead and walked out of the hospital room.

Gold lost track of time again. He watched the TV that hung from his wall, nurses came and went, adjusting a drip here, administering a pill there and slowly the aches in his body subsided.

After a few hours, well, he thought it felt like a few hours, the veteran newspaperman, Arnie Woolfson and the attorney, Lesley-Ann Trobe, returned to Gold's hospital room.

Gold had an urgent question for both of them.

"Guys, something very urgent has been on my mind. Who the hell's paying for the hospital?"

The two visitors exchanged glances. This was, after all, America, where unlike the UK, healthcare is a luxury alongside Fabergé Eggs or beach houses in Malibu.

Woolfson answered. "Who do you think? *You* are. We filled in the forms as much as we could. You have travel insurance we assumed, so that'll have health cover, right?"

Trobe chimed in. "Hope ya ain't expecting us to chip in. This is gonna cost a-plenty."

Gold wasn't particularly reassured by these responses, but even in his still-befuddled state, he seemed to recall Good Foot Productions insisting he had adequate medical cover on his travels. Larry seemed surprisingly adamant on that point.

"So kid, you feeling up to telling us what in the name of tarnation happened out in the forest. You scared the crap out of us."

Gold smiled at Woolfson. At least he seemed pleased to see him.

"Sure. I'll tell you, but I just don't think you're going to believe me. And I'm not telling the police the same story. As far as the authorities are concerned I got lost, or passed out . . . I dunno . . . something like that."

"Try us," added Lesley-Ann dryly.

It was now or never. Either they would think him certifiable under whatever Mental Health Act applied in Pennsylvania – or they would believe him. Gold drew a breath like a diver standing on the high-dive board and plunged in, head first.

He told them everything. Every last detail. He omitted nothing. There was no point. He was in too deep now. He seemed to be talking for a very long time. He only stopped his monologue to take badly-needed sips of water.

Eventually, he finished. He felt drained.

His visitors said nothing. Their faces were masks of incredulity. The room seemed to fill with the hum and occasional beeps of the monitor linked to Gold's arm.

It was Lesley-Ann who finally broke the silence.

"Are all you Brits this fucked-up? And I used to think my ex was a fantasist. Jesus Christ, you really, I mean *really*, need help."

Gold lay back on his pillows. Of course. Why would any sane person believe such a tale?

Arnie Woolfson cleared his throat in a theatrical manner, the way nervous people do when about to speak in public.

"I believe you."

Gold looked at him with incredulity. "What? Really? You do?"

Lesley-Ann muttered something softly that sounded like you must be kidding.

"Yes, Nick. I do. I believe you. You know why? Because no one in their right mind would make up a story so implausible, so crazy and expect anyone to believe a single word of it. So either you are the best straight-faced liar since Mr 'I did not have sexual relations with that woman' Clinton or you belong in a secure mental facility . . . or you're telling the truth. I'm opting for the last one."

Gold replied. "It is the truth. Every word of it. And believe me when I say I don't want it to be."

"Oh, what? You don't want to wear a red cape and be The Gatekeeper? You don't wanna save the entire world?" Lesley-Ann's tone was dripping with vitriol.

Gold really didn't need this. "No, actually, I *don't* want to be The Gatekeeper, I have no idea what I am supposed to do, I haven't the faintest notion how to save the world, I'm still hoping it's all a huge mistake."

"The only mistake is me wasting days of my time on this bullshit wild goose chase. Arnie, you do what you want, I'm outta here. I've got a client to get off a murder rap. Nick, may I thank you for making me realise just how normal I am. Right now, I'm blowing this popstand."

With that, Lesley-Ann Trobe, attorney-at-law, stood up and walked rapidly out of the room, not bothering to close the door.

Gold suddenly felt utterly drained, a level of exhaustion he'd never experienced before.

"I'll come and see you in the morning, Nick. Pay no heed to her. She's a lawyer. They're all sonsofbitches. You get some rest now, y'hear kid? Tomorrow's another day. You've been to hell and back . . . literally. Things will seem clearer in the morning. They always do. G'night Nick."

With that, Arnie Woolfson also left the room.

Nick Gold, saviour of earth, was quite alone. For some inexplicable reason, he found himself crying softly.

TWENTY-THREE

"So shall the world go on, To good malignant, to bad men benign, Under her own weight groaning."
– John Milton, Paradise Lost

The Uber dropped Lesley-Ann Trobe off at the bar close to her apartment. It was her regular hangout, a typical bar to be found in a thousand towns across the states. It wasn't exactly Cheers but the bartender knew her name and preferences. The moment he saw her enter, he started to prepare her regular drink – a Grey Goose vodka tonic, with ice of course, and a healthy slice of lime. She looked pissed, her normally attractive face furrowed with an expression that proclaimed very clearly Leave Me Alone.

"Rough day LAT?" enquired the barman. He could always engage her in conversation.

"Yeah, Stevie, you could say that. You ever had much to do with English guys? I mean, are they all screwed up off the scale or what?"

The barman shrugged enigmatically. "Nah. Not really. Met a few. They were OK I guess. Wanted warm beer for christsake. Told 'em we serve it cold like nature intended. Shall I set you up another?"

He motioned to the V&T that LAT was demolishing.

"Thanks. I kinda need it tonight."

The attorney sipped her drink and motioned to Stevie to bring over some salted pretzels in a bowl.

"Yeah, finding that Brit after three days was a lucky break, huh?" the barman said. "Amazing the guy survived."

Lesley-Ann nodded. "Amazing. The little shit just won't die. The biggest comeback since Cher."

She sipped her drink and ate the pretzels. Her mind was elsewhere.

"So, you know him? The Brit? He grinding your gears, or what?"

Another slug of the vodka. "Oh yeah. Grinding them and wearing them right out. I thought Brits were, you know, like meant to be smart, or formal, clever, you know, like that Stephen Fry guy, but this one . . . Jeez, he must have been in the bathroom when they were handing out brains. I've never known anyone talk such garbage morning, noon and night. It never stops. I mean, Stevie, between you and me, I think he's as crazy as they come."

The bartender. Always a mixture of philosopher, therapist, adviser and best-ever buddy. Usually after a few drinks.

"So why'd ya hang around with him?"

A perfectly logical enquiry.

"I hang around with this douchebag . . . no, wait, he hangs around with me. Yeah, that's it. And the reason is I gotta win this goddam case. I gotta get Loretta off the hook. Or she's gonna fry. I can feel it."

The barman was polishing glasses and putting them neatly back on the mirrored shelves behind him.

"Ya think she did it? I do. I think that crazy bitch did it, no offence Lesley-Ann."

"Hmm. None taken. You know what? I just don't know. But that doesn't matter. My job is to defend her in court and I'm gonna do just that."

Her words were now very slightly slurred.

The attorney and the bartender exchanged views, exchanged drinks, discussed the state of American politics, talked about whether a person really can bite the face off another – and if so, did it taste like chicken? – and ate salted pretzels. A typical scene in any bar across America.

"Hey, I don't know if you've noticed, Counselor, but you're

now the only person in the joint, so it's probably time to go. Whaddya say?"

Lesley-Ann looked at her watch. "Oh crap. Sorry, Stevie. Didn't know it was so late. I'll call an Uber and head home. Thanks for listening."

The night air outside the bar did little to refresh Lesley-Ann. She had downed several drinks in pretty quick succession. Three? Four? She couldn't remember. And Steve was pretty generous with the vodka measures.

She glanced at her phone. The Uber app indicated that the driver, having initially been two minutes away, was now 15 minutes from arriving.

"Shit! At this time of night. Really?"

In a decision that was partly coerced by the alcohol, the lateness of the hour, and her unwillingness to stay waiting for a car that might now never come, Lesley-Ann started to walk home. After all the recent drama, a little R&R and normality like walking was much to be welcomed.

A few minutes later, as she passed a darkened doorway of a furniture store, a voice called out from the shadows.

"Hey lady, you got any spare change?"

Lesley-Ann paused, turned and could make out a vagrant, his features obscured by the dimly-lit shop entrance, sitting on the step of the store. As it happened, she had used the last of her change on the cigarette machine in the bar. And she wasn't going to split a twenty.

"I'm really sorry, but I haven't. I'll catch you next time."

The shape in the darkness moved.

"Oh come on lady. It wouldn't kill ya to give me some goddam change. Come on."

"If I had it, I'd give it to you. But I really don't. Sorry."

Lesley-Ann walked on, picking up her pace.

The dark shape stood up and stepped out of the shadows. He called to her as she walked up the street.

"How's ya boyfriend doin' in the hospital? Dumbass Brit."

Lesley-Ann froze. How the hell did a vagrant know about Nick? But it was more than that. The voice was menacing, snarling, angry. The streets were deserted. It was late. This wasn't the time to be alone. There was something very off about the vagrant. She started to walk even faster, willing herself not to run. Instinctively, Lesley-Ann knew the vagrant was now following her, the sound of his footsteps echoing off the closed shops.

"Hey you. Where the fuck you running off to? I'm talking to you, you nosey fucking lawyer bitch." The voice was gruff, deep and very menacing.

Despite being at least twenty yards ahead of him, quite inexplicably in an instant, the vagrant was standing right in front of her.

"You snoop, you pry, you meddle, you just can't leave it alone, can you?" The alcohol in her system, the lateness of the hour and the sheer shock were all contributing to slowing down her reactions.

Then, in the street light, she saw his face.

Was he wearing a Halloween mask? To her mounting horror, she realised that what she was staring at was his face, not a fright mask . . . a face whose eyes shone with hatred, widely dilated and dancing pupils, wherein was located pure evil.

But that wasn't what made Lesley-Ann Trobe want to scream out loud.

The face wasn't human.

Perhaps it had been once, but it wasn't now.

Maggots crawled in and out of its mouth. The skin on its face hung like strips of pastrami, dangling as it moved its head. And the smell. It was the overpowering stench of putrefaction, of rotting flesh that belonged in a coffin deep in the ground.

Lesley-Ann fought not to vomit.

The creatures's expression, if that was what it was, was that of a rabid dog as it attacks. The mouth grimaced in unadulterated fury. Then she saw the teeth as the vagrant brought his head closer to hers. His breath was as fetid as a sewer and made her gag again. Another trick of the light and the martinis? No. The teeth were triangular, pointed, serrated like . . . like a shark's. It seemed to her, as a thousand thoughts raced through her mind, that the man's mouth expanded to allow the teeth to move forward, to expose them further so that they could fulfil their potential for utter carnage.

Finally, the adrenalin kicked in.

"OK. OK. You can take what you want. Stop. Please. Stop."

But it didn't want to stop. It could smell blood and fear. It could see her heart racing in her chest. It could feel her terror.

"Do you know what I am, Lesley-Ann? Do you? Do you know where I've come from . . . just for you? I want to rip your face clean off. I can taste it right now. Sweet. Succulent. And I wanna do that so bad. But I won't. Not allowed. Not right now. Later."

Somehow the lawyer managed to speak in a whisper.

"What do you want?"

The creature in front of her moved its mouth, baring the pointed teeth even more. "What I want is for you, and the old man at the newspaper office and your Brit boyfriend, to fuck off. What I want is for you to stop whatever you think you're doing. I want the Brit gone. I want you to leave it . . . all of it . . . alone. Ya hear me? You leave it be."

The attorney managed to nod. She was unable to speak.

The shock of this made her knees buckle. As much as she wanted to run, she found herself kneeling on the sidewalk, trying to gulp air into her lungs. The creature stood over her. She closed her eyes tight, willing this to end.

Had the shock affected her hearing? The crude rasping voice changed. Now it was deep, almost re-assuring yet both threatening and commanding. Perhaps it had affected her sense of smell, too. The repulsive, rancid breath of the attacker seemed to have been replaced by the unmistakable scent of very expensive aftershave.

"Lesley, Lesley, Lesley . . . there are more things in heaven and earth, Attornio, than are dreamt of in your philosophy. Some things are best left well alone. Do not be a meddlesome priest. Walk away and walk away now. Tonight. You will have nothing further to do with the Englishman, or you will suffer his fate, too. And that seriously won't be pretty. Do you understand me? Oh . . . and by the way . . . while I have your rapt attention Ms Trobe, the only reason I'm letting you live is that I may have need of you . . . defence attorneys don't grow on trees . . . but some could so easily be hanging from one. It's been, as they say, real."

Then Lesley-Ann Trobe found she was alone, kneeling on the sidewalk late at night. She struggled to control her breathing, her racing heart, the sweat pouring from her forehead and under her arms. The shock of the attack was making her feel nauseous. Her throat felt constricted. She dared to open her eyes. The street was quite deserted. Nothing moved.

Finally, her mind converged on just one thought.

Tears of relief blurred her vision. She wiped them away. In that single moment, the clarity of realisation swept through her. Whatever the vagrant was, it was not human. Was not of the earth. Was an emissary. And she knew, right there and then, that everything Nick Gold had told her was true. That from now on her life would be forever changed.

And with that thought in her mind, she vomited the entire contents of her stomach.

TWENTY-FOUR

"The childhood shows the man, As morning shows the day."
– John Milton, Paradise Regained

The next morning, Nick Gold had an unexpected visitor. He was enjoying his breakfast of cereal and yoghurt with some fresh fruit (it seemed that American hospitals served rather better fare than their British counterparts) when the door to his hospital room burst open. Despite the heavy hinge-mechanism, it was pushed open with such force that it almost hit the return wall.

"You little shit!"

Gold put down the spoon that was half-way to his mouth.

"And a good morning to you, Lesley-Ann. I can't help but observe you're in another of your famously sunny moods."

But the attorney was in no mood for badinage.

"Who the fuck *are* you? I mean who are you *really*?"

Gold looked puzzled.

"Don't give me your, I'm just a poor boy, nobody loves me."

Gold couldn't help himself. "Spare him his life from this monstrosity."

The effect was like pouring petrol onto a bonfire.

"I am fucking serious! Stop messing with me! Who are you?"

But Gold was on a roll. "Ooh-ooh, ooh-ooh . . . who are you . . . ooh-ooh."

There was something about Lesley-Ann's expression that told Gold he was about as near to being killed as he'd ever been. Time to stop poking the junk-yard dog with a stick.

"Lesley-Ann, I'm not sure what the heck you poured on your cornflakes this morning . . . acid I'm guessing . . . but I have no idea what you're asking me. You know exactly who I am. Are you drunk?"

The garden bonfire grew into the towering inferno.

"Drunk? Of course I'm not fucking drunk you moron. It's nine o'clock in the morning. Are you telling me that you're Nick Gold, you work on British TV, and you're investigating in the USA for a new TV series?"

"Yes. I'm flattered that you remembered."

"You're lying."

Now it was the patient who lost his patience.

"In case you haven't noticed, I'm in a hospital bed. From that you may safely deduce, Columbo, that I'm not very well. Apparently, I was lost in one of your delightful forests for three sodding days and nights. I nearly died. So do me an enormous personal favour and take yourself, and your attitude, the hell out of here before I call a nurse and have you thrown out."

The tirade seemed to quench the fire. The blazing light went out of the attorney's eyes.

Gold spoke after a moment. "Would you care to tell me what this Spanish Inquisition is all about? Or are we just feeling a bit PMT?"

"Don't you fucking *dare* go there!"

"I'll take that as a no, then. So, what?"

LAT sat down on a chair by the bed. On closer inspection, Gold realised she looked terrible. She was, in the words of a very old song he recalled his Dad liked, a whiter shade of pale.

"Something . . . happened last night. Something I can't explain. But it changed my life."

"Well, those Jehovah Witnesses are damn compelling."

Without warning, Lesley-Ann lashed out at Gold, striking him hard on the chest. He defended himself as she tried to hit his face with clenched fists.

"Jesus! Back off, you crazy bitch! Stop it! Calm down for God's sake!"

Saying calm down to anyone in the history of humanity has never, ever worked.

Gold gripped her wrists to stem the onslaught. This was insane. Hopefully she wasn't planning to change careers and become a hospital visitor. The last fight he'd had with a girl was at school when he insisted that Oasis were a better band than the Spice Girls.

Lesley-Ann suddenly did the utterly unexpected. She calmed down. It was as if all the energy had instantly drained from her body. She slumped back into the chair and sort of sat there. A dishevelled heap of misery and spent anger.

"Can I get you a cup of tea?" As any Englishman will tell you, tea solves everything from a broken manicured fingernail to global conflict.

To Gold's surprise, Lesley-Ann replied, "Yes, that would be nice, thank you."

Gold found this more disturbing than the assault. He rang the bell, a nurse entered, and he very politely asked for tea for two. Great hospital.

"I'm sorry if I made light of what happened to you . . . whatever it was. I apologise. I'm a little –"

"Shit?"

"I was going to say out of sorts. So, are you going to tell me or what?"

Gold then listened to one of the strangest monologues he'd ever heard in his life. The flow was only interrupted by the timely arrival of the tea. Unlike the UK, there were no obligatory biscuits.

After she finished recounting her story, the room was filled with silence.

They sipped their tea as if Lesley-Ann had just described a day shopping at Bloomingdales. The silence was only occasionally broken by Gold's very English clearing of the throat noises, much beloved at awkward dinner parties or blind dates.

"So . . . er . . . apart from that, how was your evening?"

Lesley-Ann spat out a mouthful of tea. "You are such a total ass!"

Gold smiled, partly because the tension had been broken, but mostly because the tea-spitting was pure comedy gold. He struggled to be a little more comfortable in the hospital bed, not renowned for their let's-stay-in-bed-all-day-and-watch-TV-and-read-the-papers level of cosiness.

"So what now?" asked the lawyer.

"Oh. Sorry. I thought for a second there, you were going to plump up my pillows."

Lesley-Ann pulled a face. "What is it with you Brits? Are you all obsessed with sex?"

Gold stared. "What? Er, no. Plumping my pillows is not a euphemism. It means re-arranging my pillows . . . the ones on my bed."

Was the attorney actually blushing now?

"Yeah, I knew that . . . obviously," came the lame response.

Gold shifted once again. "Now? Well, I guess you ought to get on with saving your client from a lethal injection, and as soon as I'm feeling a little better, I'll be on my way."

Lesley-Ann Trobe looked suddenly troubled.

"What do you mean on your way? Where? When?"

Gold was puzzled by her reaction. No one ever said he was a relationship guru.

"As soon as I feel OK again . . . like tomorrow or the day after. Depends on flights."

"Flights?" She seemed surprised.

"Yes. Flight. As in airplane. I wasn't planning on walking to Turkmenistan."

The lawyer leaned forward in the hospital chair. "Turk what? Is that even a place?"

"No, I thought I'd inject myself into a Tintin adventure. Bless you Americans and your fabulous, all-encompassing knowledge of geography. Yes, it is a place. And that's where I'm going."

There was a pause. Gold instantly knew it was the quiet before the storm, in the same way you knew that thunder would follow a lightning flash.

It started very quietly.

"That's where *we're* going."

Gold looked at Lesley-Ann with an expression that combined incredulity and annoyance.

"We? Excuse me? *We?* That is *not* going to happen. You cannot be my wingman any more, Maverick. It's been nice knowing you . . . well, we both know I'm lying here . . . but this trip doesn't concern you. The production company will not pay for you to tag along and I'm sure as hell not springing for it. So I think your idea just fell at the first fence."

Gold lay back on his un-plumped pillows, out of breath from his rant.

"You're amazing, Nick."

Gold was stunned.

"Really?"

"Yes, really. The way you can insert so many film references and bullshit metaphors into one sentence. Amazing. Listen up, Indiana fucking Jones, if you weren't in hospital, I would lay one on you for that remark. Not my business? Really? Some fucking freak with teeth out of *Jaws 2* threatens to eat my face right off but it's not my business? You disappear in a forest for three fucking days –"

"Lesley-Ann, do you have to swear all the time?"

"Fuck you. Listen to me. You disappear for three days and nights basically in front of our eyes and just re-appear like magic and it's not my business? You recognise a guy in a photo who's been dead for a billion years yet you met him in Turkey recently and it's none of my business? My client is on trial for a murder she apparently didn't commit and it's still none of my business? You wanna run all that by me again?"

For once Gold had no pat response to stem the flow of the tirade.

"So that'll be a no then, Counselor?"

It was a blessing that the door opened and in walked Arnie Woolfson, looking even more dishevelled than usual if such a thing were possible.

"Hi kids. What gives?"

Four little words. Normally innocuous, Today, not so much.

Woolfson sat in total silence as Trobe told her grotesque tale, leaving out none of the detail. Truth be told Gold started to feel pretty queasy when she got to the face like pastrami strips part. After ten minutes, the attorney stopped and looked at the veteran newspaperman. He sat motionless. Then, very gently, his shoulders began to shake. The shaking grew in intensity and they realised, to their astonishment, that Arnie Woolfson, hardened journalist, was crying. Tears were streaming from his eyes and down his cheeks. He reached into his jacket and pulled out a handkerchief, dabbing it at his eyes.

It was touching. And it was really embarrassing, especially for Gold, who despite his own transgression, was aware that men are prohibited by law from crying in the United Kingdom.

It was Lesley-Ann who broke the awkward silence.

"You OK, Arnie?"

The newspaperman put his handkerchief away and looked at her, his eyes still moist.

"I'm sorry 'bout that ya'll. It kinda got to me. It's weird you know, to learn suddenly that a hardened world-weary cynic like you now believes me."

"Gee! Well, thanks for the compliment, Arnie."

Woolfson ignored the sarcasm, or maybe Americans really just didn't get irony.

"I've endured years and years of people calling me a crank, a nutjob, a goddam ol' fool, but I was right . . . I. Was. Right."

His voice trailed off.

Lesley-Ann gently put her hand on his arm.

"Yeah, Arnie . . . you were right."

Gold found some words to throw into the mix. "Yes, it's a bit overpowering when you've been vindicated after enduring derision for eons."

Lesley-Ann looked at him. "Jesus . . . did they give you a thesaurus enema this morning?"

"Guys. I don't know what to say. This is just extraordinary. What do you plan to do next, Nick? Follow it up?"

Lesley-Ann inwardly bridled at being left out but internalised her displeasure. Badly.

"I'm going . . . actually it seems *we're* going . . . to Turkmenistan. I'm pretty sure that's where the next gate is."

Arnie Woolfson asked, "How come? What makes you so sure?"

Nick grunted. "I'm not entirely sure. It's a hunch. A feeling. A gut instinct."

"Yeah, we get it, Nostradamus," chipped in the attorney, still simmering with quiet pissed-offness.

Gold continued unabashed. "There is a fire over there. It's huge, I mean like really enormous."

"Why don't they call the local fire crew? Won't it be out by the time we get there?" asked Lesley-Ann.

"Unlikely," replied Gold, "it's been burning since 1971. Scientists set fire to it . . . allegedly . . . and it's been burning ever since. It was an oil exploration site and then it all went tits up."

"It went what?" demanded Lesley-Ann.

"It went exceptionally wrong. OK? There was an almighty explosion, so the story goes, and everyone on the oil exploration site was killed. All except one guy."

"Lucky him," murmured Arnie.

"Not so much. The experience apparently drove him quite mad."

"In what way?" asked the reporter.

"Oh . . . he told everyone he could . . . that he saw demons coming out of the crater."

TWENTY-FIVE

"A dungeon horrible, on all sides round, As one great furnace flamed; yet from those flames No light; but rather darkness visible Served only to discover sights of woe"

– John Milton, Paradise Lost

Gold had been musing, while recuperating in hospital, how he could best utilise the services, the experience and knowledge of Arnie Woolfson. He had come to like, even admire, the grizzled veteran journalist. He was pugnacious, truculent and determined, qualities that Gold had ascribed to himself. One thing was for sure, Arnie was a great researcher. Of that, there was no doubt. He dug in the way old school journalists used to do. For Arnie, skimming a few pages on the Internet did not count as full research. He was a 'let's go to the library, let's talk to people' kind of guy.

Later that day, Gold called Arnie Woolfson from his hospital room.

"Arnie? It's Nick Gold here. You OK?"

He didn't bother to wait for a response.

"Been thinking and wonder if you could do me a favour?"

Again no pause.

"I'm stuck here for a little longer but I don't want the trail to go cold. I'm sure, as a journalist, you understand that."

Finally a response.

"Nick, my young friend, stop with the bullshit. I'm too old and too damn tired to listen to it. Just tell me what you need and skip the pre-amble, son."

Son? Gold was irritated at being patronised, but the prescribed sedatives kept him in check.

"I need you to dig up everything you can on one Anatoly Semenov, the survivor of the '71 explosion in the desert. Background, history, family et cetera."

"Oh gee, Nick. Thanks for explaining what I'm supposed to do. I've only been doing this job since before you were even crapping in your diapers. I'm in the office now, I'll stay late, might as well use their internet and electricity rather than mine. I've got other stuff I gotta do as well. I'll call y'all in the morning."

Hours later and Arnie Woolfson was still in the offices of *The York Dispatch*. It was now late and the offices were pretty much deserted.

In a far corner, a cleaner was on her cell phone talking to her son making sure that he was finishing his homework and that there was pizza in the fridge. She was a woman of indeterminate age, anywhere between thirty-five and fifty, her careworn face indicating years of unrelenting toil that had been the hallmark of her life.

"Alejandro, don't you go ordering no more pizza., finish what's left. If you're still hungry, there's some hotdogs and subrolls. Mama will be back in an hour. *Te amo. Sé bueno.*"

Woolfson was oblivious to this maternal conversation. He was on the trail. Research was the lifeblood of Woolfson. He thrived on it. There were always so many avenues to explore, one fact leading to another until the full story emerged and could be exposed. Like so many Americans, Arnie had heeded the warnings of the Surgeon-General and quit smoking. Seated at his desk, keying in search requests, his fingers longed to hold a Lucky Strike, but not even vaping was allowed in the office. Woolfson referred to the rules as the workplace health fascists when his craving for nicotine was particularly strong. Assured that her son was not going to send out for a Domino's pepperoni with cheese stuffed crusts, the cleaner returned to her work.

Arnie was now quite alone. The next shift of eagle-eyed news-hounds weren't due for several hours. This was how he liked it. Peace and quiet. The perfect atmosphere for concentrated thinking and research. No distractions.

So he was not best pleased when the screen on his ancient MacBook began to flicker.

"Fuck! Not now!" he said to the offending machine. *The sheer impudence of inanimate objects.*

The screen settled down. Arnie keyed in some search parameters and waited for the results.

They appeared.

'Hello Arnie.'

"What the hell?" *I don't even have emails or messenger open.*

He tried again.

'Persistent old bastard, aren't you?' appeared on the screen.

"Leapin' Lazarus! What the hell?"

If in doubt, re-boot.

Arnie switched off the laptop, waited the obligatory sixty seconds, and powered it up again.

"Goddamn technology. Gimme a Remington and a sheet of paper any day."

Good. There was the familiar start up page, the icons, the task bar, the digital clock in the corner. All looked fine. As it should be.

Woolfson double-clicked on the search engine button and waited a second for it to load.

Text appeared on the screen. 'Take the hint old man. Keep your nose out. Stop now.'

The words were a red rag to an already enraged bull.

Infuriated by the hacker, Woolfson slapped the edge of the screen in frustration.

"Fucking idiot kids!"

Again, he keyed in a search question.

No text appeared this time. At last.

The screen was filled with film footage of the Darvaza gas crater, the inferno at the natural gas field in Derweze, Turkmenistan. It was spectacular. Arnie Woolfson stared at the screen as the true immensity of the fire that had raged since 1971 was brought home in vivid technicolour.

The brain is an extraordinary organ. Just by watching the images on screen, his office felt hotter. It was as if he could actually smell the burning gas.

"It's quite something, isn't it?"

The voice made Woolfson jump. He thought he was entirely alone. Looking up from the laptop screen, he saw the cleaner standing there. He hadn't heard her approach. In fact, he'd hardly noticed her before now.

"What?" he replied.

"The Davarza Gas Crater . . . it's quite a sight. You can almost feel the heat and flames just by looking at it."

The cleaner's voice no longer bore her strong Latino accent of earlier. Now it was cultured. Calm. Authoritative.

Woolfson was taken aback. "Er, yeah, I guess so. You know about it then, do you? I'm researching it."

The cleaner nodded her head. "Yes, Arnie. We know you are."

Woolfson was alarmed. This wasn't right. Damn it, it wasn't right at all.

"We? Who the hell are y'all?"

"I'm a cleaner. I clean things. That's my job. Cleaning stuff up. You know, offices, homes . . . people who get in the way."

Woolfson was now beginning to feel genuinely frightened. There was something exceptionally intimidating about this woman, yet her appearance, if at odds with her voice, was entirely normal.

"I reckon I don't follow you right now, ma'am," said Arnie Woolfson as he instinctively moved away a few inches.

"Ah, but we follow you, Arnie. That's the point. And, to be

perfectly frank, you're becoming an irritation, a nuisance, like a damn mosquito that keeps buzzing around."

Woolfson was really struggling now. It was all so confusing. An Hispanic cleaner with the voice of a British newsreader, the fact that she knew him, the growing nature of her threats.

"I think y'all better leave, ma'am," said Woolfson, mustering all of his rapidly waning courage.

The cleaner smiled. "Oh, I will be leaving. But not just yet, Arnie. You see, you just would not take the hint. We tried. We really did. But oh no, the great investigative reporter, the legendary newshound, just had to go on digging. Shoving his snout in where it truly did not belong. So now, you need to be cleaned up."

Woolfson was by now deeply frightened.

"Get ya'll the fuck out of here, you crazy bitch."

"Nice language. Not very politically correct if I may say. But then you always were an old-fashioned sort of guy. So I thought an old-fashioned departure might be in order. You like fire, Arnie? You liked looking at that huge inferno out in the desert? It is rather fascinating, isn't it?"

Woolfson started to back away from the cleaner.

"Gosh, just look at this office. What a mess. Paper, paper everywhere. One match and this place would go up like a 4th July firework. And speaking of fireworks, let's get this party started, shall we?"

Without warning, and without the cleaner even seeming to move, Arnie Woolfson was thrown back against a metal filing cabinet. His arms were roughly pulled behind him and bound to the handle of one of the metal drawers.

"What in damnation?!" he yelled.

"History. You like history Arnie, don't you? Always going on about the good old days. How things were so much better back then. Well, how about we go back . . . way back . . . I thought Oxford in England would be appropriate. Isn't that where your best pal Nick Gold studied? Of course, he wasn't there in 1555.

That's even before your time, old man. But what a time that was. It was . . . glorious. The Oxford Martyrs, Hugh Latimer, Thomas Crammer and Nicholas Ridley. And Arnie, just like you, they just didn't know when to quit."

"I can quit. For god's sake. I can stop. Please!" yelled Woolfson.

"Too late, I'm afraid. Dig, dig, dig. Poke, poke, poke. No. You're . . . in the way. When Latimer and Ridley were burned at the stake, the executioners were kind enough to tie little bags of gunpowder around their necks so their agony of being burnt alive wasn't too prolonged. Nice touch. But I'm all out of gunpowder today. Lemon Scent Pledge, dusters yes, but sadly for you, no gunpowder. So unfortunately, this is going to be agonising. What can one say in these circumstance?"

Woolfson was sobbing now. "Please . . . I'm begging you . . . please . . . don't do this . . ."

"It's all your fault, Arnie. Meddling around with things way above your pay grade, you, that Englishman and the lawyer. The Three Martyr-teers."

The cleaner looked around Woolfson's office and as she did so, the papers that were on every surface started to fly across it, as if blown by a strong wind. They piled up around Woolfson's feet and then covered first his legs, his waist, until they reached his shoulders.

"Stop it. Please!" pleaded Woolfson.

Woolfson's pitiful entreaties fell on deaf ears. The cleaner intoned, "Be of good cheer, Ridley; and play the man. We shall this day, by God's grace, light up such a candle in England, as, I trust, will never be put out."

With that, she casually poured liquid from a container onto a duster, lit the duster with a single match, and threw it onto the pyre of paper.

Woolfson howled in more pain than he knew was possible as the flames roared into life around him.

The cleaner stood watching impassively as if seeing a man being burnt alive a few feet in front of her was an everyday event and of no particular consequence. Woolfson's agonised screams, it would seem, were of no more interest than a dog barking in the distance.

Woolfson's flesh began to melt, the seeping fat from his tissues acting as an accelerant, causing the flames to engulf his head. Soon, but not soon enough, he quietened as the shock, pain and trauma rendered him mercifully unconscious. The smoke and carbon monoxide inhalation would finish the job.

The cleaner turned away and walked out of Woolfson's office into the main work area of the newspaper. She took out her phone and dialled her son once again. "Alejandro, is Mama, you done your homework like I told you? *Bueno.* OK, *Bomboncita*, Mama is finished early, so I will see you soon, yes, *mi corazón? Ahorre una pizza para su madre. Te veré pronto. Te quiero.*"

And with that, she dusted a corner of a desk that she'd missed earlier and, like Elvis, quietly left the building.

When the early morning shift came into the offices of *The York Dispatch,* they found their veteran newspaperman sitting in his chair, his head slumped back. The office was untouched.

The York County Coroner, a Miss C. Sumeray, pronounced the cause of death as cardiac arrest.

A few days after the autopsy, Gold and Lesley-Ann found themselves at 700 North George Street in York Pennsylvania at Prospect Hill cemetery. Nick had been discharged from hospital and, true to their word, Good Foot Productions had covered the enormous medical bills through their medical insurance policy.

Arnie Woolfson's funeral was well-attended. The newspaperman was well-liked and begrudgingly respected by his peers and co-workers. His widow seemed inconsolable and hung desperately onto the arms of two younger family members.

Nick and Lesley-Ann stood towards the back of the mourners at the graveside. They had a very different reason to be mourning the loss of their colleague.

“Cardiac arrest? You satisfied with that?” asked Gold.

“I know this coroner, she’s good. Knows her stuff,” replied LAT, “but am I satisfied? Are you kidding me? You disappear for three days, I get stalked on the street by the Phantom of the Opera and now Arnie just happens to drop dead? What the hell have we got ourselves into, Nick?”

“I know. You think we should quit while we’re still vaguely ahead?”

The attorney looked at him with her piecing green eyes. “Fuck that!”

TWENTY-SIX

"Knowledge forbidden? Suspicious, reasonless. Why should their Lord Envy them that? Can it be a sin to know? Can it be death?"
– John Milton, Paradise Lost

A few days later Gold and Trobe were on board a flight to Ashgabat. Both were still shocked at Arnie Woolfson's sudden demise. They were also astounded to learn that there was a flight from Pennsylvania that covered the six thousand three hundred miles in a snappy thirteen hours and six minutes. Gold had been in lengthy WhatsApp conversations with Larry, persuading the owner of Good Foot Productions that this was money well-spent – in fact, the results of his recce were beyond belief.

It wasn't an easy sell. But when he had the bit between his teeth, Gold was an exceptionally persuasive salesman. It was the part about a crater the size of Soho that proved to be the clincher, that and the endless photos that Gold had been sending from his mobile phone. Oddly enough, none of them featuring Lesley-Ann Trobe.

Like most things in life, the flight was anything but direct. The Turkish Airlines plane stopped in Toronto and Istanbul before landing at its final destination of Ashgabat. In addition to the long flight and seemingly endless stopovers, the nine-hour time difference made Gold and Lesley-Ann's ability to deal with the epic journey even harder. There are only so many films you can watch on a plane before you want to open the exit door at 35,000 feet and step outside. Luckily, the plane had its full complement of screaming babies, truculent toddlers and large passengers who did their utmost to block the aisles and occupy the toilets for unseemly long periods of time.

Gold had booked them into the Ozugkent Hotel which looked great online and pretty good in real life. The pair were so exhausted by the journey that a B&B in Skegness would have felt like paradise.

Booking the hotel had presented Gold with the first of many problems he was to encounter – the thorny issue of sleeping arrangements.

There was no way that Good Foot Productions were going to spend one single manat on Lesley-Ann Trobe. As far as they were concerned, she didn't exist. No, Gold hadn't heard of the manat either, but it turned out to be the currency of Turkmenistan.

The problem was resolved by Lesley-Ann announcing she had altered the booking and they each had their own room. This was simultaneously good and bad news, but under the circumstances Gold wasn't too fussed. After all, this was a woman whose idea of post-coital intimacy was to eat a chilli dog the size of a zeppelin and then piss off in an Uber. Gold consoled himself with this image before he fell into a deep dreamless sleep.

Next morning, after a surprisingly excellent breakfast, of which the highlight was the traditional delicious Turkmen bread called *chorek*. As Gold lived in Balham in South London, he was no stranger to artisan bread, usually a great excuse to charge eye-watering prices for so-so loaves – but these guys took bread-making to a whole new level.

Cooking *chorek* is considered an art and in a Turkmenistan house *chorek* is treated with respect as it were a special guest. A bit like Mr. Hovis. Turkmen consider bread and salt sacred – while stepping on them will bring misfortune.

Over the next few days Gold was to think he must have stepped in a pile of salt the height of the Eiger.

The hotel had made the arrangements for a hired 4x4 to be delivered to the front entrance after breakfast. With their bags stowed in the back, Gold and his jet-lagged companion set off to drive the one hundred and sixty miles to Derweze, the location of the crater.

The roads varied from superb to non-existent and the 4x4 came into its own, unlike when cruising around the rough, uncharted, mountainous terrain of Central London.

The thing about driving through a desert is each rock looks pretty much like the next one. It was barren, it was hot and service stations boasting KFC, M&S and Starbucks were noticeable by their absence.

"So how come they're letting us go to see this crater? Did you get special permission or something?" Lesley-Ann's question had cut across an Ed Sheeran song that was incongruously playing on a local radio station.

"I didn't need to. It's a tourist destination now. Over fifty thousand people have driven out to see it. It's a big deal around here."

"Why the hell would anyone except us want to see this cra –?"

The lawyer stopped talking.

"Holy fuck!"

"Ah, I see you're impressed then, or were you expecting a George Foreman BBQ?"

There was much to be impressed by.

The Darvaza gas crater was, by any standard, impressive. Scary. Huge. Volatile. A diameter of 226 feet – the size of an American football field – and a depth of 98 feet.

For once, Lesley-Ann stopped being a lawyer and became a tourist.

"Shall we go see?" enquired Nick.

She nodded. They left the 4x4 and walked towards the unnatural phenomena. The heat of the Karakum Desert was powerful and the sun burned down unrelentingly. In Gold's head, the theme tune from *Lawrence of Arabia* started to play.

"How we gonna find him? This guy you talked about on the plane. The survivor. Do we have an address?"

"Sure we do. I just Googled lone survivor of huge gas blast in remote desert and up it came, plus his email address."

There was a delicious second before Lesley-Ann realised Gold was being his usual sarcastic self.

"Hilarious. Would you mind actually answering my question or are you planning on being Don Rickles all day?"

Gold smiled in response. She'd referenced the late Donald J Rickles! There might be hope for them after all.

"I got the office in London to dig around and research the man I need to see . . . OK . . . *we* need to see." Gold hadn't even needed to look to feel the Defence Attorney's eyes burning into him.

"When the explosion happened back in 1971, everyone was killed – all the petro-scientists, the drilling crew, the guards – I mean *everyone*. It was a total disaster. One bloke, a kid named Anatoly Semenov, survived. He was some kind of intern or trainee kind of guy. You know, a gofer."

Lesley-Ann nodded as they stood watching the extraordinary sight in front of them.

"That's good, right?"

"Yeah. Well, good and bad. He survived all right, but the event made him crazy."

"You mean angry? At the lack of health and safety?"

Gold laughed derisively. "It was 1971. Health and safety back then was bring a lunch box to work and don't fuck up. Do you ever stop being an attorney?"

Lesley-Ann was about to retort but Gold continued without pausing.

"No, I mean crazy like crazy . . . nuts . . . off his head. He was airlifted out of here apparently and kept away from the world in a secured facility. Seemed the Russkies didn't want him talking to anyone."

Lesley-Ann turned to him.

"Why not? What were they afraid of?"

"Everything. It was a shit storm. The big, much-lauded oil discovery that was going to supply Mother Russia for the next gazillion years had literally gone up in flames – which was embarrassing enough. Dozens of highly-skilled scientists had been reduced to well-done steak, and now there was a lunatic telling anyone who'd listen that it wasn't an accident."

"You mean sabotage? Who . . . Nixon and Kissinger?"

Gold smiled to himself. "No. Even worse. The Devil."

It was hot here in the desert, but suddenly Lesley-Ann Trobe felt a shiver run down her spine.

"What? What do you mean, the Devil?"

"You know, the Devil, Lucifer, Beelzebub, the Horned One, Ozzie Osbourne, *The Omen*, *The Exorcist* –"

Trobe stopped him.

"Yeah, I got it after Lucifer, thanks. What did this Anatoly guy say that he saw that freaked out his commie pals?"

Gold gave her a very European look. "Do you ever forget you're an American? We're all pals now. Communism was a phase, you know, like a mullet hairstyle or tie-dye t-shirts. What freaked out, as you so eloquently put it, the Russians was that this kid was saying it wasn't the exploration team that caused the explosion. It came from the pit itself. And straight afterwards, the place was overrun by monsters, creatures that looked almost human but weren't. They had –"

Gold paused, realising what he was about to say wouldn't go down very well.

"Yes. They had what?"

"Teeth."

"Teeth?"

"Yes. Not teeth like you or me. Teeth like a shark, like Dracula . . . teeth that apparently ripped the entire crew to shreds. That's what killed them, not the explosion . . . according to Anatoly. But he might be a crazy-guy of course."

Lesley-Ann spun on Nick. "Were you trying to protect me? Are you kidding me? It's not 1955 anymore, or is it still that in ye olde London Town? I don't need protecting thanks. Teeth. I get it. Like the guy outside the bar that tried to kill me. Like *his* teeth . . . right?"

Nick nodded. "Yes. It sounds very similar. And it matches the story Joanne Walsh told me back in London, and what happened to me in Turkey. And let's not forget your client. There's a dental theme here all right."

"A *dental* theme? That's the best you can come up with?" Lesley-Ann shot him a look. "Please don't tell me that Anatoly Whateverhisnameis is still locked up in an asylum in Russia? I'm on the clock here Nick, I can't afford to be running around the world like some sort of Tom Hanks' side-kick in a Dan Brown movie."

"No. Obviously not. I hate those films. We've been digging deep back in Soho –"

"What's New York got to do with this?"

Gold rolled his eyes. You can take the woman out of Pennsylvania but . . .

"Soho . . . as in London Soho, not South of Houston Soho. Anatoly Semenov was finally released from Ramenskyon Psychiatric Hospital near Moscow in 2013. And guess why?"

Lesley-Ann looked blank. An expression that rarely crossed her face. "He got better? He recanted? He was going to be a contestant on *Russia's Got Talent*? I haven't the faintest idea . . . enlighten me."

Gold took out his mobile phone, keyed in a web address and handed the phone to the attorney.

As she read the article, her expression became one of incredulity. Not again. It just wasn't possible.

Fatal Fire At Moscow Psychiatric Hospital

At least 38 people were killed, including 36 patients and two doctors, after fires raged through a psychiatric hospital outside Moscow in the village of Ramenskyon, 70 miles north of Moscow in Moscow Oblast. The fire broke out on 26 April 2013 at 2:30am Moscow Time (22:30 UTC).

29 people were burned alive, killing some patients in their beds and others who were trapped by barred windows. Only three people survived, including two patients and a nurse.

The fire ignited on the 2nd floor of the two-storey building in a patient's bed. Three doctors and one nurse ran to the bed but were burned alive immediately. The fire raged through the 2nd floor and killed everyone on that floor. Six minutes later, the 2nd floor collapsed and crushed patients on the ground floor. Four minutes later, the fire services reached the hospital and spent the next three hours extinguishing the blaze. When the fire finally settled in the morning, the fire brigade broke into the building and searched for survivors but only found three injured people alive: a nurse on the 1st floor and two patients on the ground floor.

Gold took the phone back from Lesley-Ann. "And guess who was one of the two patients that survived? Step forward Mr Anatoly Semenov. So, we have a fire in an asylum in Hallam Pennsylvania and now we have a replica seventy miles outside of Moscow. Call me crazy but one might almost see a pattern emerging here."

Trobe was staring at the burning crater. If anything on earth was a living embodiment of the human visualisation of Hell, this was it. It was mesmerising.

After a short while, as the article she'd just read sank in, she spoke.

"I get that the asylum . . . hospital . . . whatever . . . burned down but why did they release Anatoly? Why not just move him to another secure facility?"

Gold turned to face her. "Because 'Tovarishch' Semenov told them that the same creatures that came out of the pit right here in the Darvaza gas crater in 1971 were sent to kill him in the Ramenskyon Psychiatric Hospital in April 2013. In short, the authorities were crapping themselves."

"But . . . it could just have been a coincidence? Wrong place, wrong time?"

Gold nodded. "Yeah, absolutely. Just like it was a coincidence that Lee Harvey Oswald knew that the President would pass by the Texas School Book Depository so he could shoot him when the route hadn't been published."

Trobe frowned. Why were the Brits still so obsessed with Kennedy's assassination? It was after all several lifetimes ago.

"To get back to the case in hand, Oliver Stone, apart from the view and topping up my tan, why are we here exactly?"

"Because," replied Nick "he came back. Anatoly Semenov came right back to where it all started for him. Here. And we are going to speak to him."

Trobe frowned. "You speak Russian?"

"*Nyet*. Not a wordski. But Comrade Semenov has learned to speak English. He had sod all else to do in the psych hospital for all those years. He also speaks German, Italian, French and, impressively, Mandarin. And how do I know this? Is The Gatekeeper psychic? No, because Anatoly publishes a blog. He won't let it go, but Putin's pals can't be arsed to use Polonium on him and laugh it off as the ramblings of a lunatic. He lives close to here."

"By the crater?" asked Lesley-Ann.

"I said he was nuts, not insane. No, of course not. A couple of miles away. Shall we go?"

They returned to the 4x4 and set off to where the offices of Good Foot Productions had discovered was the last known location of Anatoly Semenov, sole survivor of the Derweze Explosion, and one of three survivors of the Ramenskyon Hospital fire.

One might think he was an unusually lucky man.

After a few miles, using a combination of satnav, a printed map and a huge dollop of luck, Gold and Trobe arrived at a place that called itself a village but made Derweze and its three hundred and fifty inhabitants look like São Paulo. It consisted of a few ramshackle buildings where in the UK people would hesitate to store anything but their lawnmower – but out here, in the Karakum Desert, fifteen and half thousand square miles of bugger all, they passed as houses. Gold made a mental note never to moan about the size of his flat in Balham again.

He stopped the 4x4 but kept the engine running; global warning be damned, he needed the aircon.

"This must be the place."

Lesley-Ann looked at him puzzled.

"And you know this because –?"

"Visual clue number one: a satellite dish. Visual clue number two: a satellite dish. Thank you. I'm here all week."

"You're really enjoying this, aren't you! Driving around like some goddam movie hero. Look out, here comes The Gatekeeper! Working out who's gonna play you in the movie – Dwayne Johnson . . . Jason Statham?"

Gold had suddenly had his fill of the endless needling.

"Lesley-Ann, just shut up. Please! Just, for once, shut it. No, I'm not enjoying this if you must know. I was nearly killed. You were nearly killed. I'm suddenly informed by an Archangel . . . an *Archangel* no less . . . that I'm The Gatekeeper. I don't even fully know what that means. It's somehow up to me, Nick Gold from Balham, to keep the Gates of Hell closed. I haven't the first faintest fucking idea what I am supposed to do, but apparently the entire fate of humanity rests on my shoulders. You know how that feels? It sucks. Warp Factor Eight on the Suck Scale. Everything . . . but *everything* . . . I have ever believed in has been turned upside down and inside out. So, either I'm having the worst mental meltdown since Britney shaved her head, or somehow all of this is true, in which case you and I are in deep, deep, deep shit. Because I'm a TV presenter on a bogus TV series and forgive me, but when was the last time one of those saved the planet?"

He stopped, his chest rising and falling with the effort of his outburst.

Then the strangest thing happened. Without warning, Lesley-Ann Trobe, attorney at law, leant across from her seat and kissed him passionately on his mouth. It was a long, full-on kiss that seemed to last for about a month.

She sat back. Gold looked at her in total astonishment.

"When you're not being a smart-arse or a total jerk-off, when you speak the truth properly, I kinda like you, Nick."

"I'll, er, bear that in mind," was all Gold could mumble.

"Shall we go in . . . you know . . . as we're here and all?" enquired Lesley-Ann.

All Gold could do was nod.

They exited the 4x4 and the heat of the desert hit them harder than at the launderette Gold used occasionally back home.

They walked up to the door of the building (it would be too much for even a London estate agent to describe it as a house) where they'd seen the large industrial-sized satellite dish.

"Shall we ring?" asked Lesley-Ann.

"Ring? You think this place has a door bell? I'd better break it to you now, but there's unlikely to be a jacuzzi or indoor pool either."

"Fuck you!" came the witty response and without missing a beat Lesley-Ann banged on the door as if she was the Metropolitan Police on a drugs raid.

"Nice touch," added Gold dryly, still smarting.

Nothing.

The door remained closed and the heat grew more intense.

Lesley-Ann banged on the door again, if anything even harder.

A voice bellowed from the other side of the pale wooden door.

"Подожди минуту! Кто это? Что ты хочешь!?"

Gold and Trobe looked at each other. Bugger. Neither of them understood a single word. It could be anything from 'I didn't order a Tesco home delivery today' to 'I have a loaded Kalashnikov AK-47 Assault Rifle and I'm about to fire'.

It was Gold who took the initiative. "Mr Semenov? Hello. I'm Nick Gold from London . . . England . . . and I'd very much like to speak with you please."

Silence.

"Кто?"

Gold hazarded a guess.

"Nick Gold . . . from London in the UK . . . I'd like to speak with you please, Mr Semenov. We've come a very long way . . ."

"From a galaxy far, far away," added Lesley-Ann.

The tone of the voice behind the door changed.

"Какие! Ты Ник Голд. Ник Голд . . . the Paranormal Detective?"

"You have got to be fucking kidding me! He's *heard* of you?"

Gold shot her a glance. It was a mixture of pride and hurt.

"Yes, Mr Semenov. It's me. Nick Gold, Paranormal Detective. From the television series. Might we come in . . . please?"

"Jesus! Why not send him a boxed set of your DVDs while you're at it?"

The door suddenly swung open and there, in the doorframe, was Anatoly Semenov, sole survivor of the Derweze Disaster of 1971.

"Nick Gold . . . here . . . at my house! This is fantastic!"

"I think I'm gonna puke," muttered the lawyer.

Gold shook the proffered hand and introduced Lesley-Ann in a tone where the subtext said hanger-on rather than defence attorney. Never underestimate the planet-sized egos of TV presenters.

Anatoly Semenov was sixty-six-years-old; he had been just twenty when he had left Moscow for the desert. It would be fair to say that time had not been kind – but then a Russian Psychiatric Hospital has never appeared on Trip Advisor under Spas to Be Pampered In.

His grey hair was long in a heavy metal band way, and just as unkempt. There was a few days' worth of stubble on his face and the Shepard Fairey 'OBEY' Andre the Giant T-shirt seemed bizarrely out of place.

"Come in Mr Gold and Miss Towel, please."

"It's Trobe . . . Lesley-Ann *Trobe.*" The ego of lawyers was right up there with TV presenters.

They entered. Whatever they were expecting to see, this wasn't it. What the hell?

Gold had seen less equipment in a TV studio. There were screens everywhere. On one wall was a bank of computer servers with a fan attempting to cool them (Gold was puzzled how the place had electricity and concluded that Semenov must have his own petrol generator nearby). Keyboards were arranged on various rickety wooden tables, laptops were strewn around – it looked like the aftermath of a fifty per cent off sale at a branch of PC World.

Anatoly noticed the surprised expression on both his visitors' faces. He laughed. A deep, rumbling roar of a laugh.

"Surprised huh?" he said in perfect English with a slight twang of an American accent. "Not what you expected, yes?"

"Er . . . no," replied Lesley-Ann, who was struggling to take in this cornucopia of computerised wizardry.

"I like to keep low-key, yes? I keep under, how you say, the radish."

"Radar," suggested Gold helpfully.

"Yes. Forgive me. I get very few visitors from England, so my English is, what's the phrase . . . a trifle rusty."

A trifle rusty? This guy was amazing, thought Gold.

"Mr Gold . . . may I say it is great honour that you, of all people, have travelled far to come see me. I am great admirer of your television show. I liked, best of all, the one you made in, er, how you say, Borley Rectory. Very scary. I nearly poop in pants. I cannot believe that Paranormal Detective is here . . . in my home . . . in desert. What an honour."

Lesley-Ann Trobe looked like she'd just eaten gone-off shellfish and was about to vomit.

"That is very kind of you, Anatoly Semenov." (Gold had

adopted the Russian manner of addressing a person by their full name.) "It is, for us too, an honour to meet a man such as yourself. You have endured many hardships and yet you survive. You are an inspiration to us."

If Lesley-Ann looked sick before, she now resembled someone in the last stages of the plague.

"What are you, Gandalf suddenly?" muttered Lesley-Ann at Nick's flowery phraseology.

Anatoly seemed to fill the space in the room that wasn't already full of computers, screens, keyboards, servers, books, paperwork, mousepads, screen cleaning wipes, cables, headphones and everything in between. It was as though he had raided every car boot sale from here to Peckham.

"You live here?" asked Lesley-Ann, in a tone that said, *tell me you don't live in this dump where I wouldn't let my dog, if I had one, sleep overnight*.

"No moron. He has a suite at the Bellagio in Vegas. Jesus!" whispered Gold in reply.

"Yes! This my home! Pretty neat, huh?" boomed the reply, oblivious to the subtext of the question.

Neat wouldn't be the first adjective that sprang to the visitors' minds.

Gold couldn't stop staring at the vast array of equipment. It was not just extraordinary but utterly incongruous considering where they were – the middle of nowhere, and then some.

"You wonder, Mr Nick Gold, where equipment is from, yes?"

Gold shrugged in a *you got me* way.

"I buy from all over world. Online. Service very good. Sometimes I go to town to get special things."

"I'm guessing special things doesn't cover a duster and broom," muttered the attorney, earning her a sharp look of rebuke from Gold.

"Anatoly Semenov . . . forgive me for asking . . . no disrespect is intended . . . but all this equipment . . . it looks very . . . expensive," said Gold.

Lesley-Ann Trobe had had enough. "Jesus! What my companion is asking you is how the hell can you afford all of this?"

Gold rolled his eyes in embarrassment. That really was the difference between a Brit and an American. One dances around the edge and the other goes straight for the jugular.

Anatoly let out another huge, rumbling laugh. "I go to Derweze and I beg. I sit near crater and beg the tourists."

"Oh, that's awful," instantly replied Gold, his voice full of sympathy.

Again, the booming laugh.

"I'm just, how you say, fucking with you. I use crowdfunding. It work a treat."

The two visitors exchanged astonished glances.

"Crowdfunding?" asked Lesley-Ann.

"Sure. You think I live in stone age? It is easy. I set up page online and people all over world, they put in money. They love what I do. They love me. As you Americans say, 'what's not to love?' Everyone all over world love the supernatural, the . . . unexplained . . . the spikey stuff."

"Spooky. The spooky stuff," corrected Lesley-Ann. Gold was suddenly really regretting letting her tag along. Could she be any more confrontational? She was in the guy's house, not in court for god's sake.

"You like tea? Or coffee? Or drugs? I highly recommend the hashish . . . very good!"

Gold responded. "Er, no thanks. Very kind of you. Coffee would be fine. Thank you."

They were both surprised when Anatoly disappeared into another room, presumably a kitchen but it could have been a missile silo for all they knew, and returned with a Nespresso Coffee Machine. He smiled at their confusion.

"Oh, you think I come back with primus stove? No, I like this.

That George Clooney, he very handsome man, no? I like him so I buy this."

Gold thought if Gorgeous George only knew the global effect his advertising was having.

The coffee was made and poured into cups that had seen better days. Lesley-Ann didn't give a damn about protocol and wiped the cup very obviously on the tail of her denim shirt before putting it to her mouth.

"So! Why you here Mr Nick Gold, Paranormal Detective?"

Gold cleared his throat. "Anatoly, I think you can help us. We are in the middle of an investigation that, for reasons that I'll explain, has you right in the middle of it."

Anatoly Semenov's chest immediately puffed with pride. The great Paranormal Detective, Mr Nick Gold, needed *him*! This was a dream come true.

It was, naturally, Lesley-Ann who burst the ego-boosting bubble.

"Yeah . . . like you survived the explosion at the oil rig in Derweze in '71 and the fire in the nut . . . in the, er, hospital outside Moscow (like most Americans, she pronounced it Moss-Gow) back in 2013. So, what gives?"

Gold suspected that his companion was not on the shortlist for the US Diplomatic Corps but given the current situation in Washington, maybe she was first in line.

Anatoly Semenov suddenly looked grave. His face took on an expression of worn-out fatigue. But his eyes, oh his eyes, they burned with an inner fire.

"You want to ask me what happened, yes? You want to know how I, Anatoly Semenov, survived? You want truth or polite version that you would hear over your English cup of tea?"

Gold didn't wait for Little Miss Foot-in-Mouth to respond.

"Anatoloy, we have travelled tens of thousands of miles around the world to discover the truth behind the story. We think we know, but we need to hear it from you. You were there. You saw what happened, and we believe that there are people out there who don't want the truth to be told."

"Gee, Agent Mulder, is the truth still out there?"

Nick was really, really regretting bringing the sarcastic, wise-cracking attorney along now. What gem would she utter next – you guys deserved Stalin . . . the Gulags aren't as bad as Detroit . . . we shoulda nuked you over Cuba in '62?

Anatoly Semenov walked over to the coffee machine and made another expresso for himself. He took his first sip and he spoke. His voice was even, calm, even soothing. The eyes still burned, but it was clear he wanted Nick Gold from England to believe him. The woman? She could go screw herself.

He sat down at a large iMac and pressed a few keys to bring up a photo slideshow. Anatoly narrated for his visitors.

"This is Derweze oil exploration when I arrive from Moscow. I was twenty. Young. Full of the things young men dream of. But mostly I wanted to get away from home. It was not good there. My best friend from school days, Afanasy, showed me article about the oil project. Money. Sunshine. A new start. I went. Afanasy not accepted by officials. It was good. I like it. I was the person who did all the little jobs that the great scientists would not do. That were beneath them. You know, make tea, make coffee, clean kitchen area, wash down the digging equipment. I didn't care. I wasn't in grey Omsk, I was away from home, I was getting paid. I saw blue sky every morning."

"Mr Semenov, the explosion that killed everyone but you . . . what happened?" Lesley-Ann must have missed the university lecture on Subtlety and Manners in the 21st Century.

The photos on the screen continued their automatic slideshow. It showed happy, smiling young men and women, equipment, desert landscapes, a young Anatoly laughing with crew members. They had the air of twenty-year-olds without a care in the world, having fun and getting paid for it.

The exploration set-up was impressive even all these years

later – huge drilling rigs, trucks, a small village of prefab buildings, some large tents. It had been a very serious undertaking.

"That day, I was ordered to be at the drill head. I felt honoured to be given responsibility. It was not technical work you understand, mostly washing, cleaning and applying lubricant to the machinery itself. But I was young and it was better than washing up cups and plates, yes?"

Lesley-Ann adopted a more respectful tone. She might be a lawyer, but she was also smart; getting the best out of a witness was her area of specialty.

"So Anatoly, you saw the explosion up close?"

Anatoly took another rather long sip of his espresso; clearly, he needed to buy a little time before he answered. He seemed to be mentally examining what he was about to say next. When he did speak, it was in a hushed monotone.

"There was no explosion. That was story Moscow used to stop anyone talking about truth. It was story world could understand. The truth they could not handle. You know, like when Jack Nicholson he say 'The truth . . . you couldn't handle the truth,' to Tim Cruise."

"Tom. *Tom* Cruise." The American couldn't help herself.

Gold shot her another glance.

"Please tell us what happened, Anatoly. It's so important. Then we can tell you everything that we've learned." When Gold said everything he was not going to reveal that he was, apparently, The Gatekeeper. That would be like Bruce Wayne blurting out that he was Batman. Spoiler alert.

Anatoly Semenov ran a hand through his long, grey hair. Gold couldn't help but think he reminded him of Jerry Garcia or the Big Lebowski. From a pocket, Anatoly brought out a pack of local cigarettes and lit one. The pungent tobacco smoke filled the room. They didn't muck about with low-strength in Turkmenistan. Lesley-Ann coughed. Gold inwardly chuckled.

"It was normal day, yes. Sun shining. All good. Drilling going well. I listening to cassette of Rolling Stones while we work. We singing along to Mick Jagger. We feeling good. Then . . . then –"

His voice trailed off. Whatever was coming was obviously not the shipping forecast.

He took a deep breath. Would his visitors believe him? Would they think he belonged in another psychiatric hospital? His mind was made up. This was, after all, the great Paranormal Detective. He, of all people, would believe.

"Then I think I see something . . . something down by the place where the drill goes into ground. I not believe it. I call to my superior. He takes look. We both see same thing."

"What? What was it you saw?" piped up Lesley-Ann.

"A man. A man was down there. The man, he look up at me. I yell to drilling team 'stop . . . stop . . . man has fallen into drill area!' That is what I think. It was accident. We save life, yes?"

Gold and Trobe nodded in agreement to give Semenov some encouragement. This was evidently a still painful memory that had had monstrous implications for the remainder of his life.

"The drill team, they stop straight away. We are waving our arms to tell them to come help. More people come. One of the crew he reach down to grab man's hand to pull him up, you understand? To save him. We are in panic. I am only twenty-years-old, and this was first time I see something like this."

The ash glowed crimson as Anatoly took a long drag on his cigarette.

"That was last time I see the crew member."

The room was silent except for the whir of the fan and the gentle humming of the many servers. It was Gold who spoke and broke the reverie.

"The last time? Why was that?"

Semenov's voice was full of pain and regret, the memory as fresh now as if he was talking about something that had happened yesterday.

"The man . . . what we thought was a man . . . grabbed my

colleague's hand . . . and pulled him down. Every night, I still I hear him scream. As he fell, I saw the man open his mouth and rip into my colleague's face. The blood . . . the blood was everywhere. When I shut my eyes, I see those teeth. Not human teeth. Teeth like shark. Pointed. Jagged. Sharp. Then I see that the creature . . . the monster . . . I don't know what to call it . . . was not alone. There were more. Many more. They clawed at the drill equipment, the metal shaft, and they start to rise up from the earth . . . dozens of them. They attack the drilling crew . . . they claw at their faces, their arms . . . whatever they could reach. Within moments, the floor of the drilling area was red with blood. Wherever I look I see blood. The men are screaming, shouting, running, slipping on the blood. The military guards they see what is happening and commander he give order to fire. Now all I hear is the screaming and sound of automatic fire. One minute I listening to Rolling Stones, next I am in a war."

Gold and Trobe sat very quietly. This was why they had come all these miles across the Karakum Desert – to hear the truth from the one man who knew it.

Semenov lit another cigarette, his hands were shaking slightly as he recounted the nightmare that he had lived through, and he alone had survived.

"I panic. I ran. I ran as fast as I could…I could not understand what was happening. I didn't see the metal barrier. I run into it. That was it. I was unconscious. I fall into small area between two of the buildings where petro-scientists work. It save my life."

"Gold spoke. "It saved your life because the creatures missed you?"

Anatoly nodded. "Yes, that is correct. I was hidden in small space between buildings. They not see me. Why? I do not know to this day. But, somehow I was spared. Me. Only me."

"What happened when you came round?" Lesley-Ann asked.

Semenov looked blank.

"When you woke up from being hit on the head," she added by way of explanation.

Another long drag on the cigarette.

"I still in small space between buildings. I was slim then, not like now. I open eyes and everywhere is fire, flames, smoke. I get up, I feel still dizzy, yes? I start to walk round camp. I not believe what I see. Bodies everywhere. Half eaten, faces missing, arms torn off, eyes not in heads. And the blood. It was everywhere. I kept slipping on it. Soon I too covered in blood. I throw up. I throw up many times."

"I see. I think we get the picture," said Lesley-Ann who was beginning to feel rather queasy herself.

Gold however needed to know more. He needed to know everything.

"Was anyone left alive apart from you, Anatoly?"

The Russian shook his head, a mixture of regret and disbelief on his deeply lined face.

"No, no one. Everyone dead. I sat down to try to understand what had happened, but it was too much. I just cried. I cry for long time. I thought I had gone mad . . . that it was a dream . . . that I would wake up and we would be laughing and listening to Western music again. But we never would."

"What happened next?" asked Gold gently.

"I don't know how long I sit there. Minutes. Hours. I don't remember. Then I hear helicopters. I look up. Russian army helicopters. Four of them. Big ones. You know, the Mil Mi-8 and the Sikorsky S-67. We used to spot them from time to time, bringing in personnel to the drilling site. They land. Troops get out. Many soldiers. They were wearing breathing masks. I wave at them. They point their guns at me. I thought they were going to shoot. But they not shoot. They get medical officer to look at me, then I was put in helicopter. The doctors put needle in arm and then nothing."

"They flew you to the hospital?" asked Lesley-Ann.

Semenov laughed. A mirthless, bitter laugh.

"Hospital? This is Russian military, not your Greenpeace. No. I wake up in a cell. Outside I see armed guards. I have no idea where I am. They take me to interrogation room and six military officials question me, over and over and over again. Days, weeks pass. I have no watch. I have no daylight. They ask me same questions, 'what happened . . . who attacked the site . . . why are you alive and everyone else dead?'"

Gold stood up. "Mind if I make myself another coffee?" The tension in the room was getting to him. Nothing like a shot of caffeine to calm the nerves.

Semenov gave a gesture to go ahead.

As Gold prepared his coffee (he didn't bother to ask Lesley-Ann if she wanted one, she'd been as useful as an ashtray on a motorbike today), he asked the million-dollar question.

"Did you tell them the truth?"

The effect was startling. Anatoly Semenov jumped up from his chair and shouted.

"Yes! Yes, I told them what happened! I told them a hundred, a thousand times! I kept telling them. But still they question me!"

Gold and Trobe were startled by the sudden outburst. It was the attorney who reacted to the situation quickest.

"But Mr Semenov, they didn't believe you. Am I right? Or did they believe you but wanted you silenced?"

The attorney's professional tone and words seemed to have a calming effect. Anatoly sat down once more.

"They say to me that I lie. They say camp was attacked by terrorists. Maybe from Chechnya, maybe a local warlord. It made no difference. The Kremlin put out the gas explosion story to the world and I was put away from the world. In a hospital for crazy people."

"We prefer to call them mentally challenged, Mr Semenov," said the American.

"Oh. Is that so? Were you there? No? Then may I invite you to shut the fuck up, Miss Trobe. No offence."

The attorney, who looked like she'd just been slapped, was going to respond, but thought better of it. She didn't even like going for a general health check-up, so to be locked away in a psych ward for years on end without trial was incomprehensible to her.

"No offence taken, Anatoly Semenov," she replied.

The consummate professional when required.

The Russian continued. "They locked me away. Year after year. Sometimes new faces would come to visit me in the hospital and ask me more questions. Some were just anxious to understand, others thought I was a mass-murderer or worse still, a traitor to the *Rodina*. Always I gave them the same answers – the truth."

Lesley-Ann spoke with new respect in her voice. "That is just awful. All those wasted years. I'm so sorry."

The response was not what she was expecting.

"Wasted? Now it is *you* who is crazy. They give me books. I study languages. I study history. I study the paranormal. They need me, you see. They need me to give them an explanation. So I did. I told them what I had learned. All was OK until that night when they came back for me."

"Who did?" asked Gold.

"The same creatures I saw at Derweze. They tore the hospital apart, killing everyone in their search for me."

"But why? Why did they come back then, in 2013? All those years after their attack on the oil exploration compound?" asked Lesley-Ann.

Semenov smiled. "Simples. I knew too much. My research over decades was too dangerous for them. I had to be, how you say, silenced."

"And once again you were spared. Saved. Alive amongst so much death," stated Lesley-Ann with a quizzical note in her voice.

"Yes. A miracle. Truly a miracle."

Lesley-Ann pulled a face. Her view on these two miracles was becoming clear.

Anatoly Semenov continued. "After the fire at the hospital, when they thought I was no more use to them, Putin and his gang order that I be set free."

Gold looked puzzled. "Forgive me Anatoly, but I'm confused. I thought they might have just . . . well, you know . . . disposed of you."

Anatoly Semenov laughed, his shoulders shaking with mirth.

"Dispose of me? No way that happen. Mr Nick Gold – I am world's leading expert on a very special subject for President Putin and the Kremlin."

"Really?" replied Gold, none the wiser. "What subject is that?"

Semenov gave a smile.

"The undead of course."

TWENTY-SEVEN

"He left it in thy power, ordaind thy will By nature free, not over-rul'd by Fate Inextricable, or strict necessity;"
– John Milton, Paradise Lost

Gold needed fresh air. The combination of the intensity of Semenov's narrative, his hard-core cigarette smoke and the fact that the room was packed full of screens and servers all made even the baking heat of the Karakum Desert desirable.

Attorney Trobe followed him out of the door.

"So, our comrade in there is Putin's go-to-guy for all things *Twilight Zone?*" she asked Gold.

Gold was at that moment wishing he hadn't given up smoking. "Well, it's not so strange. Remember, it was the Soviets who first put a man in space back in 1961, Yuri Gagarin. That floored you Americans. Almost as much as when they were the first to put a satellite into space – Sputnik in 1957."

"Is there a point to this or are you just enjoying gloating at us poor, dumb Americans?"

Gold didn't bite on the verbal bait.

"My point is this. The Soviets never let the Cold War die. The West and the Russians have been investigating the paranormal since before WWII. Both sides wanted an edge. Remember that the Allies and the Soviets acquired all the top Nazi scientists at the end of the War. And we all know how batshit crazy the Nazis were about the paranormal and the occult."

"Yeah. Thanks. I saw *Raiders of the Lost Ark*."

Gold sighed. "The Soviets were taken with the possibility of psychokinesis, you know, using mental imagery to move objects. They saw it as a way of screwing up the electrical systems on an intercontinental ballistic missile guidance program. It centred really on the Soviet belief in bioplasma."

Lesley-Ann was way out of her depth but like many people, sought to camouflage her lack of knowledge with hostility.

"Let me know when we're back talking English."

Gold continued unabashed. "The Soviets were more inclined to believe that paranormal phenomena might be the result of bioenergetics – the energy given off by the metabolic processes of living things. They thought people gave off bioplasma."

"In English, *please*!"

"It's a theoretical energy field. They thought under certain conditions a person was capable of emitting charged radiation. Their research was way ahead of the West. Still is, as far as I know."

Lesley-Ann had found some gum in her pocket and was chewing in that particularly irritating way that people trying to be cool affect.

"So, the Russians let our pal in there go because he was useful and one of his insane theories might be right? The Kremlin might still even be funding him in case he comes up with a real winner?"

Gold nodded. "Maybe, and I'm just guessing here, they saw the total devastation these . . . things . . . caused and thought they'd make a pretty handy weapon. The undead can't be counted as casualties in conflict. They keep him around because he might, just might, be able to help weaponise the paranormal."

Lesley-Ann continued to chew relentlessly on her gum. "Can we go inside now the lecture's over? I'm fucking frying out here."

When they returned, Anatoly Semenov resumed the duties of the perfect host. Fresh mint tea was ready to be served, an assortment of delicious pastries were on a rather delightful decorative plate and, most incongruously, there was a packet of Chocolate Hobnobs. Gold stared at them.

"Internet," was all that their host replied. "Cannot beat British biscuits, no offence to our American friend."

Lesley-Ann pulled a face.

"Thank you, Anatoly for your hospitality . . . Lesley-Ann and I are very grateful. Aren't we?"

Lesley-Ann took the hint. "Yes, indeed. It is awesome."

Gold winced. Awesome, the most over-employed word used in the wrong context of all time.

"Nick, Lesley-Ann, let me show you this. I think it help." Anatoly turned to one of the larger screens and brought up photos of what seemed to be an abandoned village surrounded by lush green fields.

"This is what remains of the medieval village of Wharram Percy. It's in your England, Nick – in a place called Yorkshire. Have you heard of such place?"

Gold smiled. "Yorkshire? Yes, I've even been to it. It's up north. Please carry on."

"I show you this because you know why it is abandoned?"

Gold and Trobe shook their heads in unison.

"The Walking Dead."

"What . . . the TV series? They left an entire village because they thought the show sucked?"

There were times when Gold wondered just how difficult the American Bar Exams might actually be.

"Zombies, Lesley-Ann. The undead. This is not a new thing you know. Zombies have long been of fascination to us, yes? I talk of far longer than the horror movies by George Romero and his *Night of the Living Dead* from almost fifty years ago. I am telling you that in mediaeval times, they were scared shit of them."

"Shit scared. You get shit scared of something." The ever-helpful lawyer.

"You must excuse my English. Not my best language. My Mandarin is better. So, let me explain. At a recent site where they dig things up from the past, yes . . ."

"Archaeological."

Gold gave the attorney his best death stare.

"As you say. Yes. What did they discover? I tell you. Look at this. The mutilated and burned bones of seventeen people buried in a pit outside the deserted medieval village of Wharram Percy, in Yorkshire England."

"What does that prove, Anatoly?" asked the defence attorney.

Being in a psychiatric hospital for decades obviously develops enormous patience in a patient. Semenov just smiled.

"These mutilations were carried out on the bodies after they dead. The experts think they were cut up out of fear that the dead might rise and walk among the living."

Gold was intrigued.

"What period are we talking about?"

Anatoly was in his element. "Radiocarbon dating says the bones are from the eleventh to the thirteenth centuries."

"So pretty old, then," added Lesley-Ann helpfully.

"Indeed. Very old. That is my point. But here is what I find of interest as well. Blade marks, mostly from knives not swords or axes, were left on the body and the head sometime just after death. The burning of the bones also was around the time of death. Some had their heads cut off. The researchers say all of this, er, things, was to protect against revenants."

"Revenants. Like in the film where Leo gets the shit kicked out of him by a bear?" asked Gold.

Anatoly smiled. "I too love that film. Scorsese, he very clever man. But I prefer *Goodfellas* or maybe *Casino*."

Lesley-Ann interjected. "Sorry to break up the Marty love-fest but *The Revenant* was directed by Alejandro González Iñárritu – he's Mexican, you know, as in wall."

Both men looked crestfallen.

Semenov ploughed on.

"Revenants – literally the returned, essentially the walking dead – appear in English written sources from the eleventh to the thirteenth centuries. Wait, let me show you. I have book here . . . somewhere . . . I find it."

The visitors did as they were bid. After much grunting and what they presumed to be swearing in Russian from their host, he returned with a leather-bound book in his hand. "I like history. You like, yes? This book I asked Kremlin to supply. So they did."

"It looks old," remarked the lawyer.

Gold groaned inwardly. Americans! The entire White House staff probably thought the Great Wall in China was built in the 1960s.

Semenov addressed his audience. This was a truly wonderful day. He had company. He actually had people to talk to. Not just on Skype, but right here in his home.

He started to read.

'The Wharram Percy burials are reminiscent of an account in Geoffrey of Burton's 12th-century Miracles of St Modwenna.'

Lesley-Ann interrupted. "Sorry to butt in here, but can we sort of cut to the chase. I'm sure the entire book is absolutely fascinating but, you know, we're kinda on the clock here."

Semenov looked slightly crestfallen. Gold could have happily shot her.

"Of course. I cut to chase. It seems, yes, that two men run away to the nearby village of Drakelow in your Derbyshire and die soon after, only to rise from the grave the following night carrying their coffins on their backs. Terrorise villagers who are mysteriously found dead in the morning. Pretty good huh? I learn it. So this continues night after night until most of the village has been killed. So, what to do? The survivors dig up the corpses of the two men, tear out and burn their hearts and cut off their heads and place them between their legs."

Gold interjected. "Wasn't this story used to suggest that the practice of placing severed heads between the legs of Anglo-Saxon and Romano-British burials was protection against revenants? The burning of specific body parts or the whole corpse seems to have been much more crucial to destroying twelfth century revenants than decapitation."

The lawyer looked at the TV presenter. He actually *knew* stuff.

Semenov was delighted with his guest's interest. "Yes. Blade marks were found on some ribs in the Wharram Percy pit. They could be attempt to remove heart for burning."

Lesley-Ann was tired of being a third wheel. "So these revenants. Are they common or what?"

Semenov explained. "No, not before Norman Conquest, but suddenly they appear in the late-eleventh and twelfth centuries. I think my good friend Mr Nick Gold will know that. The revenant and ghost stories in twelfth and thirteenth centuries is when people start to believe in penance and purgatory."

Anatoly was in his element. "The Wharram Percy burials are due to fear of walking dead. In Middle Ages these fears very real. Local people may have been dug up from local cemetery by people who knew them in life, mutilated, burned, and reburied beyond the village area."

He consulted the book once more and read aloud.

> *Wharram Percy, like the village of Drakelow, was eventually abandoned. The stigma of revenants was enough to haunt the village for centuries afterward.*

Semenov closed the book with a dramatic gesture.

"Wow! Who knew, eh?" was the summary from Lesley-Ann while Gold was a little more expansive.

"So, this entire idea of the undead, the walking dead, zombies, goes way, way back. Interesting. Anatoly, let me tell you why we are *really* here. On reflection, I need to share this with you. It's important that you understand what happened to you . . . well, it happened to us too. *Both* of us."

Over the next hour, Gold and Trobe told Anatoly Semenov everything they knew. Gold left out nothing, even his grim experience with Mehmet, the Turkish tour guide's wife and how, according to Barachiel the Archangel, he was The Gatekeeper. For her part, Lesley-Ann was no less candid, as she described the attack outside the bar. They also talked, with sadness in their voices, of the sudden death of their colleague Arnie Woolfson. His passing was still very raw to them both.

Outside it was now dark. There is dark and there is desert dark. No ambient light. No cars. No shop windows or illuminated advertising hoardings. Nothing. It is as though you are seeing the night sky for the first time. Human beings, looking up from their blue planet, can see two thousand stars at night. A far lower number than logic would suggest, but true none the less. Out here, in the Karakum Desert, that number seemed to be two hundred thousand. It wasn't, of course, but to Gold and Lesley-Ann, as they stood in the cool night air, it seemed that way. But then Gold had acquired a rather more profound knowledge of the nature of the Universe.

"Can we trust this guy?" Lesley-Ann asked.

"It's a little late to ask me that now, don't you think?

The lawyer was determined. "He was banged up in a psych ward for God knows how long, maybe he is crazy . . . or worse . . . one of *them*. Why was he spared not once but twice? Freud said there is no such thing as coincidence."

"Yeah. Sigmund also said that sometimes a cigar is just a cigar. Clearly, he'd never smoked a Partagas Serie D No. 4. Look, Lesley-Ann, what's the worst that can happen? If Anatoly wanted us dead, then he's had hours to do it. And it's not like the neighbours are going to hear anything."

Lesley-Ann let out an exasperated sigh. For once, she couldn't argue with what passed for Gold's logic.

They went back inside.

Anatoly Semenov had all the lights on now, plus candles. It

reminded Gold of those restaurants in South London where they try to recreate – and fail to – the atmosphere and look of the Middle East. This was the real deal. More food had been laid out: meats, bread, what looked like a large bowl of hummus and two bottles of red wine. Nick wondered if he had a branch of Waitrose out the back they'd failed to notice. Maybe he ordered it all online. He seemed to live most of his life on it.

"You are hungry? I have prepared a simple supper. We have much to talk about, yes?"

They nodded in agreement. Lesley-Ann asked where the bathroom was (as Americans never ask for the toilet). Alone with Nick, Semenov spoke with a twinkle in his eye.

"Your girlfriend? She very, how you say, spunky."

There are some phrases that have a Grand Canyon's worth of difference between the USA and the UK. Gold quickly banished the mental image that had sprung to mind.

"Er, she's not my girlfriend . . . not really . . . we're travelling together to investigate all of this. We are. Really."

Anatoly laughed. "So, you no fuck her? Shame. She quite hot. In my country, we all think most Englishmen are impotent. Not like Russian men."

Gold was about to respond when Lesley-Ann returned, unaware she'd just broken the world record time for a female going to the ladies.

"Nick, so you are not just the great Paranormal Detective, but now also The Gatekeeper. It is big honour. Big responsibility. You must be proud."

Gold shook his head. "God no! I don't want the job. I certainly didn't volunteer for it. I'm sure there's been a mistake and it's not meant to be me."

What Anatoly Semenov said next astounded both of his visitors.

"Oh yes. It is meant to be you, Nick Gold. There is no mistake. You are The Gatekeeper for sure."

Gold stared at him opened-mouthed. It was Lesley-Ann who, as ever, broke the silence.

"Are you shitting us?"

By way of reply, Semenov asked them "Have either of you heard of The Lost Books of the Bible?"

Gold nodded. The attorney didn't.

"But for many years I research, yes? First in books, then on Internet. Now both. I look at thousands of documents, articles, magazines. I have nothing else to do. I am scholar, you understand me? There are many Lost Books. One appears in the Bible – Numbers 21:14. 'Wherefore it is said in the book of the Wars of the Lord, what he did in the Red sea, and in the brooks of Arnon.'"

Lesley-Ann sat up, almost choking on a large piece of bread on which she had spread an equally large dollop of hummus.

"Arnon? Seriously?"

"Yes, like your friend, Mr Woolfson in the United States of America."

"You *knew* him?" Lesley-Ann was incredulous.

"We email each other. He big researcher too, yes. I was sad to read of his death. Yes, the books of Arnon. It is a sign."

"What exactly is the book of the Wars of the Lord?" asked Lesley-Ann.

Semenov started keying words onto one of his many computers. He was like the Jean-Michel Jarre of PCs once he was working.

"Look, I explain." Up on screen appeared: *'The so-called lost books of the Bible are those documents that are mentioned in the Bible in such a way that it is evident they were considered authentic and valuable but that are not found in the Bible today. Sometimes called missing scriptures'.*

Anatoly was into his stride now. "Do you know how many words there are in the Bible? Nearly three quarters of a million. It one of longest books ever written, yes? But . . . but the Bible is not complete. No. Not at all. There are seventeen missing books that were *not* included. Seventeen!"

Lesley-Ann looked at Gold. He nodded in confirmation. She had had enough trouble reading the Bible as it was, let alone with the addition of another seventeen lost books.

"One of these seventeen missing books is The Book of Wars of The Lord. In this book, which I have read many times, it tells us of the battle between Good and Evil. Between God and Lucifer."

"Anatoly, are we in for a Bible study class tutorial, because frankly it's not really my thing," piped up Lesley-Ann.

Semenov's face froze into a bitter smile. He replied in a very measured tone.

"Is that so Miss Trobe? Tell me . . . if you don't believe in gravity, does it affect the world? No, it exists. If you refuse to believe in gravity, does it affect Universe? No. You will still fall from a skyscraper. So quite frankly I don't give a shit if it's your thing or not. You can listen and prepare yourself or you can go outside and not be prepared. Me . . . I don't care. Not my problem. Nick Gold is my concern . . . Nick Gold, The Gatekeeper. Now if you excuse me, I have much to explain and tell him from my decades of research. Stay or go or sit in corner and eat hummus. All same to me."

Lesley-Ann's face turned puce. She could not remember the last time she had been spoken to in such a rude, discourteous manner. Who the fuck did this Russian think he was? Egotistical chauvinist prick. Fuck him! Seriously, fuck him!

"My apologies Mr Semenov. You have my full attention."

Inner dialogue is a marvellous thing. If it's kept inside your head.

"Good," was the one-word response.

"To find origin of Lucifer, we look at Old Testament. In the Hebrew, the name Lucifer is translated from the Hebrew word *helel*. Do you know what that means?"

The lawyer took a stab in the dark. "Avoid at all costs because he's a seriously bad dude and will rip your lungs out of your chest?"

Anatoly smiled indulgently. "No, Miss Trobe, it means *brightness*. Lucifer's name means *morning star* or *star of the morning* or *bright star*. It tells us, yes, in *Isaiah*."

"Lucifer Morningstar. Sounds like a Van Morrison album title," responded Lesley-Ann, who was keen to show remorse and get back on the horse.

Another indulgent smile.

It was Gold's turn to educate the attorney. "Lucifer is just another name for Satan. Satan is head of the evil world-system. He was the real power behind the rulers of Tyre, Babylon, Persia, Greece, Rome, Nazi Germany, Cambodia – every evil ruler that we see in the history of the world."

"Seriously?" asked Lesley-Ann.

Anatoly Semenov nodded gravely.

"So, and I'm out of my depth here Anatoly, how did Lucifer get to be so smart?" asked the American.

Semenov smiled. "Yes. Yes! Good question! I have answer. Lucifer, this angel . . . yes, *angel* . . . is the highest creature God ever created. How we know this? It in Bible. God says, '*You were the seal of perfection, full of wisdom, and perfect in beauty.*'"

Semenov went on.

"You must understand, yes, Satan was the wisest creature God ever created. No other angel, no other being, was created with the intelligence that God gave to this creature. God says that this creation is '*perfect in beauty*'. Apart from the Holy Trinity: Father, Son and Holy Spirit, this creature is today the highest being."

Lesley-Ann looked puzzled, her face a bewildered frown. "Whoa, hang on there a minute Billy Graham, how come if God is so smart, he made Satan in the first place? I mean, if God knows everything, as we are told, then this was one mahoosive mistake, right?"

"I will explain you, in a minute. I research. I read. I look at texts . . . not mobile phone texts, I mean the texts written by the scholars. The answers are all there. In Ezekiel 28:14 it says, 'You were the anointed Cherub'. The word cherub is singular for cherubim, the very symbol of God's Holy presence and His unapproachable majesty. These cherubim occupy a unique position. In the Garden of Eden, after Adam and Eve had been sent out, God placed cherubim to guard the Tree of Life."

"Yeah, that worked out well," murmured Lesley-Ann.

"Anatoly," interjected Nick "this could be all fable, right? Myth. Legend. The Garden of Eden. The snake. The apple. Adam and Eve. These are stories. They're not an accurate history. I mean, God made the Heaven and Earth in seven days? The bloody M25 motorway took eleven sodding years and it's only one hundred and twenty-one miles long."

Semenov looked at Nick Gold with intensity. "God didn't take seven days to make the Earth. It means that God took seven attempts to make the Earth *right*! The first six were . . . how you say . . . crap."

"Wait! There are *six* crap Earths out there? asked an incredulous Lesley-Ann.

Semenov just smiled. "Six, six hundred, six million. Who knows?"

Gold spoke up. "Lesley-Ann, are you familiar with the Kabbalah?"

She shrugged. "Other than Madonna follows it, no I'm not."

Gold smiled. "OK. I studied it when I was researching Comparative Religious Studies during my degree. So, in Hebrew Scripture and within the mystical tradition known as Kabbalah, there are numerous references to worlds other than our own, with life on them. It's fascinating stuff. I mean, think about this, OK? Back in the eighteenth century, the Book of the Covenant was written by a Rabbi Horowitz. He emphatically says that God created an infinite number of worlds, of physical, spiritual and inter-dimensional nature. And get this, Rabbi Horowitz refers specifically to 18,000 physical planets. In the Talmud, there's reference to something like 1018 stars in the observable universe. And you know what? That's a figure that is very close to the accepted number that can now be seen in the night sky."

Lesley-Ann smiled at Gold. "And I thought you were an idiot. I stand corrected, Professor Gold."

"It may not even be seven worlds, by the way, it may be seven cycles of humanity. Let's hope we're not in the seventh, because that, my friend, is the end of the human race."

"Is that it?" asked Lesley-Ann.

"It? That doesn't even scratch the surface. When we read about 'days' and 'years' they don't mean time in the way we understand them. A divine day equals one thousand earth years; a divine year is 365,250 earth years. Now's here's the freaky bit. If we do the maths, Adam would have been born when the earth was 42,000 divine years old. The universe can then be calculated to be 42,000 times 365,250 years old, which equals 15,340,500,000 years."

"And your point is?" LAT asked.

"My point, Lesley-Ann, is this number is uncannily close to the fifteen billion years calculated by today's cosmologists . . . since the Big Bang!"

Semenov broke into applause. "Yes, Nick Gold. Yes! You get it!"

Gold made a small ironic bow, acknowledging the applause, which enabled Lesley-Ann to kick him swiftly in the ass.

Semenov grabbed the moment. "The point you *must* understand, this very important if you want a chance to survive, is that Satan was a cherub. His job was to guard and protect the very throne of God. Satan had the highest of all positions."

Lesley-Ann was getting more confused. "Well, that seems a pretty good deal. He's numero uno. The big cheese. El Heffe. What was his problem?"

"His *problem*, as you say, was it was a position which he despised. In the book of Ezekiel, we see the highest of God's creatures, perfect in wisdom, beautiful beyond description, a musician with an exalted position."

"And?" asked Lesley-Ann, tucking in to a particularly delicious-looking pastry of almonds and honey.

"And . . . this beautiful creation also had a *free will*."

"Bummer," responded the lawyer, taking another large bite from the dessert in the desert.

Gold looked at her. Was she actually taking this seriously? Why in the name of Gloria Steinem did he agree that she could tag along? What was he thinking? Gold believed that Anatoly Semenov was genuine. If he really was The Gatekeeper, whatever the hell that meant, then he better get genned-up on the subject to at least stand a chance of a scintilla of success. Semenov seemed like his best shot.

"As you say, Miss Trobe, a bummer indeed. I find answer in Isaiah 14:12. Lucifer makes a choice, yes?"

"To be a bad guy . . . big time?" she suggested.

"No. Not to be bad guy. He says, 'I will ascend to heaven; I will raise my throne above the stars of God; I will make myself like the Most High'. You understand what I say, no? He does not want to be God's servant. He does not want to do what he was created to do. He wants to *be* God!"

The room was suddenly very quiet. Finally, the heart of the problem, explained in just five one syllable words.

Anatoly had their full attention. "He wants to be served and there are millions who have chosen to do just that, to serve him. They listened to his lies and chose to follow him. His first follower? Eve. She listened. She lost."

Lesley-Ann had stopped eating. "So, if I've got this right and remember a single thing from the Bible, God gets totally annoyed and throws Lucifer out of Heaven. It was a boardroom coup that went way wrong. Right?"

"A boardroom coup . . . I like that," responded Semenov,

smiling. If we use your, what is word . . . analogy . . . the other directors didn't do so great either. Lucifer convinced a third of the angels to follow him in rebellion against God. How we know? It says so in Isaiah 14:12-15, Ezekiel 28:13-16 and Revelation 12:7-9. Because of Lucifer's rebellion, his name gets changed to Satan – it means adversary. His followers, the fallen angels, they now known as demons."

The three of them talked through the night, boosted by Semenov's particularly excellent coffee, the best Gold had tasted outside of the Algerian Coffee Store on Old Compton Street in London's Soho. Semenov, with Gold's added input, explained, as a tutor to a student, how Satan and his demons were not ready to give up in their fight against God. From the moment Adam and Eve disobeyed the one thing they were instructed to do, deceived by Satan, so began the battle of light versus darkness; right versus wrong; good versus evil.

The Great Deceiver and his agents brought darkness and oppression disguised as light and liberty.

This battle of God versus Satan has been raging for over six thousand years. All that was missing was for Lucifer to build the Death Star.

It was nearly dawn. Tiny shafts of light were making their inevitable way through the chinks in the home of the Russian. The three of them were exhausted. Gold felt as if his brain had turned to a pizza while Lesley-Ann realised how, in comparison, completing her IRS 1040 form was relatively straightforward. Semenov suggested that they went outside to watch the night melt away into another spectacular desert dawn. The sky was purple. A cool breeze blew into their tired faces. As the sky changed colour, it was as if the world was waking up.

"Now, finally we come to you, Nick Gold, the Paranormal Detective, The Gatekeeper. It is like this. Every twenty years, why twenty I don't know, no one does, Lucifer attacks the earth. *This* earth. The other earths are not our problem, yes? So, a

Gatekeeper is appointed. An ordinary man or woman. A representative of humankind. Not a person of high rank. Just a person. Their role is simple – to show that Good can still prevail, that Satan is not, as it says in *Corinthians*, '*the god of this age*'. That is your role."

"So . . . nothing too heavy then," replied Gold, breathing in the much-needed fresh dawn air. "I keep explaining to anyone who'll listen that this must be a mistake. Why me?"

"Because," was all that Semenov said.

"Well, that explains everything. *Because*. Great. What could possibly go wrong now I'm armed with that in-depth piece of knowledge?"

Lesley-Ann had been unusually quiet for the past thirty minutes, seemingly lost in her own thoughts.

"Anatoly, Nick must close The Gates of Hell, right? I know . . . I know . . . batshit crazy . . . so we're going to go back to Derweze and that'll be our Alamo?"

Semenov looked perplexed.

"Derweze? No, no, no. Not there. That is not your battleground."

"So what now? We have to travel all over the world closing all these gates? How the hell are we going to do that? Get sponsored by British Airways or Richard Branson?" asked Gold.

"Come with me."

With that Anatoly Semenov turned smartly on his heels and walked back into his home.

TWENTY-EIGHT

"Go; for thy stay, not free, absents thee more."
– John Milton, Paradise Lost

"The Gates of Hell. You have been going to them, yes?"

Gold and Trobe nodded. "Yup. Hierapolis, near Pamukkale in Turkey, Hallam Township in Pennsylvania USA and here at Derweze in Turkmenistan. All three."

Anatoly burst out laughing. They stared at him. What was so amusing?

"You guys. You crack me up, yes. I study for decades but you know everything about everything. You say all three. You forgot the fourth."

The expression you could have heard a pin drop seems unlikely in the modern world. But in this ramshackle house, containing countless terabytes of digital information, it was true. The silence was almost overpowering.

"Excuse me? What?" Lesley-Ann finally said. "Run that by me again."

"The fourth gate. You not been there."

"What fourth gate? What do you mean?" asked Gold in a slightly querulous, yet anxious tone.

Semenov pulled out a cigarette, of which he seemed to have an inexhaustible supply.

"When they put me away in the hospital outside Moscow back in '71, at first I thought I was going mad. I did not want to believe that what I saw at the oil drilling was real. It turn me upside down, inside out. But, thing is, I know it to be true, yes. Once I know I not crazy I, bit by bit, little by little, start my years of research. I ask for books. At first they tell me no. But slowly they allow me. Each time a new leader come, I get a few more books. Brezhnev was good, Andropov, ex-KGB, not so much. Konstantin Chernenko was OK, but I starting to rock under Gorbachev, a good guy. Yeltsin was drunk so much of time I get many books and when Putin arrived first time in 1991, then I of great use to Kremlin."

"Why?" asked Lesley-Ann, whose knowledge of the shifting, serpentine sands of Russian politics was a little rusty.

"As I explain to you, because of the secrets that they thought I might uncover. Think of it – an army of demons. That put shits up North Koreans, Chinese, breakaway states, right? Remember, we lost twenty million alone in World War Two. If Kremlin could mobilise twenty million undead troops, all of whom would want revenge, well you understand what I'm saying."

Gold was musing over these truly awful figures. He knew the Germans had tried to exterminate the population of Russia, a favour that Russia was happy to repay once the tide of the conflict changed. Russia, wide and flat, so that there was literally nowhere to hide or take cover from incoming fire. A vast slaughterhouse.

"And did you find the key? The secret to unlocking this hell on earth?" Gold had asked the big question.

Semenov dragged on his cigarette, the acrid smoke danced in the morning light.

"You like movies, Nick? I love them. Watch all time. Remember in *The Godfather* when Don Vito Corleone say, 'A friend should always underestimate your virtues and an enemy overestimate your faults.' That good advice. I listen. I learn."

Lesley-Ann added "I love that film. Godfather Part I and Part II. Godfather Part III, what a pile of crap. But Anatoly, that doesn't answer Nick's question. Did you tell them what they wanted to know?"

Anatoly Semenov stood up, scratched his head, made a vague

attempt to smooth out his long, straggly grey hair and stretched.

"I believe correct phrase is 'are you fucking mad?' The Kremlin, those men in secret meetings, they think they can control this, to be its master, like this was vicious dog that they could train to obey. The demons answer to one person and one person alone – Satan. No one controls him. No one. Not even God."

"But they let you go?" asked Nick.

"Sure. I give them enough clues, hints, ideas, but nothing that would allow them access to the Gates. You have the clues, Nick The Gatekeeper. You just not see them . . . yet."

Lesley-Ann stared at Gold as if he's just grown another head, which considering their recent experiences, would not be a total surprise.

"You have clues?" she demanded.

It was Nick's turn to stand up. Anything was better than sitting there feeling like an idiot. Clues? He didn't have the first idea what Semenov was referring to. At least if he paced around the cramped room, it might look as if he was cogitating on the conundrum.

"You haven't the faintest idea, have you Nick?" Lesley-Ann, with her sharp legal mind, had seen through Gold's pantomime in a nanosecond. There was no point in denying it.

"Not the foggiest."

"Huh?"

"No. Not the slightest."

Lost in translation.

It was Anatoly who came to Gold's rescue. "Think Nick. Please, think carefully. When you were with Barachiel, did he say anything that might be of use? Was there a place? A name?"

Nick Gold was tired. He didn't recall ever being so tired before in his thirty-two years. His mind, what he thought was left of it at any rate, was whirring through the conversations he had had with the Archangel – first in Balham in South London, not a series of words one would normally put together he mused, then in Turkey and finally in Hallam USA. So much had been said. Was there something that he'd missed in their conversations?

"Nick, you OK?" enquired Lesley-Ann solicitously. He had a pained expression on his face, as if trying to remember what was hurting. "What should Nick be trying to recall, Anatoly? Would it be obvious? Would it be something from the Bible? From Greek mythology? Did he see something? Can you give him a steer?"

Something was nagging at Nick's memory. Something that was tantalisingly close to the surface, so near he felt he could reach out and touch it, but it shifted, changed, morphed into nothingness.

"Anatoly, in all your research, did you draw up a map of the locations of the Gates? You say there are four?" went on Lesley-Ann.

Semenov looked crestfallen. "Yes, there are four that I believe I have discovered . . . but there are also many *possible* other ones all over world – Fengdu in China, known as the City of Ghosts; the Masaya Volcano in Nicaragua; the Lacus Curtius in Rome, Italy; St Patrick's Purgatory on Station Island in Ireland; there's even one in Iceland, possibly – Mount Hekla, a very active volcano from the twelfth century. There are more too."

Iceland! Gold assumed Semenov meant the country not the supermarket chain, as that would be just too weird.

"Fuck me!" exploded Gold "You have got to be joking! We can't run around like some demented TV Holiday show to all these places. We haven't got the time and we certainly wouldn't get the budget from Good Foot Productions. There must be another way or this is hopeless."

Semenov stood up and disappeared into the back area of his house out of sight. Trobe and Gold sat in silence, both feeling exhausted and more than a little depressed.

Semenov reappeared, carrying something in his hand.

"When I need to think," he announced, "you know what I find help me? Cigar. That's what. Cigar. It relax me, and when I relaxed I can think clear, you understand?"

They nodded.

"Very important to have cigar in good condition. If it dry out, crap. No good to smoke. I have these sent from Sautter of Mount Street in London. On Internet, yes. Shop sell aged and vintage Cuban cigars, so as a Russian I feel I give support. I watch their videos when I need break. It help me with my English too."

Well, this was fascinating, thought Gold. Yes indeed. This was just the perfect time to get a lecture on sodding cigars.

Anatoly was enthused, inspired by his passion for smoking a good Havana. Considering he smoked cigarettes that appeared to be made from nuclear waste, it was a wonder he could taste the difference between an expensive Cohiba, Partagas or Monte Cristo.

"Now as I say, here in desert, it very hot."

A remark that caused Gold to bite his tongue. His mood was darkening, brought on by exhaustion and frustration.

"So very, very, *very* important to keep moist and in tip of the top condition. I use humidor which I also buy from the shop in your Mayfair, but also I keep them in this."

With a flourish worthy of a Las Vegas magician, he produced a metal cylinder.

"I not open this until I want to smoke. I keep them always in their tube –"

What had he just said?

"You do *what?*" asked Nick who suddenly looked as though someone had plugged him into the electricity supply.

Semenov looked puzzled. Of course, he knew his guests would be utterly fascinated by his profound knowledge of all things appertaining to cigars, but even he, the great cigar aficionado, didn't expect this reaction.

"I said I keep them in a tube."

"Tube! You keep them in a *tube*!" Gold exclaimed and, without warning, jumped up and hugged a bemused Anatoly Semenov.

Lesley-Ann was perplexed. Had the Brit just lost it totally? It was a goddam cigar for God's sake. What was the big deal?

Nick turned to her grinning. "I know what the clue was that Barachiel gave me. I know which Gate of Hell I must close!"

TWENTY-NINE

"In thoughts more elevate, and reasoned high Of Providence, Foreknowledge, Will, and Fate: Fixed fate, free will, foreknowledge absolute, And found no end, in wandering mazes lost."
– John Milton, Paradise Lost

The effect on the room was explosive.

Nick Gold was like a man possessed, rushing around the room like an illicit lover in a French farce who'd just heard the husband's unexpected key in the front door. In fact, he was moving with such alacrity that the husband in question must have been returning home early from a Special Forces mission.

"What the hell is up with you?" asked Lesley-Ann, shooting a WTF look at Anatoly. Semenov, for his part, was looking at Nick Gold with a sense of respect – no wonder they called him the Paranormal Detective. Had he known his colleague was thinking this, Nick would not have had the heart to tell him that his boss Larry had dreamed the name up. He'd also come up with Sporty, Scary, Ginger, Posh and Baby for a girl band back in 1995 originally called Touch.

"We have to go. Now!" was all that Gold replied, as if such an exhortation was a sufficient explanation in itself.

"Whoa there, Barry Allen, would you at least tell us *where* we have to go to?"

But faster than a speeding bullet! More powerful than a locomotive! Able to leap tall buildings at a single bound, Nick Gold was having none of it.

"I'll explain on the way."

Gold grabbed a yellow legal pad off Semenov's desk and started to write furiously, covering several sides of paper in his untidy scrawl.

"Anatoly, this is what I need you to check for me. Do your brilliant research, you know, the way you do, and then email it to me. I'll be doing plenty of my own."

Anatoly Semenov looked both delighted and dismayed simultaneously – no mean feat. "So, Nick, you no want me to come with?"

Gold was not insensitive to how Semenov had helped so far nor that they would still need his assistance in the near future.

"Anatoly Semenov, my dear friend, *muy drug* . . . you have extended your friendship and hospitality to two strangers. For this you have our eternal gratitude."

"Oh great . . . now I'm in a scene from *Dr Zhivago*. Jeez!" muttered Lesley-Ann under her breath.

Gold continued.

"Your struggle, your story, is now *our* story. We will tell it to the world."

"Oh give me a break, you pompous asshole," muttered the irritated attorney.

"But your great gift, no . . . your towering *talent* . . . means that you can help us, and the *world* . . . best by staying here in this . . . this *centre* of knowledge, of communication, of research. We need you, Anatoly Semenov . . . will you help us?"

Semenov seemed to swell with pride. Was that a tiny tear in the corner of his left eye?

"Nick Gold, my new friend . . . my dear friend . . . I will stay here in the Command Centre. I will help you in the battle you must face. I will give you the information you will need."

"Oh for the love of God . . . get a room you two," continued Lesley-Ann's almost internal commentary.

The two men gave each other a bromance hug that wouldn't have been out of place on Brokeback Mountain accompanied by much manly back-slapping. Lesley-Ann felt like the ugly bridesmaid the bride had had to invite because they were related.

Semenov untangled himself from Gold and went over to Lesley-Ann. "My Yankee friend . . . I wish you God speed. I like you. As you Americans say, you are full to top with spunk."

"Er . . . thanks," she replied, and, like Nick before her, trying to erase a very unfortunate mental image.

Anatoly now gave the lawyer a mighty bear-hug, picking her off her feet and swinging her around 360 degrees. Try this in an American office and there wouldn't be a truck big enough to carry all the lawsuits, she thought.

With the goodbyes finally concluded, Gold and Trobe headed out to where they'd parked the hired 4x4, threw their bags into the back seat and set off back to the Ozugkent Hotel in Ashgabat.

In the car, the silence was rather oppressive.

"You two moving in together any time soon?"

Gold rolled his eyes. Why was everything a damn competition?

"He liked you, too. He's more of an, er, man's man."

"Oh gosh? Really? Who knew. Excuse me while I reset my watch to 1959."

Gold knew there was no point in entering a debate about glass ceilings at this juncture. The attorney would just have to suck it up.

"Any chance, Robert Langdon, that you might be in the mood to share your epiphany? You know . . . as we're driving in a desert and there's fuck all else to do unless you want to play I Spy with words beginning with rock and sand."

Gold turned to her and gave his best attempt at a charming smile. It was a long drive, he was tired and he didn't need to participate in a bitchfest all the way back to the hotel.

"Did you just fart?"

"No! I was smiling at you."

More silence.

"Fine, Lesley-Ann. Of course, I'm going to fill you in . . . get you up to speed I mean."

She turned in her seat and her body language said deafeningly, 'I'm listening and this had better be good.'

Tough room.

Gold began. The road, or what passed as a road was largely empty, so he could relax, talk and drive simultaneously.

"If I am The Gatekeeper, which I must stress I have zero desire to be, then, like it or not, and as nuts as it sounds, I'm going to have to, somehow, deal with it. All the complaining in the world isn't going to make this bloody thing go away. It's like income tax. If you ignore it, the bastards will still come after you. So . . . something at the back of my mind has been buzzing around like . . . like . . . a thing that buzzes. It started in London and, as it turns out, was confirmed by Barachiel in a throw-away remark he made."

"Yes? Can you do me a solid here and not drag this out?"

Gold looked offended.

Really tough room.

"Fine," he went on. "No problem. Let me give you the edited highlights then, shall I?"

He didn't wait for a response.

Gold sighed. "I was sitting on the Tube. It's what the London Underground train system is called."

"Nick, I know what the damn Tube is."

Gold nodded. "Of course. I forgot. So, I was sitting in . . . a carriage on the Tube and there were some tourists sitting opposite me. They were looking at a map of the London Underground tube network. And something started to form in my mind . . . and then it was gone. Not my mind, the *thought* I was trying to form."

"May I just say how riveting this is, Nick?"

"Lesley-Ann, either you want me to tell you or you don't. I am one hundred percent down with dropping you off at the hotel and saying a heartfelt cheerio, goodbye, so long and *adios*. In the words of the song *Vienna*, it means nothing to me."

"Nice 1981 reference there, grandad. Shut up and keep talking."

There was no point in pointing out the contradiction.

"Anyhow . . . I couldn't work out why it disturbed me when I saw the tourists looking at their map of the London Underground. Made no sense. Then, when Anatoly came in with his cigars it hit me . . . the thing that Barachiel said to me that I had taken no notice of."

"Which was?"

"Beck."

A frown crossed Lesley-Ann's face.

"Beck? Like in Jeff Beck, the rock guitarist? Or like the guy named Beck that beat Beyoncé and Sam Smith to win the 2015 Grammy for Album of the Year, Beck?"

Now it was Gold's turn to look puzzled.

"What? No . . . no. Neither of them. Beck as in Harry Beck."

"The kid with the hair in One Direction?"

"Jesus! No! That's Harry freaking Styles! Harry Beck!"

"I fucking heard you the first time! Harry Beck! Fine. Great! Who the fuck is Harry Beck?"

Gold took a long intake of breath. Calm Nick . . . calm.

"Harry Beck was a total genius. Back in the 1920s, he worked as an engineering draughtsman at the London Underground Signals Office. In 1931, this guy had a brainwave to end all brainwaves. He proposed a radical new design to illustrate the London Underground system which was growing like Japanese knotweed. The network had become just too big to represent geographically, you know, putting it all on like a map."

"I know what geographically means."

"Good for you. So, Beck's brilliant plan was to tidy the map up by straightening the lines, using diagonals and evening-out the distance between all the stations. He got the idea from looking at his old electrical circuit diagrams. Naturally it was rejected by the powers that be at first but was eventually published and adopted across the Tube in 1933."

Lesley-Ann stared at him. "And you know all this because? Are you some sort of train spotter or something?"

"No, Lesley-Ann. You say you know what the Tube is, right? I'm a Londoner. Like most of London's citizens, I practically live on the Tube. That 1933 design is iconic. It's now used by virtually every subway system in the world. It's fucking brilliant . . . and it's British! That's how I know!"

"Is this the part when you tell me that you guys invented Shakespeare, Parliament and tea?"

"As opposed to junk food, fizzy drinks and Trump. No, it's not."

Silence.

"So, er, what exactly did your best pal Barachiel say to you?"

"My *pal*? Stop busting my balls, will you? He's not my pal and believe me, if I could get out of this, I would. It's not like signing up for a mobile phone contract. What he said, and I think it was pretty much the last thing while I was . . . I was . . . you know, gone, was something like 'do you think that a nation as huge as Hell has just one entrance? There are gates all over the world. You know this. The answer is Mr Beck'."

"That was it?"

The 4x4 hit a particularly vicious pothole, which considering the general state of the road, was saying something.

"Yeah, that was it. All of it."

"And?"

"And . . . I've realised that what was bugging me when I was on the Tube in London was the layout of Hell. Why all these gates? Why people assumed there was just, you know, one gate? Of course there isn't just one, there's freaking loads of them . . . it's like the London Underground, it all joins up, but on a huge scale. What Barachiel was telling me was that the gate of Hell that I have to defend was in London . . . and part of the Tube system. That's where Lucifer is going to try his hand this time round."

Lesley-Ann started to play with her hair. Gold thought it was kind of sexy and irritating in equal measure.

"So, here's the thing, Nick – why can't good old Barachiel,

who, to be clear, is so *not* your pal, just tell you which damn place to go to. What's with the Scooby Doo clues crap?"

"Well, and you'll have to forgive me here, Lesley-Ann, as of five minutes ago I was a TV presenter and now I'm the bloody Gatekeeper tasked with saving the world from being over-run by throat-ripping demons, the answer is . . . I haven't got a clue . . . no pun intended. I don't know. I guess that's the way that this works. Maybe it's like a test of some sort. Maybe Barachiel has to see if I'm, I don't know, worthy of the role. God knows!"

"Yeah . . . speaking of which . . . how come you haven't heard from him?"

"Who?"

"*Him*. You know. *God*."

Gold slammed on the brakes off the 4x4 and steered it to the side of the road.

"What the fuck?" yelled the lawyer.

"Is this some sort of joke to you? Are you getting a big kick out of riding me at every opportunity to get a cheap laugh?"

Gold was furious. The lack of sleep, the strain of the situation, the insanity of it all was taking a heavy toll.

"Really? *How come I haven't heard from God?* Hilarious. Laugh it up, Counselor. Do you think I believed any of this to start with? I can't remember the last time I prayed, went to church, believed in *any* of it. Not for years. Not since I was a kid. Not since my step-parents brought me up. Then, boom, out of nowhere I meet an Archangel and he shows me Hell. I *saw* it. And you know what? It scared the living shit out of me. It was . . . it was . . . just . . . terrible."

Gold seemed to be finding it hard to speak; emotions were washing over him and he seemed to be drowning in them.

"It's very, very hard to have everything you believed in . . . in my case, *nothing*, totally overturned. The things you, I, mocked, to suddenly be true. I can't process this. I don't know how to deal with it. I have no answers. But . . . but if I keep running, if I keep moving then I don't have to *think*. Because, you see, if I think, I really believe I will go quite mad. It's like Nietzsche said, 'if you stare into the abyss, the abyss stares back at you'."

Nick put his head back onto the headrest on the seat of the 4x4. Beads of sweat had formed on his brow, his breathing was laboured. His eyes were closed. He sat motionless.

The only sound was the wind occasionally gently buffeting the windscreen.

"I'm sorry."

They were not words Gold was expecting to hear.

Slowly he opened his eyes and turned towards Lesley-Ann.

"Me too."

She leant forward and gently kissed Gold on the cheek.

"So now what?" she asked.

Gold seemed to regain some of his composure. The atmosphere in the 4x4 was as if a pressure-valve had just been released. Neither of them knew why. But that's life. Sometimes stuff just happens.

Gold finally replied. "Now I go to London. Anatoly will be emailing or WhatsApping me his research. You know what he told me while you were in the loo? He told me that his name Semenov is derived from the male name Semen or Simeon. Semen in Hebrew means God that hears."

"Go figure."

Gold went on. "You will, I guess, be heading back to Pennsylvania to save your client from the Chair, or lethal injection or however you dispose of murderers in your State. She must be crapping herself that you've pissed off to the middle of nowhere."

"Are you fucking insane?"

"Excuse me?"

"What? You think I'm not coming to London? You think you can pack me off with a thanks little girl but this is man's work? I'm seeing this through. So get used to it. And I swear to God, if you go Sly Stallone on me with but this could get dangerous I will punch you in the nuts!"

Gold exhaled.

"So that's a no then?"

"Screw you. Start the damn car and drive."

As they drove, mile after boring mile, Gold thought it might be a good idea to try a light convivial conversational gambit. It's in an Englishman's DNA.

"Well, I think you'll enjoy London. It'll be fun to show you around."

"Oh gosh, thanks Nick. That's so sweet of you. Because obviously, I've never been to your big city before and, gee it would be swell having a man show me around as I'm from such a small hick town back home."

Why had he bothered?

"I assume from your tone that you've visited London then? Just a wild stab in the dark on my part, obviously."

"Duh! Yeah, like about ten times."

"Oh. Were you an air hostess before the law had the pleasure of your company?"

Boom! In your face! Mic drop!

A mile went by in total silence. Gold 1, Trobe Nil.

Then, quite unexpectedly, Lesley-Ann spoke.

"Air hostess . . . good one. I didn't grow up in Hallam, Pennsylvania, I grew up in Greenwich, Connecticut. East Coast. My mother was a lawyer, my father an accountant, good old Ma and Pa. I went to Columbia University in NYC, read law, graduated top of my class. My loving parents used some muscle. Joined a major firm in Manhattan. Yadda yadda yadda."

"And?"

"It went great. I was great. The rising star they called me. The Golden Girl. Everything I touched turned to gold. I was set to be the youngest partner on the firm's letterhead."

Gold interjected. "But you decided that the corporate world

wasn't for you and you wanted to stand up for the little people. To make a difference?"

"Fuck no!" replied Lesley-Ann. "Are you nuts? I was making a fortune. I married the head of corporate affairs. We lived on the Westside in a loft conversion. I drove a Beemer. What's not to like?"

Gold felt he'd been punched in the stomach.

"You were married?"

"Oh gosh Nick, did I forget to mention that? Apologies. Yes sweetheart, I was married. So what?"

Nick was flummoxed.

"So, er . . . nothing. Good for you. Yay."

"Asshole. Anyway, one day we get a new client. Huge. I mean e-fucking-normous. Pharmaceutical company. Billings will be in the millions. Head of the firm assigns me to the account. Golden Girl you see. Me and David, my husband, the go-to-couple, the A-Team."

David. Gold hated him straight away.

"I'm assuming this doesn't have a happy ending?"

"Funny you should say that. David fucks up. There's a clause in a contract that runs to a hundred pages or more. It's a new drug. In the testing stages. Kids with cancer. The worst scenario, right? Kid dies. Drug has side-effects that were unforeseen. But the pharma company knows they're bullet-proof because of the contract these desperate parents have been only too happy to sign. You would, right?"

Gold nodded in assent.

"But the mother of the dead kid won't let it go. She sues. Get's some firecracker of a lawyer from Midtown who happens to hate the pharmaceutical industry. Fuck knows why. Maybe it didn't clear up his acne as a kid and he never got laid. Who knows? But no one gives a shit because the golden couple made sure the contract was watertight. Except . . . except it wasn't. David had screwed up on one tiny clause. It went to court. Cost the pharma company tens of millions. They were pissed. Cost our firm the client who in turn sued us. So now they were pissed."

"That's rough. Wasn't great that the child died, if I may say. So David was fired, I'm guessing?"

Lesley-Ann let out a mirthless laugh.

"No, Nick. Not quite. The cocksucker pinned the blame on me. Persuaded the firm's partners it was all my fault. He was a very persuasive guy. Very. And the lifestyle was more attractive than I was. I was replaceable. The money wasn't."

Gold was finding this all a bit much to take in. "But you argued your side of it, right? You told them what really happened?"

Another, even longer, more bitter mirthless laugh.

"You wouldn't last one hour in a top Manhattan law firm, my friend. Do you think they gave a fuck? They believed him. He was, as I said, *very* persuasive. I was threatened with every lawsuit you can name, and then some, or told to get the fuck out of Dodge and never, ever, come back. David was a networker you see. No other firm was gonna touch me. So I left. He stayed. The end. Roll credits."

"I'm . . . I'm so sorry." Gold was lost for words. He was right not to have liked David from the very start.

"Yeah. Me too. Now can you get us out of this damn desert? I need a drink."

"Join the club. Just so you know, I'm not David. Not in any way. Some things just aren't replaceable."

As the 4x4 lurched off once again, Lesley-Ann Trobe allowed herself just a hint of a smile.

THIRTY

> *"Who first seduc'd them to that foul revolt? Th'* infernal Serpent*; he it was, whose guile Stird up with Envy and Revenge, deceiv'd The Mother of Mankind,"*
>
> – John Milton, Paradise Lost

After what seemed an eternity, they finally pulled up outside the Ozugkent Hotel in Ashgabat. Lesley-Ann headed straight for the bar while Gold had to handle the onslaught of 'Mr Gold, you are back, we were so worried about you being lost in the desert and the car hire company were very concerned' from the front desk team. After assuring everyone that he and Ms (or was it Mrs? he suddenly wondered) Trobe were absolutely fine and there was nothing to worry about, Gold joined the lawyer in the bar area. She was downing a large glass of Diet Coke with ice and lemon with another one already lined-up on the bar counter.

Gold ordered the same. Clearly neither of them had watched *Ice Cold in Alex.*

"I'm going to have to call London. I need to give them an update. This will have run way over budget for the recce."

Lesley-Ann put down her drink. "You're about to face Lucifer and his minions, and I don't mean the cute little animated movie things, and you're worried about budgets?"

Gold looked at her. She might be a whip-smart attorney but it was evident she knew the square root of fuck-all about television production.

"Yes. Oddly enough I am worried about budgets. You know why?

Because if Larry thinks I'm taking the piss and can't see a return on the company's large investment, several things will happen: they'll fire my arse, they'll cancel the show, and more to the point they will dump me out here in wherever the hell we are today. Just like Malcolm Maclaren did to Johnny Rotten and the Sex Pistols; decided he'd had enough and dumped them in LA without a penny while he swanned off back to London. I know this: I went to a talk John Lydon gave at the British Library. He told the story himself."

Lesley-Ann stared at him.

"I'm sorry . . . what part of Armageddon are you not a-gedding here?"

Now it was Gold's turn to stare.

"I get it all. Remember, I'm the one who saw Hell. Not you."

"Clearly you've never met my ex-husband."

"No, I doubt I'll ever have that singular pleasure. I'm being logical. Stay with me before you Karen Walker me. We, I, whatever, need to get back to London and finish this. I need the funds. I need the backing. I can't do this alone. And when it's done, I'll have one hell of a TV series. It'll fast-track my career."

The attorney stared. What was it with these media types?

"Yes, I forgot. Your career. Obviously that comes way before stopping Lucifer's attempt to flood the world with an endless supply of zombie, undead . . . things. I'm delighted we've got that in its correct perspective. I'm going to my room and have a very long bath. You do your TV thing on the phone. And get me an upgrade on the flight to London."

With that Lesley-Ann swept out of the bar with a style that betrayed how she'd watched far too many Bette Davis and Joan Crawford films during lonely nights in Pennsylvania.

Gold finished his drink, ordered another and took it up to his room. Checking that the time zone difference was acceptable, he put a call through to the offices of Good Foot Productions. After the obligatory how are you nonsense with the receptionist, Gold was put through to Larry's office.

"Nick Gold – my very own Paranormal Detective. How ya doing, buddy?"

Larry sounded ebullient.

"Great, thanks Larry. How the devil are you?" Always best to show respect to the folks who hold the chequebooks.

"I'm like a dog with two tails. All good in the hood. So get me up to speed. What's occurring?"

Nick Gold proceeded to recount to Larry the PG-rated version of events. Obviously, it was a step too far to include everything . . . like Barachiel making guest appearances, that he was The Gatekeeper . . . stuff like that.

What was left was an exciting follow the breadcrumbs, chase the Macguffin type tale designed to whet the appetite of Gold's boss in London and keep the wheels of industry a-rolling along. By that, Gold meant a further injection of production company cash.

As he reached the end of his monologue, which had only been interrupted by a few 'Hmms', 'really', 'you're kidding' from Larry in London, Gold's stomach knotted up. The lack of reaction was concerning. Was Larry hacked off with the project? Would he call it quits and pull the plug? Was he, Nick, about to feel the way Johnny Rotten had in LA?

Larry's voice came through loud and clear. "Nick, get yourself back here and come in and see us. Let's talk it all through face to face. I've got a feeling about this."

A good feeling. A bad feeling? A here's your P45, now piss off feeling?

Gold simply replied with a fake chirpy tone. "Absolutely Larry. Looking forward to catching up."

If in doubt, play dumb. And that was that.

Gold then called through to Lesley-Ann's room and a tired voice answered. Gold didn't bother with the Oh, did I wake you? pleasantries.

"I'm heading back on the first flight I can get to London. Got to see the big boss in the office. And then, fingers crossed, I'll have some info through from Anatoly. What are your plans? You coming along?"

"*Coming along?* What am I? The love interest in a James Bond movie? Yes, obviously I'm coming along. Tell me what flight has availability and I'll book it online. Now can I go back to sleep?"

Click. The phone went dead.

After the usual excitement that accompanies booking anything online, getting rid of the infuriating pop-up ads, being informed via a countdown clock that you had just ten minutes left to complete the purchase and, of course, inadvertently clicking on the wrong option, Gold had his seat booked. He called Lesley-Ann with the flight details and went to have a shower.

Later that day, Trobe and Gold were onboard their flight to London Heathrow. Lesley-Ann had managed to book the seat next to him so they sat in fairly amicable, companionable silence watching films or sleeping.

Once through immigration, which at Heathrow is as welcoming as the plague but takes longer to survive, Gold got straight down to business. Airports do that to a person.

"Look, I have to go straight into town to meet with my boss at the office. What are you going to do? Did you book a hotel or something? We could meet later for dinner."

Lesley-Ann looked at him like he had, once again, just grown another head right there in the baggage reclaim area.

"What am I going to do? I wanna meet this famous boss of yours. I'd love to see who is insane enough to employ you. And no, I didn't book a hotel. I figured I could crash on your sofa for a few days. I promise to leave the toilet seat up for you."

Americans. Straight to the point.

The British version of Lesley-Ann's self-invite would have contained several, 'if it's not too much trouble', 'if I'm not imposing', 'I was wondering if', 'do you think I might possibly' and 'you'll not even notice that I'm there plus I'm a dab hand at cooking'.

Gold just muttered whatever and walked to the taxi rank.

With the boundless joy of the M4 motorway and the A4 that leads into central London and makes every visitor to the UK want to jump right back on board the next flight home, the two arrived at Soho's Dean Street and entered the offices of Good Foot Productions.

A few minutes before their arrival, Mitzi, the receptionist with a first from Warwick University, had overheard a furious row emanating from her boss's office. Despite the polished wooden door being firmly closed, Larry's raised tones were clearly audible. Evidently he was on the phone to Adam Farthing. The interchange was so loud and so interesting that Mitzi was forced to remove her earphones, stop listening to her audiobook of *Instant Influence and Charisma* by Paul McKenna and tune into what was transpiring a few feet away. Interestingly, the book would prove invaluable as, within a few years, Mitzi was CEO of Netflix, although somehow she felt that Larry's offer of a few well-placed calls had somehow oiled the wheels of industry.

"So what are you saying, Adam. Just to be clear. That I should shut down Gold's budget?"

Larry's speakerphone was on full volume, and Adam's voice was clearly audible.

"Yes. You know my view. I think the company has been far too generous. He's a loose cannon. Who knows what he's been up to? Who can tell how prudently the company money has been spent? You know, Larry, frankly I am getting very close to having more than enough of Mr Gold and his world tour of bullshit. It's ridiculous. Sorry, but it is. There's going to come a time, Larry, when you're going to have to make a choice. Him or me. I'm serious. Someone who can really add to the company or a wildcard who doesn't have your best interests at heart. Not like me. He's running around on a crazy hunch that will lead to absolutely nothing. You'll see. Nothing. It's a total waste of company money."

"Need I remind you, Adam, that by the company money, you mean *my* money."

"Yes of course, Larry. I appreciate that."

"So, again, in the pursuit of clarity, you're telling me how to spend my money?"

The tone of Adam's voice changed dramatically. The bombast instantly mutated into servility.

"No, of course not, I would never dream of doing that, Larry. It is entirely yours to do with as you please. I would never dream of criticising you. Never."

There was a pause.

"That's good to know, Adam. And very wise. Now go do what you do so well and make us all fucking rich. Oh, and Adam, please don't ever put me in a position where I have to choose."

The click of the receiver was loud.

He was finishing another phone call but beckoned them in.

"Vladimir . . . no problem . . . always a pleasure. We're on for a spot of bear hunting next time I'm over? Take care. Speak soon. Bye."

Larry put the phone down and jumped up from his leather executive swivel chair from behind his antique polished rosewood desk.

"Nick, you crazy bastard! Come here!"

He enveloped Gold in a breath-exhaling hug accompanied by much back-slapping.

"And this must be Lesley-Ann. Welcome to London, Mrs Trobe."

Nick didn't recall mentioning Lesley-Ann's marital status, nor come to think of it, her surname. In all the excitement and travelling, he had probably let it slip.

"Sit down guys. Tea? More coffee? Shall I send to Bar Italia for some Panini? It's to die for. They do this thing with Parma Ham . . . well, it's off the scale."

"Thanks Larry, but we ate on the plane."

Larry took out a large cigar from the humidor on his desk. "Yeah, I know – no smoking in the office. Fuck 'em."

He cut the end of the cigar and spent a while using a long wooden cigar match to light it. After the first luxurious puff, he said, "Sorry the office is a bit quieter than usual, Lesley-Ann. Some of the team are out on the road. We're looking at a new series called *That Riviera Touch* – the name's a tribute to the More-cambe and Wise film. Loved them. Yeah, it's about ex-pats who've made it big out there and their Riviera lifestyle. You know, cars, boats, clothes, sun . . . the usual, you will never achieve any of this that our punters lap up without a sense of irony. So, what's new, guys? Any more ideas to throw into the show?"

Nick couldn't help himself, betraying the inner insecurity of everyone in showbiz.

"So, you still like my idea?"

Larry took another long puff on his Havana cigar.

"Like it? I fucking *love* it. That's why we're still funding the recce and its development. It's got legs. I think it could even make it onto terrestrial television. Big time. You know what . . . fuck it . . . I'll call the DG now and fix something up."

"The DG?" enquired Lesley-Ann, a fish totally out of water.

Nick jumped in. "The Director-General of the BBC. The top man. Larry's just kidding. No one gets to speak to him. You don't even get to speak to a Head of Department. You spend days just trying to make contact with a nineteen-year-old intern there."

While he was speaking, Larry was hitting a number that was evidently on speed dial.

"Tone? Larry. Yes, great thanks. How you fixed tomorrow for lunch? Got a killer new series I want you to hear about."

There was a pause.

"Well, that sounds about as interesting as watching paint dry. Accountants, they're all bloody bean-counters. Shall we say twelve-thirty at Claridge's? Great . . . I'll see you there. Looking forward to it. Love to Cynthia."

Larry put the phone down. "So, Lesley-Ann, what do you make of our Boy Wonder here?"

Awkward.

"Well," she began, "he's certainly an interesting guy to hang around with."

Larry laughed.

"And they say Americans don't get irony! Yes, interesting. But let me ask you, what's *your* interest in all of this? Delighted to meet you by the way."

Lesley-Ann looked at Nick Gold's boss. The suit was obviously hand-made. It fitted to perfection. The shirt was clearly the best with an expensive silk tie to complete the ensemble. The fingernails were manicured and the hair, slightly greying, had been exposed to a barber who knew his or her craft expertly. He had the easy manner that the truly successful and wealthy exude. He seemed charming and welcoming. Not what she was expecting from the way Nick had spoken about him. Actually, for an older guy, maybe mid-forties she estimated, he was in very good shape and pretty easy on the eye. There was no middle-age paunch, his face seemed remarkably line-free yet bore no tell-tale signs of having been under the knife and his shoulders and chest indicated that he worked out regularly. When he moved around his office, he was light on his feet and, to Lesley-Ann's surprise, had a quiet gracefulness that belied his six feet height and muscular build. His movements were unhurried and fluid. He was a player, of that she was in no doubt. A man with the confidence to insist on getting his own way by sheer force of personality. But it was his eyes, above all, that fascinated Lesley-Ann. They were piercing and deep violet – eyes that could penetrate your very soul. He was the most beautiful man she had seen in her entire life. And, for reasons Lesley-Ann could not properly articulate, the most frightening.

"My interest? Well Nick's a, er, live wire to be around, and I'm in the middle of a case back home and his research may be of help to my client."

"I see. And what has your client done? Speeding ticket? Voted Republican? I'm just kidding. What has she done?"

"Well, she's been charged with murder. Allegedly killed her husband."

"And did she do it?" asked Larry, leaning forward.

Lesley-Ann ran her fingers through her hair. "Interesting question. The police think they have a slam-dunk case. I'm not so sure. She's very convincing – if she's lying."

Larry smiled. "The trust of the innocent is the liar's most useful tool."

"Shakespeare?" asked Gold.

"Stephen King," replied Larry.

"Well, as they say, the jury is out on this one, Larry. But it's my job to defend her to the best of my ability, so that's why I'm here. Gathering any possible defence evidence and argument that I can."

"I'm sure you'll get all your answers while you're here, Lesley-Ann. You're in very capable hands with Nick. He's our number one boy. Within a few months he'll be a household name. Lucky that I have him on a tight contract!"

He laughed.

But he meant it. Showbiz is always fun until the contract arrives. Then the show goes and it's just biz.

"I'll drink to that," chimed in Gold, who had felt a little excluded from this semi-love-fest.

"Speaking of which, you guys must be exhausted. Go and have lunch on me. There's a great Vietnamese restaurant opened just around the corner. Keep me posted, Nick. I'll speak to some of the team in France later today and bring them up to speed. I know you ate on the plane, but trust me, the *Ca Kho To* is heavenly. Have fun you two. Nick . . . good job. Keep it up. I think, no, I *know*, you're really onto something here. Keep at it. Lesley-Ann, I'm sure we'll meet again."

With that, Nick and Lesley-Ann said their goodbyes and thank-yous and went off for lunch. Larry was right, as usual. The *Ca Kho To* was utterly delicious.

THIRTY-ONE

"Alone, and without guide, half lost, I seek What readiest path leads where your gloomy bounds
Confine with Heav'n;"

– John Milton, Paradise Lost

After lunch, Nick deliberately caught the Tube from Leicester Square and took the Northern Line direct to Balham in South London so that Lesley-Ann could understand how the city relied on public transport. London boasted twenty-one thousand famous black cabs, eight thousand instantly-recognisable red buses and until recently, around forty-four thousand Uber drivers. Transport for London was still the fastest way of traveling from A to B in London.

Nick talked her through the Tube map that they'd picked up for free at the station. Harry Beck's brilliantly innovative diagrammatic layout looked better than ever. It was timeless, an icon and well worth the ten pounds, ten shillings fee Mr Beck received for the task in 1931.

When they arrived at his local station, Gold explained to his soon-to-be lodger that the largest number of people killed by a single wartime bomb was sixty-eight, right here at Balham Station. Lesley-Ann looked shocked. Most Americans, Gold knew, had no idea that the shortest distance across the English Channel to France is a mere twenty miles. That was all that had separated Britain from the largest army ever created in modern times. Twenty miles from German occupation and total annihilation.

Once back at Nick's flat, Lesley-Ann could see that it was

pretty much a man cave, which said volumes about the way Nick had been living his life for the last couple of years.

As is the way of the modern world, both turned on their laptops, checking social media to see what everyone had eaten for lunch, what the cat had been up to and who was blocking whom.

It's life, Jim, but not as we know it.

"Great!" exclaimed Gold. "Anatoly Semenov has been hard at work. Top bloke."

Lesley-Ann winced. Did Brits really say bloke? Was Dick Van Dyke lurking just beneath every Englishman's skin waiting to start dancing around chimney pots?

"He's dug up a ton of info about the London Underground. Loads of facts and figures that he thinks will help us narrow it down."

"Narrow what down, exactly?"

Gold looked up from his screen. "Which station on the Underground I have to go to. Where, you know, he'll be. With his fang pals."

"*He* being Lucifer? And, so I'm getting this, you have to work out which one it is? Well, that shouldn't be too tricky. Knock yourself out, Philip Marlowe. I read up on your tube thing. There are two hundred and seventy stations and two hundred and fifty miles of track. I'd take sandwiches if I were you."

Gold resisted the temptation to throw a book at her. "I'm not saying it's easy. If it was easy, then *anyone* could do this."

Lesley-Ann laughed out loud. "Yeah, right. And, of course, you're not just anyone, you're The Gatekeeper. Da da!"

"Seriously? Piss off!"

"Oh, grow a pair Peter Parker. Where are you actually going to start? Suppose you hang out at the wrong tube station and old Lucifer sneaks up the escalators with his pals at another one?"

Gold looked unhappy. "Yes, that, oddly enough, had crossed my mind. Which is why I am following up on a suggestion that Anatoly made."

"Which is?"

Gold spread out the fold-out tube map.

"It needs to be narrowed down. Maybe he'll hit a major station, but perhaps he'll be more cautious. Think about it. The Asylum at Hallam Pennsylvania was off the beaten track, and then some. Hierapolis was hardly Grand Central Station, or Waterloo, as we're in England. The Derweze Crater is in the middle of the freaking desert, so, if he follows the pattern, the Gate won't be an obvious choice. It'll be far more obscure. It'll give him the time to do whatever he has up his skeletor sleeve."

The attorney nodded.

"Nick, can I ask you a question? You're on TV right. You're single, yeah? You make a decent living I'm guessing. So, my question is, why are you living here? In this apartment? Wouldn't a guy like you have a, I dunno, a house or something? In central London, not out here in the boondocks?"

The lighted match had been thrown on the spilt gallons of petrol.

Gold blew his lid. For the next twenty minutes Lesley-Ann Trobe was subjected to one of the worst experiences of her life – a full explanatory discourse on London property prices, the importance of location, access to public transport, the gentrification of the urban sprawl. It was a monologue delivered with passion and in-depth knowledge.

At its conclusion, Lesley-Ann was armed with enough information to start her own estate agency.

"Thanks for that, Nick. I feel truly enlightened. Lucky me."

Gold smiled. His work here was done.

"Shall we grab a dinner and some shut-eye? I'm pooped."

Lesley-Ann looked aghast.

"Pooped . . . tired."

She looked relieved.

They left Nick's flat and wandered down to the conveniently located Day of the Raj restaurant and proceeded to demolish several beers, starters, various breads, some main courses and a few side dishes. It surprised them both how hungry they were. Lunch seemed hours ago.

As they walked back up to his flat, Nick began to ponder on the sleeping arrangement at Casa Gold. They'd had an enjoyable dinner and he'd made her laugh. Several times in fact. Should he make a move? Would she feel rejected if he didn't? Would she kick him in the nuts if he did? He decided to see how things panned out.

Back at the flat, Lesley-Ann didn't want a nightcap nor a cup of tea, nor indeed coffee.

"Well then, I'll bid you *adieu*. I'll be off . . . to bed. Sure you've got everything you need? Another pillow? I have more blankets or a duvet if you'd prefer?"

Lesley-Ann assured him that she was fine and had all that she would require for a good night's sleep.

And that was that. The rich vein of potential romance clearly had been exhaustively mined.

Gold said his goodnights and went off to bed. He was just dozing off nicely when the bedroom door opened.

"Really, are *all* you Brits gay?

For several hours, Gold did his utmost to disprove that particular urban myth.

The next morning, over toast and Marmite, the latter drawing a repulsed cry of 'what the fuck is this shit?' from his appalled lodger, Gold set out the plan for the day.

"Between what I've been looking up and the lengthy email from Anatoly, we have an appointment this morning at Transport Museum at Covent Garden. We're meeting a Professor Clifford."

"Who's he?" asked the lodger, still wearing her bedhead hairstyle with some aplomb.

"He is a *she*. Professor Clifford is, I gather, the foremost authority on London's underground railway system – the Tube.

She's agreed to see us. I got the office to email her that it was essential to our research. The museum will get a mention, she'll get an on-screen credit. Happy days all round."

They set off later, after Gold had once more disproved the lawyer's assertion that all Englishmen were repressed, and caught the Tube to Covent Garden.

"Is this the Mary Poppins place? I wonder whatever happened to the little girl in the movie? Jane Banks? I wanted to be her when I was a little kid and saw it on TV for the first time."

"I've no idea. Rather before my time. By a century or so. And you're mixing up *Mary Poppins* with *My Fair Lady* which *was* set here."

The duo entered the Transport Museum, which was situated right on the Piazza at Covent Garden. The area's days as the capital's centre for fruit and vegetables were long gone. Now it was a popular tourist destination and boasted dozens of excellent restaurants. And some not quite so great.

At the reception, they asked for Professor Clifford and were told to wait for a few minutes. After a while, they were escorted to a small office away from the public areas. Behind a desk covered in papers, files, pencils and, yes, a pencil sharpener sat a blonde woman in her early forties. She stood up and formally shook hands with Nick and Lesley-Ann.

"Have you been offered tea?" she enquired.

Lesley-Ann was struggling to come to terms with the British obsession with tea. Even Nick, once they were here in London, had offered her endless cups of tea every few minutes or so it seemed. It must be hard-wired into the nation's DNA.

Tea was brought and served in rather fetching mugs from the museum's shop, depicting portions of the Underground map.

"I've read your email carefully, Mr Gold," announced Professor Clifford, adjusting her designer glasses as she re-read it. "I think I can help you and your . . . friend."

"That's great," responded Gold rather too much like an eager schoolboy.

Professor Clifford started to fold out papers and schematics.

"I must say that your programme sounds rather fun. Ghosts and all that. Marvellous."

Gold beamed enthusiastically. "Well, we certainly enjoy making them. They seem to be popular. And thank you so much for your help. It is much appreciated."

Lesley-Ann sat there. Was this the way business was conducted in England? How much politeness could anyone take without screaming?

"I think this is where you should start looking," said the professor as she pushed a number of papers across her desk towards Gold. It seemed the lawyer had become invisible.

Gold started to look at the information placed before him.

"Was that what you were looking for, Mr Gold?"

Indeed it was.

"I'm so sorry, I didn't catch your name." The question was aimed at Lesley-Ann.

"Trobe. Lesley-Ann Trobe."

"Ah, American I see. Judging by your accent."

The lawyer immediately realised that the professor was some sort of genius.

"Got that right, Prof."

Prof was not a term used to address English academics outside of Hollywood films. A cloud passed across Professor Clifford's face. But it was soon replaced as she got into her stride on her specialized subject.

"There are two hundred and seventy functioning stations across our network here in London, but at least forty overground and underground stations that are still in existence but are no longer used for travel."

"Why were they closed?" asked Lesley-Ann desperate for something, anything, to say.

"They were closed for a variety of reasons, from low passenger numbers to re-routing. All these stations have very interesting histories. Some offered a vital refuge throughout the wars. London got it rather bad, Miss Trobe you see."

"Yes, I know," replied the attorney.

Professor Clifford was well into it now. "During World War Two, many stations were used as public shelters and underground offices for London Underground and government staff. Down Street station was transformed into an underground facility with phone lines, and even hosted a meeting of the War Cabinet. Another station, Brompton Road, was sold to the War Office in 1938 and is still used by the Ministry of Defence today."

"Fascinating," said Lesley-Ann, with all the sincerity of a politician.

"Stations have also played a part in Britain's cultural life. Aldwych station, for example, was used to house the National Gallery's collection during World War One and British Museum artefacts during World War Two.

"Of course, we are quite modern in our outlook here at Transport for London. For instance, Aldwych station has been used as a film location for productions as different as The Prodigy's *Firestarter* music video, *Sherlock* with that rather delightful Benedict Cumberbatch chap, and the zombie film, *28 Weeks Later*. Zombies . . . I've no idea why the public are so fascinated with them. Total nonsense of course."

"Oh, indeed. Total nonsense," chimed in Lesley-Ann. "What kind of idiot would want to see a film about them, or worse still, read a book about them, eh?"

Professor Clifford smiled at her foreign visitor. "Quite so, Miss Trobe. Quite so."

Gold was ignoring the verbal jousting that was taking place and was staring intently at the papers in front of him.

"Yes, that's the list of disused stations that your office requested Mr Gold. I must remember to look out for your programmes on television. I regret to say I'm more of a *Midsomer Murders* type of viewer myself."

But Gold wasn't listening.

"There are so many. Sod it! So bloody many!"

"Excuse me, Mr Gold? Do we have a problem?" enquired Professor Clifford.

Gold looked up. "Oh, sorry. I'm looking at this list of disused Tube stations . . . it goes on forever. I had no idea."

"Well as I said, there are forty. What in particular are you looking for? Perhaps I can narrow it down for you. Be of assistance, so to speak."

Yeah, I bet you'd love that, thought Lesley-Ann.

"We're thinking of a disused station that is central but kinda out of the way. So, Aldwych would be way too obvious, er . . . to choose. You know. Everyone knows it through TV and movies and stuff," added Lesley-Ann helpfully.

"Let me see. May I look over your shoulder, Mr Gold? Two heads being better than one and all that."

Jeez! Why don't you just give him a blow job while you're at it, thought Mrs Trobe.

"Sure," replied Nick, utterly oblivious to anything except his thoughts.

The professor moved around the desk. "Now, let me see. Ah well, we have Down Street. Useless even in its own lifetime. Opened in 1907 and closed in 1932, lack of use you see. It was between Green Park and Hyde Park on the Piccadilly line. The idea was to give the wealthy citizens of Mayfair easy access to the tube network – until some genius worked out that the inter-war years rich were entirely disdainful of travelling underground. Snobs, you know how it is. Well, possibly not you, Miss Trobe."

"Mrs, Mrs Trobe."

Keep pushing sister. One more crack outta you, hun.

"Then there's Mark Lane Station, which opened in 1884; it ran right through until 1967, when nearby Tower Hill was opened to deal with the huge number of commuters. Sad really. Nothing left now. Mark Lane was completely stripped down following its closure, its tunnels reduced to cold concrete cellars."

"Yeah. Tragic. Tell me, Professor, are we going to go through each of the forty stations in such detail? You know, just asking here."

Gold shot Lesley-Ann a look indicating that she was being less than helpful. Otherwise known as STFU.

Professor Clifford, for her part, gave the American a look that would have floored Darth Vader.

"So many to choose from, Mr Gold. Brill, Brompton Road, British Museum, City Road, Hounslow Town . . . it's a cornucopia of choices."

Yeah, we know you're a freaking professor. Keep it simple, internalized the lawyer.

Lesley-Ann stood up. Screw this. She went and stood next to the professor.

"Guys, let's break this down. It's gotta be in central London for maximum effect . . . .er, for the TV series I mean, so let's forget the ones out in the sticks. So, what's close to the action but one that no one knows?"

"By sticks I assume you mean suburbs? I myself live on the Essex border. It is most charming, Mrs Trobe. Actually, there are parts of Essex that you would fit right into."

"What's this here? replied Lesley-Ann, her lack of knowledge of the counties on the edge of London insulating her from the barb.

Professor Clifford adjusted her glasses.

"Ah yes. Yes indeed. Very interesting. King William Street."

Gold looked up. "Interesting how, Professor?"

"Well, King William Street was the original, but I have to say, short-lived northern terminus of the City and South London Railway. This was significant as the first deep-level underground railway in London and one of the component parts of the Northern

Line, or, as it's known to Londoners, the Misery Line. It was located within the actual City of London, on King William Street."

Professor Clifford chuckled. "Funnily enough, despite being a short-lived station, it was in operation longer than King William who was actually on the throne for just seven years."

"Gosh, fancy that," responded Lesley-Ann.

Professor Clifford had an audience. She was, as they say, on a roll.

"King William Street Station opened on 18 December 1890 and was constructed from a large masonry station tunnel, accessed from the surface by a lift shaft or a spiral staircase. There were two platforms, one on each side of the single, central track, one for passengers entering and the other for passengers leaving the trains. That system was later called the Spanish solution. No idea why, I'm afraid. Not the foggiest."

"Oh dear," muttered Lesley-Ann.

"The station tunnel itself is situated beneath Monument Street and runs east-west across King William Street, ending beneath Arthur Street. The approach tunnels had sharp curves and steep gradients to go underneath the River Thames, while also remaining under public rights-of-way. Anyway, the station was closed on 24 February 1900."

Gold had remained silent during the professor's discourse.

"What's there now? Is anything left?"

"Funny you should ask, Mr Gold. The original station building was demolished in the 1930s, although the parts of the station below ground were converted for use as a public air-raid shelter during the war."

Gold had a gleam in his eye. His enthusiasm and excitement was palpable and oddly seemed to fill the professor's small office.

"Professor, if we wanted to film down there, would it be possible? Is there any way that we could access the station?"

Professor Clifford took off her glasses and polished them on her Hermes scarf while she thought.

"Yes. Theoretically that would be possible, I suppose. Let me double-check. Give me a moment, would you?"

She went to her laptop, stared intently at the screen while she keyed in some information and, after a few moments, straightened up with a satisfied look on her face.

"Yes, it's possible. It can be accessed today via a manhole butting on to Regis House. That's a newish office building. There's the original cast iron spiral staircase leading down to platform level. You can't use the lift or the lift shaft anymore, they filled it in with concrete during the construction of the original Regis House."

Gold nodded to indicated that he was taking all this in.

"The original running tunnels north of Borough station are still there, although when the Jubilee line extension was built in the 1990s, the old southbound tunnel was cut through as part of the construction works at London Bridge station. These running tunnels now act as a ventilation shaft for London Bridge station."

There was a faraway look in Gold's eyes. Professor Clifford was subconsciously expecting a round of applause, but there was nothing.

Lesley-Ann realised that she had to step into the void.

"Professor Clifford, you have been absolutely terrific. We are enormously grateful."

The Professor looked at the American as if she had just turned into a member of the Royal family.

"Well . . . er . . . that's very kind of you, er . . . Mrs Trobe. Yes, thank you. We try to do our best don't you know. I'm, er, pleased that I could help. When do you think the show will be on television, you know, so I can remember to set a series link?"

"Well, you can never be too accurate with dates, but I'd estimate early next year. Spring maybe."

The lawyer had absolutely no idea what the hell she was talking about, but it served to fill in the awkward gap caused by Nick apparently going into a catatonic trance.

"Wouldn't you say that's about right, Nick? Nick? Nick!"

Gold snapped out of it at the third calling of his name.

"Er, yeah. Sure. Definitely."

Lesley-Ann smiled winningly at Professor Clifford who, despite her best efforts, looked bemused.

"So, Nick, is there anything else you'd like to ask the professor? I'm conscious we've taken up a lot of her valuable time."

Gold still seemed in a daze.

"Nope. I think that pretty much wraps it up. Yeah. Thank you so much Professor Clifford. You've been a huge help. Really, you've been great."

Without warning. Gold leant over and kissed the astonished professor on both cheeks. Lesley-Ann, attempting to recover the situation, proffered an outstretched hand and shook the professor's in a professional, business-like manner.

The professor, for her part, looked as if Captain Kirk had just beamed down into her office from the Starship Enterprise with Spock, McCoy and Sulu in tow.

Lesley-Ann ushered Nick Gold out of the cramped office, out of the Transport Museum and into the daylight of Covent Garden.

Once they were a safe distance away from the venue, the attorney spun on Gold.

"What the fuck's the matter with you? Do you have any idea how embarrassing that was back there? I was dying!"

Gold, in return, looked her straight in the eyes.

"I've got it, Lesley-Ann. I know it."

"You know what, you freak?"

"I know where I must face Lucifer."

THIRTY-TWO

"But what more oft in Nations grown corrupt, And by thir vices brought to servitude, Than to love Bondage more than Liberty, Bondage with ease than strenuous liberty;"

– John Milton, Samson Agonistes

Lesley-Ann ushered Gold into the nearest coffee shop she could find in Covent Garden. She ordered two double espressos and brought them to the table. Waitresses in London were about as ubiquitous as horse and carts.

"What in the name of Rain Man were you doing back there? Seriously, what happened? Did you have a fit? Are you OK? Have you gone all Charlie Sheen on me? Do you have a violent torpedo of truth rammed up your arse?"

Gold sipped his espresso slowly and deliberately. He still seemed lost in thought.

"Hello! Anyone in there? Ground control to Major Nick."

Gold looked up. In the light of the coffee shop, he looked older. Maybe it was the shadows.

"I'm sorry about that, you know, back there. It was a bit overwhelming."

"It was a bit fucking embarrassing too. You gonna share?"

Gold nodded. "Yes, of course. The thing is, it all hit me at once. It was like a light bulb switching on, a pivotal, seminal moment, a –"

"Yeah, I think I've got that part! I meant, are you gonna share what your eureka moment was?"

Again, Gold nodded and seemed to perk up.

"I was looking at the list of disused stations that the professor was showing us. All the time, I was thinking which one would it be? Where would be the least likely but also the most obvious?

The lawyer crinkled her nose.

"Er, yeah . . . right."

Gold understood her confusion. "What I mean is that in every other time the undead, demons, whatever the hell they are, turn up it's in a fairly out of the way place – so they wouldn't arrive at Piccadilly Circus or Times Square."

"But why not? They can choose any of the Gates of Hell. You've said it's like a subway but on a monstrous scale."

Gold pondered the question. "Yeah, I know. No idea. Maybe Barachiel knows? Maybe it's some heaven versus hell war gaming rule. Like *The Hunger Games* or something?

Lesley-Ann stood up, walked over to the coffee shop counter and ordered two raisin Danish pastries. Theology made her hungry – not for knowledge, just for Danish. She returned with two plates.

"Thought you might like this. They look fresh. I've been thinking, and at the risk of stating the blindingly obvious, why don't you get in touch with your pal Archangel Barachiel and get the low down on what to do? Isn't that the smart thing to do?"

Gold took a bite out of his raisin Danish.

"First, I am tired of telling you that he's not my pal as you keep calling him. Secondly, and this may come as a shock, it's not like I can go see Commissioner Gordon at Police Headquarters, climb up on to the roof and shine the Barachiel-Man signal. He's not Bruce Wayne in disguise. He's not on speed dial, I can't email him and I very much doubt he's got a WhatsApp account. I have no say on when or where he turns up. He just does. Or doesn't. OK?"

Trobe quietly munched on her Danish, dabbing her mouth with a paper napkin to remove any vestigial crumbs.

"Whatever."

"*Whatever*? Are you fourteen?" Gold had never been a fan of Valley Girl Speak.

"Moving on, Alfred, you evidently have come to a conclusion. Which is?"

Gold took a last gulp of espresso.

"OK, consider this. Who runs the UK?"

Excellent. The perfect time for a discussion on socio-economics.

Lesley-Ann decided to play along.

"The Queen of England."

Gold rolled his eyes, not bothering to disguise his irritation.

"Don't be ridiculous. You're a lawyer, you worked in Manhattan. Think!"

The ex-corporate lawyer tried her luck once more.

"Fine. Apologies to Liz. How about the Government? Your Members of Parliament or whatever they're called."

More eye rolling. "Think! I'm talking about who *really* runs the UK. Not the crap we're fed. Who really holds the power?"

Lesley-Ann blew out her cheeks as if she was Miles Davis at the Blue Note.

"I give up. Why don't we save time and you just tell me?"

Gold realised he was losing his audience. Even losing one was too much for a TV presenter's ego.

"The City."

The attorney looked blank.

"The City," repeated Gold.

Trobe began to drum her fingers on the plastic-covered table.

"Yes, I'm familiar with the word city. I'm just not following you."

"In the UK . . . in London, the centre of finance, the hub of all things to do with money, is in a specific area of London. It's called simply the City. Sometimes it's called the Square Mile. It's like your Wall Street. It controls everything."

The light dawned in Lesley-Ann's eyes.

"Ah, you mean the Bank of England. I get you."

Gold shook his head emphatically.

"No, forget that. The Bank of England is nothing. It's a façade. It's showbiz. I'm talking about the real power brokers. It's where three hundred thousand people work every single day. It's been there since around 47AD, since history started to be recorded here. The same area."

Lesley-Ann was now giving Nick Gold her full attention. The thing lawyers do when an expert witness is on the stand.

"Let me put this in perspective," said Gold. "Every day nearly four trillion US dollars are traded globally. Trading in London is responsible for getting on for half of that. Nearly half of the total of the world's trading.

"How the fuck do you know this crap?" asked the bewildered yet, to her fury, impressed, visitor.

"I'm an investigative journalist . . . sure, laugh all you want, but I read. I research. I watch."

Lesley-Ann put her index finger into the espresso cup, ran it around, and put the content into her mouth. Gold found it simultaneously annoying, childish and exceptionally erotic.

Unaware of her actions, the attorney pressed on.

"So, we've established that the City, as you call it, is worth a shit load of money. OK. I get that. So how does this help you pinpoint the right Underground station to play Gunfight at the OK Corral?"

"Because, Counselor, seven of the eleven London Underground lines run through the City, serving eleven stations. And guess what's right in the middle of that? King William Street Station! Yes, the one that's been closed since 1900. It accounts for so much."

Again, a blank look from Lesley-Ann.

"Toxic waste."

"Excuse me?"

"Toxic waste," repeated Gold. "The poisonous by-products of manufacturing, farming, septic systems, construction, automotive garages, laboratories, hospitals . . . basically the shit they all produce. The waste harms humans, animals, and plants if they come into contact with these toxins buried in the ground."

"OK, Al Gore. So?"

Gold was speaking hurriedly now, belying the veneer of his cynical attitude that hid his true intellect.

"The station was closed in 1900. Right? Does that date mean anything to you? No, it wouldn't. But it does to me. Back in series two of Paranormal Detective, I did an episode on haunted London, you know, the usual crap about ghosts being seen just about everywhere except in an Apple Store. I did a lot of research. You know how you get distracted when you research stuff? So I really got into the whole thing about the City. And I kept thinking, how come the City suddenly started to go so toxic after 1900?"

Lesley-Ann stood up yet again, wandered over to the counter and came back with two Diet Cokes. Comfort food.

"Toxic how?" she asked, sucking on the straw in the can. Gold took out his laptop, opened it up, and after a short while, spun it around so his companion could see the screen.

"Here's my headline notes from that show. I wrote far more of course. Well, they didn't end up in the show, I kind of made them for myself.

'The Baring Crisis. In November 1890 the City and nation were shocked to learn that Baring Brothers had been rescued from collapse.'

Gold looked up. "Does that mean anything to you. Barings? Ring any bells? OK, they stretched themselves very very badly by underwriting a series of Argentinean bonds. They were one of the City's most renowned and trusted merchant banks."

Gold spun the laptop around on the café table so Lesley-Ann could have a better view of the screen.

*

'1895 – Jabez Spencer Balfour was one of Britain's earliest self-made millionaire businessmen.'

"This guy made a fortune from a complicated inter-connected group of property companies that operated as a large-scale long-running Ponzi scheme. In November 1892, the Liberator Building Society, Balfour's principal company, failed, leaving thousands of small savers totally penniless. Sound familiar? Ponzi scheme? Mr Madoff?

'1904 – Whitaker Wright made a vast fortune from the promotion of overseas mining companies.'

"Oh yeah. Another classic. The collapse of London & Globe Finance Corporation, this guy Wright's financial flagship, in December 1900 caused total panic on the London Stock Exchange and bankrupted twenty firms of stockbrokers. Wright skipped town, was arrested in New York and tried in January 1904. No surprise, he was found guilty of fraud and sentenced to seven years. He committed suicide at the Royal Courts of Justice minutes after his conviction by biting a cyanide capsule hidden in his mouth."

The attorney was intrigued. Here was a discernible pattern.

'1922 – Horatio Bottomley was a flamboyant company promoter, swindler, newspaper proprietor and Member of Parliament.'

"In 1922, this guy was convicted of twenty-three charges of fraud, perjury and false-accounting, and sentenced to seven years. He left thousands of small investors without a penny. You getting where I'm coming from now?"

'1929 – Clarence Hatry – a significant City financier – downfall in September 1929.'

*

"You know what happened because of this? It so eroded investor confidence it triggered the Wall Street Crash of October 1929. That's no small potatoes."

'1931 – The chairman of the Royal Mail Steam Packet Company, Lord Kylsant, and a partner in Price Waterhouse, a leading City accountancy firm, were charged with publishing a false prospectus with intent to deceive investors.'

"Nice huh?" Gold was in full, confident stride. "It goes on and on. Just look!"

'1987 – The Guinness Scandal.'
'1991 – Bank of Credit and Commerce International: 150,000 depositors lost $2 billion.'

"Remember this charmer?"

'1991 – Robert Maxwell, found drowned beside his luxury yacht near the Canary Islands.'

"Oh yeah, Maxwell's publishing and newspaper empire was bust, owing £2.8 billion to its bankers. There was a £530 million hole in the pension funds of his 16,000 employees. Nice guy."

'1995 – The sudden collapse of Barings, one of the City's oldest and most prestigious firms. Losses were estimated at £500 million.'

"It doesn't stop there, Lesley-Ann. Think back just a few years. The dot.com boom and bust; the Enron scandal; the fall of Northern Rock; the collapse of Lehman Brothers, the global banking crisis and, of course Bernard Madoff's massive fraud. You know how much that guy took? Sixty-five billion dollars. Billion!"

Gold turned the laptop around and closed the lid.

"Toxic waste. You see what I'm saying? This isn't random, there's a clearly discernible pattern here. This is real. It leaks up from underground. It started around the time of King William Street Station's closure and it's never stopped. Still hasn't. It's just like the birds that fly close to Hierapolis by the temple that all drop dead. It's the same thing here but on a far bigger scale. If we see that these events are all linked, then you have to believe that something is causing them. And it comes from below the ground and seeps up. Everything has been leading up to this point. I mean *everything*. Human history has been blindly following a path that leads us all straight off a cliff."

Lesley-Ann took a particularly loud slurp of her Diet Coke. "Off a cliff how?" she asked.

Gold took a deep breath. It was a very valid question. But for him, the answer was obvious. "Rampant, unrestricted capitalism."

The lawyer jerked her head up. "Don't tell me you're a goddam Commie! You work. You get paid. You boast that you're only in it for the money. At least I'm honest about it. I told you the moment we met back in Pennsylvania."

Gold smiled at the memory. "Yes. Yes you did. And no, I'm not a Commie, as you quaintly put it. You think I'm a fanboy of Stalin, Pol Pot, Mao? Total monsters! No, what I'm saying is that there is a cause and effect in action here. Capitalism gone crazy. Unchecked. No moral compass. People don't matter anymore, they're just numbers. I'm not moaning that there's rich people around . . . shit, I'd like to be rich. But there are limits. This crazy free-for-all has brought about the most colossal wealth inequality."

"So? Get off you're freeloading ass and work."

Gold stared at her for a moment. "You are completely missing my point. It's not about sponging off the state. It's not about having some inalienable right to be rich. Or happy. This gap, this huge chasm, means that social mobility is almost impossible now. There's no way out. No way up. It causes despair . . . and despair leads to anarchy. Why do you think on-line gambling is the world's biggest growth industry? Why do we queue like lemmings to buy lottery tickets? It's much worse than all of that; it undermines democracy. Without democracy, all bets are off. Evil can walk right in. True evil."

"Crap!" replied Lesley-Ann sharply.

"I wish it was. But it's true. Think about it, Lesley-Ann. Just for a moment, think about it. World War Two, the last just honourable war. We were facing annihilation by fanatics. We were fighting to save our country, our entire way of life. Now tell me what we've been fighting for in the Middle East year after year? Liberty? Freeing the oppressed? No. Money. We blow it up, you re-build it. We are where we are because this is where we were always heading."

"Nick, I have no idea why we fought Gulf One, Gulf Two, Afghanistan, Syria, Libya. OK, it seems crazy to me. I'll give you that. But are you saying our troops are evil because I'm going to walk right out of here if you are? They're fucking brave, every last woman and man."

Nick held up a hand in an attempt to pacify the clearly angry attorney.

"No, I'm absolutely not saying that. It's not them. They go where they're told to. They don't vote on it. It's not like 'Shall we go to the Bahamas or Iraq?'"

Lesley-Ann simmered down slightly.

"You know, I know, that cut through the BS saving civilisation line and the bare truth is that the pursuit of money is the root cause of so much unrest, conflict, death. It breeds irrational nationalism. It encourages the We're fantastic and everyone else sucks belief system. And hey, before you know it, the very processes of democracy have been bought by a hidden elite who are indecently rich. So rich they can put virtually anyone they like in the White House."

The lawyer looked at Gold with a mixture of indignation, disbelief and admiration.

"That's how I know which Gate of Hell I need to close. That's what all of this has been leading us towards. As they always say, follow the money."

Lesley-Ann took one last long, and again somewhat noisy, suck on the straw of her soft drink.

"What do we do now, Nick?"

Gold smiled. "Know your enemy and know yourself and you can fight a hundred battles without disaster."

"Yes, Sushi," responded Lesley-Ann.

"Sun Tzu," came the reply.

THIRTY-THREE

"Henceforth an individual solace dear; Part of my Soul I seek thee, and thee claim My other half: with that thy gentle hand Seisd mine, I yielded, and from that time see How beauty is excelld by manly grace."

– John Milton, Paradise Lost

Gold was determined that although Lesley-Ann had boasted how many times she had previously visited London, and thus had no need of his services as a travel guide, she had never seen his city through his eyes – the eyes of a true Londoner. For him, London was, and always would be, the greatest city in the world. Its 8.7 million inhabitants were extraordinary, brave, resilient, tough, smart and often very, very funny. If Hitler had failed to destroy the nation's capital and subject the population to despair, then, whatever it took to be The Gatekeeper, Gold was going to do his best. Same shit, different day.

They left the café in Covent Garden and, surprisingly for the UK, the weather wasn't bad. Chalk up another miracle.

"Let's walk," he said.

"What's the matter? Lost your Mussel Card?"

"Oyster Card . . . it's called an Oyster Card. No, I want to show you some stuff. I think you'll like it."

Lesley-Ann gave him a look that unequivocally said the opposite.

They left the cobbled streets of Covent Garden and walked down the narrow streets beyond the piazza. The shops displayed a seemingly endless variety of goods that would tempt the most jaded soul. In Floral Street, Gold showed her the wonderful Tintin Shop, dedicated to the cartoon boy detective.

"What, are you five?" she enquired.

There was no point in even replying.

On Maiden Lane, he stopped outside a restaurant.

"Do you know what this is?"

"I'm going to guess a restaurant."

"No, not just a restaurant . . . Rules, the oldest restaurant in London. It's been here since 1798. 'Rakes, dandies and superior intelligences who comprise its clientele' they said when it opened. You like game?"

"I'm into baseball."

Americans.

They continued walking, Gold giving a learned commentary of the city that he loved. Despite her sarcastic responses, Lesley-Ann knew that finally she was seeing the real Nick Gold. No longer the flippant, facile guy full of ennui, but a man fully engaged with life, sharing the places that meant most to him now and would throughout his life – wherever it took him. He wanted her to catch his enthusiasm; to see beyond mere bricks and mortar into the very heart and soul of the capital.

They walked on and turned down Catherine Street.

"Let me present the Theatre Royal, Drury Lane. We just call it Drury Lane."

"And I'm seeing this because?"

"Because, my dear Mrs Trobe, it has been here since 1663 and is the oldest theatre site in London that is still in use. Every single day. Oh, please remind me, what were you doing across the Pond in 1663? Ah yes, our King Charles the Second had just signed the Carolina Charter. No, not ringing a bell? Jeez! King Charles II owed an enormous debt to his pals who helped restore the monarchy, so as a big thank you he rewarded eight of them with a grant of land that included what is now North and South Carolina. Me, I'd have taken them out for dinner and maybe a show."

"How come you know all this stuff?"

"Because those who cannot learn from history are doomed to repeat it."

Lesley-Ann, if she was being truthful, was actually enjoying this amble through town. Yes, she'd been to London many times, but that was for work, which meant offices, sandwiches around a boardroom table and soulless commercial hotels that could be anywhere on the planet. This was the real London, steeped in a history that spoke to you at every street corner.

"And on your left, ladies and gentlemen, I present the Savoy Hotel, the first luxury hotel in the United Kingdom. It was revolutionary. You know why? 'Cos it had electric lights, electric lifts . . . sorry, elevators, and oh yeah . . . bathrooms in most of the rooms with constant hot and cold running water. Guess who the first manager was? César Ritz."

"Like the crackers?"

"Like the Ritz Hotels . . . oh . . . you were messing with me. Good one. Actually you should feel right at home here, being American. Know why?"

She shook her head, enjoying this pop quiz.

"Because the front entrance to the hotel is the only place in the whole of the UK where you drive on the right. Fact. I thank you."

Finally, they reached Waterloo Bridge and walked half way across. Gold gently held her arm and motioned her to stop.

"This is the best view of London. Any Londoner would tell you that if they really knew their city. Waterloo Bridge."

"Like that song? *Waterloo Sunset*."

"Yup, the very same. Ray Davies got it so right."

From the centre of the bridge, one of twelve in central London that span the Thames, they looked up and down the river. Gold pointed out some of the notable buildings from St Paul's Cathedral to the Cheese Grater, from the historical to the ultra-modern, from the wondrous to the woeful. Lesley-Ann really did admire the sweep of the city from this vantage point.

"You really love this place, Nick, don't you?"

He smiled. "Yes. Yes I do. It's my home. It's where I was born. It's where I'll die."

Lesley-Ann shivered and then lightly touched his arm. "You don't know that."

"Yes, I do."

She didn't respond.

"Look around you, Lesley-Ann. Millions of people going about their lives. Full of hopes and dreams. Planning their futures. Minding their own business, just getting on with it. And not one of them, not one, has a clue that it could all be over in the blink of an eye. Everything gone. I can't let that happen. It's worth fighting for. It's worth making the effort. I have to try . . . or I will always carry the guilt of knowing that I did nothing and lost . . . lost all of this."

He swept his arm across the view.

They walked on, talked on, and as they did so, there came a moment when, ever so subtlety, ever so quietly, they saw in each other's eyes how their minds had touched and although it had taken a while they were falling in love.

Later that afternoon, they went to Good Foot Productions where Nick had arranged for them to collect a GoPro camera. He needed the GoPro Hero5 Black as he wanted to make sure he could capture any footage whatever the circumstance, and this was the best weapon of choice. That was providing he could stay alive. The devil, as always, was in the detail.

The camera was waiting for them on the reception desk. Larry wandered out of his office.

"Nick Gold! How's it hanging?"

Larry looked as urbane and stylish as ever. His charcoal grey Gieves & Hawkes bespoke suit, which wouldn't have seen much change from £5,000, fitted perfectly. If anything, he looked younger than ever. His piercing violet eyes shone with energy and there was a definite spring in his elegant, noiseless, step.

Gold was surprised. "Hi Larry. Good to see you. I thought that you might be in the South of France for, what was it called, *That Riviera Touch*?"

"Huh? Ah yes, I was. Just for a few hours. Hence the slight tan. Flew back this morning. I had to leave and get back here on a personal matter. Anyway, I don't like not being in the shop. And how is our valiant American lawyer today? Taking in the sights?"

"Valiant? That'll be me," she replied in a rather cheesy, chirpy tone which grated on Gold's ears.

"Actually, I was shooting the breeze with the kids here and we thought, and just hear me out, that this would make a terrific little series. It's got a sassy lawyer, a mysterious murder case, maybe dark forces are at work, it has international travel . . . it works huh, Nick?"

Nick Gold, Paranormal Detective, TV presenter and egotist, was silently seething. Would he wander into a courtroom and steal Lesley-Ann's thunder? Now the pushy cow was elbowing her way into his world. His! Fucking bloody nerve!

"Sounds great, Larry," replied Nick.

It's showbiz. It's how it works.

"Yeah, knew you'd love it. It's been a while since we had a hot lawyer on a doco fly-on-the-wall series."

This was the precise moment when the hot lawyer in question would stand up to redress the male chauvinism that dominated the media. When she would speak for the thousands of her sisters who had been seen as eye-candy or autocue-cuties, who had been looked at as merely sexualised objects, and not for the brains and abilities that they possessed. She would take her place in a proud, long line that included Erica Jong, Germaine Greer, Janet Street-Porter, Gloria Steinem, Bella Abzug and Betty Friedan. Hash tag Time's Up.

"Really? That'd be neat," she said.

Gold thought he was going to projectile vomit.

"Anyway, what are you up to now, Nick? I see you're borrowing one of our cameras. Do you need Adam to come along with you?"

Shit! Gold had totally forgotten about the irritating Mr Adam Farthing.

"No, I'm just trying some stuff out. No need to bother Adam with it. Just some ideas I'm playing with to maybe add in to the new series. Give it a possible new feel in some scenes. Just need to try it first."

Larry nodded.

"Sure. Let 'em go, let 'em be happy."

A Larry catchphrase.

"Well, good to see you as always, Nick. Nice to see you again, Counselor. Happy hunting."

They left Soho and returned to Gold's flat. Once there, Gold started further research online. His first port of call was the site Ordnance Survey Maps, London, Five Feet to the Mile, 1893–1896. Then after making a series of notes in his Moleskin notebook, he studied London Masterplan in Nine Sheets, Ordnance Survey Landranger 176 Map West London and Ordnance Survey Landranger 177 Map East London. His notes were now complete.

Then, to Lesley-Ann's total astonishment, she looked over his shoulder, an infuriating habit, and saw he was scrolling through interpretations of the Book of Revelation.

"Are you kidding me? A little late for redemption, don't you think?"

Gold was reading and making notes on the writing of John, the Apostle, while in exile on the Isle of Patmos in about 95 A.D.

"I'm not looking for redemption. I'm trying to fully understand what I'm facing here. I wouldn't be much of a Gatekeeper if I hadn't dusted off my theology."

"Er, yeah . . . I guess so. Is it helpful?"

"Let's say it's as cryptic as I recall it being. It's like the Francis Ford Coppola of the Bible, with some action scenes directed by Michael Bay. Subtle it ain't. It is a book of wars, but war always ends in peace. So that's good. It is a book of the rewards of the righteous. I guess in the end it's about optimism. Everywhere God overcomes Satan."

"Amen to that, baby. Amen to that. You've had tougher battles. Your step-parents, you survived them."

Gold nodded. "Sadly, as far as training goes, they weren't exactly supernatural. Actually, they weren't super-anything."

"But you're here to tell the tale. So remind me again, this book is gonna help you how exactly?"

The attorney wasn't letting it go.

"Because, it's all a bit Uri Geller. Revelations points out, look here at my note, that there will be an end of conflict, that God will triumph, that the enemies of our souls will be punished and that the followers of God will be eternally rewarded."

"Good to know, Nick. Now, what's the plan? Now that I mention it, what's Plan A, Plan B and the extra back-up plan?"

Gold sat very quietly before answering.

"There's only Plan A. And, between you and me, even that is not technically what you'd call a plan."

"Well, can I hear it at least?"

"It's pretty straightforward. I go down to where King William Street Station used to be, get in there –"

Lesley-Ann waited.

"Get in there and –?"

Gold gave a slight smile. "That's pretty much it."

The attorney ran her hands through her long dark hair and exhaled loudly.

"Well, you got me there. That is, for sure, one hell of a plan. It's complex, it's subtle and I like the way you've thought this through. Are you planning to bring along Face, Mr T and Murdoch or are you going alone, Hannibal?"

Gold started to answer.

"Are you totally one hundred percent fucking insane? What's the goddamn matter with you?" Lesley-Ann yelled, her voice filling every crevice of Gold's small flat.

"Why not just throw yourself under a truck? It'd be quicker. That's not a plan. That's just plain stupid!"

Gold rubbed the stubble on his chin in the way men do when they need time before answering anything from did you have sex with your intern? to do you fancy poached or scrambled eggs?

Gold finally spoke, having lined up his thoughts into something resembling order.

"Here's the thing, Lesley-Ann. There's no manual for this. There's nothing online under How To Be The Gatekeeper. Had I been selected to be a zoo keeper, a park keeper or maybe a goalkeeper, I'd be in with a chance. I still have no precise idea what to do or even what I'm expected to do. So, having thought about it, I'm just, well, going to be there to suck it and see."

Lesley-Ann took a moment. "You do understand, don't you, that there's a good chance you're going to die? Why do this? You don't need to."

For an instant, Gold was taken aback by the thought that perhaps, deep beneath her vitriol-spitting, Kevlar-encased exterior, she might actually care for him. Timing is a funny old thing. It's not necessarily linear nor always based on logic, but it was at that precise moment that it dawned on him that he really cared for Lesley-Ann Trobe. Deeply.

Gold shook his head. "But I do. I have no choice. It's the random lottery of life and it picked me. If I don't go, then how will I live with myself? What would I be living for? Besides, if I am The Gatekeeper, a job I want as much as I need another arse, then Lucifer or one of his chums will come for me wherever I am. So, I might as well make a stand at a place of my choosing."

"Listen to yourself!" Lesley-Ann was despairing. "*Make a stand?* What Middle Earth, Game of Thrones crap is this? You haven't got some, I dunno, invisibility cloak, or a magic wand, or tame dragon. This is just insane!"

Gold stood up and stretched. And as he did so he looked at the lawyer.

"You OK? Why are you looking at me like that?" she asked.

"Like what?"

"Like a cross between a Mini-Schnauzer puppy and a deer."

To his embarrassment, Gold realised that he must have let a look of tenderness escape.

"Please feel free to stay here as long as you like. The spare keys are in my bedside table. Rent's paid up front for three months but you'll be back in the States long before that, I guess, doing your Law and Order thing."

"What the fuck are you talking about? What, you think I'm sitting on my ass here watching TV tonight? Forget it! I'm coming with."

Now it was Gold's turn to get annoyed. "One word – no. That's not happening. OK, it's so not happening. You've just bollocked me, assuring me that my plan is shit and I'm going to die, so . . . duh . . . you're tagging along too. I don't think so."

Lesley-Ann walked across the room, put her hands on either side of his face and kissed him fully and passionately on the mouth.

"I'm coming with you. Get your coat," was all she said.

Gold couldn't argue with impeccable logic like that.

THIRTY-FOUR

"Thus it shall befall Him, who to worth in women over-trusting, Lets her will rule: restraint she will not brook; And left to herself, if evil thence ensue She first his weak indulgence will accuse."

– John Milton, Paradise Lost

Adam Farthing was furious. The situation with Nick Gold had been burning him for days now. It was ridiculous. Gold was nothing but a jumped-up hack, a light-weight Z-lister who thought he could breeze through life with flip remarks and sarcastic comebacks. Unlike Adam, he wasn't a professional, he didn't take his craft seriously, he wasn't a team player and to top it all off, he was plain bloody rude. The little shit! Adam had joined Good Foot Productions to make great television programmes, to hone his considerable talents, even if he said so himself. He hadn't wanted to even touch stupid Paranormal Detective with a barge pole, but Larry had made the decision for him, and there was no point in arguing so early on in their relationship. He had to demonstrate that he was a good soldier, that he was a real team player, a good guy, someone that could be relied on. So with a smile and a You got it, boss! he'd accepted being attached to the project as director. But fuck me, that sodding Gold was a total bastard. Why in the name of God had he opened up to him in Bar Italia? What a stupid mistake. The entire episode with his dead grandfather had been buried . . . much like his grandfather. Tiredness, a trick of the light, who knows, but right now that freaky little incident was the least of his problems. Gold! That man with his irritating easy manner was standing in his way. And to make it worse, Larry was buying into his crap. Larry, of all people! Oh yes Nick, please swan around Turkey, oh sure Nick, please be my guest and enjoy the USA on my money, hey Nick, why not spend some time in Turkmenistan and let me pay you for it. Fuck him and fuck this situation. Enough was enough.

Bolstered by several beers from the fridge, he dialled Larry's mobile. It rang just once.

"Adam. Always a pleasure dear boy. Is this a social call or are you going to impart news of great delight to me?"

"Hello, Larry. Look, I'm really sorry to bother you but I really have to talk about Nick Gold with you."

There was a slight pause.

"Do you now? Well, pray tell, what's grinding your gears, as they say across the pond?"

"I don't know where to start, Larry. I mean, you know how much I value your advice and how much I enjoy being part of Good Foot Productions. In fact, I'd like to think that we'd built up not just a commercial and creative relationship, but that we're friends."

Silence.

Adam Farthing was beginning to wish he'd never made his anger- and beer-fuelled call. But he was committed now. And he was right. He was doing the right thing.

"Larry, I'm a total team player. You know that. But I have to speak my mind. Nick Gold is out of control. This running around the world is . . . is ridiculous. I'm sorry, but it is."

"I authorised it." The tone was hard.

"Yes. Yes, of course. I fully appreciate that. And I fully respect your decision."

"In which case, love, why are you calling me?"

Oh crap. This was going badly. Come on Adam. Come on!

"I'm calling because I care, Larry. I care about the company. I care about our reputation in the industry. And I care about you.

Gold is taking you for a ride. This total rubbish about the dead coming back to life and slaughtering people. It's superstitious crap."

"Well, dear boy, how very sweet and kind of you to be looking after my interests so diligently. I see I have underestimated you. So, Adam, what do you propose I do?"

Saved! Yes!

"Well Larry, I think you should cut Gold off right now. Stop the money. Stop the project. We could go after other projects that I know one hundred percent will work."

There was a pause.

"And if I don't?"

Shit!

"Well, I may have to resign. I assure you that's the last thing I want to do. But really, this situation cannot be allowed to continue."

"No, Adam. You're quite right. It can't."

Relief!

"Thank you, Larry. Thank you so much. You know I only have your best interests at heart."

"Of course you do, dear boy. I know that. Well, thank you for your call. It's been most illuminating. You can rest assured I'm going to take on board everything that you've said. You have a splendid evening now. Cheerio."

Result!

He had been bold and at a stroke cut Gold off at the knees. Goodbye Gold. Take your smart-arse ways and piss off. Adam Farthing grabbed another beer from the fridge. He felt good. No, he felt *great*. He needed to celebrate this famous victory and he knew exactly the right way to do it. He'd call the agency and spend a pleasant couple of hours with one of their girls.

Adam Farthing, for all his bluster and bombast, was a deeply insecure human being. Rather than face rejection from a girl on a date, he'd come to prefer buying their services by the hour. With them, he could be whatever he needed to be. They could be in charge: tell him what to do; paddle him; beat him – and they would never complain no matter how perverse his desires became. It somehow filled the hollowness of his soul.

Farthing dialled the agency number he had committed to memory, and requested an out- rather than an in-call. To hell with it, why should he have to go out? Let the bitch come to him.

He went to the bathroom, generously applied aftershave, brushed his teeth and waited. After forty-five minutes, the door-bell rang and he pressed the entry-phone to admit his visitor.

The agency hadn't let him down. Chantal, that was the name this one was using, was five-feet-six-inches tall, blonde, buxom and carrying an expensive leather holdall.

They shook hands. So very British.

"Can I get you a drink?"

Chantal was taking off her coat to reveal she was wearing long black latex gloves, an underbust latex spanking dress and leather knee-high boots with four-inch heels. Farthing liked what he saw. "No thanks. I thought we could, you know, get to know each other straight away. How's that work for you?"

"That works just fine."

"Well why don't you lead into the bedroom, baby and let's get this party started."

The beer, her perfume, getting rid of Gold, being in sync with Larry, all combined to make Adam Farthing feel bold, adventure-some, even euphoric. He went to kiss her.

"Uh-uh honey. First the cash, then the lash. Business before pleasure. A girl's gotta eat, and not just cock. House rules."

Farthing handed her an envelope containing the amount agreed with the agency.

"I'm not even going to count it, baby. You've got an honest face. In fact, your face is so honest, I can't wait to be sitting on it."

Oh she's good, thought Farthing. Yet another sound decision made tonight. He was on a roll.

Chantal began to undress him. Clearly she wasn't from a nunnery as her fingers made light work of the buttons and zips until he was naked.

"Now why don't you be a good boy and lie down on the bed, baby and let momma go to work?"

He didn't need a second invitation.

Without asking permission, Chantal reached into her holdall and produced handcuffs which she swiftly put on Farthing's wrist and then secured him to the bedstead.

"You boys. Always making decision after decision. Tonight let's just say that I'm behind the wheel."

She went to work. She was, after all, a professional. Actually, she was a dental hygienist from Hendon who now had a very nice flat in Swiss Cottage, a brand-new Audi convertible, took three holidays a year all because London was full of sad bastards who'd happily pay for her services. Of course, she was very good and much in demand.

She wasn't just good. She was fantastic thought Adam Farthing as she teased him, toyed with him, brought him to arousal running the base of her Heavy Handle Silicone Core Whip the length of his body and talked in a way that he yearned to hear.

"How's that, baby?" she asked as she straddled him.

"Fantastic. It's fantastic," gasped Farthing.

"How would you like it to be even better, baby? Hmm? I've got something very special just for you. I shouldn't really, but what the hell? Sounds good?"

Adam was so drunk, aroused and befuddled that he could only nod.

Once again Chantal reached into her copious, yet fashionable bag, and withdrew a dull grey metal flask.

"I'd never normally do this to one of my clients, baby, but you know, there's something special about you, and you deserve

Chantal's special treatment. Have you been a naughty boy? Hmm. Have you?"

Farthing nodded. This was just great.

Chantal smiled. "I thought so. Do you know what happens to naughty boys?"

His breathing was now very laboured. He shook his head.

"Well baby, they get punished."

Adam Farthing closed his eyes and waited for the slaps to come, slaps he craved. What he couldn't see was Chantal swiftly unscrewing the metal flask.

He felt her fingers exploring his mouth; a finger was inserted. He opened his mouth a little wider . . . and did not understand the nature of true agony until a flask of molten lead was poured down his throat.

Large amounts of steam appeared instantly from every orifice of Adam Farthing's face, and within ten seconds, the lead had solidified, completely filling his larynx. His internal organs had ruptured, his lungs were scorched and, for a millisecond, he felt himself choking from the steam.

Chantal climbed off the now lifeless, but still smouldering form. She removed the handcuffs and got dressed. The elbow-length black latex gloves that Adam Farthing had specifically requested ensured his flat contained none of her fingerprints.

"Job done?" she asked.

Standing all this time in the corner of the room, a silent witness, Adam Farthing's grandfather nodded. "Yes, my dear. Job done."

THIRTY-FIVE

"While yet we live, scarce one short hour perhaps, Between us two let there be peace, both joining, As joined in injuries, and enmity Against a foe by doom express assigned us, That cruel serpent."

– John Milton, Paradise Lost

Recognising that this might be his last night on earth, Gold splashed out and ordered an Uber to take them to the area where the disused King William Street Tube Station was located. Several things occurred to him as their driver, a cheerful chap called Mohammed, discussed why Britain was the greatest country in the world with his American passenger. First, why had he never thought of making a will? Probably a little late to worry about that now. Secondly, why had Lesley-Ann flipped from arguing to kissing so swiftly? Was that a New York thing? Thirdly, how did he feel about the attorney? Half the time he wanted to throttle her, the other half to ask her to move in. Fourthly, and finally, had he switched the light off in the bedroom?

Then there was the small matter of what was he going to do tonight if he actually had to face Satan and his motley crew. He decided not to ponder on that for too long. God knows, and right now, God was being pretty button-lipped about the entire affair. In some ways, this was like the worst blind date in the world, except the chances were that Gold would recognise Lucifer, even in a crowded bar. The horns and cloven feet were a bit of a clue.

Then there was the question that most men of thirty-two don't often ask themselves – what if I die? Not the enormous metaphysical and theological questions that had anguished mankind since the dawn of time but, more importantly, would it hurt?

As the dark London streets rolled by, Nick Gold wondered if anyone would miss him. That was a depressing avenue to wander down especially as he wasn't sure of the answer.

"And it has been very lovely to meet you. Good luck with all that you do. I hope you enjoy my beautiful country. Try to get to Brighton while you are here. Very lovely."

Gold realised the Uber, the ubiquitous Toyota Prius in which he was a passenger, had stopped and Mohammed was saying his farewells to Lesley-Ann.

"I will give you both a five-star rating," were his parting words as they exited onto the pavement and the Prius whispered off into the night.

"Well that was fun," chimed in Lesley-Ann. "Did you know Her Majesty the Queen has been on the British throne for sixty-five years and that she is such an amazing woman? That was one big fan just now."

"Yeah. Long time." Nerves were finally getting to Gold.

"So, what now?" asked the American. "You got everything in that bag – map, torch, camera, garlic, wooden stake?"

"Yeah."

"Well, OK Mr Convivial Conversationalist, let's go, shall we? I don't really like hanging about on deserted city streets. Makes me jumpy."

Considering what they were potentially about to face, the irony of that statement was not lost on Gold.

They walked along in silence. Lesley-Ann was impressed by the area that surrounded them. It was the very heart of London. Not the tourist Trafalgar Square, Buckingham Palace, Regent Street part, but the very soul of the City.

They walked past the Monument to the Great Fire of London of 1666, which started in the King's Bakery in the aptly named Pudding Lane. When the fire started on 2nd September, the Lord

Mayor of London, Sir Thomas Bloodworth, was woken up to be told about the fire, he replied "Pish! A woman might piss it out!"

He was wrong. The fire raged for days. Hundreds of thousands of people were left homeless. Eighty-nine parish churches, the Guildhall, numerous other public buildings, jails, markets and fifty-seven halls were reduced to burnt-out shells. The loss of property was, at the time, estimated at between five and seven million pounds, which today would equate to over a billion.

A new London emerged from the ashes. The two hundred feet high Monument, designed by Sir Christopher Wren, who also designed St Paul's Cathedral, was built on the initiative of King Charles II.

Another monument marks the spot where the fire stopped: the Golden Boy of Pye Corner in Smithfield. According to the inscription, it was evidence of God's wrath on the City of London for the sin of gluttony that the fire started at Pudding Lane and stopped at Pye Corner.

The City . . . sin . . . gluttony . . . some things don't change over time.

They walked up Monument Street and turned right onto King William Street, crossing Cannon Street with Monument Tube station on their right.

There it was, an eleven-floored large modern building clearly marked Regis House on King William Street itself. The last Regis House had been demolished in 1995 and this was its replacement, opened in 1998.

Lesley-Ann exclaimed, "This must be the place!"

The visual clue, hardly testing of Hercule Poirot, was a fairly elaborate rectangular blue plaque which bore the inscription 'Site of King William Street Underground Station. First City Terminus 1890-1900'.

"Bravo Dr Watson. Who'd have thought, eh?"

"Fuck you," a response not thus far found in the works of Sir Arthur Conan Doyle.

"And that is what we need," said Gold. He was looking at a large circular metal manhole cover. "From the diagram we saw at Professor Clifford's office, my own research, and that being Fish Street Hill over there, this must be the right one."

"Just like that!" replied Mrs. Trobe. "The gods must be smiling on us tonight."

"I'll settle for just one," came Gold's rather terse reply.

London boasts around four hundred and twenty thousand CCTV cameras, one for every fourteen people in the capital. To many, they provide peace of mind and security. To Gold and Lesley-Ann, they provided a monumental pain in the arse.

Proverbs 16:27: *Idle hands are the devil's workshop*. Not wishing to join any Satanic micro-manufacturing plant, Gold took out a long heavy metal tyre iron that he'd bought in a local branch of Halfords earlier in the day.

With Lesley-Ann standing between him and the nearest CCTV camera, Gold struggled to lift the manhole cover.

"Fuck! It's stuck!" he exclaimed.

"Pull harder."

"Thanks, Lesley-Ann. That hadn't occurred to me. Thank God you're here."

"Wanna hand?"

With reluctance, Gold acquiesced.

They both pushed hard on the tyre iron, grunting with effort. Finally the metal cover, which appeared to weigh a ton and be welded in place, lifted a fraction. They pushed down harder and it rose another couple of inches until they could get a hold of it and pull it aside. The sound of the metal scraping on the concrete pavement sounded like an AC/DC concert to Gold's ears in the silence of this part of the deserted City.

They were in.

The smell of dank, dark, unused places wafted up. It was an odour that made their hearts beat a little faster. No one ever has happy associations with that smell. It smelled of loss, of being forgotten, of darkness and, frankly, of fear.

"After you, Gatekeeper," invited Lesley-Ann.

Gold looked at her. Somehow, opening the large metal manhole cover, and experiencing that first unpleasant waft, had made it all far too real.

"Yeah. Thanks," was all Gold could muster.

They had come prepared. As prepared as one can be before going to have a tête-à-tête with the Devil. Or his disciples. Or indeed anyone brave and stupid enough to force open a manhole cover and descend underground in central London. It wasn't just the smell and the dark. It was what else lurked down there.

Gold knew from his haunted London show researches that there were at least three and a half million urban rats in the UK. Rats that were termed streetwise. Whether they wore hoodies and hung around on street corners looking hardcore was not clear. Then there were the mice. Untold millions of them. Gold had read a study by Professor Bill Wisden from Imperial College. 'Tube mice are amongst the toughest of their species. They forage for food on the tracks, survive the deafening noise of the tube trains, and evade Transport for London's efforts to eradicate them. Soon they will also be sleep deprived. The planned 24-hour tube operation will mean that the mice will evolve to be more stress resistant. Tube mice will have an even shorter and more brutal life.'

Which was pretty much how Gold was now viewing his immediate future.

The two subterranean explorers put on their LED headband torches and switched on their high-powered TrustFire High Port Super Bright 8500 Lumen Flashlights that Nick had purchased on eBay.

The light from their torches both helped and hindered. It helped in as much as they could at least see through the Stygian gloom, but it hindered in that the shadows cast by the LEDs played absolute havoc with their imagination. Darkness seemed to hide every horror imaginable. It was as if your worst nightmares were lurking, waiting to pounce, to bite, to gouge every few yards.

Neither Trobe nor Gold were wearing a Fitbit but their heart rates would have been off the scale as the thumping in their respective chests testified.

Very slowly, and accompanied by various interspersed mutterings of, "Oh this sucks . . . this is the worst idea since your last stupid idea . . . what the hell are we doing? . . . did you hear that?" the duo walked gingerly on.

"This looks like it," whispered Gold.

"Why are you whispering?" asked Lesley-Ann, also in a whisper.

"Because I am so creeped out I don't think I can speak any louder."

"What looks like what?"

Gold shone his torch on a door which bore a very faded sign proclaiming Emergency Stairs.

"This is what it shows on the plans we saw," informed Gold to an enthralled audience of one.

They moved closer and Gold placed his hand on the rusted handle. He pulled.

Nothing.

He pulled harder, repeatedly – grunting increasingly loudly with the effort as he did so.

"Bugger!"

"Have you tried pushing?" came an American voice from out of the gloom.

Well, that was not embarrassing in the least as, with a creak of long-rusted hinges, the door opened.

As he pushed it.

Passing through the emergency door in the basement of Regis House, they found themselves at the top of the old emergency stairs and, step by slow step, they descended the seventy-five feet to the station below.

To their surprise, the emergency stairs appeared to be not only original but in remarkably good condition considering their age. Even the handrail on their left seemed sturdy.

The spiral stairs ended thirty feet above the old disused platform of King William Street Underground station. From that point Gold and Trobe descended a concrete stairway that ran down to platform level. In the torchlight, they could see that the platform still retained its original cream and patterned tiling scheme that was used on the early City and South London tube railway stations.

As they walked along, even slower now, they could make out posters from the Second World War left in situ. Gold was reminded that the station had been used as an air raid shelter when the Luftwaffe had tried to turn London into rubble and ash night after night.

> *'Spare a thought for your fellow shelterers and refrain from making any unnecessary noise. Please remember others may be asleep although you are not.'*

Looking up at the poster, Gold and Trobe stopped for a moment. They could barely imagine the nightly horrors of sleeping here underground, not knowing what would be waiting for you in the dawn, whether your home would still be standing, and who might have been injured or killed as the bombs fell – anonymously, relentlessly, randomly. In truth, thirty-two thousand civilians would die and a further eighty-seven thousand suffer injury. In the 1940s, the Underground platforms were a brief life-preserving sanctuary in an otherwise insane world. Hitler and his goons had sought to break British morale, but the raids only helped galvanise the will of the British people for the remainder of the war.

The torch beams picked out another wartime poster, a cartoon in colour depicting a couple gossiping over a restaurant table with Hitler hiding underneath with pen and paper poised to take notes. The man was saying to the woman, 'Of course, there's no harm in you knowing!'.

Underneath came the stern admonition: 'Careless Talk Costs Lives'.

At the east end of the disused station was a side room that still, somehow, had tiled walls and a tiled ceiling. It was a toilet. There was still tiling along a walkway running on the south side of the station. Oddly, there was still a kitchen, bereft of any equipment, and close by a sixty-four feet shaft that was built in 1940.

That was it. Without jackhammers and pneumatic drills, the sealed brickwork prevented the duo from making any further progress.

"So, what now?" asked the attorney. Gold noticed that the torch in her hand was shaking, causing its beam to move erratically over the surfaces of the disused platform.

"Now we wait."

THIRTY-SIX

"God doth not need
Either man's work or his own gifts; who best
Bear his mild yoke, they serve him best. His state
Is Kingly. Thousands at his bidding speed
And post o'er Land and Ocean without rest:
They also serve who only stand and wait."
– John Milton, Sonnet 19

It was cold down here. The air not only smelled stale, it *felt* stale against their faces. This was not a place for the living. Everything about it had a sense of mourning. The passing of the great idea of the station in the first place, the memories of those who huddled in their masses years later seemed etched into the brickwork and concrete. There was no sound. No light. It was a place abandoned, forgotten and desolate.

Nick kept checking the time on his watch in the torchlight to try to gauge how long they had been waiting. Afraid to move, afraid not to move.

"If your pal Barachiel was ever going to appear, this would really be a great time," Lesley-Ann said in a quiet, nervous voice. The fact was, anyone, under virtually any circumstance finding themselves in the abandoned King William Street station, would have felt highly on-edge. That Gold and Trobe were there to face the absolute of absolute unknowns took their fearful anticipation to a whole different level.

"How long are we going to wait?"

"How long's a piece of string?" replied Gold.

"What?"

"Old English expression. We wait until something happens."

"Whatever. And then what?"

"Then I'm hoping I get inspired. If I'm meant to be here, then it might be clear what I must do. I don't know."

Their silence deepened and their trepidation grew.

"Nick . . . are you scared?"

There was a pause.

"No, I'm not scared. I'm terrified. If you want to know, I'm having trouble breathing."

"Thank you for being honest. I thought it was just me."

Nick felt Lesley-Ann's hand slip into his. He squeezed it back in a gesture of solidarity.

Suddenly, there was a sound. A sound that they had not heard before, not since they descended from the mundane world above.

It was a scraping. Like mice foraging in a cupboard, but on a massive scale. Then the unmistakable sound of an animal, breathing heavily. Something large. Very large.

"Did you hear that?" whispered Gold.

"Yes," was all Lesley-Ann could say. Even that lone syllable seemed to get stuck in her throat.

It was as if a reptile was dragging its heavy body across the concrete platform. Between breaths now it seemed to be issuing guttural growls and intemperate snarls.

"Oh Christ!" muttered Gold.

He shone the torch in the direction of the sound. The LED headband lights had already given away their location. He had no desire to do what he was about to, but it felt better to see what they were about to face.

The light from the torch picked out nothing. The platform seemed as deserted as when they had first arrived.

Then, bit by bit, Gold realised why he couldn't see the source of the noise. Whatever it was, it wasn't coming from the platform itself; whatever or whoever they were – they were coming from the ceiling.

The *tapetum lucidum* of a hundred red eyes reflected in the torch light.

Then one by one they heard the unmistakable sound of flesh landing on the platform, dropping like obscene raindrops – splat, splat, splat.

At last the torches revealed what had been making the noises.

Creatures that used to be human, now trapped in a netherworld of eternal pain, blood, fangs and revenge. Men, women and children. Snarling like rabid dogs, blood-tinged saliva dripping, their mouths pulled back in a rictus that displayed what should have been teeth but were, in fact, rows of triangular razor-sharp fangs. They were still wearing their funeral clothes – cancer victims in coffin-ready designer suits; car crash victims with grotesquely broken bodies; suicides in underwear, nightwear, even dressing gowns; bomb victims with missing limbs or the structural integrity of jellyfish after their bones had been pulverised by concussive shock; here was an aeroplane crash victim still wearing the complimentary slippers and travel socks provided by the airline; and several executed criminals in bright orange jump suits, arms and legs still pinioned. All taken before what they considered their time.

Gold and Trobe stared in profound horror at the *danse macabre* emerging before them.

So, this was what an eternity of nothingness did to the human spirit. This was the ultimate expression of mortal men who craved immortality. The creatures had evolved from people who had families, friends, and lovers into monsters, more akin to huge insects or nihilistic troglodytes than human beings. The way they moved, the sounds they made were closer to cockroaches or large beetles than people. Yet it was their clinging on to the very last vestiges of humanity that made the sight even more disturbing and terrifying.

A little girl, who could have been no more than five, and whose long blonde hair tumbled sweetly over a Peppa Pig sweatshirt, smiled at them. Trobe, without thought, instinctively stepped forward smiling in return, reaching out a welcoming hand. Without warning the girl opened her mouth, bared her knife blade-sharp teeth and vociferated an ear-shattering sustained scream of inchoate fury.

Lesley-Ann Trobe and Nick Gold knew they were about to die. This horde, this swarm, of once human remains, was going to literally tear them to shreds. Would it be quick? Would they feel every bite, every rip, every part of their flesh being torn apart?

"Oh God!" was all Nick could manage. "I am so sorry. Forgive me."

"Oh, I don't think that's very likely, do you?"

From the darkness at the end of the platform came a voice. Soft, restful, inviting, persuasive yet quietly, and unmistakably, commanding.

The undead quietened down, their advance halted less than fifteen feet from Nick and Lesley-Ann.

The voice . . . Nick knew it. Surely he knew it?

The horde grew silent and began to move apart, leaving a gap between them. Now the only sound Gold and Trobe could hear was their own blood pumping so fast it filled their ears. Their chests physically hurt as their hearts raced. Adrenalin coursed through their systems.

They both felt utterly nauseous and an obscure but pervasive sense of wrongness suffused their souls.

They were both very, very frightened.

The sudden change from the animal-like cacophony to total silence was abrupt and unnerving. Footsteps were steadily, deliberately and slowly advancing.

Gold thought he was going to pass out through fear and tension. Perhaps he almost wished for it. So he wouldn't feel the first bite into his neck or face.

The footsteps stopped. In the pool of torch light emerged a face.

"Hello Nick. What's a nice boy like you doing in a place like this?"

Gold and Lesley-Ann stared, neither of them able to utter a word.

It simply could not be.

"What? No smart-arse reply? No witty badinage? No well-practised spontaneous come back? I'm disappointed."

Gold could only stare as he felt his entire life unravelling.

"Not even a hello?"

Gold tried to speak but his mouth was dryer than the Karakum Desert.

Finally, he managed to spit out one word. "Larry!"

Dressed in an immaculate hand-made Mark Powell Saville Row suit, Santoni Double Buckle leather shoes, Turnbull and Asser handmade shirt and a silk Hermes tie, there, in this forgotten, long-dead part of subterranean London, stood Larry Shaitan, CEO of Good Foot Productions.

"Ah, Mrs Trobe. A pleasure to see you again. I see young Nick here has persuaded you to come along for the ride. That's what I so admire about you Americans, your get-up-and-go, can-do spirit."

"You knew my name," replied Lesley-Ann almost to herself. She was standing as though she had been carved out of marble. "You said she . . . what's *she* done? In your office. I never mentioned my client was a woman."

Gold, reeling, wasn't following.

"A minor slip-up on my part," responded Larry. "I was thinking about the phone call I'd just put through to . . . " he paused, as if catching himself, "a friend of mine . . . in the States. Old golfing buddy. Good for you, Counselor, for spotting that. Sharp. I like that. I guess that's why they pay you the big bucks, right? Or did, once upon a time, should we say."

During this exchange, Gold's mind was racing, yet coming up with nothing.

Lamely, he asked the inevitable question, and was himself struck by just how banal it sounded."

"Larry, what are you doing here?"

Larry burst out laughing. The sound echoed around the disused tube station, bouncing off the bare walls and floor. The undead skittered and inched forward as if anticipating their abominable lusts would soon be satisfied.

"And you have the sheer audacity to call yourself the Paranormal Detective. My dear chap, you couldn't detect a whore in a bordello."

The well-practised charming smile faded.

"Why do *you* think I'm here, Mrs Trobe, or may I take the liberty of calling you Lesley-Ann?"

"Because whatever you are, you're not human."

Larry Shaitan pondered the response. The creatures continued to stir uneasily around him. One or two barked and growled.

Shaitan merely clicked his fingers once, as if summoning a waiter, and the pack fell silent instantly.

Again, the smile that had sealed so many deals.

"Poor Nick. Always five steps behind. And there's you thinking you're so smart, so streetwise, so savvy. The perfect example of the human condition – always knowing precisely the square root of fuck all."

Lesley-Ann spoke, her voice tremulous. "What do you want with us?"

Larry rubbed his perfectly-shaved chin. He liked to visit Geo. F. Trumper on Jermyn Street at least twice a week.

"Me? Absolutely nothing? You two have interrupted a perfectly excellent late-night dinner at Bibendum with a dear friend and his husband to celebrate the launch of Elt . . . , sorry I *must* learn to be more discrete, a new album. The new chef Claude Bosi really does have a magical touch. His little *amuse bouche* of a mini cornet of foie gras ice cream was divine, as indeed was the eggshell filled with curry powder-spiked coconut foam. You simply must try the duck jelly as a starter next time you go, it has caviar and smoked sturgeon. Ambrosial actually."

Larry paused.

"Hmm. Actually, that's rather silly of me. They're won't be a next time, will there? Ah well, two more down. Makes it easier to get a table."

Gold thought he was now finally past the tipping point of madness. He was amidst a vision of Hell and listening to the menu from an exclusive London restaurant. But then, he thought, nothing made sense any more.

"So why are you here?" ventured Lesley-Ann. "Why not just kill us earlier when you had the chance?"

Larry burst out laughing. The masses on either side of him stirred and launched into their own bastardised form of laughter that sounded like a perversion of chittering insects. The effect was chilling.

"*When I had the chance*? I could have disposed of you at any time of my choosing. I don't require, as you so quaintly put it, a chance. No, my dear girl, I am here because of him . . . young Mr Gold, or should I refer to him by his new sobriquet, The Gatekeeper?"

More laughter, more scraping, more chittering.

"You knew?" was Nick's response to this.

Larry looked genuinely perplexed. Slight frown lines appeared on his face, despite the best efforts of Botox.

"You really haven't got a fucking clue, have you? Did I know? *Did I know*! I know *everything*!"

The word everything was as deafening as thunder. It reverberated around the station as if to emphasise its truth. It was so loud it hurt Lesley-Ann and Gold's ears. Their heads rang with the sound.

"You thought you could flim-flam me, Nick? You thought you could pull the wool over these millennia-old eyes? I invented bullshit, Nick. I created it. 'Go on sweetheart, eat the apple, what's the worst that could happen, eh Eve?' 'Come on Judas, what's he ever done for you?' 'Sure Gavrilo Princip, pull the trigger on Archduke Franz Ferdinand and Sophie, Duchess of Hohenberg. There won't be any consequences'."

Gold and Lesley-Ann stared. The enormity of what was before them was opening up like a vast cavern. Or was it really, finally, the abyss?

"But . . . but if you knew I was The Gatekeeper, then why allow me to get so far?" Gold was so very lost now.

"Well, my dear boy, that's the game. That's the fun. That's the nonsense that He and I play out every twenty years. He knows it's going to happen, I know that He knows . . . and so it goes on. So here we are. Why on earth did you think it was so easy to get the money to fund your running around the world? Do you really think any sane production company would behave like that?"

"But what about Adam Farthing? Does he . . . does he . . . know?"

Larry glanced at the Rolex Cosmograph Daytona he'd been given by a very grateful member of a middle eastern royal family for his help in ensuring the emergence of Daesh.

"Damn. Is that the time? I must be in Moscow in half an hour. Still, I hardly have to concern myself with queues at immigration. What were you saying? Ah yes, Adam. Sadly young Adam was being, what shall I say, an irritant. Can you believe that he was questioning my judgement? Anyway, it's sorted now, I poured oil on his troubled waters . . . well, not oil exactly."

"This just cannot be possible," cried out Lesley-Ann.

The man in front of them laughed. "Not possible? Really? Your narrow, plaintive ignorance is beyond measure – pathetic in fact. You see all of this? You see me? You see my followers, and yet you have the temerity to instruct me on what is, and isn't, possible? Talking to you is like teaching an ant quantum physics. You only know this tiny little world, this sad little planet spinning around pointlessly in this infinitesimal Universe. I rule countless universes, all of them, all of the time. Do you yet fail to understand? I am infinite. Or did you, in your ludicrous ignorance, assume only good old Daddy has the exclusive rights to that? It's all a bit much isn't it, for a cynic like you, Nick? Pathetically arguing against the God of the Gaps brigade."

Gold responded. "I thought it was a legitimate argument. Just because there are some features of the natural world that science is still at a loss to explain, there is no need to rush to claim that it can only be explained by God. Science produces hypotheses, and the believers beat a retreat. I believe we should not put God into the gaps."

"And would you just know it, Mr Oxford Theologian, you are so wrong. I fill the gaps. Me. Why's that? Because I'm always around – here, there, everyfuckingwhere. It makes me laugh – science versus God. Both sides so desperate to be always proved right. And yet . . . and yet . . . here I am. Oh, and by the way, nice to see that you can actually string a sentence together and you're not a complete media muppet. I laid it out for you all. Larry Shaitan. Not one of you got the joke: Shaitan is the Arabic name for Satan. Thick as pea soup, all of you."

Gold spoke. His voice carried no conviction whatsoever. "You won't win. There will be others after me. Good always defeats Evil."

Larry's laughter seemed almost maniacal.

"Of course, keep telling yourself that. Lets you humans sleep at night. Listen Mr Gatekeeper, you know why I will win? Because of you. Because of who you are. Because of the very core of human nature. You think I'm the evil one? No, I'm not. You are."

"You created evil," replied Lesley-Ann. "It's you, not us."

Larry gave a snort of derision.

"You are so simple. Naive. Humanity always reduces everything to a dichotomy: black and white; true or false; good or evil. That's why I succeed, century after century. You think I make people evil? That I force them to do my bidding? That's the joy of it. They *want* to do it, they cannot wait. I merely whisper a suggestion in their ear, show them what might be, what they could accomplish. They perform the acts, I don't."

"Bullshit!" responded Gold. When you know your own death is imminent, one is emboldened and manners fall to the wayside.

Larry glanced at his watch again. "Places to go, people to be," he muttered. "Let me, and I've no idea why I should bother, enlighten you. I see a weedy little Austrian child in Braunau am Inn called Schicklgruber. A moody little boy. He grew hostile towards his father, I liked that. Very relatable. Wanted to be a painter. Unfortunately, he wasn't any good. Turned down twice by the Viennese Academy of Fine Arts. Now he's embittered, angry, lonely. Perfect."

Larry paused, as if reflecting on a cherished memory.

"So, I put him in touch with the Mayor of Vienna, Karl Lueger, one of my earlier experiments. Paid off rather more than I could possibly have anticipated. WWI breaks out (another one my top ten hits) and this runt of a human being avoids Austrian military service declaring he's unfit, but then joins the 16th Bavarian Infantry Regiment serving throughout the conflict as a corporal. Suddenly, he's brave. I wanted to give the little guy a boost, you see, two Iron Crosses.

"Germany surrenders, he's furious, feels betrayed. Again, good. Now I just happen to bump into him at a coffee house. Listen to his bullshit over some strudel. 'Why don't you help Germany?' I suggest. That was all I did. Nothing more. Just put the idea into his head. He goes to prison. He writes *Mein Kampf* – total bollocks of course, but sold five million copies in a year – and . . . well, off we go."

"What the fuck do you mean off we go? You murdered millions . . . millions!" Gold could hardly restrain himself.

Larry looked genuinely shocked. "*I* murdered millions? *Me*? I did nothing. I sat with a bitter, twisted the world-hates-me little nobody in a cafe and in the immortal words of Prez Barack merely said, Yes you can. Humans did the rest. It was nothing to do with me. I mean, those camps, I hadn't even thought of that. OK, I admit I suggested the swastika. I'd been sitting on it for over 5,000 years when it was the Sanskrit swastika, which means, get this, good fortune, or well-being – there's an irony for you. Then good old boy archaeologist Heinrich Schliemann discovered the hooked cross, more irony, on the site of ancient Troy. Didn't work out so well for them, but there you go. Old Heinrich connected it with similar shapes found on pottery in Germany, put two and two together and made five and announced that it was a significant religious symbol of our remote ancestors. Total crap of course but the Nazis bloody loved it, lapped it up. That's humanity for you."

Gold realised that Lesley-Ann was gripping his hand so tightly that it was making his fingers go numb. Creeping into his mind was the thought he was trying to avoid – what was he supposed to do? What was The Gatekeeper's plan of action to prevent further earthly carnage?

He genuinely didn't know. There was no flash of inspiration. Life was suddenly and irreversibly quite unfathomable.

"But you lost. We won. The allies won. Good defeated evil," said the attorney.

"I lost? Did I? What happened? You Americans, and the Russians, stole the finest Nazi scientists, built rockets, created atomic and hydrogen weapons, started the Cold War. A win-win in my view. Did I do that? Nope. Did *you* do that? Sure did. And if I lost, Mrs Trobe, if such a thing were possible, then pray tell, where was my Father during all of this? On vacation? Having a sabbatical? Six million turned to ash in the ovens, forty-five million civilians dead, fifteen million dead in combat, that's sixty million killed, and what did He do? I'll tell you – nothing! And you all still think He's great. Which is why I'm still here. And always will be."

The creatures surrounding Larry stirred in their approval, shuffling, scraping, chittering.

Lesley-Ann instinctively stepped back.

"You worship an absentee landlord. Where is He? And come to think of it, where's your dear friend Barachiel? You'd think, as he started you on this path, he'd have the good grace to be here, you know, lend some moral support. But no, nowhere to be seen. Typical. At least I'm here. I'm always here. I'm everywhere. I make the effort. I go the extra mile. I'm in the courts, in the parliaments, in the military and, of course, in the media. You might say *The Sun* shines out of my arse."

"If anyone is bitter and twisted, it's you, Larry," said Gold.

The words fell into silence. Larry seemed suddenly to grow in height, in physique, his presence now filling more of the disused station platform. The subtle changes in his face were alarming. Gone was the smooth, expensive, well-manicured face. Now it was harder, more purposeful. Hawk-like.

To Gold's ears it seemed that the even tone of his voice had changed. It had shrugged off the urbane entitled sound of the British upper class. Now it was a harsh discordant shriek tinged with emotion and anger.

"I was His favourite. I was the highest of all the Angels, the anointed Cherub. I was the most beautiful of all His creations. He told me. Told me right to my face! I only wanted the best for all of us. I knew He wasn't up to the job. I was. It's all there in the Book of Job. It spells it out for you. I had access to heaven and to the throne of God. *One day the angels came to present themselves before the Lord, and Satan also came with them. The Lord said to Satan, 'Where have you come from?' Satan answered the Lord, 'From roaming through the earth and going back and forth in it.'* I was still moving freely between Heaven and Earth, speaking to Him directly and answering for his activities."

Larry was still growing. Looming ever larger in this subterranean station.

"Why did I fall from heaven? They tell you I fell because of my pride, that I desired to be God, not to be a servant of God. It wasn't pride. I knew I would do a far better job. And what was my reward for trying? He threw me out. I was cast out!"

Gold was looking up at the apparition before them. It was now immense. No longer human. No longer of this earth. It shifted shape, morphing from one being to another. Dark, cloaked, winged, clawed.

"So all of this because you've got daddy issues?" yelled Lesley-Ann.

The silence that ensued was terrible. The creatures on the concrete platform stood stock still. Gold's heart beat even faster.

"You dare to mock me?" The immense terrible figure stooped and leaning over Lesley-Ann whispered in a voice that could be heard across the Universe. "How are your daddy issues these days? Do you still recall fondly those nights when Mom was out playing bridge with her fancy friends in Westport Connecticut and Daddy would visit your bedroom in your lovely home in Greenwich? Well Counselor?"

"Fuck you, fuck you!" screamed Lesley-Ann.

What had been Larry laughed. "There we see it. The poor little girl still angry after all these years. My heart aches for you. No, really, it does. Just so unfair."

Lesley-Ann was crying, sobbing uncontrollably. The being that was before them had entered her very soul and found her darkest secret. Gold looked on in a mixture of surprise and shock. There were no words.

"Oh dear, I seem to have upset our American friend."

Larry Shaitan had resumed his human form.

"Anyway boys and girls, *tempus fugit*. And I really am on the clock this evening. So, shall we end this little charade? Whaddya say?"

Gold reached for Lesley-Ann's hand. She had stopped crying.

Gold thought he might start any moment. So this was it? The terminus. In a cold, dark, disused Underground station.

"How does it end? Do you offer us a Faustian deal?" Gold looked straight into Larry's eyes.

Larry pulled a cigarette from a solid gold case which bore the initials LM and lit it with a gold Dunhill lighter.

"I really should quit . . . but what the hell. You know what I admire about you, Nick?"

Gold shook his head.

"Nothing. You're shallow, vain, self-centred, disingenuous and, at the heart of it all, you're a coward. And what a waste. You had the smarts to go to Oxford, to study theology, to maybe even make a difference. To help people to *think*. And I made all that happen, yes I did, just for you. Poor Mummy and Daddy had to go, they were far too nice. Dangerous road that North Circular. So say hello to Hazel and Lloyd Carson. Perfect. Religious. Righteous. I wanted a real adversary. For once I wanted The Gatekeeper to understand . . . to really understand. To be worthy of their role. And that was you, Nick. But no, that was just too arduous, too much of an ask. Too much bloody hard work. So you trade in your talent to front-up shit TV to the dumb-arse masses. And you talk to me about Faustian deals? But hey, don't take my word for it. Come on down, it's time to play *The Guilt is Right*!"

There was a movement on the platform as the creatures scuttled aside to let a figure through. The torch light was not bright enough to mark out who it was until the figure stood next to Larry.

"Hello Nick. Of all the disused tube stations in all the world, you had to walk into mine."

"Oh dear God," was all Gold could reply.

"Close. But no cigar. Lesley-Ann, how rude of me. I'm Nick's ex, Suzie. How lovely to meet you. I see he hasn't lost his touch – still taking his dates to all the best places."

Lesley-Ann stared at Suzie. She was svelte, dressed in a clearly expensive, yet under-stated, designer trouser suit and was groomed to perfection. She looked ethereal. Simply stunning.

"Doesn't she look terrific, Nick?" said Larry, without a trace of irony. My Persephone as I like to think of her. If I had a heart, Suzie would have a very special place in it, as I do in hers. Let's face it Nick old boy, she chose to be with me rather than endure living with you. Free choice. Bet you miss that make-up sex, eh? God knows, I would."

Suzie spoke. "Larry, well let's call him Larry for convenience, was telling me, Nick, that you're the . . . what was it now, oh yes – The Door Keeper."

"Gatekeeper," corrected Gold. Even dead, she could still get under his skin.

"You see, Lesley-Ann, you don't know Nick like I do. I mean, you're not his type. You're far too intelligent, smart, self-assured, independent. You're not in awe of his charm, wit and TV career. He'll only let you down. That's his speciality. Isn't that right, Nick?"

Gold really had had enough.

"Larry, Lucifer, whatever, if you're going to kill me, just fucking do it. I don't need to listen to this shit. Yes, I'm The Gatekeeper, but guess what, I have no idea what that means, but you already know that. So let's just finish this stupid game of yours shall we?"

"Whoa Nick . . . when did you grow a pair?" replied Suzie on Larry's behalf. "Quite the handsome hero, aren't we?"

Lesley-Ann, to everyone's surprise, stepped forward.

"You know the difference between you and me, Suzie? I'm alive and you're dead. I choose to help others while you, in your self-centred screwed-up world, chose the easy way out. Jesus, Nietzsche must have had you in mind: 'For every sufferer instinctively seeks a cause for his suffering; still more precisely, a perpetrator, still more specifically, a guilty perpetrator who is susceptible to suffering.' So, who's the fucking coward now, bitch?"

Suzie gave a truly blood-chilling snarl, bared her razor teeth and sprang forward to gouge at Lesley-Ann's face.

"Stop!" The word was deafening within the enclosed space. Larry stepped forward and without even looking at her, slapped Suzie very hard across her face. She fell onto the platform floor.

"No one touches these two except me. Do you all understand?"

There were murmurings of Yes, my Lord from the assembled creatures.

"My apologies. It must be the excitement and unbridled joy of seeing you again, Nick. Kids today, eh? Fine. Shall we proceed? Gatekeeper – this is what happens. You have a very simple choice. Make the right one, I go away . . . sort of . . . make the wrong one and, well, these good folk come up with me and, how shall I put it, truly piss on London's parade."

Nick had no idea what to do or say.

"What is the choice?"

Larry smiled and spoke as if he was ordering a vodka martini at the Savoy's American Bar.

"I kill Lesley-Ann. Or you kill Lesley-Ann."

Gold felt as if his heart had been entombed in ice. He felt ruined.

"What? You . . . fucking what?"

Larry brushed an imaginary speck of dirt of his immaculately tailored lapel.

"Oh, I'm sorry. Wasn't I clear enough. The woman dies. You kill her or I do. That's it. In a nutshell."

"That's not a choice, you bastard. It's murder. What kind of choice is that supposed to be? What will it achieve? Prove you're a monster? We already *know* that."

"That's the deal, my friend. It is what The Gatekeeper must do. I didn't ask you to take the job. I may have helped you prepare for it when you were young but that was all, I assure you. That's down to Barachiel, who I can't help but notice, still hasn't had the courtesy to show up. *Quelle surprise*."

"Do I get a say in this? You're going to kill us both anyway. You're just playing with us. Get a kick out of it, do you? You want me to end up like that thing?" Lesley-Ann pointed to Suzie who had now stood up and was scowling at her and Nick. Suzie's eyes had turned jet black; two unfathomable lakes of clearly unhinged unmitigated hatred.

"Ah, Americans. God bless 'em. Always the talent for the dramatic. Tick tock, Nicholas. What's it to be?"

Gold bowed his head. "And if I kill her, this Gate of Hell is sealed?"

Lucifer nodded.

"And if you kill her?"

Lucifer gave an elegant shrug of his shoulders. "You do the math."

"How?"

"Entirely your choice, old boy. Makes no difference to me."

Gold stepped forward. "Do you have a gun?"

Larry smiled. "Do I have a gun? I control universes beyond your imagination. I'm not a gang-banger from East LA. I have quite literally everything."

Gold felt a sudden weight in his hand. He looked down. There, in his right hand, was a Colt Python .357 Magnum, its silver eight-inch barrel gleaming in the torch light. The prancing horses on the handle spoke to its Old West heritage.

"I thought we'd go old school," was all that Larry said.

Gold weighed the revolver in his hand. It was heavier than he would have imagined.

"I've never fired a gun before. Never even held one," he said.

"They'd piss themselves in Texas if they heard that. I took the liberty of loading it with Radically Invasive Projectile, or R.I.P. bullets. Had them adapted specially for the Colt. They're fabulous, Nick. They splinter into eight eviscerating shards to take out all your vital organs. That's their tag line, not mine, by the way. They launched them at the Las Vegas SHOT Show in January. They've been dubbed 'the last round you will ever need'. Been dying to see them in action."

Gold turned towards Lesley-Ann and raised the gun.

"Nick, for fuck's sake . . . don't . . . please . . . for the love of God!"

"Oh, I don't think my Father is going to help you now, my dear. Just aim and squeeze the trigger ever so gently Nick. The gun will do all the work."

"I'm so sorry Lesley-Ann. I truly am."

And with that Nick Gold, the Paranormal Detective, put the steel barrel of the Colt into his mouth and blew the top of his head clean off.

THIRTY-SEVEN

"Thus was the applause they meant, Turn'd to exploding hiss, triumph to shame Cast on themselves from their own mouths"
– John Milton, Paradise Lost

The sound of the round being fired in the enclosed concrete station was deafening. The heavy revolver dropped from Nick Gold's dead hand as he fell to the platform. Blood gushed from where the top of where his head had been and flowed out across the grey, dirty surface of the platform, mingling with the detritus of decades of neglect. It pooled in a lake, a red circular lake of blood, brain and bone.

As the echoes died away, silence prevailed. All the participants stood still, shocked into immobility by this act of self-violence.

Lesley-Ann was frozen, her mouth open in a silent scream. Now she put her hands to either side of her head and started to rock backwards and forwards in paralysed grief.

It was Lucifer who broke the tableau.

"Noooo!" he screamed, his cry filling the air. "That's not the way it's meant to happen! This is not fair! You cheat! You vain, self-sacrificing little fuck. You couldn't help yourself, could you? You egocentric prick! Even now, it's all about you! Your death . . . it's . . . it's tainted! You fucking cheated me!"

Lesley-Ann stared at him in utter disbelief and confusion.

Larry had transformed once again into a dark, black shifting shape with eyes that burned as red as coals. Its tendrils flew against the walls of the station. Its cloak, or perhaps it was its body – Lesley-Ann was unable to discern – whipped into a frenzy, catching some of the creatures in its fury and sending them flying. The creatures themselves stared as their Master exploded with unfettered rage, tiny embers of fire catching on the clothes of some of the creatures on the platform as they cowered in dread. The sound emanating from this whirlwind was feral and chilling.

"You always were such a bad loser, Lucifer Morningstar."

The voice was calm, even mellifluous.

Lesley-Ann, running purely on adrenalin, turned to see who was speaking. The platform was suddenly brighter, illuminated by a light, the source of which seemed to come from everywhere.

The whirlwind ceased. Gradually the inchoate shape began to re-form as Larry Shaitan. The look on his face, when it came into focus, was one of pure loathing and disgust.

"Barachiel!"

Lesley-Ann stared, her emotions running between terror, hope, and anger.

Barachiel was in human form and walked silently across the platform towards Larry.

"A little late to the party, aren't we? What kept you? Down on your knees worshipping Him?"

Barachiel shook his head, dismissing the insult as one would from a small misspoken child.

Larry was regaining his composure. The effortless charm, the easy manner, the believability draping themselves over him like a favourite cashmere coat.

"Poor old Nick. He really wasn't up to the job you gave him. The Gatekeeper. My Father always had a taste for the melodramatic," Lucifer laughed quietly.

"I think Nick Gold was more than up to the task, Lucifer," replied Barachiel, now only a few feet away from the enemy he had fought across the millennia.

"Really. I love your idea of success, Barry. Blowing your brains out. Taking the easy way out. We really must discuss this sometime, maybe in my domain?"

Barachiel looked at Gold's body. The blood had stopped flowing.

"The last round you will ever need. They weren't kidding. That is some mess," said Larry in an admiring tone.

Lesley-Ann was sobbing. The shock was beginning to take its toll. Large tears fell down her cheeks. She made no attempt to stem the flow. What was the point?

"After all this time, Lucifer, after all your Father tried to teach you, you have still learned nothing."

"Yeah? How is good old Dad these days? Missing me? Ready to abdicate? Let someone who knows what they're actually doing take over the family business?"

Barachiel shook his head in sad dismay.

"Anyway, your Gatekeeper fucked-up big time. I believe that is the correct phrase. So we will be on our way. Nice try Barry, close, but no Bolivar Royal Coronas. Let's do this again in another twenty years. As we always do. My friends here have a very busy night ahead of them."

The creatures, emboldened by Satan's words, started up a series of loud rhythmic rasps and chitters.

Lesley-Ann literally jumped at the sound.

"One moment, Lucifer!" Barachiel spoke with a tone that commanded respect and would not be gainsaid.

"I don't think so, not this time, Barachiel. Face it, God is dead."

"Lucifer. I suggest you finish all the quotation, not just the part that you hold on to like a drowning man holds on to the wreckage of his boat. 'God is dead. God remains dead. And we have killed him. Yet his shadow still looms. How shall we comfort ourselves, the murderers of all murderers? What was holiest and mightiest of all that the world has yet owned has bled to death under our knives: who will wipe the blood off us? What water is there for us to clean ourselves? What festivals of atonement, what sacred games shall we have to invent? Is not the greatness of this deed too great for us? Must we ourselves not become gods simply to appear worthy of it?'"

Lucifer looked into Barachiel's eyes. "Sacrifice?"

Barachiel nodded. "Yes, sacrifice. 'The magnitude of a progress is gauged by the greatness of the sacrifice that it requires'."

"Don't go quoting fucking Friedrich Nietzsche at me. I taught him!" exploded Larry.

"But not well enough. Nick Gold was willing to act to save this woman. You call it vanity. You say his death is tainted. You are wrong. He was prepared to pay the ultimate price to secure her safety and her freedom. He put her before himself in a selfless act of courage. He is a true heir to the title of The Gatekeeper."

Larry's chest was heaving with fury.

"He chose the coward's way out, the spineless little shit."

"No, he did not. 'Man is not equally moral at all hours, this is well known. If his morality is judged to be the capability for great self-sacrificing resolutions and self-denial, which, when continuous and grown habitual, are called holiness'. Did you teach him that, too? Nick Gold's act was pure, brave and noble. He fulfilled his duty as The Gatekeeper."

Once more, Satan started to morph into his true, monstrous form. Lesley-Ann pressed herself against the wall of the platform, now in such a state of confusion and shock that she could barely function.

"You will not deny me, Barachiel!" screamed Lucifer as he filled the station.

"And you, Lucifer, will not defy your Father . . . nor me!" With that, a blaze of white light, brighter than the sun, yet painless to the eyes, came forth out of Barachiel. It filled every crevice of the disused station. The forlorn creatures tried to shield their eyes from the brightness and spontaneously started to back away. Barachiel, before Lesley-Ann's eyes, grew into his true magnificent celestial form. His wings unfolded, light spreading even further as they did so.

"Away from me, Satan!" Barachiel declared. "For it is written: Worship the Lord your God and serve Him only."

Like a supernova, the light grew in intensity. For an instant, it was the brightest light in the Universe.

Now all Lesley-Ann could see was white light, of an unimaginable purity and intensity. It should have rendered her blind.

But there was no pain. The light was beautiful. It bathed her, cleansed her, comforted her.

Slowly it started to fade. And was finally gone.

The King William Street Underground station was deserted but for Barachiel in human form, Lesley-Ann Trobe . . . and the broken, bloodied corpse of Nick Gold.

Lesley-Ann realised that she had been holding her breath, and exhaled violently, trying to pump air into her lungs.

Barachiel turned to her. "Are you all right?"

There really was no answer to that.

Gently, as if her footsteps might wake him, she approached Gold's body.

"Jesus! Nick . . . Nick, why?"

Barachiel walked towards her. "He died for all of us. He understood in that final moment what being The Gatekeeper truly meant. What he had to sacrifice to close the Gate of Hell."

Lesley-Ann could not stop staring at the body. As a criminal defence attorney she had grown used to examining an endless stream of unmoderated, graphic photographic evidence, but looking at the destroyed remains of someone you knew, someone you cared for deeply was a very different experience. She felt hollow, drained of all feeling and emotion. There was simply nothing left inside her. And then, rising within her like a wave that rushes to throw itself on the shore, she knew. She knew in that moment what she had been denying to herself. That she had at some indistinguishable moment fallen in love with Nick Gold. Yes, she had started to love Nick Gold. He had always been the one, ever since he walked into her office, unannounced, in Pennsylvania. She knew that with a clarity and certainty that would live with her forever.

After what seemed to her an age she managed to speak.

"That's it? Lucifer has gone? The world's safe for another twenty years?"

"No, the world is never safe and Lucifer is everywhere. All around us. But the Gates of Hell are now sealed. Until the next time."

Lesley-Ann stared at the gun lying on the platform.

"And you think that's a good deal, do you? You think Nick's death is just fine? That all of this, this madness was worth it?"

She straightened herself up. "Maybe Larry was right. Maybe there is no difference between you and Him. It's all the same. You demand sacrifice, you demand death. Tell me how that makes you good? You weren't even here. You stood by and let this happen. You let him die."

Archangel Barachiel spoke very softly. "No, Lesley-Ann, I was here all the time. It was not my place to intervene. It was my place to see that mankind understood the choice it was confronted with. That Nick would, ultimately, choose good over evil. That he would find the courage to save those he loved."

"And what makes you any better than Lucifer?"

"The difference is that God is love. That is all it has ever been."

"Fine. So show me the love you so proudly boast of. You're God's right-hand man so you claim. Make it right. Bring him back. Bring my Nick back to me. Make him alive!"

Barachiel walked across to her and put his hand on her arm. "That is not the way it must be. Nicholas Gold has gone. The Gate has been closed. He understood, in those last few seconds, the true nature of being The Gatekeeper. He was selfless and he was brave. He didn't flinch from his duty. He died for you."

Lesley-Ann's body shook with racking sobs.

"I'm begging you . . . begging you, please . . . bring him back."

Barachiel shook his head slowly. "I cannot undo this. To do so would unleash a horror on this world beyond your imagination, even after what you've witnessed tonight. You must sense it, Ms Trobe. You must see how it is. You must feel the hatred, the divisions, the enmities, neighbour against neighbour, posturing dictators all too ready to unleash weapons of vast destructive power, the dispossessed ready to rise up feeling they have nothing left to lose, the followers of some twisted, corrupted faiths intent on committing endless atrocities. And where are the leaders? Where are the men and women of reason? Where are those whose shining light acts as a moral compass that can be followed in safety and honour? No, Lesley-Ann, these are dark times, dangerous times. The Gatekeeper is needed now more than ever."

"But he's gone. He's lying there dead. There is no Gatekeeper now."

Barachiel smiled. A small gentle smile tinged with sadness. "Yes, this Gatekeeper has passed. But I cannot risk that the next twenty years passes without another ready to act. The world is far, far too fragile, too volatile, too easily seduced by those who promise everything yet deliver only suffering. It requires courage, it requires of a person a quickness of thought and steadfastness in deed. It requires one willing to learn. To study."

"I am not sure what you are saying?"

"It is you."

What the fu –"

"Lesley-Ann, you are The Gatekeeper now."

THIRTY-EIGHT

"Death is not (wherefore dream'st thou thus?) The son of night and Erebus: Not was of fell Erynnis born On gulfs where Chaos rules forlorn. But sent from God, his presence leaves, To gather home his ripen'd sheaves,"

– John Milton, The Complete Poetry

EIGHT YEARS LATER

She knew it would be her last glimpse of the outside world as she shuffled, leg-ironed and handcuffed, through the final noisily unlocked gates of the maximum-security State Correctional Institute, Muncy in Lycoming County and across the yard before climbing into the secure cage at the rear of a modified Ford Transit Connect. Stopping for a few seconds to take a deep breath of a rare bounty of fresh air, she knew that the sixty-eight mile, one and a half-hour drive to the Field Hospital SCI Rockview was the mere prologue to her last-ever journey on Earth: her one-way pre-planned trip to oblivion. She hoped she would get a glimpse of the façade of Muncy that had so impressed her on arrival eight years ago, when it had reminded her of pictures she'd seen of an Ivy League college rather than a prison. She also hoped she might catch a glimpse of the Longanton Wesleyan Church where, in what felt like a different universe, she and Doug had gotten married. On the journey, she would have plenty of time to think about how she had come to be at Muncy and what awaited her in the coming days, but then time, now fast running out, was what she'd had too much of for the last eight years. Locked in her cell twenty-two hours a day with only sporadic out-of-cell exercise in a ten-by-ten yard caged courtyard – and always with two officer escorts – as frightened as she was now, she felt a growing sense of relief and an upwelling of serenity. Time to put her trust in the Lord, even if he'd been serially absent these last few years.

It was always highly likely that the twelve members of the jury at her trial would reject her defence. The argument that her dead Daddy was the guilty party unsurprisingly fell on deaf ears, despite the valiant efforts of defence attorney, Lesley-Ann Trobe and later the Atlantic Centre for Capital Representation, who had taken up her cause. While the jury held fast to the opinion that dead people, by and large, did not return to kill family members, wives – in fits of jealousy and anger – often killed husbands. Just as Loretta had the night the old Chevy broke down in Hallam. Of that, the jury had no doubt. During the sentencing phase, they also formed the not unexpected view that this particular murder was entirely abhorrent and without mitigation. Crime scene photographs helped make that case. The jury unanimously agreed that the death penalty was the only right and proper course of action, if merely *pour encourager les autres* from rending asunder life partners and blaming it on their lately or not so lately departed nearest and dearest. Judge Dwayne A. Haskell Jr fully concurred.

When all legal arguments had been exhausted and there were no further avenues of appeal for Loretta's legal team to pursue, other than a late-hour call to the Governor to seek last minute clemency – this to a Governor who had gone on record saying that if he had his way, public hanging should be reinstated for such a despicable crime – they knew all hope had departed. Loretta Johnstone was doomed.

When the day of the execution came, Congresswoman Lesley-Ann Trobe visited her erstwhile client on death row at Rockview. Loretta's holding cell was just twenty feet from the execution chamber itself.

"I'm so sorry, Loretta. I really am."

The inmate had aged visibly. Loretta's tired, pale, but otherwise expressionless face clearly showed she had, inwardly, resigned herself to her fate.

"You all tried, honey. Y'all gave it your best shot. And I am grateful for that. But I have to ask you one thing, OK? Do you still believe I didn't do it?"

Lesley-Ann looked straight into Loretta's eyes. "I'm sure, without a shadow of doubt, that you are innocent. Believe me when I tell you, I *know* you did not kill your husband."

For a millisecond Loretta Johnstone smiled.

"Thanks honey, it means a lot to me, but you seem so certain, Lesley-Ann. How come?"

"Loretta, honey, you wouldn't believe me if I told you."

Lesley-Ann sighed and pulled her chair nearer the floor-to-ceiling bars of the cinder block holding cell. She rested her head against the cool metal and reaching through, gently rested a hand on Loretta's thigh.

"Hey ma'am! No touching. You know the rules," shouted the guard.

As a condemned prisoner facing imminent execution, Loretta was under twenty-four-hour surveillance and visitation rules were being strictly observed. Her life was ending, there were just a few hours remaining and everything was closing in as her world retreated to these stark four walls and the awareness of what lay a few feet away on the other side of a plain metal door.

Lesley-Ann bit her tongue. Now was not the time to get into an argument with an officious correctional officer.

"You were always a churchgoer, right Loretta? You believe in God? He may not be answering your prayers right now, but you figure He walks alongside you as you walk through the darkest valley? You know how the psalm goes on? 'I will fear no evil, for you are with me; your rod and your staff, they comfort me'."

"Well, seeing my dead Daddy and all, kinda made me wonder

what in God's name He was a playin' at. But I guess He has His plan and my pastor says I'm gonna get to know all the answers in just a few hours in any case." A wry smile accompanied this last statement.

Lesley-Ann couldn't help but admire the bravery of this very ordinary woman caught up in the most extraordinary of events.

"Loretta, sweetheart, we don't have time for me to tell you all that happened after we met with Nick, the Brit, in the lockup, but you have to understand that where you're going is gonna be just fine. I was no bible-reading girl, but I've seen enough in the last few years to *know* that there is a Hell – a real, agonising, unearthly realm – and if that's true, so must there be a Heaven, which is your next taxi stop. So you take comfort in knowing that while Daddy is elsewhere . . . Doug is waiting right there for you."

Loretta wrinkled her nose and pushed an untidy greasy fringe out of her eyes.

"I hope my dog Elvis is awaitin' on me. That would be great, but Doug . . . no, I think I am well passed havin' any of those feelings left in me."

The sudden scrape as the guard pushed her chair back and stood to attention caused both women to jump to their feet. The door at the end of the corridor swung open as Warden Barrett, followed by two uniformed officers, walked in. Dead-eyed and clearly well-versed in dealing with the protocols of the final hours of prisoners in the execution house, he was all business.

"OK, Congresswoman Trobe, it's time for you to join the other witnesses. The officer will show you where they are gathered. There's plenty of coffees and pastries."

Which was, by any standards, Lesley-Ann thought, about the most inappropriate thing anyone could say in the circumstances.

The Warden turned his attention to the prisoner. Relaxing for the briefest of moments, he smiled. "You OK, Loretta?"

She nodded while looking past the Warden through the bars of her cell at the still open door. A thought struck her. Life is an endless set of choices at a myriad of forks in the road. If she were to walk through that door and turn left, no doubt it would, with some twists and turns and much door-unlocking, lead to the outside world where the Pennsylvanian evening was cool and breezy with high scudding clouds. When was the last time she'd seen uninterrupted sky? But turn right through that door, as she must do soon, and all she would find was an obscene mockery of a clinic. A gurney, central lines, syringes and monitoring equipment. The only purpose of the doctors – to assist her death.

She was snapped back to reality as the Warden explained that in an hour or so, the team would be along to make the final arrangements. Some would be unpleasantly intimate and two female correction officers would take charge of that part of the process. "Don't you worry about anything now, Loretta. We'll all be goin' through this together," the Warden intoned.

Loretta merely nodded and sat down on her bunk again. One hour: an aeon, an instant.

Soon enough, too soon, the tie-down team were pushing into her cell and gently taking her arms. She was marched quickly to the bathroom and pushed and pulled into diapers and a clean orange jump suit. Her arms and legs were secured with handcuffs and leg irons and, surrounded by four officers, she shuffled the remaining length of the corridor and into the execution chamber. Her cuffs and leg irons were removed and she was lifted onto the gurney before she had time to react. Two strong arms held her shoulders as she was efficiently strapped down.

Raising her head, she could see the Warden standing next to a large wall-mounted telephone. An open line should the Governor, or the Supreme Court, choose to stage a last-minute intervention. The clock above the Warden's head read 18:55.

A middle-aged tight-faced female technician stepped towards her and without saying a word began to swab her wrists before inserting a cannula in each arm. The pain was momentary. A heart rate monitor was affixed to her chest. The technician withdrew behind a screen.

Loretta was startled by a noise as an electric motor raised the blinds to her right. Now she could see the witnesses sat on metal chairs in a starkly-lit unwelcoming white-washed room. Lesley-Ann was at the front, just a few feet away. The women smiled at each other; Lesley-Ann confident that Loretta would shortly be in an altogether better place and Loretta strangely comforted by her ex-lawyer and friend's certainty. Of both her innocence and by her strange metaphysical assurances.

Warden Barret stepped forward; Loretta noted how the Director of Corrections moved next to the phone. How much they must rehearse all this, thought Loretta. Kind of them really.

Clearing his throat, and for the first time looking a little nervous, the Warden spoke.

"Loretta Shereen Johnstone, you have been found guilty of murder in the first degree by the state of Pennsylvania and by the order of the court have been sentenced to death by lethal injection on this day. Do you have anything you would like to say before sentence is carried out?"

Loretta stared at the ceiling for an uncomfortably long time.

"Loretta? Do you want to say something?"

She turned her head and looked at the witnesses.

"My son, I see you. My, how you've grown. I love you. Live a happy life. Only the sky and the green grass goes on forever, and today is a good day to die. Please do not mourn my death or my life. I hold no bitterness to no one. Just remember the light. I'm gonna let this light shine. Let it shine. Let the light shine. Okay Warden, let's do it. I love y'all."

And with that Loretta turned her head and let it rest back on the gurney, staring at the celing.

Warden Barret stepped back and nodded.

Everything was silent in the execution chamber apart from the gentle susurration of the air-conditioning unit.

For a minute, two minutes nothing seemed to happen.

Then Loretta gasped.

"I can taste it already. I'm starting to go."

And with that she closed her eyes and shuddered.

The clock read 19:02.

Unobserved, in the corner of the execution chamber, stood Nick Gold. He gently lifted Loretta from the gurney and brushed the fringe from her eyes.

"Wasn't too bad was it? You'll have a bit of a headache for a day or so. Annoying or what? Dead – and still drugs do your head in. Anyway, come on, there are people looking forward to seeing you again . . . Oh, and here comes Elvis. Your dog that is. The other one's a bit more difficult to get an appointment with. But we will. We've got all the time in the world."

EPILOGUE

"And now the sun with more effectual beams
Had cheered the face of earth, and dried the wet
From drooping plant, or dropping tree; the birds,
Who all things now behold more fresh and green,
After a night of storm so ruinous,
Cleared up their choicest notes in bush and spray,
To gratulate the sweet return of morn."
– John Milton, Paradise Lost

NINETEEN YEARS SINCE THE DEATH OF NICK GOLD

She heard the door open quietly behind her but couldn't bring herself, quite yet, to turn away from the floor-to-ceiling window. The view was extraordinary. Here, on the third-floor of Colorado's Capitol building, she could look down the half-mile length of Civic Centre Park towards the Denver City and County Building that would, henceforth, be the future seat of government of the (rather less than) United States of America. She found it impossible to gauge the size of the crowd. Someone had said they were expecting over a million people to attend, but in truth it was a topic few wanted to debate given the toxicity surrounding the history of the subject. For a New York native, who had spent years in Washington before the evacuation, the early morning cornflower blue skies and bright sunlight still felt unnatural. She could see how almost all of the vast crowd were dressed in a style derived from the grey and sandstone-red environment suits the two-hundred strong Martian colonists were making so fashionable and ubiquitous. In retrospect, it was ironic to think how hostile the debate had become about whether the US component of the colonists could or could not insist on having a 'postal vote'. Plenty, both on Mars and in the US, argued that, as they were never going to return, they should henceforth be considered extra-nationals. Inwardly, she thought this would be the last election where off-worlders had any sort of vote or influence. Out of orbit, out of mind.

The day was colder than the seasonal average so she would need her Burberry cashmere trench coat later. At fifty-one, she was still a strikingly beautiful woman of whom it was said by countless media commentators could wear a bio-degradable bin liner and make it look good. Though far from vain, she felt she had earned the right to indulge a little in keeping up appearances. Her height, gym- and yoga-derived elegance and just fractionally less than beautiful face, which somehow added to her appeal, combined with her raven hair (a colour she admitted benefitted from some pretty regular attention by her hairdresser) could still stop men dead in their tracks. And some women, too.

The sound of a gentle clearing of the throat finally persuaded her to turn her back on the once-in-a-lifetime vista. While she had aged not only gracefully over the last twenty years, and arguably emerged, butterfly-like, into a whole new strata of beauty, the man standing in front of the door had not aged at all. Literally.

Indescribably handsome, graceful, he stood taller than somehow he should, with an air of confidence that seemed not at all misplaced. "You OK?" he said in a deep heavenly choir of a voice.

"I guess so. No chance we can back out now and go hiking in the Rocky Mountains, right? Or maybe come back next week when things have quietened down? Or binge-watch some antique TV shows from back in the day?"

A gentle laugh was the only reply.

Sighing, she walked over to the ridiculously ornate couch that divided the room. She had been given this, the Governor's office, for her personal use for the last ten days, much to the Governor's profound annoyance. He in turn had seconded the Lieutenant Governor's abode and so the process had cascaded down the building until, presumably, the Head of Parks and Recreation was finally holed-up in a lawnmower shed somewhere across town.

With the look of a stillborn smile, she waved her arm. "Come and sit. Talk to me. I guess we've got a little while before the circus begins."

"I just saw the head of the organising committee vectoring towards the breakfast buffet. He won't stop until he's hoovered up enough to feed the State of Maine. Speaking of which, I just got the latest. Everything's gone east of Bangor. A second surge has taken out Ellsworth, Trenton, Jonesboro. All under . . . for good."

"Shit! That's pretty much the whole East Coast lost. That's it. We've got ourselves a brand new geography. Those high-rise scavenger communities see themselves as the equivalent of the Old West pioneers and I don't see anyway short of full military engagement to stop them. Go East, young man and what . . . re-occupy the last vestiges of man's folly in New York and Boston? Live a life entirely divorced from society's norms and demands. No interest in being part of the collective that is the remaining United States. How long before they, too, declare themselves independent?"

"It's item number twenty-seven in your in-tray for tomorrow."

She sat back with a grimace. "I dread to think what items one to twenty-six are. I can hardly wait. How in the name of God, no offence, did it come to this? Seriously, how did I end up here? Was this always the divine, you know . . . His . . . plan?"

"Nah, it's just the way things panned-out. Kinda just happened. You should know by now everything is in humanity's hands. I'm just here to act as occasional advisor. Even up the odds a little. Weight the dice."

"Occasional! Really? Where the hell were you when peak oil finally tanked the world's economy while our genius leaders had made sure wide-scale renewables were legislated virtually out of existence?"

"Well, you did come to your senses. Took a while. But you got there. Look around you now, a post-carbon world with virtually unlimited energy – and, remember, you were part of the movement that helped drive it."

"We came to our senses, as you so quaintly put it, after fifteen percent of the world's population starved to death and the Middle East and Russia asserted their new-found geopolitical significance and consequently were bombed to buggery and back. And talking about driving – must I really travel in a chauffeur-driven limo this afternoon? I haven't been in an ape-driven car for ten years. Has it even got V2V communication? I won't feel safe."

"It's a small nod to tradition. We need some symbolism about returning to halcyon days. That kind of thing. You know that the seven ConfedStates are holding their own 'anti-celebration' today and –"

"What are those good ole boys going to do? Hang black mannequins from lamp posts while whistling Dixie?"

"Something like that. Actually, I kinda like that tune. Of course, with whole chunks of South Carolina, Florida, and Louisiana under water, I would have thought any celebrations in the Seven States will be somewhat dampened shall we say."

"I'll do the jokes, you concentrate on getting me through the next twelve months – alive and sane."

"Well, we know what's coming, but what we don't know yet is where or how. Just believe in yourself. Think of the campaigns and skirmishes you have won over the last nineteen years. I have complete faith in you."

She was about to tell him that was all very well when he held up his hand and, reaching into his beautifully tailored jacket, took out an iHol. Although she was sure he needed no human-devised connected device to know what was happening (here or throughout the Universe she assumed), the man seemed enamored of each new iteration of technology. One of the perks of the job, he had once said.

A fully three-dimensional figure, who would have been entirely convincing as a human visitor had she not been two feet tall and stopped at the waist suddenly hovered in front of them.

"Ma'am, I have the British Prime Minister standing by. He would like a quick word if that's acceptable?"

Ma'am . . . Jeez. Well, that all changes today I guess. "Sure, put him on, honey." She was never quite certain she had the protocol of speaking to AIs fully down. Honey seemed to work. Something that kids took to like ducks to water still felt alien to her. The two-foot woman vanished and, after a brief atmospheric scintillation, was replaced by a full-sized British politician.

"Good afternoon Ms P–"

"Uh-uh. Not yet. What can I do for you, Prime Minister?"

"A bit of a heads-up really. I have just appointed a new Secretary of State for Foreign and Commonwealth Affairs following the sad and entirely unanticipated demise of his predecessor. Most extraordinary business . . . first recorded instance of an automated home-help murdering their owner. Quite extraordinary. Sorry, I digress. Anyway, I've given the job to a back bencher, a Welsh fellow called Thomas Diafol. No Cabinet experience but the best speaker I've ever heard. No end of a stink about it over here, I can tell you. However, I have my reasons. Thing is, the chap says he's met you before – something about a pleasant interlude on London's Underground? No idea, frankly. Anyway, he happens to be in your fair city right now and would love to come along to the celebratory lunch today. Is that all okey-dokey with you and your people?"

She turned to the man on the couch and raised her eyebrows. He looked thoughtful, but nodded.

"Sure, tell him to ask for my Chief-of-Staff and he'll come down and ensure he gets past the watch dogs."

"Marvellous. May I wish you a wonderful day and assure you that you have the full backing of the British people."

And with that he was gone.

"What the fu–?"

"Well, that's the Brits for you. Circumscribed by procedure and traditions, but always capable of surprising the heck out of you. It's time we made a move. I've had your coat brought down; do you have your copy of *The Federalist Papers* ready for the Chief Justice?"

"Yeah, it's on the desk over there. It was either that or Harry Potter. The way this country has torn itself apart over the last ten years, it's difficult to say which is the bigger fantasy story."

They walked out of the office along a series of corridors clad in Colorado red onyx and down two flights of marble-floored stairs, their journey marked by respectful nods, brief bursts of applause and the odd moment of flag waving. The new flag, of course.

When they reached the main entrance hall with its walls hung with portraits of every US President, she couldn't help but crane her neck and look straight up the one hundred and eighty feet to the top of the dome. It seemed apt; a far distant cupola as unreachable as the moon, which just about summed-up her feelings about what she was going to have to achieve in the coming months. Well, if you aim for the moon and miss, you're still amongst the stars.

Here was the crowd stood in the hallway. Hundreds of the great, good, not so good and downright malevolent who would soon be seated on the platform. The organising committee, night after night, had agonised over precedent. A parting like that of the biblical Red Sea opened before her, and with the man a step behind her, she walked through a tide of applause out and into the bright, but still chill, Denver air.

Now the noise was incredible. A wall of sound literally shook the building.

The hologram screens floating above the crowd showed drone shots of smiling, laughing faces found at random, especially children, all wearing mutable tattoos that shimmered between the new US flag, emotes and every conceivable artistic design. Now the screens were showing cheerfully waving colonists on mars and the moon.

She took her seat and breathed deeply.

It seemed like only a few moments before she found herself standing in front of Laura Montez, Chief Justice of the United States, with her hand resting on *The Federalist Papers*.

"I Lesley-Ann Trobe, do solemnly affirm that I will faithfully execute the office of President of the United States and will to the best of my ability, preserve, protect and defend the Constitution of the United States."

The bells of the Civic Centre across the park began to chime midday and she could hear the twenty-one gun salute bark as the United States Marines band struck up Hail to the Chief.

Behind her, she was sure she had heard her chief-of-staff, Barachiel (Barry Angel to everyone else) whisper, "Way to go Gatekeeper. Let's get this show on the road, Ms President."

ACKNOWLEDGEMENTS

To my partner Siobhan, for enduring this relentless maelstrom. You are truly a saint.

To my children, Lauren, Scott, Charles and James for being my role models and bringing me so much joy.

To my literary agent and friend Jonathan Hayden for believing. The endless meetings, screaming matches and brutal emails were all worth it. We kept the faith.

To Teresa Quinlan at LovePR London. This is all your fault.

To Larry Viner and Lloyd Beiny for always making me laugh.

Finally, to my constant companion Ebony, the Mini-Schnauzer, whose insistence on being walked twice a day kept me sane. Almost.

Born in London and educated at Dulwich College and the London School of Economics where he studied Law, Sony Award Winner Russ Kane was the voice of Capital Radio's Flying Eye for 20 years. Today Russ broadcasts on BBC Radio London. He is the founder of The Espresso Bar help forum on Facebook and co-founded Men's Radio Station (www.mensradiostation.com) which focusses on men's mental health and well-being, working alongside Women's Radio Station.

Russ Kane's 90-minute one-man stand-up show Kaned Laughter has been performed to sell-out audiences in London, Los Angeles and the Edinburgh Fringe Festival.

With a background as an advertising copywriter, both in London and New York, Russ specialised in the corporate sector and amassed fifteen international writing awards for his work, including the Gold Medal at the New York Film and Television Festival.

In 2002, his autobiography *Shout At The Moon* was published.

The Gatekeeper is his debut novel. His Mini-Schnauzer loved the endless balls of paper thrown across the room.

Twitter: @russellkane

INVASION

Russ Kane

"There are two types of UFOs, the ones we build, and the ones they build"

– Ben R. Rich, Director of
Lockheed Martin's Skunk Works

It is a troubled time. Humanity has fallen prey to populist nationalist sentiment and democracy is under threat like never before. To top it all, too little action too late means climate change is now an immediate threat as coastal cities disappear, water wars break out and unmanageable levels of migration cause societal upheaval on a scale not witnessed since the end of the Second World War. Never before has the world seemed such a fragmented, frightening place to live.

Something has to be done. And it has.

In total secrecy, a group of scientists, film-makers and communication experts have been working in a remote facility in Canada. Funded by a discrete assortment of software billionaires, the group are seeking a way to unite the planet.

It's a huge task but they have an equally huge plan.

A staged alien invasion to bring humanity to it senses.

Thanks to their ability to manipulate the technology that searches deep space, the group will create the manifestation of a number of intelligently-controlled UFOs heading on a direct course for earth. All the calculations will indicate that the craft are scheduled to arrive in earth orbit in five years' time.

The false-flag information is released and instantly goes viral.

But the results are not like those in films. Instead, once the 24-hour news cycle has moved on, the end result is a dangerous mixture of global apathy and religious mania.

Some of the world's governments quickly learn that this alien contact is simply untrue – an elaborate technical lie. But some governments, including that of the United States, see it as a once-in-a lifetime opportunity to clamp down on the populace by perpetuating the lie.

Lesley-Ann Trobe, back in New York and now both a human rights lawyer and high-profile environmental activist, is approached by a notorious conspiracy theorist who, for once in his life, is telling the truth. His sister, who works at the Calgary facility and has turned whistle-blower is terrified by the arrogance and misplaced certainty she sees among her colleagues. She has urged her brother to get the truth out before it is too late.

Shortly afterwards, the entire Calgary enterprise is involved in a devastating accident which leaves no survivors.

Now Lesley-Ann Trobe has very little time to disprove the government's own conspiracy and to find a way to ensure the draconian measures being enacted against science, religion and personal freedom are thwarted. The people have a right to know the truth, but at what cost?

INVASION WILL BE PUBLISHED IN 2020

Printed in Dunstable, United Kingdom

66918205R00231